Spaulding Taylor is the pen previously published by fiction. A professional cellist who performed for with orchestras including the BBC Symphony and Royal Philharmonic Orchestras, he is married with one daughter, addicted to playing tennis and spends part of every year in Crete.

LAST STAR STANDING

SPAULDING TAYLOR

unbound

This edition first published in 2021

Unbound
TC Group, Level 1, Devonshire House, One Mayfair Place
London W1J 8AJ
www.unbound.com
All rights reserved

ISBN (eBook): 978-1-78965-098-3
ISBN (Paperback): 978-1-78965-097-6

Cover design by Irena Czusz

Printed and bound in Great Britain by Clays Ltd, Elcograf S.p.A.

Spaulding Taylor would be very grateful if you found time to review this
book, either on Amazon or on Goodreads. (Just 'A good read' is enough!)
#LastStarStanding

For my father

SUPER PATRONS

Richard Allen
Vanessa Allen
Adam Balkwill
Mary Banks
Hilary Birch
Keith Bramich
Michael & Jeanie Carter
Andy Charman
Sally Codling
Amanda Collison
Claire Constable
Wendy Crust
Martine Culbertson
Doreen DaSilva
Jane Daters
Clare & Chris Deighton
Clare Deniz
Jessica Duchen
Julia Edmondson
Fiona Fogden
Jo Goddard
Donna Guillemette

Charles Haywood
Dorothy Haywood
Marion Hitchcock
Rhonda Hollinberger
Nancy Hollinshead
John Housewright
Chris Jeffery
Gillian Kuroiwa
Andrew Laing
Colin Lawson
Benedict Leonard
Dennis Malone
John & Kay McLaughlin
Kerry McMenamin
Rachel McVeigh
Simon McVeigh
Stephen Neiman
Carl Nicholas
Thomas G. Noblett
Daniel Ogilvie
Jennifer Overhausa
Chris Richardson
Philip & Heather Rowson
Mandy Selby
Frank Sheppard
Cheryl Sourbeer
David W. Stewart
Jack Taylor
Priscilla Taylor
Jane Terepin
Ann van Allen-Russell
Anita Vasan
Grainne Wade

Stephen Wade
David Watts
Warren Whitley
Jan Whitwill
Frances Willenbrock
Martha Wills
David Wray
Han Yu

1

I was looking up several hundred metres into a tiny square of sky.

My elbow, encrusted with dried blood, still ached from the ropes they used to bind me. I couldn't move much, but I could still twist my torso and I doubted that any bones were broken. On the downside, my lips were cracked like dry glue, and my thirst was intense.

Most of all, I was furious. I'd never thought that the blinking Xirfell would capture me. I think I'd always assumed that – despite being the feared rulers of an embarrassing number of galaxies – they were basically just too thick. For this reason, in all of broken Earth, there could be no more pissed-off prisoner than me.

How had it happened? Well, I was teaching – those fat little pundling faces lifted to mine – when the testers entered, shuddering the ancient door back on its hinges. I spotted their leader instantly – some trick of stance, perhaps.

'What do you want?' I asked, but one of his underlings had already pinned me – deadening every tendon, immobilising every muscle. I remember thinking, Fuck, fuck, fuck.

Though I also felt remorse for all those times I had objected, 'But why didn't they fight?' Because – in that moment – the answer was obvious. Each of my breaths felt dredged up from my feet, as if every oxygen molecule had been separately petrified. I couldn't have fought a medium-sized caterpillar.

I suspect it was nerves that crowded that entire class of pundlings into one: pundling 3034, middle of the front row, the one who pinched his pen so anxiously, a pundling with rounder eyes than most. My attention was reserved for the leading tester, who had released his eel-like zuge – oiled, weaponised, glittering – apparently bent on escape. Though it couldn't escape, of course. Instead, it curled itself sulkily around the tester's muscular arm.

'Do you see the zuge?' he demanded of my class.

Nobody dared to answer. I attempted to protest – but my vocal cords had been jellified. Meanwhile, the tester flicked the zuge's snaky head, causing its rows of eyes to blink resentfully round the room.

He asked the class, 'Do you know what a zuge is?'

They did, I felt sure. Every eye was centred on it, on its fluidity, on the living colours pulsing through it. It writhed bitterly, though I knew that it was only half-alive: they're bred not far away from where I grew up. The microchip replacing its brain was invisible, but I spotted the scar at the top of its skull.

'Do I have a volunteer to assist in a demonstration?' sneered the tester.

Not 3034, I thought, but perhaps it was fate. I watched helplessly as the fat little pundling toddled obediently from his desk, shoulders slumped, flabby lips wobbling, eyes even more apprehensive than usual. The rest of the class remained focussed on the zuge – those liquid lights – as if hypnotised.

The tester raised his arm and I tried to shut my eyes. It was almost certainly an urban myth, but supposedly, after a glimpse of that pearl-black fang, one can never sleep easy again. But my eyelids refused to close. Instead I waited for the spiteful barb, for 3034's drawn-out, wild-curled dance of death.

Which didn't happen.

Instead, a pulse appeared to rock through the tester as the zuge slicked back into his glove. He rasped, 'Kindness stilled my hand. Sit down, 3034.' And as 3034, still blinking, obeyed, he added, 'You will wonder why we're taking your teacher from you. Do not tax your brains with such matters. All that we do is for your good. Your welfare is your beneficent King's sole concern.'

Which must be why he feeds pundlings to his disgusting blurgs then.

The tester wheeled around to face me.

Ah, death, I thought, with a strange combination of terror and yearning.

It started with a deep ache in the small of my back, and spread outward and upward, like a germ, like a flower. I was only to return to consciousness beneath that square of sky.

2

My first prison meal was delivered by an undersized pundling, who put an iced straw to my lips. There were grains in the liquid – maybe sand, maybe worse – but I was so thirsty that I downed every drop.

The pundling fed me but refused to make eye contact. I was left still starving, though less for food – that graininess lingered – than for companionship. I wondered how many similar prisons surrounded me. Hundreds? Hundreds of thousands? Was I privileged or punished by that reminder of cloud and sky?

The entrance whooshed open. I couldn't turn my head but was alert to every signal – from the zip-swish of the door to that tang of sour, fetid air. A cloak brushed past me; a figure that, with speeding heart, I recognised. Despite the rumours, Ravene still lived.

She was attended by a blurg – blubbery rings, oozing tentacles, gluey gait, the sickly-sweet scent of rotting prawns. The detritus from its rings was being neatly collected by a small pundling.

Meanwhile Ravene, in silks so glorious that every silkworm had probably been knighted, swivelled before me. Stroking her lower lip, frowning, she looked every inch the ranking princess. I recalled that constellation of tiny freckles above her elbow and closed my eyes to drown out the recollection, the warm glory of flesh on flesh. Had it really been a decade?

'Aiden. It has been many years.' Her voice was the same – if anything, a still creamier contralto.

'How could I forget?'

'I wondered if I'd changed.'

'No, you look terrific. But could you possibly lose the sidekick? Surely I'm bound enough for safety here!'

'Why should I?'

'Perhaps because I retain some residual sense of smell?'

She laughed and dismissed the blurg, which oiled away. 'Happier now?' she asked and then, very casually, 'I still have my zuge with me. You look tired, Aiden.'

'I was fucking pinned, didn't they tell you?'

'No. But what were you doing teaching pundlings, anyway?'

'I like pundlings. Anyway, I have to work somewhere. I was expelled from the Academy after they found out about us.'

She could still blush. If she had been enhanced, at least she'd chosen to retain some human traits. How human *was* she, these days? I wondered. To subdue my boyish reaction, I said roughly, 'There were rumours you were dead.'

'Did you believe them?'

'A little.'

'Enough to be sorry?'

Was she flirting? – It was tough to tell, because flirting had always been Ravene's default mode. But there was far more at stake here than an old flame. I was no longer the kid I'd been at the Academy. Instead, I was thirty, an operative of the rebellion, and sworn to fight her father, her regime, her entire race… And, given the secrets I had to protect, the sooner I roused her into finishing me off, the better.

With that airiness I so well remembered, she pressed, 'So, were you sorry?'

I had been sorry, as I recalled, but fired back, 'Why the hell should I have been sorry?'

And braced myself for the zuge, those long lines of pulsing eyes, that single fang.

Instead, she leaned against the wall – she'd been a famous leaner in our college days – and polished a nail with diamonds embedded in it. (They'd found a new mine on some wrecked planet, massive fuss in the news.)

'I just wondered. You're one of the rebels, I know. That's why Father ordered your arrest.'

'Your father still lives?'

'He's late in his third incarnation, but yes, he still lives.'

The King hadn't been much in evidence lately, so this counted as bad news. I said, 'The old buzzard always had it in for me. Ever since the Academy.'

Ravene flashed the smile that used to intoxicate me. I suspected that her human half was recollecting old times, but I wasn't getting my hopes up. It was the thought of torture that set the skin on the back of my neck crawling, which was why I needed to goad her into releasing her zuge. Fat chance I'd have of betraying anybody if every white blood cell I'd got was bursting through my skin… And Ravene had always had a shortish fuse.

'We had some good times, didn't we, Ravene?'

'We were innocents then.'

'Shame you betrayed me.'

'You were betrayed by a colleague, not a princess! We both were.'

Despite the circumstances, I still felt a dart of shock. That bastard Judd? Or Harrison? I was desperate to know. But the smarter part of me latched onto the 'princess'.

'You seem to have talked your way out of trouble with Daddy pretty brilliantly.'

My provocation was rewarded by that stunning smile. I recalled the satiny texture of her skin, the electric warmth of those lips. But I'd made my choice – and every decision since had led me straight to this metallic chair.

'Would you rather that I had betrayed you?' she asked.

'Well, it might have made more sense. You were always easily bored.'

She paced. 'I was not bored with you, Aiden – not at all! But one of your friends – also in the history department—'

'Which one?'

'I can't remember names.'

'Try. Male or female?'

'Male.'

'Dark or fair?'

'Dark brown hair. And very boring.'

That bastard Harrison! I'd always wondered.

Ravene, of course, had already lost interest. Instead, she strode around restlessly. 'Because we were together – though it was a few years ago – perhaps the King remembers? Perhaps that's why he sent me to kill you. Me!'

There was just a moment when I almost admired the old bastard. There was an elegance – an irony – in his choice of Ravene. I took a deep breath and remembered that I belonged to myself no longer. If I ever did – if we ever do.

'Then get it over with,' I told her roughly.

'What do you mean?'

'Do what you were ordered to do!'

'Fiery as ever!' she murmured, drawing back her long sleeve.

I waited, recalling the only other zuge I'd ever seen, 3034's fat anxious face, the stricken silence in my classroom. I closed my eyes, superstitious as a child, that I might not see the fang.

When I opened them, Ravene was far closer than I had realised.

She said, strangely, 'Wait!' A soft swathe of turquoise hair was falling across my face. It was a wonderful kiss, almost animalistic.

Instead of a last meal, a last kiss. Fine by me.

Ravene felt starved of human contact – but for several seconds I forgot to notice, I was so fired, so surging, so lost. And when she pulled away, I was captured by those irises: the left side blue, the right green, divided down the middle as precariously as by a surgeon.

I shut my eyes again, waiting for that crushing fang.

Instead I heard the door whoosh closed and, when I opened my eyes again, I was alone.

3

The invaders – variously termed 'the ancients', inaccurately the 'moon men' and finally the Xirfell – arrived a decade ago, in 2084, exactly seventeen years after the end of WWIII.

There was precious little resistance – either in the remainder of the Americas or in the lands of the Old Ones. In short, the ease with which the Earth fell, which many believed the result of brilliant timing, always seemed to me like pure dumb luck.

It was an Earth hardly worth the trouble that Ravene's father had conquered: hunger, famine, devastation and misery were everywhere, and billions had died, along with the ocean's entire ecosystem, and so many trees that the planet may be irrecoverable. Ravene had confided, during the period of our intimacy, that the Xirfell's original plan had been to establish a few sterile outposts, plant a few monuments to the King's supreme genius and then shove off to some more promising planet, leaving the survivors to fight or to rot, as they chose.

She didn't know what made them change their minds.

If the Earth was mostly wrecked, the northern hemisphere was spectacularly so. Still, there remained a few areas for the Xirfell to plunder, particularly in the Arctic, Antarctic, Siberia, northern Canada and Australasia – which the Xirfell renamed G13 – a sector spared the worst of every serious war. It was in G13 that the

9

Xirfell first set up their command structure, and G13 where I first encountered them.

To my mind, they've always seemed a strange combination: culturally naïve, scientifically advanced, emotionally simple.

Their knowledge was impressive, not only of weapons capable of making ours look like slingshots, but also of alien creatures of astonishing gifts: some capable of intuitively divining the presence of minerals deep in the earth, others with the capacity to destroy any bloody thing. They'd also invented robotniks so advanced that I often wondered – other than out of the sheer hilarious thrill of the chase – why they even bothered with our galaxy, having already got about a quadrillion servants from their own.

The Xirfell were however culturally disappointing. For example, they were strangely taken with the detritus of our newest ruins – London, Shanghai, New York. The far more ancient ruins that Londoners and New Yorkers admired they trashed without regret: the Acropolis, the pyramids, Pompeii… Ravene once airily remarked – though as I recall she thought it hilarious – that her father preferred making history to studying it.

This comment was made during our idyll at the Academy, the only university in the world to survive WWIII. This institution had been allowed to continue by a King sated of easy victories, and desperate for both amusement and distraction. Though I was never sure that the Xirfell ever quite grasped that, at the Australasian Academy, they were mostly dealing with the also-rans. The geniuses I'd known or heard of had all perished in the earliest days of the invasion at Harvard, Oxford, Peking University and MIT.

Or perhaps they'd all been driven underground, and were still subsisting in ruins and caves? – It was possible. Not even the Xirfell could murder everybody.

I was interrupted in my recollecting – but not by Ravene. Instead there reared up from behind me one of those noiseless aliens known as blundicants. Far more like a gigantic jellyfish than anything land-based, they move with the ease of the waterborne. Imagine a gluey blob with perhaps eighty fist-sized limbs, two or three metres high. This one was both phosphorescent and diaphanous – the organs repulsively shifting beneath that hood of skin.

As its attending testers tramped in behind, I thought, Oh, fuck, so it is torture, after all.

I knew that blundicants have one weapon against which all humans and even part-humans are helpless: they can latch onto a creature's backbone and access its brain. They weren't mind-readers – that would have been game over – but they were as close to being mind-readers as any creature in the Xirfell's galaxy, our own, or all the wrecked ones in-between.

And I had more dread of having my brain hacked than most. Not because I'm some kind of a frigging genius but because I had something rare there: my memory sliver.

The memory sliver was an upgrade which I'd been given at the Academy, when the Xirfell, surfeited of destruction, selected a few human students to experiment on. To this day I have a minute, supposedly indestructible, implant inside my skull, on which I inscribe my personal diary, through thought commands alone. Over the last decade, I'd grown more and more intrigued by this process, as a full and frank record for posterity – *The Mad Rebel's Tale*, anybody? – and it must've survived my death because – hey – you're reading it.

Basically, I wanted to leave behind some kind of testimony – of affirmation, even – that not everybody on Earth chucked in the towel after the Xirfell had triumphed. That there really had been a rebellion, and that I was one of its operatives, and that being a rebel was the single thing I was proudest of in the whole of my messy, chaotic life.

Anyway, in my case, the memory sliver operation worked –

along with a couple of minor physical upgrades, nothing life-altering – but the other students were less lucky, so the Xirfell abandoned the idea.

But would the blundicant nose it out – even destroy it? – I wasn't entirely clear how their mind-melding worked.

I straightened into alertness as the alien circled, nerve-rackingly close, at first blocking the sky, then releasing it. Suddenly, shockingly, I found myself released from the bondage of the chair. Although, before I could so much as twitch a bicep, the blundicant had locked itself onto my spine.

I steeled myself – uselessly, of course. What the jellyfishy thing used for muscle I had no idea, but it was crushingly efficient. Next I felt something crawling through the spinal fluid, all the way from the bottom of my spine to my crown. A boneless chill eased into my neck, tingling my scalp and pulsing icily around my head. Without speech, I was addressed, brain to brain.

–Can you hear me? It silently wanted to know.

Like an idiot, I yelled aloud, 'You'll get nothing out of me!'

It ordered me, wordlessly, to address it only on the inside. If I understood I was to nod. Eventually, grudgingly, I nodded.

–It's for your own protection. I know it may seem strange, but I am a friend, Aiden.

–Like fuck you are.

I was scrambling to erect blocks in my brain, walls that might protect the secrets of my rebel cell – safe houses, meeting places, secret names, sympathisers whose names I knew. What if – unconsciously – I was about to betray them all?

Then the blundicant 'spoke' again inside me.

–I realise that this is difficult to believe, Aiden, but I really am a friend – to you and to the rebellion.

–Of course you fucking are. Why don't you just finish peeling my brain back like a blinking onion and piss off?

But then it breathed, inside my brain:

–Harpalian.

I stiffened, for if my blood name was in their hands, then it was all over – for me, for Malthus, for Priscilla, perhaps even for the rebellion itself. The creature had stolen my *name* – my only consolation being that it hadn't been my own doing, that it had been stolen.

Once I'd finished swearing, one of the testers growled, 'Shall I punish him, sir?'

'No, not yet,' the spectre-thing said hastily. His inner voice remained quiet, even patient.

–I gave you your true name not to upset you, but to prove myself a friend – a fellow member of the rebellion – though I hold a relatively high office in the regime. In fact, I've been sent by the King, who believes me loyal, to scour your brain for rebel intelligence. I come with some hope – not much, but a little.

Automatically I glanced up but could see nothing beyond the bulbous blobs oozing to either side of me, as he was latched onto my spine. I directed my still-furious mind inwards.

–Prove it. Prove that this isn't just some massive con.

–I can prove nothing. Your own instincts must guide you. Either I am one of them, and playing games with your psyche in hopes of learning more – they know something of the truth already, I'm afraid – or else I'm a rebel agent, your comrade in arms, united with Omyestra, and striving to overthrow the regime.

Omyestra, of course, was Priscilla's blood name, and she the nearest thing I still had on Earth to a mother. Priscilla! What I wouldn't give to see those deep hazel eyes again!

But the blundicant could have swiped Omyestra from the same part of my brain as Harpalian, right?

There were no certainties left; still, I had to decide. I almost pitied the blundicant: its appearance was against it, its invasiveness too – who wouldn't feel violated? But what if it was telling the truth?

It was not unheard of, not impossible: after all, even Nazi Germany had boasted a handful of Party members willing to assassinate Hitler. There had been rumours of creatures secretly on the side of the resistance since forever – even a few, supposedly, within the Golden Circle itself. (What had he said? 'I hold a relatively high office...')

I couldn't help wondering what office that might be.

–How do I know that Priscilla's name wasn't oozed out of me by those clammy globules of yours?

–It might have been. You must simply decide to trust me – or not. I would only say this, you have no other hope. At least, none that I can determine.

A well-spoken monster, I couldn't help thinking – or maybe elegant English was part of its act? Personally, when I feel something strongly, I tend to swear.

I remembered what Sebastian taught me – Sebastian, betrayed and murdered but ever our leader. ('Erect barriers before, after and during... Prepare fake stories, and feed them these first... Go deeply into your truest self – there will your answers lie.')

But where was the 'truth' in this metallic cage? I took a deep breath and a gamble.

And inside, I told the creature,

–Game on.

4

The next bit proved a severe test, mostly of my acting ability.

Back at the Academy, I'd been a tolerable character actor – never a star – except during a pretty rubbish student revival of that ancient classic, *Fiddler on the Roof.* And I'd only starred then because the actor playing Tevye got denounced and imprisoned, casting – as you could imagine – rather a pall over the proceedings.

But the first thing the blundicant 'told' me after I relented was that I needed to pretend to be in pain, or at least discomfort, to avoid his being suspected by the regime. His orders were to extract information, by any means – his credibility was at stake. The creature suggested that I call him MF, his own name being unpronounceable, and warned that we were being monitored from every side. Then he spoke very bluntly.

–I have bad news. Malthus is dead – no, friend, use that anger. Try to wrench away from me.

But I was too upset to pretend. Never to see old Malthus again – those kind eyes, those sloping shoulders, that attenuated profile with the pipe! Yes, there had been rumours. But there are always rumours on a planet rife with deliberate misinformation. MF continued.

–He died a hero.

–Of course he did! – He lived a hero, too.

–Then imagine I killed him. Summon up your anger. Acknowledge it – own it.

After I had cursed freely, he added,

–You should also know that another has been sworn in as leader in his place.

But not me, I thought, with a spurt of jealousy. Although not really leadership material – too impulsive, too volatile, too much of a risktaker – part of me had still hoped, even longed, to be the next one chosen.

MF didn't comment, but he probably sensed my jealousy. Instead he said,

–The rebellion is now headed by Martin McNamara. You know him, I believe.

It's tough having to constantly show myself in so unflattering a light. However – though we'd practically grown up together – Martin was never a friend, and – on my side at least – the dislike had always been spiced with jealousy. Of course, I respected him: physically powerful, mentally cagey, white Anglo, confident, stable, fit – the boy had it all, compared to a half-Indigenous orphan like me. It was simply that we had attended the same school, had together survived the Academy cull and had jointly risen through the ranks of the rebellion without finding a single thing about each other to like. I imagined Martin taking the oath of leadership, Martin receiving the congratulations of all our acquaintance, Martin being embraced by my girlfriend, Petra…

MF urged me to wince, something I managed without effort.

–Martin, eh? Well, well. There could have been worse choices. Me, for instance.

But this was unfair. Here I was in prison, with Martin probably exerting every sinew on my behalf – and all I could do was to snipe at the bastard. So I added,

–Is Petra OK? – She must be devastated about Malthus.

–Petra is safe. Though mourning her uncle, of course. And I'm also allowed to give you some good news: we have a sympathiser in the Golden Circle.

–That's not good news, that's a disaster – that never works. We've been here before, MF. Before your time, probably.

–This creature is honest.

–We believed the other one honest as well.

MF was kidding himself if he trusted anyone in the Golden Circle to be truly a member of the rebellion. For several years there had even been a policy against any member of the rebellion rising to such giddy heights, because the regime's loyalty tests were so punishing that no human could withstand them... Then I remembered.

–Creature, did you say? Do you mean an alien?

–Could you grit your teeth, friend, as if trying not to scream? Excellent. Now, have you heard of the rulers of the pundlings?

–That would be the Xirfell themselves.

–On Earth, naturally. But on their own planet, E356, the pundlings were also ruled.

Well, they would be, wouldn't they, the splodgy little fatheads, I couldn't help thinking. Which was unfair, as they were so gentle and so loveable. I recalled 3034 with a stab of remorse.

–So, who rules them in their home galaxy, if not the Xirfell?

–A people you won't have encountered, as they can't endure Earth temperatures.

–Then how the hell could one of them be here, and in the Golden Circle too?

Unruffled, MF explained that the creature, a peitrel known as Leelack, was kept in something that resembled a frozen pool. On the pundlings' planet there were great billowing expanses of this icy substance, but on Earth Leelack's movements were restricted, as she couldn't breathe air for long, and Earth's was anyway so polluted. I tried to imagine the fat little pundlings scooting around a planet half-covered with icy slime – perhaps that was why they didn't need shoes? – but remained sceptical.

–How long has she been in the Golden Circle?

–For several years, one of the secret members.

This was not unknown: some Golden Circle members encouraged near-cultish followings – others preferred complete privacy. Sometimes the first we ever heard about a Golden Circle member was when they were denounced as traitors and scheduled for execution.

–Sebastian himself enlisted her.

–And what do they look like, these icy creatures?

–She rarely leaves her quarters, so I have never met Leelack.

–But surely you must know?

–I have heard that they are amber in colour and surpassingly beautiful.

–Unlike you, then.

At which MF mildly proposed that I have another go at struggling.

My immediate thought was that Ravene was unlikely to be keen on a being possibly even more stunning than her – I predicted trouble for the sea-fishy creature. But acting felt tougher than ever, given all that the blundicant had told me. Of course, Malthus' death was a blow – and so – between ourselves – was Martin's promotion. But MF had not only failed to detect the memory sliver, he had also gifted me with a sliver of hope. MF was one of us; Petra was safe – and this Leelack compelled my imagination. She must be deep, and deeply strong, to have passed all their tests and still be with us!

Which was why, despite Malthus's death, I felt flooded with sudden lightness. MF must have noticed because he wryly observed,

–You're not a very good actor, are you?

–And never was. But now – when I begin to feel some flicker

of hope – I'm so utterly useless, stuck here! Why wasn't I warned about the chance of my arrest? I could have gone undercover – headed off on some mission – anything!

–No one knew. Why don't you blame me? Curse, yell, moan, so that they imagine I'm torturing you – but then I must leave you, to supply a report for the King.

–But you'll come back?

–I will try. Also, be alert for pundling 7784, who is with us. He may have messages, either from me or from Martin himself.

Even as he detached himself, two testers were crushing me back into that loathsome chair, while I committed pundling 7784 to memory.

In some ways I longed for MF to go, for I ached from my spine upwards – but it was hellish lonely in that chair. Lonely enough to make even Ravene, who was careless as a cat and could quite easily kill me, feel like a friend.

I never much enjoy being on my own – I feel most alive when commanding a team. Perhaps MF sensed this, because he moved before me and I saw, this time with much less revulsion, his organs rocking into each other beneath that gluey plasma. But then he was gone.

A pundling arrived, with food. Another removed my waste. And I remembered.

5

I hadn't been attracted to Petra, at first. She was too skinny, with those thin lips, budlike breasts, athlete's legs and defiant air. It had been during a meeting – Sebastian's last, as it happened, for he was arrested soon afterwards – when I first noticed her.

Sebastian said, 'We can expect no more help from Sefu and his team, under their current circumstances, and the situation in G9 is very bad. We don't know how much intelligence the recent defector gave the Xirfell, either. We need to return to what we do best: small operations, small cells, and perhaps small victories also.'

Priscilla agreed but added, 'But we must remain open to any unexpected opportunities. To strike where possible – to resist where necessary.'

Ichthus said gloomily, 'Mass uprisings must be much less likely.'

'Someday,' said Priscilla, 'these will happen. But we can't know when.'

Petra's hand shot skywards. Too pale, too intense, too thin – not my type. But there was something about her, all the same.

'Yes, Petra?'

'I think that we should take more risks, in terms of publicity.

Most of the people in my lodgings have hardly heard of the rebellion, though I'm sure there are sympathisers there.'

Now this contribution was pretty much shot down in flames, but I found it so appealing that I approached her afterwards and said, 'I really liked what you said in the meeting, Petra.'

Her face looked far less bony, her eyes far brighter, when she blushed.

'It seems such a waste not to seize every chance – and who knows what might spark the revolution? Historically, it always happens so unpredictably!'

'Also, unless we take a few risks, we'll never go down in legend and song.'

'Who cares about *that*?'

'Um, me, I'm afraid.'

She unleashed a mischievous smile. 'I'd heard you might.'

'Personally, I think there ought to be more individual initiatives,' I added, almost without thought, because she was exciting me.

And I was aware that she knew this. And that she was aware that I was aware. And it all ended, as of course I meant it to, much later that night, with my lips locked onto her tiny breasts, and her arms around my hot neck, and my prick at first cosseted in her mouth and finally utterly triumphant inside, and my preference for voluptuous women wildly overturned.

Now the rebellion didn't forbid this kind of thing, but it wasn't exactly encouraged either, so we agreed to keep the affair a secret. Something we managed so badly that it was only a couple of days before Malthus, second in importance only to Sebastian himself, took me aside and told me that 'it was known' that I'd been with his niece.

I didn't know what to say. Sheer respect for the man handicapped me.

'I'm sorry. But she—'

He put a broad hand on my shoulder. 'Petra is strong and real and wonderful. But it's potentially a great distraction for you both, and at a very critical time. We're depending on you, Aiden. Probably far more than you think.'

This speech made me ridiculously, crazily, childishly happy – really, I'd rarely felt so happy – and just recalling it moved me deeply, especially when I remembered that he could never put his hand on my shoulder again.

After this, Petra and I restrained ourselves, but after another meeting, it happened again, and I'd never felt anything so intense, not even with Ravene – perhaps because with Petra there was none of the titillating electrical strangeness that there was with a half-alien. (Still weirder was the fact that, due to the Xirfell's accelerated lifecycles, Ravene had been, in human years, a mere toddler when we were together, though appearing at least twenty.)

But from the moment Petra's lips touched mine it was as if a charge had fired me. Pale as she was, she felt golden in my arms; everything I did seemed to answer her. In those days, we became hungrily and even dangerously obsessed with each other, and maybe – to be honest – I did lose the plot for a while.

I also felt guilty, because of what Malthus had said. But the times were crazy – the politics were crazy – and the rules are suspended in wartime. And gradually Petra and I became rather less absorbed in each other and started paying more attention to our tasks – not only various rebel missions, but also keeping up our 'cover' personas in the world outside.

Perhaps the gene for stability was somehow omitted from my DNA, but the next time I found myself really obsessing about Petra was when Martin McNamara went after her.

Early for a council meeting, I was just entering the cave – one of the twenty or so venues we used, in random rotation – when I spotted Martin and Petra were already there. Instinctively,

I slipped back out of sight, just as he said under his breath, 'You grow more beautiful every day, Petra.'

Now I accept that I ought to have announced my presence – and immediately too. Instead, I waited, at the edge of the cave entrance, just out of sight.

Petra said, 'No, I grow thinner and thinner, like a cat.'

'You do have eyes rather like a cat's – slanted, elegant.'

'My mother used to tell me that. I always doubted it was a compliment.'

'Of course it was a compliment.'

'I don't know where I've put the folder for sector four. It should have been in the third row, but you know what Iolanthe's like.'

'Why don't you just put that file down?'

'Martin, please. Don't.'

'You know how I feel. Kiss me.'

'I – I can't.'

'Your uncle wouldn't mind.'

'Aiden would.'

'Aiden! Yes, well – useful fellow in a brawl – a fantastic shot – but you know how rash he is. No tact, no discipline, utterly reckless – always going off practically getting himself killed! Why should any sane person choose Aiden?'

She very quietly said, 'You don't always… choose.'

'What do you mean?'

'You don't always choose – logically.'

'No, of course not, but are you really sure—'

'Sure of what?'

'Well, are you sure that it isn't just, well, the fascination of his being an Indigenous person?'

'What earthly difference does *that* make?'

'It can possess a rather exotic appeal. And you do realise that he's been with the princess herself?'

'I wouldn't care if he'd been with a tester!'

'But humans are rendered sterile in these cases!'

'Well, who'd want to bring a child into this world, anyway?'

I should mention that Martin had called his shots perfectly correctly here: I can never have a child. Coupling with Ravene – only half-human though sexually virtuosic – had taken that from me. Though she'd never pretended otherwise: in fact, she had even warned me. In her fashion, Ravene's quite an honest creature.

Maybe more honest than I was, eavesdropping outside that cave... I can still vividly summon up the smell – bat droppings, the dregs of Malthus's pipe, Priscilla's stale green tea.

I missed the next bit due to being distracted by the howling of wild edoys, those weird, hyena-like aliens. By the time I started paying attention again there seemed to be a scuffle going on. Surely Martin wouldn't do anything requiring me to interfere? – I balled my fists in my pockets.

I strongly suspect that Petra slapped him – though I'll never be able to prove it – because then I heard a rather sulky, 'OK, OK, you made your point.'

I moved off – silently, not a cracked twig – but, once back in the wilderness, I found it impossible to concentrate. Instead I wandered around, feeling confused and unworthy, but also in a kind of a glory. For, although Petra hadn't said that she loved me – I'd noticed that, as you probably did too – still, she was faithful.

Then I got attacked by one of those super-rats that had thrived since the invasion. The size of a Labrador, riddled with germs and probably rabies, it tried to nail me without so much as a sporting warning. I was in just the mood to trample the brute to death, though it measured the better part of a metre and its teeth were fearsome.

I thought, They'll probably outlast us all.

The reason for my temper might have been because, although I had disliked Martin for years before he made a pass at my girlfriend, he was also, in that unspoken 'pecking order' of the resistance, more highly thought of – something of which Petra ('You don't always … choose') had seemed unsettlingly aware.

Not simply better-born, but less mercurial, more intellectually incisive, more emotionally controlled. On the other hand, his being White and my being Indigenous was a non-issue, at least within the rebellion. So much so that I'd thought it odd that Martin had even mentioned my ethnicity, along with the impossibility of my fathering children. (But had Petra really meant what she had said, about not wanting any? After all, many women did want children…)

Anyway, the whole incident bugged the hell out of me, which was probably why the giant rat got his. Delaying my return to the cave until the last possible moment, I continued to wander instead.

All around, weeds were busily reclaiming most of suburban Sydney, the previous name for Australasia's capital. Houses, gardens, swimming pools and tennis courts were all in the process of being swallowed up by radioactive vegetation, while some of the wild snakes were of extraordinary size, judging by one snakeskin I stumbled upon. The air, of course, was still thick, fetid, vaguely metallic, but there was some comfort in the triumph of the indomitable wilderness. The ivy and kudzu, at least, resolutely refused to die.

As for my eavesdropping, I contented myself by vowing that I would try harder to control my temperament. (How well have I done? – Not very.)

At this point two pundlings arrived with my usual prison meal, sandier and gristlier than ever. But MF had gifted me that sliver of hope, so I gulped it down as fast as I could, in hopes of not registering the taste.

6

I woke up, dashed by drops of rain, to realise that I was being shaved, well out of the pundlings' usually unvarying routine. The reason for this became obvious when, a half-hour later, I was visited by King Hebdith himself.

The upside – I must be more important than my own mother ever thought me. The downside? – I was probably about to be fucking executed. Steeling myself, I couldn't help noticing how much harder it was to accept death than it had been before MF had appeared.

Before MF, I'd even ordered Ravene to kill me, so that I could betray nobody. At this point, though, I felt confident – maybe over-confident. I had to force myself to recall my training – to deepen my breathing, to ground myself.

The King was heavily attended. In addition to no fewer than ten testers of unusual size and impressiveness, each the rough equivalent of five or so battle-hardened human warriors, he was also accompanied by two Xirfell, three humans or part-humans, a couple of robotniks and a squat, pudgy-legged, strangely cuddly spider. This creature, perhaps fifteen centimetres wide, was curled smugly in the royal lap, emitting pigeon-like coos. I wanted to hit it with a brick.

I thought, The first party since my arrest, five days ago. Possibly my last party, also.

At first there was manic activity, due to the lack of a suitable resting place for the King's backside. (There was a chair, but one reckoned too humble for the royal rump.) I watched as a couple of perspiring pundlings appeared, bearing an embroidered throne between them. Once ensconced, the King was within my line of vision, spider-creature on his lap – one muscular hand just smoothing it.

When Ravene's father had first conquered Earth, the Xirfell had apparently resembled the result of an unlikely erotic collision between a rhinoceros and an anteater – presumably this was what the Xirfell looked like, in their own galaxy? Many body-borrowing, body-altering operations later, he was one of the handsomest middle-aged humans I'd ever seen – tanned and tall, broad of shoulder, strong of face, with a short beard and wonderfully wide-set – almost *too* wide-set – blue-black eyes. Only the slit-down-the-middle irises remained from his previous incarnation. (Perhaps his current body was stolen? – Technology had made even this possible.)

A decade ago, as ruler of our wrecked planet and conqueror of any number of others, the King could wed whomever he chose, and thousands of gorgeous young women and exquisite aliens were paraded before him, in a scene vaguely reminiscent of the American South in the days of the slave trade.

Out of these – absolutely against the form book – he had selected Ravene's mother: a more delicate, yet still entrancing, version of the leggy Ravene. Whom he had used and abused, adored but still supplemented with thousands of others – each preferred in their turn – until they did something displeasing, when he had the unnerving habit of tossing them to his blurgs.

Despite this, the King had never forgotten Ravene's mother, Queen Angharad. Which was presumably why, her cancer inoculation having failed and the Queen having died, he persisted in retaining Ravene as his heir, to the annoyance of any number of ambitious rivals, equally his offspring. There was also a hideous memorial to his first wife and a week each year dedicated to mourning her, though she had been unremarkable except for her shyness – a tiny Welsh beauty, visibly distressed at being singled-out by the new dictator-King.

All this rushed through my brain as I surveyed King Hebdith, in person, for the first time.

What had Ravene said? – his third and final incarnation. The Xirfell's energies faded with each incarnation: their colouring less vital, the reality dimmer. Though he was still a fine figure of a man, the old bastard, grown fleshy on his triumphs and wearing attire vaguely suggestive of ancient Rome. In his dress, his attitude, even his posture, he struck me as a middle-aged child – self-centred, vengeful, vain, the centre of his own warped universe. And, when I recalled Sebastian and the rest, I absolutely hungered to feel his dark pulsing blood within my fists.

I thought, Steady on, Aiden. Not your job to save the world.

'So, here we have the troublemaker, Tenten,' were his first words, at which his entourage glared as one in my direction. Even the spider-creature seemed to stir disapprovingly in the royal lap.

I was OK with this. I would rather, of course, have been leader of the rebellion, or maybe one of the rebel leaders of the simmering insurrections of G6 or G9, but I could live with 'troublemaker'. Rhetorically, to his testers, he added, 'Where do we breed these traitors?'

I told him, 'I'm no traitor – to my people.'

'You are a traitor to the democratically elected leadership of this planet!' he spat. The suddenness of his rages was legendary, along with his swift changes of mood – this rebel was to die, the next to be given another chance. Mercurial, he loved to keep every servant guessing.

I said, 'But, luckily or unluckily, there's no democracy left. So, what have you come for? My life?'

'Not today. For information only.'

'You'll get no information out of me,' I retorted, hoping that this was true. 'Anyway, you sent your scummy mind-meddler only yesterday. Surely he keeps nothing from you?'

One of the testers grated – to be fair, they have ratcheted throats – 'Shall I punish him, your honour?'

'Not yet,' said Hebdith, and then, looking curiously at me. 'You should know that one of your colleagues is dead – the one called Malthus.'

Of course, I knew this only confidentially, from MF, so I had to pretend.

'You killed him!'

'He is anyway dead. And you have been spoken of as a potential successor.'

'You're joking – Me, heir to Malthus?'

'It could be just another rebel lie. Others were mentioned also.'

I wondered whether Martin McNamara was on their radar, gloomily reminding myself that I owed my first loyalty to our new leader. The crooning of the furry creature itched at my nerves, and suddenly everything seemed hopeless. MF had maybe tricked me – Malthus was dead and – just at that moment – I found that I couldn't quite believe in some stunning rebel alien, obliged to exist on ice and accepted into membership of the Golden Circle. The entire resistance suddenly seemed a ragtag collection of misfits – encircled, oppressed, outclassed – and almost certainly doomed.

But the King seemed nervy, an uneasy twitch at the corner of his mouth. This could have been paranoia – as had been rumoured before. But what if he had something to be paranoid about? Why did he blinking care who had taken over, unless he feared the rebellion, or feared what the rebellion might someday rouse the masses to do?

I tried to imagine it – spies in government, treason in the army, riots in the cities, uprisings in the wilderness. Perhaps some non-Earth species on the radar that not even the Xirfell could handle, hell-bent on their destruction... I sat up straighter just as he asked me outright, 'Who is heir to Malthus?'

'Haven't a fucking clue. How could I, stuck down here?'

A flash of fire in those bisected eyes. 'There is one called Ichthus.'

I thought, Ichthus? *Ichthus?* Ichthus, always chewing his lower lip, who must be eighty, if a day! Though eighty wasn't particularly old any longer. Yet Ichthus seemed to have been born old. Pedantic, cautious, carping old Ichthus! – not even I could be jealous of Ichthus. But maybe Ichthus could be sold to the Xirfell as the new leader?

I clenched my teeth and refused to answer. The stinging shock was instantaneous – blood trickled down my temple. The tester's whip recoiled, studded with some fiery substance that smelled of something I didn't recognise. Could be poison. Sometimes they were poisoned, sometimes not; nobody had ever accused the Xirfell of consistency. Though a part of me felt almost glad that it had started at last.

'Speak!' the ranking tester glowered.

'It's not – Ichthus!'

I was guessing that time was critical. If I could only buy MF enough time to get a warning to Ichthus, the rebellion could get him into hiding. I had only to make the regime waste enough time tearing it out of me that Ichthus had been selected, for Martin – our real leader – to be secure.

It was supposedly safer not to name Martin, not even internally. I pictured his name, and then imagined rubbing it out. Could he be with Petra, at that very moment? I couldn't help imagining it: Martin's taut, lean body and strong shoulders, those athletic thighs…

Suddenly one of the tester's whips targeted my knee – my vision momentarily spangled by the purity of the pain.

'The name!' snarled the King. 'Ichthus!'

'It isn't – Ichthus.'

Here, very luckily, I instinctively closed my eyes, because in the next second my left eyelid was torn. Fury tiding over me, I cursed freely. The King watched me, a beading of sweat on his brow. I thought, Why the fuck is *he* sweating? Isn't this the guy who allows his unfaithful concubines to be torn apart by those hyena-like edoys?

'The mind-melder said Ichthus,' rasped a tester, and I secretly blessed MF.

'What about McNamara?' demanded the King. I allowed a derisive expression to cross my face but said nothing. Another tester landed his whip on my shoulder, but the knee had been way worse and my wince was partly faked, in hopes that I might be spared a sequel. Another blow on that knee might cripple me.

The King needled me. 'Martin McNamara? Why not? What's wrong with him?'

'He's not fit to be a leader.'

'Drugs?' asked the King sharply. 'Drugs, coward?'

What on earth could I blame Martin for? – The fucker was very nearly perfect. He hadn't touched drugs even as a teen.

'Women,' I breathed.

Revenge was sweet. Though there wasn't a whole lot of truth to this, I must admit, because casual affairs were never Martin's style. Power was all he ever really wanted, and now he had it, and maybe Petra, too. But – and this was what was messing with my brain – he also had me. I was pledged, until death, to Sebastian, Malthus – and now, Martin.

Only the last one stuck in my throat.

'What about Laurentia?' demanded the King.

Now I had met the brilliant Laurentia only twice – she'd led a smallish cell before her transfer – but as I suspected that she'd come second in the ballot, it was certainly my job to trash her.

'Laurentia, the half-human. Speak!' This from the King, sweat still pulsing on his temple.

Maybe he secretly hated the sight of blood? Or might the rumours be right, that it turned him on? – I snapped, 'Certainly not Laurentia.'

'Temper?'

I thought, Even the King had heard of her temper! – and decided to use the fact, to suggest that I was weakening.

'– is not sound.'

'This accords with our intelligence,' a tester grated. 'Your Honour, shall I—'

The King said thoughtfully, 'I'm sure it's Ichthus Dmitrios. Twist the shoulder – hard, but not hard enough to dislocate… What say you to that, traitor?'

'Not – Ichthus!'

This went on for blinking hours, but I'll spare you the rest. I admitted Ichthus had been elected – though of course he hadn't – at the end of five bruising hours. I could only hope that this supplied time enough for pundling 7784 or some other operative to warn MF, and for Ichthus to go into hiding.

It had seemed even longer – some trick of the brain, perhaps.

The King had left long before the end, not long after they blindfolded me. How did I know? Because the testers briefly lost interest, and then began to get annoyed at how long I was holding out and got interested again. Also, the scraping of the King's throne, as it got towed away.

Then serene little pundlings rushed in to sew me up – the knee was worrying, the eyelid not so bad. Meanwhile, I felt privately triumphant. Though concerned for Ichthus, I was betting that I'd bought him enough time. Also, I'd never been tortured before. Call it a rite of passage.

But once my euphoria waned, I despised myself for relishing the attention. I also fretted about where Ichthus could go: a safe house, maybe Bully's? Tim's dugout, deep underground? I wondered if Martin could have held out longer than I did – and whether Petra and the others would even know that I'd been tortured.

As the light faded to black, I longed for the credits to roll, the audience to disperse and the show to be over.

7

I was left alone, barring pundlings, for two endless days, with far too much time to think. Not knowing how much longer I might have, I decided to work on my record for posterity – not that I'll have any personally, of course. After all, no other human survived the memory sliver operation and – while not pretending that mine represents deathless prose – I do guarantee an accurate record. (If only Hitler'd had one! Imagine the thrill at its discovery!)

And if, in my darker moments, I imagined the memory sliver finishing up in the centre of the pit where the King would finally toss me – or lost in the entrails of the royal blurg – I also teased myself with the notion that, someday, somehow, a couple of creatures might read it, and understand.

Now WWIII by all accounts was no picnic in the park, but the fact that it was 'merely' the rest of the world that imploded permitted Australasia to survive.

Instead, it was the Xirfell invasion – sometimes termed the Final War – that did for G13, though even calling it a war seemed a little arrogant, given that it was finished in a couple of weeks. (Final Skirmish, anyone?)

A fastish end to the Earth's long period of galactic isolation. Your basic game-changer.

The first rumours of aliens occurred when I was sixteen. My

adoptive father Duncan flew home in his zelopod and said disgustedly to his wife, 'An obvious hoax, but you wouldn't credit how many people think there's something in it. Lord, what fools these mortals be!'

And poor Sophia, her face a sticky greenish colour, said, 'Duncan, dear, I think it's true.'

Stomach plummeting, I was sent to my pod to do my homework, where I promptly vomited what remained of my dinner. But, if not a false alarm, it wasn't the real invasion, either. Every government on Earth was united in denying it, and the fascist dictatorship in question – it was somewhere in South America that the scouting Xirfell vessel had been sighted – executed every witness.

So, only a warning shot. The invasion itself was still to come.

Theories abound as to why the original Xirfell sighting was so hushed-up. There was certainly international collusion. But Duncan Tenten, an entrepreneur, was privileged in government circles – he owned about sixteen zelopods, of the sort that even women's eyes followed – and I suspect he knew more than he let on.

At any rate I returned to school, still caring mostly about rugby but near the top of the class for all that. Puberty happened. Girls happened. Sport happened too, although the World Games – successors to the Olympics – never did. Because the second time that the Xirfell came, they came for real.

Religious hysterics claimed it was the Second Coming, that the blinking Xirfell represented the Horsemen of the Apocalypse. Cynics were quick to imagine a government conspiracy to turn Australasia into a full dictatorship – which had happened almost everywhere else following the coronavirus years anyway. But others instantly recognised it for what it was: Earth's final war.

There was resistance, but it was disorganised and scrambled, fierce but divided. History will say that the Russians made the best fist of it, which is how they came to be annihilated. History will probably also claim that the Asians fought the longest, especially in their farthest-flung outposts – though America and Europe were hit earliest and hardest, by the release of crusted creatures resembling gigantic eels, capable of asphyxiating small cities, that the Xirfell dispatched once their usefulness was over.

History might also mention the original Xirfell themselves, rumoured to be so hideous that the sight of them could blind people – though this only happened to humans aged over 120, and not to all of these.

I was in the Academy's food pod when the news first broke: landings on both coasts of America and – still more crushingly – in Europe, with a separate but devastating sideswipe at Beijing. At first, lurid reports surfaced everywhere – each more horrific than the last – but later that same day the Xirfell blocked all communication, and that was even worse, because then we heard nothing.

Imprisoned within the Academy – which had instantly erected its nuclear shields – about twenty thousand of us endured isolation for over a month, the longest month of our lives, during which Earth was wrenched from human grasp.

For us, the not knowing was the hardest.

While the rest of Australasia was dying, we had nothing to do but wait. We were reduced to wandering around the halls in a parody of university life, afraid to glance out of the peepholes for fear of what we might see, though it was mostly only a dusky half-light, the smouldering end of the world. It was during this period that my adoptive parents, the Tentens, died – possibly by their own hand, for there were plenty of suicides, especially after the principal cities had been incinerated.

By the time the Xirfell found sufficient leisure to investigate our puny corner of the world, we were down to our last consignment of post-nuclear biscuits, while the Xirfell had grown sated, smug and tolerant with their victories. Probably for that reason, as a switch-up from show trials and executions, they decided to experiment on those few uncontaminated Earth-dwellers. This was why the Australasian elect – and we youthful Academy students in particular – were not only allowed but even encouraged to live.

Indigenous Aussies seemed of particular fascination. There was even a short-lived move to keep us as pets – which fell to the ground after two Xirfell were murdered by their 'pets'. For a while the biggest and strongest Indigenous Aussies were pitted against each other in the ring, with the Xirfell taking bets on the results. For all these reasons, Indigenous Aussies seem a lot rarer than we used to be.

Meanwhile, the remaining Academy university students – of every ethnicity – were rounded up and jailed. (Really, we were the lucky ones. The fate of non-students, the unskilled or the simple was to be hunted down or else left to starve.)

All the same, we didn't feel lucky. I'll never forget the cell that I shared with around seventy other Academy survivors, sustained by animal scraps, mostly raw. For ages I assumed that we'd been rounded up to die. This would have been OK by me because, what with the overcrowding, the sickness and the airlessness, existence was pretty unendurable.

Instead, powerful beings of a vaguely bull-like appearance arrived, from the Xirfell's own galaxy, to put us students through tests. (It was around this time that the name 'tester' was coined, for this specific breed of alien.) Those who failed were either lobotomised or sent to the slate fields. Those who passed most spectacularly were sent to lab-like centres, where some of the Xirfell's weirder servants were ordered to mind-meld with us.

So, MF wasn't – quite – my only experience of mind invasion.

These miniature aliens resembled twelve- or fifteen-centimetre blobs of flabby globular ectoplasm, and sported any number of short protruding stumps (maybe noses? I could never decide). They felt warm and oily, almost soothing, on one's brow – very unlike MF's spinal rake, though maybe distantly related.

I'll never forget the sensation when that first sucking tentacle connected with my head – or my state of slippery panic – what if I didn't get it back? – as my entire brain oiled sideways. The moment I perceived it in my head again was possibly the most purely joyful of my twenty years.

Numbers. Out of the entire surviving university cohort, only eighty-nine survived the miniature mind-melders. As one of the fewest of the few, I was then selected for the memory sliver experiment. So, even if I'm exploded by zuge – which could happen any second now – this tiny, indestructible implant should survive: the last fragment of me left standing.

Eventually the King decided that it would be more amusing to re-open the Academy for the benefit of his own numerous offspring, those resilient humans who had survived every test, and a few hand-picked aliens.

A different kind of experiment: a social experiment.

This was the period when I was imperially seduced by Ravene, and when Sebastian Nevsky – then the ranking history professor – recruited me for the rebellion, along with Malthus, Ichthus, Ho Chi, Laurentia, Martin, Bully, Sefu, Tim, Doreen, Hugh and all the rest.

Sebastian. How to describe Sebastian? – He was not only a historian but a passionate believer in revolution as an act of conscience. He believed it to be our duty – to humankind, even to history – to resist. Though he accepted our loyalty, he held it lightly and, in return, he gave us everything he had. Whenever I remember him – his big beard, his enormous girth, his amazing generosity – I think that nothing I could do in return could ever be enough.

8

I was interrupted by Ravene. Less shocking than the first time, of course, and accompanied by a few testers and an assortment of baby pundlings – which she had infantilized abominably. There were fifteen of these, thanks to the usual Xirfell superstition – fifteen members of the Golden Circle, fifteen ranked princes and princesses, fifteen every bloody thing – and all fifteen had been buttoned up like bulgy ballerinas in frilly tutus and satin shoes, their knees resembling bread rolls, their fat chins wobbling.

Ravene's own arresting beauty – she was in navy and jade silk – was set off perfectly by the baby pundlings, who gambled gleefully about the barren room, undeterred by the lack of anything to play with beyond each other. It revolted me: the outfits, the cherubic tumbling, the lot.

As soon as Ravene entered, she aimed a studded fingernail at several places around the walls. Maybe some devices had been implanted there? I instantly committed these to memory, recalling MF's mention of monitoring devices. She was guarded – because of course I was so frigging dangerous, bound to the chair – by two testers equipped with whips. To be honest, I rather focused on the whips, as my knee was yet to recover.

Ravene seated herself on the only chair, tugging one of the little pudgeballs onto her lap, where it gleefully fiddled with her turquoise hair. The hair appeared to have minute gems set into it: must have made combing torture. I recalled Petra's ponytail with a sudden emotional charge. Probably, I'd never see her again.

'And so, dear Aiden! Are you well?'

'Fantastic. Remind me what this nightclub's called again?'

'But you're injured! I told them not to hurt you!'

'Must be great to have servants so thoroughly to be trusted.'

'What happened to your knee?'

'I fell on the tennis court. What else could have fucking happened?'

The knee was – frankly – murder. The Xirfell might have been astonishing at genetics but they were crap at minor injuries; also, that particular effort had gone most of the way to the bone.

Ravene, in pretty distress, dropped the pundling, who rolled cheerfully back to her fellows. You can't beat a pundling for philosophy.

'But Father promised!'

'Yeah. Like he promised not to carpet-nuke most of planet Earth.'

'Aiden, be quiet, this is serious. They're going to put you on trial.'

'Well, let's hope it's a mega trial. I've been a fucking bit-player long enough.'

Despite this, my heart still lurched. They were going to *try* me? – What the hell was the point of that? There must be some point, otherwise they'd just zuge me and have done with it... Though, come to think of it, it had been several years since they'd last put a member of the rebellion on trial...

She said nothing, so I added, 'But really, Ravene, I can't see the point. I plead guilty! I'm part of the resistance – I've sworn to be! What's a frigging trial going to prove?'

She hesitated, biting her pretty lip, but there was no provocation in it. Finally, she said, 'It's not for treason, Aiden. You're being tried for murder. Someone called Malfous, I think.'

Malthus. I suddenly felt sick with fear, but not for myself. Suddenly I understood the King's interest in a middle-ranked rebel, your basic operative. The resistance, you see, had millions of secret supporters, perhaps billions. For this reason alone, a trial for treason would almost certainly have backfired. In comparison, trying a rebel for murdering one of his own leaders was utterly – even obscenely – brilliant. Who could sympathise with an asshole like that? I could practically draft the press release personally: 'Our distasteful duty… The inner workings of a villainous rebel cell… Back-stabbings, murderous jealousies… addictions to strange and macabre rituals… in-fighting, incest, fornication…'

The list could go on and on.

God, yes, it would play – especially in those already-skittish areas on the fringes of the insurrection zones. In a heartbeat, the efforts of years would be lost. Those who still believed in revolution would lose hope, and secret sympathisers would drift away, either into the actual wilderness, or else into the wilderness of despair. And after my conviction there would be no public execution. Instead I'd be zuged underground and reported an ignoble suicide – or publicised as having been murdered in some ugly prison brawl.

'Who was Malfous?' repeated Ravene. I hadn't really heard the first time.

'One of the greats. Brilliant at languages, brilliant at strategy. Tall guy, bald, thin, a gentle giant. I loved him.'

'Then why did you murder him?' she asked, with that Xirfell simplicity.

'Don't be so fucking ridiculous! I haven't even seen him for over a year! He was forced into hiding after your father put out a warrant with a two thousand-kadrill reward, wasn't he?'

'So, he was turned in?'

'For that kind of money? What do you think?'

'And you had nothing to do with it?'

Had she always been quite this stupid? Or was she drugged, maybe? – Impossible to tell, with those divided irises. I said dangerously, 'Sure I did, Ravene. I turned him in personally. I loved him, remember?'

'You mean "no". That makes sense,' said Ravene, sliding her foot thoughtfully in those emerald sandals. 'But they say you were already in custody when you murdered him.'

'And a pretty fist I'd make of murdering a medium-sized mosquito from this chair!'

Although – I couldn't help thinking – some people would believe it. They wouldn't know about the chair, the isolation, the swirls of radiation, the howling of edoys from the surface above. Instead, they'd vaguely imagine a knife fight in a dank prison corridor, a vicious strangling in a prison-yard.

Also, I'm known to be impulsive, because I am.

God, what a mess I'd made of my life! – in being expelled from the Academy over Ravene, in refusing Malthus's advice about going into hiding, and in messing about at the pundling college, just waiting to be captured. I could imagine my future: I'd be hung out to dry in a show-trial – afterwards, they'd kill me. The only bright spot I could see was that I'd get to speak at my trial. Even if it was just for five blinking minutes – I'd have my moment.

But would I be able to use it? The quality Sebastian had rated me for was bloody-minded recklessness – in his words, 'courage to the point of stupidity'. I'd known a few orators back in the Academy – Sefu had been brilliant, Laurentia reportedly still more so – but I hadn't been one of them.

Still, I'd have my moment.

At this point Ravene murmured something, but it turned out she was only dispatching the testers, along with the mini-pundling ballerinas. At this, I perked up. It might be that some lingering remnant of feeling remained, or that she had something private to tell me. She approached. Even at such a moment – I'm human – it was impossible not to admire her sinuous beauty.

There was a twentieth-century brand – Batman – that was revived when I was a child. Most generations seem to have some take on Batman. Anyway, if you ever happened to catch it, you'd be able to visualise Ravene perfectly: Ravene *is* Catwoman. If you missed it, I haven't enough patience to go into details. Dumb series, I must admit, but it appealed to the youthful Aiden just fine.

She lifted my chin, as if she wanted to study my eyes. What was she looking for? And what was that witching subliminal scent? – Pheromones have so much to answer for! Her manicured fingers traced the outline of my lip, that scar above my eyelid. I was trembling like a youngster on the edge of discovery.

She was tilting my head back, her lips ruffling the nerves of my face, shivering my wounded throat, caressing the section that the pundling had missed on my morning shave. When she kissed me I recalled that almost electric pleasure, which I'd once believed had spoiled all human females for me, that delicious half-strangeness. How warm her lips were! As our tongues wound together, the only thing moving faster than my pulse was my brain.

Could she be about to release me from the chair? And if I went along with the seduction – my body's vote overwhelmingly in favour – might escape be possible? Of course, I was supposed to kill her...

She straddled my lap and effortlessly slipped my primed prick inside her springy tautness. And suddenly I was twenty again and my body straining against hers – against its bonds too. Breathing fast, she was pulling me deeper. She was slowing me – slowing me, to time it more perfectly. She did this until it was almost unbearable, the uprush unstoppable...

Oh God Oh Christ Oh Petra. What have I done?

9

What I was really looking for, of course, was a reason. A night spent tossing and turning under fog-blinded stars had shed no light on why Ravene had chosen to seduce me. She could have no shortage of partners at her command, with her starry rank and glorious looks – one of her half-sisters supposedly maintained an entire stable of healthy young Xirfell guys to service her. Ravene, as far as I knew, had resisted this – though, as King Hebdith's appointed heir, she might not be permitted the same freedom, either.

Now mine has been considered a handsome face: the brown-black eyes deep-set, the nose aquiline, the jawline strong, the skin – that tawny Indigenous shade – unexceptionable. And I was still pretty trim, despite what felt like months underground.

Still, I was thirty, worn-out, battle-scarred. Had the element of risk attracted Ravene? She'd always been a risk-taker: we'd once done it on the Academy principal's desk, though I'd felt too nervy to enjoy it. Or was seducing me purely opportunistic? After all, how many people had the power to disable the monitoring devices in a prison cell?

But it could also have been the pull of the past. Could my impending trial have awakened some flicker of real feeling? If so, could that feeling be made useful to the cause? Was it even possible – I tried to remember everything she'd said, but it had mostly been me showing off – that I could 'turn' the King's heir, herself?

Unable to relax, I twisted restlessly instead. Had there been a breath of feminine sympathy in her words, her tone, her hesitations? ('Aiden, be quiet, this is serious. They're going to put you on trial.') Had she only come to warn me, or had she always had something more tumultuous in mind? Had the infant pundlings only been included to make her visit appear frivolous? Also – and in retrospect this appeared strange – surely the ranking bodyguard should have given a rousing if respectful raspberry to any notion of leaving the King's heir alone with a rebel? – The fact that he hadn't might be significant.

There had long been gossip about Ravene's stepbrother Uval, and his ambitions to replace her as heir. Could we have been left alone together by someone with an interest in framing Ravene? Had every monitoring device really been disabled?

Of the two pundlings shaving me, one was new. Most creatures considered all pundlings identical – which was presumably why the Xirfell branded them – but long experience had taught me otherwise. I checked: 7784.

Ours! His eyes were the usual washed-out silver-grey, but hugely alert, his hands swift and deft. Was that the merest suspicion of a wink? He was saying something in their curly speech, after which his comrade trotted off.

'I have told him,' said 7784 under my ear, 'that the blade must be replaced. I have news from Martin. You are to be tried.'

'I know.'

7784 showed no surprise – they are a stolid race. He continued, 'The blundicant mind-melder is to return. Also, a rescue mission is being planned.'

It was all I could do not to whip my head around. 'That's mad!'

'I don't know any details,' he apologised.

'A rescue mission! How the fuck could that succeed?'

'I don't know.' Well, he wouldn't, of course. He then added, 'Do you know where the hidden monitors might be in here?'

'Roughly.'

'Could you indicate, using your gaze?'

'I can try.'

'Martin says to stay strong.'

A very juvenile part of me felt annoyed at that, but that was crazy. I might not like the guy but he'd still been frigging elected. And was he really going to attempt a rescue? Such a thing had never even been tried before. I felt sick at the idea that some of the others might die in the attempt. I thought, 'Don't let him send Petra.' Bad enough having one of us bound to a blinking chair.

As if I'd said this aloud, 7784 added, 'Petra sends steadfast love.'

Which was worse than had the shaving blade slipped and cut me to the bone. For I had dreamed in the night – but of Ravene. I recalled, with loathing, that my seed was rotting inside Ravene, while Petra was sending 'steadfast' love.

The choice of word might even matter. Martin had probably made his move – and found Petra steadfast. (But why should she have refused? No one had ever escaped the grip of the regime.) Though I could still recall her rather sad, 'You don't always… choose.'

But there I was, soon to be internationally vilified as a murderous traitor, soon to be executed – basically, dead meat.

This so infuriated me that I thought about jerking my carotid artery into the path of the bright new blade: the Xirfell cheated of their precious trial, my name unsullied, my ordeal over.

And yet Petra was 'steadfast'. The word filled me with renewed purpose, as Petra had certainly intended. Suicide was the coward's way out. And the regime would be sure to find some way of blackening my name, regardless.

7784 stood by, while his colleague meticulously repeated the shave. Meanwhile I trained my gaze, apparently at random, at the places where Ravene had believed the monitors to be. 7784 nodded, almost imperceptibly. Then off both pundlings trotted, like the twins they weren't, leaving me alone again.

But MF was coming.

I yearned for MF as an outback traveller lusts for water. He would know more about the trial than Ravene, more about the rescue mission than 7784. I also found myself hoping that MF could 'read' what had occurred with Ravene, that I wouldn't have to tell him. Though I could always protest that I'd been given very little option, or that turning her had been uppermost in my mind… There was also the worry that, once MF knew about Ravene, he'd report it to Martin and the others. It was easy to imagine Martin's wry disapproval – but would Petra understand?

She might be steadfast, but was I?

10

The very first time Sebastian ever spoke to me was in the Academy, only a few months after the Xirfell had resurrected it, and he was pretty fucking rude.

I was passing the time of day with Katie, an attractive girl whom I could never fancy, as we'd been kids together. Suddenly Professor Levsky hove into view: head of the history department, organiser of the siege during the invasion, broad of shoulder, Falstaffian of belly, blustery of beard. I admired him enormously and made a point of never skipping his lectures, but I'd never expected him to notice me, lowly undergrad that I was.

'Tenten?'

I practically stood to attention. 'Sir?'

'Author of the paper "Disraeli and the Congress of Berlin in modern context"?'

I flushed with modest pride. 'Yeah.'

'And what a disgusting load of ignorant drivel it is!'

I attempted to defend myself. 'But I thought you'd said that we should—'

'I said! I said! I'll show you what I said, young man, word for bloody word! You just come along with me!'

Crestfallen, I nodded gloomily at Katie and followed, as he stumped powerfully towards his private pod. On the way we encountered Ravene, who mouthed, 'What the fuck?' upon seeing me being borne to the scaffold.

I felt like a four-year-old shamed for not asking to go to the loo in time; I felt publicly humiliated, my modest pride in my essay dashed. I'd really thought that my essay, if not likely to cause Professor Nevsky to turn handsprings, deserved a low B. (Nevsky never gave As.) I'd grown quite interested in the Congress of Berlin during his lectures; I'd even stopped doodling, just to take it all in.

Nevsky closed his pod behind us and barked some private command to his robotnik, which caused it to blink twice and buzz off. Then he motioned me towards a chair, one of the old-fashioned kind that didn't even register your vital functions. Your basic bum-rest.

'Sorry about that,' he said, so roughly that I didn't immediately grasp that I wasn't about to be kicked off the second-most prestigious course in the Academy. 'But I had my reasons.'

'Reasons?' I asked, stupidly.

'I have a personal reason for wanting to see you alone, Tenten.'

I dismissed the usual reasons out of hand. The Academy had always been a hotbed of sexual shenanigans but Sebastian Nevsky was a family man, and I'd never heard the faintest rumour of anything extracurricular. Then he added, 'You've been under surveillance by two of my people over the past couple of months, Tenten.'

I thought, 'My' people? Who the hell were his people? I stammered, 'L-look—'

'I just wanted to find out if my hunch was right. You're sympathetic to the rebellion, aren't you?'

I drew myself up haughtily and gave it to him in the gizzard. 'Never! I revere our beloved ruler the King, his glorious and extensive family, the esteemed Golden Circle—'

Sebastian yelled, 'You're fucking their fucking princess! You're pure rebel from your fatuous little head to your fatuous little toes! Just admit it!' And here he leaned forward and jabbed me on the sternum. 'Fool! I *am* the rebellion! You can tell *me* the truth!'

My look of incredulity was probably pretty unflattering.

Now I'd heard about the rebellion and I'd often imagined them: tough, taut, trim, fit – basically, an idealised version of me. Not old Nevsky, with that messy beard, that enormous paunch and those rumpled suits... He leaned back, practically laughing his fucking beard off.

'Yes, you're looking at the leader of the resistance, Aiden. Not a hugely impressive-looking leader, but there you are. However, the rebellion itself is in fantastic shape. We're growing stronger almost daily, and on every continent. I've personally planted four cells in as many weeks.'

'Cells of resistance? Unconnected?'

'Connected only to those on the top committee, which I chair. So, were any cell to be infiltrated, the damage should be containable. It's the same principle as—'

'The Cold War.'

'You weren't too badly taught.'

'The twentieth century is my thing, WWII particularly.'

'Is it? So, what attracts you to that particular moment of human weakness and all-too-human catastrophe, Tenten?'

I hesitated, taken aback at the swift change of subject. I'd been wondering – hoping really – that he might be about to recruit me. I was also a little embarrassed because – let's be honest – WWII was one of the most perennially popular historical periods, and always had been. Whether it was Hitler's compulsive character, those diabolical camps, the crazy socio-economic situation that had started it all or the common purpose his opponents had achieved – it resonates like no other.

I probably explained this very badly, after which Nevsky set me right on a few minor points. Then he stood up and trudged heavily towards his window, which overlooked the rugby pitch.

He started deceptively lightly. 'And what is your opinion, Tenten, of Australia's penultimate prime minister, D. Justin Medlicott?'

I felt far happier with this question. A wide-open chance for a try was how I perceived it, and I rushed to nail the pass.

'The most disgusting of all of the pre-invasion leaders, Professor. He oppressed the poor, secretly organised the vote-rigging hacks, prioritised arms sales, cut taxes for his friends, starved the refugees and finally cut that outrageous deal with Zhao Jianyu. OK, he wasn't Hitler, but his targeting of the Indigenous was clearly along the same lines, and might even have ended similarly, had WWIII not intervened. They were mostly put to work—'

'Your birth mother was an Indigenous Australian, I believe.'

I was a little surprised, but then, the professor's mind was like that. It made surprising connections, challenging conjunctions – basically, it careered all over the place. This was probably the reason his lectures were so popular.

'Yes – but she gave me up for adoption when I was eight weeks old. Then the Tentens adopted me.'

'And did the Tentens never share with you the name of your father?'

'They couldn't, sir – they never knew.'

'Are you sure that neither of them knew? Wasn't it possible that Duncan Tenten knew, but decided not to tell you?'

Heart speeding, I said, 'Did you *know* Duncan Tenten, sir?'

'I did. And I had it from his own lips that your father was D. Justin Medlicott.'

There are moments when the entire world seems to rock on its hinges – my arrest was one, and so was the moment when the nuclear dome folded over the entire Academy, shutting the rest of Australasia outside. For a moment everything in sight – the professor's messy desk, the window over the wind-swept rugby pitch, the professor himself – darkened, as if a greyish film had descended.

My first thought was that I was cursed, that nobody in the world was unluckier than me.

Of course, I'd long since guessed that my birth father had been White, or maybe mostly White. But... D. Justin fucking Medlicott? That racist, fascist, sexist, arrogant, blustering, hypocritical, self-aggrandising, lying sociopath? – The D. Justin Medlicott who had declared it his 'divine purpose to reinstate the purity of White Australia'? The D. Justin Medlicott who had personally ordered more than ten thousand refugees from WWIII dumped alive into shark-infested seas?

I couldn't begin to imagine how anyone who had singlehandedly instituted the neutering of Indigenous Aussies had the fucking nerve to father a child by one. Also – not being funny, but what price his picture-perfect wife and white-blond children? (Or maybe he'd only played the White Australia card to get elected? That had been the period of the race riots, hadn't it?) I recalled that aquiline nose, that faintly sneering set of mouth, that exquisitely modulated accent, those poncey, hand-painted ties.

Once I'd finished swearing, Sebastian said sympathetically, 'I'm very sorry, Tenten. And so, to be fair to him, was Duncan Tenten. So much so that he very nearly chose to adopt another infant instead. I'm glad he stuck with you.'

'But how did it fucking *happen?* Was my mother—'

'Your mother was on Medlicott's domestic staff – an extraordinarily charismatic woman, by all accounts. He would have assumed that she'd been sterilised, but she'd escaped it somehow. Anyway, as soon as he discovered the pregnancy he had her framed for stealing a dress of his wife's, and kicked onto the street.'

Maybe it hadn't even been consensual. Maybe he'd even raped her? – a thought which turned me too sick for speech.

Sebastian was watching me closely. 'It was a condition of the adoption that the Tentens never attempt to trace your parents. But Duncan was so disturbed by what he learned about your father that he asked if I could possibly track down your mother.'

'And could you?'

'Sorry, no.'

So, Duncan had tried to help my mother – I honoured him for that. He hadn't given up on me, either. I stood up, sat down, stood up again – I didn't know what I was doing, even as I did it.

After a moment, Sebastian added, 'I know that all this is very tough to take in, but we still need to watch the time. Consider yourself chewed out and ordered to re-write one essay. Now, do you need a few days to consider, to mull it all over, to reconcile yourself to all this? Because – in case you aren't as bright as I suspected – this amounts to an official offer to recruit you.'

I passed a hand over my brow. It was a leap from a possible rape to a genuine rebellion, but – I found myself even sorrier for Australasia, and far more fired-up against its fate than I'd ever felt before.

In short, born a rebel without a cause, I'd just found my cause.

As for Ravene – and I suspected her name might still crop up – I thought about her almost with pity. Just like me, she'd lost her mother, and her father was a fucking asshole. I think I might even have had some dim but heroic idea of saving her.

Yet something about the princess still concerned me. I loved being chosen – no man more. But...

I voiced this worry aloud, 'Did you only pick me because of Ravene?'

'Of course not. I chose you because of three qualities I believe you to possess: an outstanding brain, a stubborn spirit, and a determination to make a difference – of course, you can also play the young idiot, but this too shall pass. So, do you need more time – or not?'

I took a deep breath and said, 'No, I'm up for it. Count on me.'

He absolutely beamed. But then he rapped out, 'Why? For the adventure? Because you fancy starring in your own personal thriller? Or because I've just put my life in your hands?'

Well, he had, no question. A single word, to Ravene – or indeed anybody – and he'd be zuged, his nascent rebellion well and truly done for. Later, I marvelled that he had taken so crazy a risk, for the puny reward of netting yours, the undersigned. But back then I was physically enhanced and sexually triumphant. Despite having been lazy at school, I'd still been selected for the Academy. I'd also been selected to be upgraded – and had failed to crash and burn during the operations. Perhaps most crucially, I was only twenty. At twenty, I think I took it for granted that I was a pretty great catch.

I said, 'Partly, for the adventure. And partly – to make a difference.'

'What about the princess?'

'That's just a bit of fun. It doesn't mean anything.'

'Don't drop her. She might prove useful.'

'It's way more likely she'll drop me. Ravene gets bored fast, and she's already been with me miles the longest.'

'Try to keep her intrigued. You'll get messages pretending to be from various historical societies: memorise and destroy. And now you'd better go before anyone notices how long you've been here.'

And with that I was dismissed, excitement tiding through me. Really, it was all I could do, criminally young and brutally stupid as I was, not to cartwheel all the way to the next pod.

I had been chosen by the leader of the rebellion. I'd probably be given astonishing chances to shine – even to exact revenge for those deaths – unknown – of Duncan and Sophia Tenten. In fact, all I needed was an assurance that my Disraeli paper was OK to be as high as a kite. (In the interests of posterity, I'd actually nailed a B+.)

I ran into Ravene in the hub, downing one of those revolting-smelling strength drinks. 'Was it very bad?' she asked sympathetically.

'Fucker just doesn't like me. A re-write.'

Ravene wasn't really interested. She curled her limpid foot around mine, an invitation.

'Later. I have to go to the librapod.'

She solaced herself by summoning Candice for a gossip and I escaped.

I did go to the librapod, but not to check anything. Instead, I pored over texts about Disraeli with a disordered brain. How many other men – in the whole world – were skewering a princess while assisting a rebellion? And yes, it might get a little complicated but – as Sebastian had recognised – I enjoy complications. Sebastian's offer – and learning the truth about my father – had given me a focus, an ambition, a purpose. And, in the rebellion, a family, too.

I'll never know what Sebastian was thinking that day – and perhaps it really *was* partly Ravene – but I hope he recognised raw material that he could work with.

Other than that, I can't imagine what he saw in me.

11

I was expecting MF. I was half-expecting Ravene.

Who I got was Ichthus.

I was watching the fading sunlight and trying to forget the pain in my knee when, suddenly, I was no longer alone. First a blurg slurped into view – all odorous rings, that fishy smell. It must have been highly-ranked though, for it sported a strange crimson necklace and had several pundlings engaged in clearing the rancid sludge in its wake. Behind it paced any number of testers, their thighs bulging in their tight trousers, because fashion judgement was never a Xirfell thing.

I was braced for the King long before he appeared. I was also alert – read paranoid – for whips, but the testers appeared to be unarmed. (Perhaps they didn't want me scarred before my trial?) I was gearing myself to resist but it wasn't until the entire party was organised that they unleashed something truly horrible before me.

First there was another of the door's metallic swooshes. I twisted my head – as far as I was able – and registered several of the newest robotniks: androgynous, almost three metres in height, they loomed over even the testers and were, in their mute intensity, still more intimidating. Carried between them on a litter was – Ichthus. Ichthus, whom I had set up, claiming that he was Malthus's successor as leader, when Martin had really been chosen.

Oh God, they'd caught him after all.

Ichthus was probably eighty, though there were plenty of humans of over a hundred who looked a lot younger. Also, he'd never much liked me, though he'd probably come out of the egg carping and finding fault. Despite this, he was shrewd as well as literary. He had served for years as the rebellion's underground propaganda guru and I still recalled Sebastian saying, 'Be more patient with Ichthus, my friend. Not every battle is fought with nerve and sinew.'

Despite this, I'd never succeeded in liking the guy, because Ichthus was one of those people for whom nothing was ever quite right; an ungracious, ungenerous, editorial soul – no friend to relationships in general and to sexual relationships in particular. I was pretty certain he'd warned Petra not to get involved with me.

Still, I felt desperately sorry for him. Naturally wiry, the wasted muscles of his arms drooped off the bone, and the lines of his skull stood out like those of Nazi concentration camp survivors. When he recognised me there was a twist of face. Angry? Nervy? Spiteful? – I couldn't decide.

'What, do you not salute your leader?' mocked the King.

A spurt of rage shot through me; I pushed it down. I said, 'Greetings, Ichthus.'

He glared, as if I'd split an infinitive, but said nothing.

I turned to the King. 'I greet him, but do not serve him. Ichthus is not my leader.'

'So! Is this the truth, at last?'

'Yes.'

'And the statements you gave us a few days ago – these were false?'

'Of course they were. I was being fucking tortured, wasn't I?'

Was that a flicker of sympathy on Ichthus's wan face? One of the testers muttered something unprintable. Then the King began to simmer.

'Why did you frame Ichthus, human?'

'Because I didn't fucking know you'd got him!'

'He says that Martin McNamara is the new rebel leader. Is this true?'

I met Ichthus's faded eyes but could read nothing there. Had he given up, been bought off – even gone over to the other side? – I couldn't believe it. They'd have fed him, for a start.

'Impossible,' I returned, with a curl of lip.

'Martin McNamara impossible – why? For what reason?'

'I told you. He's rigid, obsessive – and has a weakness for women.'

'Not like *you,* then?' sneered the King.

I recalled my worry about there being some monitor that not even Ravene had known about. Though the King's snide comment might also refer to the past. I snapped, 'Anyway, he's no Sebastian!'

'And – ha! – you are?'

I laughed shortly. 'Me? I'm not even in the running. For every charge against McNamara there are twenty against me.'

And the saddest part was that this was probably true.

I suddenly noticed that Ichthus was looking at me significantly. A message, a warning? Was he too terrified to speak? At this point a robotnik was ordered to turn Ichthus to face me. It had 'hands' like shark-fins, and even its smallest muscle screamed industrial power. Ichthus's mouth was forcibly opened, but to no purpose – his tongue was missing.

The King said casually, 'You observe the missing part? We give parts of no importance to the royal blurg.'

A burning retch reached my throat, I gulped it down. Two of the testers poked each other, as if it was some hilarious joke. The King continued, 'After this, Ichthus admitted that your leader is Martin McNamara. Is this true?'

'He is *not* my leader!' I retorted – possibly with conviction. (Martin the successor to Sebastian? To Malthus? Martin in the history books? – If there would be any history afterwards, if the Xirfell didn't finish it all off.) And then, I lashed out, 'What difference does it make, anyway? Why are you so effing bothered? We're puny! We're pathetic! We're no threat to you, with your fucking great testers, your lethal robotniks, your scummy mind-melders, your horrific zuges! You're fucking paranoid! Call yourself a King? Well, I call you a pathetic, fading, vindictive sociopath! So now why don't you just go ahead and zuge me, because I'm fed-up with your fucking mind-games – I'm fed-up with being allowed one fucking metre of sky – and I'm fed-up with what fucking assholes like you do to people like *him*!'

The testers were appalled. One whispered urgently to the King, another lowered his great bull head, as if considering impaling me on the back of my chair with that horn of his.

This would not be a cool way to die.

The King had reddened, a weird splash of colour beneath his cheekbone. 'Kill him!' he screamed, but nobody moved – not even the blurg, and blurgs have to keep moving, otherwise their rings fester.

Was it a revolt? Was it a set-up? Why was the King almost smiling? – Was this yet another sick joke?

'Human, are you too stupid to understand?' said the King, almost caressingly. '*You* are to do the killing. You are to kill Ichthus. That's why he has been brought here. Really, you are slow! You will incriminate yourself – here, now, forever – by killing your friend. You will live until the end of your trial for his murder. *Then* you will be allowed to die.'

'You want me to kill Ichthus?' I repeated, aghast.

'At last you have grasped the situation.'

'Well, I fucking refuse! I'm not murdering an old guy who's already had his tender bits cut off, thanks. Do your own dirty work!'

But, at the same time, I had the germ of an idea. They would have to release me, in order for me to do anything. And then, might I possibly be able to get at the King? – The testers, the robotniks, potentially even the blurg, might interfere, but...

The King muttered an order, and two robotniks skimmed towards me. They stood close, as the bands of my chair slicked back. And suddenly I was standing, slightly swaying due to having been bound for so long, calculating hard against the sudden throbbing of my heart.

It was 4.02 metres; the King leaned forward.

Back to 4.03, 4.04.

Keep still, damn you.

It was heaven, of course, to straighten my legs, but I forced myself to protest. 'I refuse. You can't force me to murder anybody!'

'If you don't, the tester will do it, and we can still blame it on you at the trial,' the King told me, with a strange, tense smile.

I thought, They still wouldn't have an actual record of my doing it – but another part of my brain was still calculating. You see, I believed the King might just have forgotten something.

'Why don't you ask your friend what he wants?' he sneered, and I slid my eyes briefly towards Ichthus.

4.27 metres, adjust 65 degrees, the side of the hand four centimetres from the base of that fat royal neck... But all I said was, 'Do you want me to do this, friend?' And the strangest thing was not that he nodded – they'd got his balls for sure and probably the lot – but that he did indeed seem like a friend.

I had always underrated him. As Sebastian had said.

I'd never liked Ichthus better than in that moment, when he was begging me to kill him. I leaned down and put my hands on either side of that rope-like neck, where the pulse was, naturally, speeding.

Did he really want to die? Does anybody? The body, of course, always votes against.

I said, 'Tell me when,' and, when he just nodded, I felt the faint scrape of bristle against my palms. There was utter silence. 4.27 metres. 4.25 metres. The King, the testers, the blurg, the robotniks, me, poor Ichthus – all caught like a sepia snap from long centuries ago. I pressed down on his artery for just a fraction of a second – then I flew.

It was 4.27 metres dead and I got the King's neck as neat as a pin, approximately a second and a half before a tester crashed his great hairy fist into my temple. Sweet Jesus, the pain!

What the King had forgotten was that, back when I received my memory sliver, they had messed about with a few physical advantages, as well. I had, since that operation, been able to launch myself several metres from a simple squat. Which had won me any number of bets in my time at the Academy.

After they prised my hands off the King's neck it all got a little wild. There must have been orders that I should survive, but one bastard slashed my left temple, which hurt worse than the swelling already stretching my jaw. Meanwhile, the senior tester ratcheted out orders for medics, and for Ichthus's removal.

Had I been noble or unkind to spare him? – I couldn't decide.

Two other testers carried out the unconscious King. He was breathing very hoarsely, with a split lip and a swollen neck but seemed very disappointingly undead as I was shoved harshly back in my chair. I also wondered, uneasily, whether they'd go ahead and kill Ichthus themselves or have another shot at making me do it. Twenty seconds might have been enough; his life hung by that fluttery a thread.

I was admiring the night sky, clearer than it often was, when the pundlings arrived, with their clammy hands and wavery speech.

They patched me up, and fed me something grey, greasy and lukewarm.

Later, much later, I fell asleep and dreamed.

12

I dreamed about my mother.

A stunning creature, with snapping black eyes, an impulsive mouth and gloriously untamed hair, she would still have faced cruel discrimination as a 'dig' or – still ruder – a 'chocco'. Female 'digs' were routinely sterilised, pre-WWIII, so I couldn't help wondering how she'd managed to avoid it.

Basically, I should never have been born.

A notion my birth mother probably strung along with, as she did her level best to get rid of me, apparently making us both seriously ill before a local charity intervened. It was they who arranged that I be given up for adoption.

This last bit I learned from Sophia and Duncan Tenten, the childless couple who adopted me at two months. (Apparently, I'd been entranced by Sophia's necklace for most of our first meeting.) My cost was crippling – for I remained in rude health despite my birth mother's best efforts – but Duncan Tenten had old-fashioned notions about his 'line' – the irony being that most lines ended between WWIII and the invasion anyway.

I had almost nothing in common with my adoptive parents. Duncan took me to rugby matches and paid for the most expensive schools. The plan was that I inherit his publishing company – a plan upended by the war. His gentle, nervous wife would probably have preferred a girl. Sophia was a conscientious mother but somehow uninvolved; she wasted a massive amount of time and energy fussing about clothes.

They were a devoted couple in a stagnant kind of fashion, as if feeling had somehow been bred out of them. My birth mother seemed very different. On my eighteenth birthday Duncan gave me two mementos from my birth mother, including a recording of her dancing in a talent competition: beautiful, rebellious, vaguely flirty with the audience. Her lips and eyes were far plumper than mine and she had hair with a life of its own – the blackest hair you ever saw, but with streaks of crimson woven through it. The way she whipped it to the music was mesmerising.

I watched this so often, looking for a reason – OK, an excuse – for my rejection. Couldn't she have just run away with me? There were still plenty of wildernesses thirty years ago. Some Non-Essential-Terrestrial workers (nettys, as they were known) kept their illegal children but no, my mother couldn't be arsed.

Maybe this was why, whenever I dream of her, she's dancing. She whirls through my dreams, that crazy hair lashing her face, and I reach out for her with inexpressible longing – to know, I think, more than anything. Why did she leave me? Why did she abandon me? Was I really so unlovable?

I always wake up without an answer. This time, though, I awoke with unusual suddenness – there was something going on outside my door. Six testers noisily entered. Then, with a surge of relief, I recognised the non-gluten-free shape of MF. (How bizarrely blundicants move, like an oil spill in slow-motion, those colliding organs.) I'd hoped they might send him – although my gloomier guess had been that they'd send a tester with a whip, to pay me out for attacking the King.

I writhed in my bonds, scowling.

He observed, 'It is pointless to object, human. Save your energy, instead!'

To which I publicly retorted, 'I'll do what I fucking well choose!' – but I was already being hauled from the chair, an operation overseen on this occasion by six testers, several robotniks and two anxious pundlings. I had clearly been upgraded to a serious danger to pedestrians and traffic, haha.

Then, that creepy sense of something oiling up my spine. It was no struggle at all to yell.

MF attempted, unsuccessfully, to dismiss his bodyguards. The ranking tester – they're born into their ranks, of course – grated back, 'Orders are to remain.'

'Then,' said MF evenly, 'remain, by all means.' And, just to me,

–Very good. As an actor, you improve.

–Thought you were never coming back, you fucking bastard.

–I see that your manners have survived yesterday's trauma.

–What's happened to Ichthus, MF?

–He's in a deeper chamber, is all I know.

–What, deeper than this?

–There are many deeper, Aiden. Far beyond the reach of sunlight. But he was still alive yesterday.

This counted as only modest relief. What if they ordered me to strangle him today? I considered this, until he reminded me to protest. I did what I could, before asking,

–Do you know about Ravene, MF?

–I know the princess. What about her?

It was tricky to explain, particularly when communicating by central nervous system alone. I did my best and, after a longish silence…

–So, she seduced you.

–Um, yeah. But were we spotted? Could there have been some embedded device she might not have known about?

–Possibly, but I suspect I would have been briefed, in that case. Please complain a bit while I think.

Well, one has to do the civil thing. A moment later I yelled in earnest, as he wrenched my spine. I think he chuckled. I, in sharp contradistinction, did not chuckle, and wished very hard that he had a shin, so that I could kick it. Finally he said,

–Of course, if it was discovered, the princess might always claim to suffer from sexual addiction, like her sister.

–And does she?

–I believe not. But all this might still count for nothing – unless you could turn her.

–Believe me, MF, that thought has occurred. But I doubt it. It's not that she's stupid – but there's this bone-headed simplicity about her. There always was.

–Could you still kill her if required? If you were freed to make love to her, perhaps?

–You're joking, right? I couldn't even kill Ichthus.

–I know.

–Are they going to try to make me kill him again?

–I haven't heard. But – seriously – do you think that you could kill the princess? Martin will need to know.

How I wished it wasn't Martin! I thought hard. Could I really kill Ravene? Finally I said,

–I just don't know.

–That twist of expression is excellent. Forgive me, I'm going to twinge your back again.

'Shit!' I yelled, to the rollicking amusement of the tester contingent.

–Whenever you think of Martin McNamara you appear to be in pain. Why?

–Let's save that one for the long winter evenings, shall we?

–The Xirfell want to know why you couldn't kill Ichthus, when he begged you to.

–I thought I could reach the King. But just tell them that pity stayed my hand.

–And when he begged you?

–So I'm fucking squeamish!

–You weren't squeamish aiming for the King.

–No, I was hoping for a more solid result there. Didn't work though, did it?

–He is recovering. He's in his final incarnation, as you probably know. Now, listen. Your trial is set for next week.

Next week. Far sooner than I'd imagined.

–Unless they postpone it again. Or unless you're rescued. The rescue may or may not come to anything, but you're to know nothing about it, in case you get tortured again. You should also know that there have been discussions about having you interviewed, live, in hopes that you incriminate yourself – or the rebellion, perhaps.

–An interview! – What kind of an interview?

–I only know that it is under consideration. Do you have any other questions?

–Petra?

–Is well, as far as I know.

We spent the last ten minutes pretending that he was dredging information out of me. I didn't act brilliantly, but it didn't matter, because the testers were mostly messing about with nocxmow, a gambling game played with living chips. Basically, their favourite thing.

Then they all left, MF included.

'Is well, as far as I know,' MF had said. No 'steadfast love', no nothing.

Maybe she'd given in to Martin after all? I could easily imagine it – I kept imagining it – his well-knit frame, his admirable calves, his no doubt admirable prick, his tanned skin... Probably at this very moment she was secretly comparing us, entirely to his advantage.

Not that Petra is racially prejudiced, not in the least. And wasn't the titillation of the different – see Ravene – often still more tempting? All the same, they'd be working together, in meetings together, attending the service for Malthus together, planning missions together... the lot.

Though I also had to admit that my last encounter with Ravene had reignited a powerful yearning for that reckless energy – sex-on-a-cliff-edge – which had entirely eclipsed Petra's boyish beauty in my head. Even my dreams had shifted from one to the other. (Wonder which one my dancer mother represented, if either?)

I fretted that MF, always intuitive, had guessed something of this. Which might have been why I didn't thank him, though I regretted this the moment he'd gone. After all, he couldn't just pitch up, he had to be ordered to come. He could be superseded by another blundicant; he could be dispatched elsewhere – he could even be zuged, should the King suspect even a fraction of the truth.

In the meantime, every time the door opened I feared it might be Ichthus, when I still hadn't made up my mind about what I should have done.

Really, I hadn't made up my mind about any bloody thing.

I couldn't help contrasting MF's recent visit with 7784's. Before: 'steadfast love' from Petra, rescue mission full steam ahead. After: nothing from Petra, rescue mission a question mark.

Of course, it was a batshit crazy idea in the first place. No one had ever been rescued from the regime, so why should I be the first? – Probably, Martin was just concerned that I might screw up my trial, wrecking the rebellion's reputation. That would explain Petra's silence perfectly.

That afternoon I dozed off and dreamed again.

I was, as so often, treading through the diseased tide of ivied jungle that was irresistibly swallowing up the dead grass, the ruined bungalows and the cratered swimming pools of G13. There – in once-idyllic suburbs – a few humans had once enjoyed a cosy, comfortable existence. Also there, shielded by the tide of radioactive wilderness lapping at every door and window, were the rebellion's favoured hideouts: crumbling cricket clubhouses, disintegrating primary schools, ancient Scout huts.

Getting to these places was frankly part of the thrill. I'd been attacked by long-clawed feral cats, stung by a five-eyed scorpion, and even attacked by one of those gigantic snakes that have pretty much made these places their playground, with no other great predator beyond the occasional crocodile – though the crocs seemed to have suffered far more than the snakes.

The fucking snakes seemed almost to have *thrived*.

Anyway, in my dream, I was crossing a humid clearing that had obviously once been a tennis court. Most of its wire enclosure had rotted away, leaving just the rusting posts, bleak sentinels from a dead past. I was kicking a soil-encrusted, half-crushed beer can when I was struck down by a wild blast of air.

Winded, I scrambled to my feet, secretly marvelling that massive jaws weren't already fastened to my leg – but the tennis court was empty, except for the cicadas, which, along with the rats, no amount of radiation seemed able to kill.

Nor had there been a lightning storm. In short, I'd been blasted into the ground by nothing and nobody. Strangest of all, I was being addressed, like Paul on the road to effing Damascus.

'Aiden.'

And, blow me down if it wasn't his voice. Not God's – Sebastian's.

I stared round. There was still nothing to be seen, and I only belatedly recalled my training and squatted down again, like an oversized toad, on the wrecked court. It was always dangerous to be out in the open – Xirfell drones could be anywhere – but I should be able to eyeball a giant snake before it nailed me. In my dream I sat hunched and motionless, a half metre or so above the ants and asked, 'Is it really you?'

'Yes.'

'But aren't you dead?'

He sounded amused. 'I was dead, of course. But I've been reincarnated.'

'What as, a blinking wind? Was it you who shoved me over?'

'No, as a spirit. You're still asleep, Aiden.'

Now this might sound strange, but sometimes when I'm asleep I'm half-aware that I'm dreaming. I've even successfully dragged myself to consciousness, when I begin the familiar nightmare that the invasion was happening all over again, and that the crushed walls of the Academy pod – that I first saw tumbling into the ocean, taking with it the entire European culture class and two of my closest friends – were crashing soundlessly into the sea.

In this case, though, I didn't want to wake up.

As for Sebastian being a spirit – well, I wasn't fussed. Did Sebastian's comment mean that Buddhism and Hinduism had got it right and all the rest wrong? – Not a clue. But I did seek reassurance on a crucial point. 'You're still Sebastian, then?'

'I am even more Sebastian than I was when you knew me.'

Weird. But OK, also.

In my dream, about a hundred ants, having formed a quorum, started doing the rumba up my leg. I said, 'Go on. I'm listening.'

'You're holding a tremendous amount of resentment.'

'My birth mother?'

His silence told me all I needed to know. I casually beheaded a few ants, but the rest failed to gather around the graveside to say how sad it all was. I couldn't remember killing ants in a dream before. I couldn't remember feeling humidity in a dream before, either. Was this really a dream, then – or some kind of bizarre vision?

'Right,' I said. 'I'll give the matter some serious thought.'

'You'll need all the strength you can muster for your trial.'

So, he knew about the trial. Well, he would, of course, having been reincarnated into a storm-force gale.

'And this – resentment – is weakening me?'

'Of course.'

Call me shallow, but I failed to see how a Xirfell show trial could have a single thing to do with my feelings about my birth mother.

Instead, I felt that old longing – the longing to have the burden taken from us, and to be allowed to sit back and cheer while some super-aliens – this time noble and saintly creatures (fat fucking chance) – emerge out of the ether, demolish the Xirfell and then unobtrusively return to their home galaxy, never to be heard of again... Basically, God-from-the-machine, as popularised by the early Greeks.

I said, 'Listen, Sebastian, I'll try. Though, as far as the trial goes, I'm not wildly optimistic. I'll probably just sit there and swear.'

'Don't put yourself down. You scraped a B+ in my course, didn't you? And I never gave A's.'

And with this I woke up, still in the chair, but with a crazy hope surging in my heart.

13

They hadn't brought Ichthus back – yet – and nobody else had shown up either. But I hadn't felt as restless as usual, because I had my dream/vision to play with, like a puppy with a bone. It amazed me how Sebastian-like his voice had been.

The dream had also hugely enriched my confidence.

Now I hadn't felt entirely deserted, ever since MF had shown up, while various other things – pundling 7784, Petra's 'steadfast' love, Ravene's not-exactly-steadfast love – had also cheered me. But I'm intensely social – life and soul of the party, as a general rule – and solitary confinement tested my nerve as well as my patience. It was tough not being able to scratch my ankle, but still tougher to have nobody to talk to. But I found that I could 'summon up' Sebastian in my head, which was a massive comfort.

I could just imagine him: paunchy, bearded, dressed in those old-fashioned suits, banging on his podium as he lectured, putting Martin down when he got snarky in committee, teasing Bully for putting sugar in his coffee, or looping his arm around Priscilla in that gentle, protective way, as if every inch of her was separately and individually precious... Basically, my spirits soared, and I teased the pundlings-of-the-day almost light-heartedly.

'So, what have we got here, then? Seabass in lemon and butter done in paper? Venison with truffle sauce?'

6598 looked bewildered, and so – to be fair – did 5324.

'It is your food, prisoner.'

'Can you tell the chef that the choice of hors d'oeuvres is getting a bit tedious?'

They conferred worriedly, then, 'You want it hotter, prisoner?'

Cruel of me to tease them; years of teaching had taught me that. They are good, loveable, conscientious creatures, but not bright. I'd never struck a really bright one yet – 7784 excepted.

'No, no, just a joke.'

'I will suggest that it is hotter tonight,' said 5324 earnestly and with that they trotted away, the endearing little sausages above their flabby knees quivering like those of very old people in swimsuits.

I endured the rest of the day without tossing and aching and longing to be able to move, as if the wind with which Sebastian knocked me down was somehow buoying me up.

14

Maybe I'm just a moody sod. The next day found me, shaky and nervy, quizzing myself nastily.

'Beginning to lose it, aren't we? Probably something in the gruel. Remember old Ichthus? He could easily have been drugged, right? As for you, you'll be rubbish at your trial, incoherent and stumbling, your childhood stammer will come back for a last hurrah, and you'll forget every single thing you had to say. You'll be shamed – internationally shamed, and – because it'll be broadcast throughout the world – the rebellion will be shamed too.'

I also remembered what Sebastian had suggested about my birth mother, and that I had promised to think about it. This I had absolutely no desire to do; I even felt annoyed at him for so tactlessly bringing the matter up. After all, if I was still pissed-off at my birth mother, that was nobody's business but my own.

I had no recollection of her, only the recording of her dancing. Instead, my first memory was of Sophia Tenten, a dogged musician, attempting 'Waltzing Matilda' on the piano. They had one of the newest ones, the kind that a button could release from the wall. (Perhaps Duncan had been hoping she would forget to release it?) – Either way, her reedy voice and uncertain fingers remained in my memory.

Up jumped the swagman and sprang into the billabong.
"You'll never catch me alive!" said he.
And his ghost may be heard as you pass by that billabong:
"Who'll come a-waltzing Matilda, with me?"

I had been maybe four, because it was their first house, less glitzy and pretentious than the one they died in. I didn't have a clue what a 'billabong' was, or that 'waltzing' meant 'wandering' – basically, I didn't have a clue about any frigging thing, except that I howled.

Yes, in my first memory, I howled like a dog.

History fails to record Sophia's reaction, but I expect she told me not to be so silly, this being her default position where emotion – any emotion – was involved. And what right had I to howl? – I'd been rescued at birth, elevated into the most elite strata of Australasian society, and given nothing but the best.

My second memory was of my fifth birthday and this one was All Aiden's Fault. Sophia had worked hard, organising a robot who supplied electronic fireworks and one of those games where you got to play an intergalactic hero.

But one of my youthful playmates had rashly bought me a telamarinic – one of those interactive, programmable pets – and I was entirely entranced. All I wanted to do was to play with it. The games, the friends, the food, the intergalactic hero bit, the fireworks – as far as the youthful Aiden was concerned, a waste of space.

A distraught Sophia reported my breach of manners to Duncan, and he was obliged to thrash me – something he hated doing. It wasn't that he hit me hard – it was the unfairness which stung. It was my birthday, for a start, but I also suspect that, on some subconscious level, I was already angry.

I was deeply unimpressed with the world when I was five.

I was also unimpressed with school. Mine was a glossy,

expensive place: golf, polo and falconry included as standard. Despite falling with an audible thud for my teacher, Miss Paxman, I was both miserable and intimidated – my stammer kicked in during my second week, and I saw off three separate speech therapists before it was cured.

I was also routinely abused for being a 'netty'. Somehow, it had been discovered that I'd been born to a Non-Essential-Terrestrial worker, something more contemptible than any ethnicity... Hey, it was that kind of a school.

Luckily, I wasn't quite alone. Two of us were deemed nettys in my school – Andy Powers and me – and I still recall bawling like a baby when we were seven and his parents were transferred to G24, then still called China, leaving me the last netty standing.

Matters began to mend in secondary school. There I took up martial arts in hopes of defending myself from the street gang members who – not realising that I was actually one of them – offered to break my jaw on a near-daily basis, thanks to my school uniform.

Martial arts translated into respectable muscles, which ended in my finally making the rugby side, and claiming the second-prettiest girl at the Leavers' Dance. I know it sounds crazy – with my birth father in command, Australasia was on its knees – but this was still one of the happiest times of my life.

Sophia took a photo of my girlfriend and me in our prom outfits: Eloise lovely in peach with just the wrong shade of lipstick, me sporting a new suit and a tight, nervy smile, and my hair in that slimed-down stage that I still blush to remember.

Despite the hushed-up Xirfell recce in South America – the one that had so alarmed Sophia – an alien invasion was the last thing on my mind. Instead, I was hugely excited to be offered a place at the Academy, though my main goal involved making their first rugby squad. Had I been allowed to complete my course – I wasn't – I doubt my degree would have been anything special.

While at the Academy I didn't see the Tentens often, though Duncan persisted in inviting me home on Sundays, so that he could drivel on about business, while Sophia fretted about her roast. I generally longed for this ordeal to be over, so I could escape to the gym on my zelopod. Later, I reproached myself for this – I should have been more grateful. But how could I have guessed, that final Sunday, that I'd never see either Duncan or Sophia again?

On my eighteenth birthday, in addition to the letter from my mother, Duncan took me aside to explain the exact nature of my inheritance. I can no longer remember much about this, and it anyway became entirely academic post-invasion.

'Who was my father?' I asked, but Duncan claimed not to know. Had even my mother known? – I couldn't help wondering. The way she danced – maybe she went out with a lot of guys?

Her letter – her one shot at motherhood – was very brief. It was ultimately incinerated in the Tentens' mansion but I still remember it perfectly.

Dear son, I dont know what the rich people will call you but I picked the name Aiden so I hope its still yours. It means fiery as you probably know. You must be grown if you are reading this and had every advantage. Its hard to be poor but you wont be and thats a good thing I can tell you. Wish I could see you. Wishing you health and happiness always, your mother.

'Wish I could see you' was all that resonated – unsurprisingly, as it was the only emotional sentence that she had allowed herself to write. Though it hit me, even at the time, how tough it must have been to be a despised member of the underclass – despite being excessively pretty. (Though looks can also be a burden, to women especially. See: D. Justin Medlicott, AC, PSM, DSC.)

I also remember feeling disappointed that someone who could

spell 'advantage' could get her apostrophes wrong but, what with the triumph of artificial intelligence, the underclass were lucky to get more than a few years' schooling by 2060. By that point there wasn't much hope for any human who didn't own a startling amount of money – in some places, the poor were simply eliminated, like feral animals. So it was marginally to its credit that, in Australasia, nettys like my mother received any education at all.

Who knew? – She might even still be alive. I might have flown over her in a zelopod or been served by her in some irradiated hole in the outback. This wasn't as crazy as it sounds, because who knew what might have happened to those remarkable looks, over thirty hard years? And how could she – or anybody – be expected to recognise someone last seen as a snivelling two-month-old?

Though I liked to imagine that some part of her fabled charisma might still have spoken to me. There had been such a glow over her features, such life-affirming energy! If you don't believe me, you can check it out here – I had it copied on the memory sliver, that minute, triumphant, indestructible thing... Indestructible, that is, unless all the galaxies get crushed together – in a final fit of impatience – by some justifiably pissed-off God.

Meanwhile, 'Waltzing Matilda' clashed with my mother's wild dance music in my mind, over the recollection of what was, in retrospect, a rather touching letter. I checked to see if the anger was still there, the anger that she had tried to abort me and failed, the anger that she had tried to give me up and succeeded.

And found that most of it seemed to have gone.

15

The next day, shortly after breakfast, several technicians and robotniks showed up, without an invitation, in order to install lighting, hoists, scaffolding, you name it.

Could this be my teleview debut?

Then several pundlings and a robotnik appeared. I was neatly patched up, and garbed in an old-fashioned 2030s-style outfit, which hid my grisly knee entirely – though the scars on my face took the pundlings quite a while to obscure.

Perhaps for this reason, the two chairs in front of me were angled artfully to camera, as if I was an aging Hollywood legend hoping to display my best side. I thought, Do I look older than thirty? If so, does it matter?

How dizzy I felt! – probably those scalding lights.

I might have just caught a half-wink from 7784, in passing, though pundlings always blink a lot, as their eyes seem to struggle with the Earth's polluted climate... Still, I was swiping all the encouragement I could get.

I was hoping that the interviewer might be MF, though I couldn't imagine any creature less camera-friendly... That see-through blubber, those wriggling organs – although maybe our own organs ooze and murmur likewise?

Trying to discipline myself, I decided that my best plan would be a charm offensive, to stop the rebellion being dissed as either starry-eyed no-hopers or else as crazed nutcases. Reasonable, suave, charming, calm – above all, calm.

Then I spotted her. Oh fuck, my interviewer was Ravene – of course it was. But what immediately struck me was that this seemed a new and different Ravene. For a start, she was strictly, even starchily, attired. Her collar extended all the way up her neck, while that sublime hair – glowing with tints like the inside of a shell – was utterly trammelled. Her chin appeared even pointier than usual, and those bisected eyes, always as large as those of some Disney heroine, looked enormous.

When she did glance over at me, those bisected eyes were entirely opaque. Now this could mean two things with Ravene, one of which is unprintable.

I was sensing the second thing, though – I was sensing fear. My guess was that we'd both been corralled into a performance in which even Ravene might have something to lose. Perhaps Uval, the stepbrother, was anticipating, even hoping, he had set her up to fail? If so, was it my duty to play along or to disrupt? Would somebody very kindly step in and lead me? Sebastian? MF? Any fucking person? (Which was in itself pretty ironic, given that I generally moan about being led.)

But I could have been wrong about Ravene – just part of that strange disconnectedness I'd felt, off and on, since breakfast. Meanwhile I amused myself with watching the robotniks revitalising the walls of my prison. By the time the cameras rolled, the impression would be that my cell was embellished with those scenic-wall devices you could alter with a thought, from jaw-dropping Amazonian waterfalls to undulating English dales.

As if.

And, as I watched, I suddenly realised that I was beginning to feel more than dizzy – almost high – spacy, uprooted. Could there have been something in my gruel? I tried to concentrate but the swimmy sensation steadily worsened. There was also a strange numbness in my mouth.

They've fucking poisoned me.

I hadn't quite fainted before a great metallic thud clamped itself on my forehead: I recognised the 'hand' of a robotnik doctor. There was the usual buzzing sensation as it monitored me. Then, clamp removed, the robotnik addressed the pundlings, very annoyingly in their own language, then buzzed off.

What had he told them? 'This asshole has only got a month to live?' Or, 'All this guy needs is a whisky sour?'

Suddenly I was surrounded by concerned pundlings. The numb, metallic taste in my mouth had intensified. The walls flickered dizzily, sickeningly, from coral reefs – as if any of those still remained – to Swiss mountains featuring tiny alpine blooms – ditto – studded with soft green sward. Only my patch of sky stayed honest, displaying the dull glow of afternoon. The cushioned chairs were still there, though Ravene seemed to have disappeared.

I breathed, 'What happened?' And a pundling whose number blurred before my gaze said reassuringly, 'Do not worry, prisoner.'

'Was I poisoned?' The way the pundling glanced at her colleague spoke volumes.

Drugged, rather than poisoned, was my guess – they'd overdone it, probably. The King would lose his temper, and a few luckless heads might roll, for someone had delayed their precious all-Earth transmission, and nearly permitted me the escape of an easy death.

Not the King's plan. I happened to know.

Though there was also a chance that pundling 7784 had been ordered to assist me to commit suicide. This could be viewed as a kindly gesture, given what had happened to poor old Ichthus. I even imagined – there was nothing wrong with my imagination, it was my body that had been torpedoed – a heartrending scene in which Petra gave way and agreed to allow 7784 to smuggle poison into my breakfast mush.

I imagined the headlines on televiews everywhere. 'INQUISITION OF REBEL TRAITOR DELAYED DUE TO UNFORESEEN CIRCUMSTANCES.' (The Xirfell have yet to learn that capital letters suggest aggression.) Or, more prosaically, 'TRANSMISSION DELAYED.'

I shut my eyes and concentrated. The King would want this interview to occur as near as possible to its advertised time. If I refused all food I could probably get away with it on an empty stomach, in full possession of whatever faculties I still possessed…

I decided, *I'm swallowing nothing.*

They didn't like it. Instead, they were determined to attempt anything – short of force-feeding – that might induce me to eat. First, they tried MF. He arrived in a hurry, organs tumbling, and connected faster than he ever had before.

–Yell, Aiden.

I obliged. Then, very bitterly, I told him,

–They fucking poisoned me.

–They drugged you, as far as I can tell.

–What's the difference?

–I can understand why you're distressed.

–You're fucking right I'm distressed! One of the most important days in my entire useless life and these assholes try to turn me into a lolling fuckwit?

–It's what any dictatorship would have done.

–Sounds as if you're pretty cool with that.

Here he meanly needled my back. It felt as if pincers were ripping my backbone open, as one might do to a cooked fish. My yells were real.

–What was *that* for?

–Sorry, overdid it a bit. This is scary for everyone, you know.

Of course it was tough: tough on MF, tough on Ichthus –
if Ichthus still lived – tough on Priscilla and Tim and Doreen
and Hugh and Bully and everybody else. Tough even on Martin.
Tough, too, on the amber sea-creature in the Golden Circle. And,
at that moment, every single one of them was depending on me.
This idea was both oppressive and exhilarating because – luck of
the draw – I had been chosen. MF continued.

–I was sent to find out why you wouldn't eat.

–They can't make me, can they? Like a blinking suffragette?

–They could, but I doubt they will. It would be hard for you to
speak if they did. But what do I tell them?

–Tell them that my stomach revolts. And don't you dare pull
that spine-thing again, not if you value your face... assuming for
the purposes of argument that you have one.

–Good luck, friend.

I waited for a word from Petra, but no luck. He added
apologetically,

–I'm afraid you'll have to scream, if I'm to retain any
credibility at all.

I yelled, with all the energy I could summon up, with barely a
calorie inside of me.

As soon as he'd gone, I wished I hadn't been so rude. I also
wished I'd asked him to order me a little uncorrupted water.
Instead I was overwhelmed by gentle pundlingitude.

'Eat, prisoner, otherwise you will faint again!'

'Prisoner, if you eat, it will do you good.'

And once I waved them away then I was in serious trouble,
because then other pundlings arrived, with real food. And how I'd
missed real food! Not only while buried underground, but ever
since the invasion.

The food at the Academy had been excellent, while Sophia had
prided herself on her old-style cookery – I'd enjoyed any number
of superbly executed roasts and casseroles at her table. But I'd

never smelled anything like the dishes arrayed temptingly in front of me. Some of the ingredients I couldn't even identify, but others I'd been missing since forever.

Before me lay a sea bass, voluptuous of interior, crisp of skin, suffused with oriental spices. Beside it were white truffle shavings over fresh pasta, with slivers of roasted artichokes and – the final temptation – something alien but divinely crunchy in appearance. I've always had an adventurous palate ('Aiden eats with an enthusiasm maths cannot command' one teacher/wit had observed), so maybe the mystery dish tempted me most of all.

In my defence, I'd eaten nothing but soy-based gruel for a fortnight, before which I'd only been dished up astonishing delicacies like gristly stew, or potatoes with all their flavour bludgeoned out of them. Although – to be fair – I'd heard of a cook in the King's own kitchen being less than gruntled, for only pickled meat from the Xirfell's home planet was in serious demand, and all her training wasted.

I couldn't help wondering which chef, thrilled with a brief so appealing, had prepared these toothsome temptations in vain. Because there I sat, both thirsty and ravenous – but mostly thirsty: had the Xirfell an iota of imagination, they could have tormented me with tepid water – but not about to give in.

The pundlings continued to press me, their flute-like voices rising.

'Prisoner! You will need strength!'

'The poor prisoner is too sick to eat!'

Then I heard one of them whisper to another, 'But he is not to die.'

I was glad to hear this.

Soon afterwards, they padded sadly away, bearing their untouched delicacies between them.

Not that I felt entirely relieved, all the same, for the idea of injections had occurred and – bound as I was – how could I

possibly fight back? A minor dose of some drug, even dental gas
– because the Xirfell could be pretty bloody simple, for a people
capable of laying waste to entire galaxies – and I'd present as
risible a spectacle as any dictator could hope for.

Meanwhile the seconds and minutes ticked by with –
presumably – the broadcast still being delayed. I guessed that
somebody was probably thinking up the least-obvious way to
inject me – though, come to think of it, what was to prevent my
mentioning having been injected while on-air?

Nothing, in my opinion.

I fired myself up by recollecting Sebastian's execution, the
zuging of Malthus, poor Ichthus's tongue. Suddenly my elbow
was being jogged. 7784, complete with shaving materials.

Two shaves in a single day? Even with a worldwide broadcast
in the offing, this felt like overkill – I wasn't in a boy band. But,
turned out, his was no ordinary shaver: it had been hollowed-out,
and the liquid inside had a garnet sheen, like some famous claret.

'Drink,' he mouthed.

Had it been any other pundling – but this one was ours – MF
had told me he was ours – and in his almond-shaped eyes was
something that looked like truth.

Was this the last drink of my life? – I had nothing to go on
but those silvery eyes. I opened my parched lips and allowed
him to siphon the lustrous stuff down my throat. Instantly, I felt
a humming power from my crown to my toes, energising yet
calming, blasting a glitter of wellbeing all the way to the nerve-
ends. 7784 instantly twisted the blade round and started to shave
me.

'You! *Tortif!*' yelled a tester. 'Get away from the prisoner!'

'So sorry, sir, but I was ordered—'

'Just get the fuck out of here before I fucking zuge you!'

And with this came the sickening slash of a glass-encrusted
whip on 7784's heavy head. He wavered, blinked, and fell –

though he was caught before he hit the floor by one of his fellows, who rushed him away.

I ached to exact revenge but the only way I could protect 7784 was by pretending. I slammed my eyelids shut, fervently hoping that a pundling could survive such a blow, while taking strange comfort from that deep look in his eyes.

Perhaps ten minutes passed, while restless waves of robotniks, testers, people and pundlings surged round, against the same bizarre backdrop of extinct alpine flowers. I caught snatches of conversations: 'That will be useless unless'... 'can delay no longer'... 'give him one of the previous'... 'The King has ordered'...

What? But her voice had sunk too low for me to hear what the King had ordered.

Finally, everything quieted down. A pundling smoothed the make-up caked over my facial wounds. A sea scent wafted past, probably Ravene. At last I was lifted – by a robotnik who marked my wrist with his power – and deposited in one of those deliciously comfy chairs.

The robotnik held me until I was bound again, though the audience presumably wouldn't see the invisible bonds pinning my torso, knees and elbows. The original burning tumult of 7784's crimson liquid still warmed me, but it had taken a quieter turn, like a river breaking its bounds and swelling over a wider expanse. I felt prepared and alert, though occasional nerves still tweaked at me.

Ravene seated herself, not allowing her eyes to meet mine. She looked pale but disquietingly lovely, and there were no attendants in sight: no robotniks, no testers, not even a pundling. The recording devices were noiseless, but the feverish light and glowing alpine blooms still dazzled my brain.

'Aiden Tenten is with us, one of the leaders of the rebellion.' Her voice was strong – possibly too strong, pitched somewhere between self-confidence and hands-up neurosis. There was also a little twitch at the corner of her mouth, which could have been nerves. Rather liking the 'leader' bit, I straightened my shoulders against the invisible bonds.

'Mr Tenten, do you deny that you have rebelled against the beneficent government of the Xirfell?'

'I do not.'

'Might I ask why?'

Christ, where to start? I plunged in.

'The Australasian government of my youth was pretty diabolical. They decimated great swathes of the country – they oppressed the weak, the uneducated and the Indigenous – they saturated the environment with chemicals – they imprisoned almost everyone who disagreed with them, and their elections were certainly rigged. But they were sensationally democratic compared to the Xirfell. The Xirfell have culled humanity, preserving only those they consider useful or intriguing. They've laid waste to the planet, kidnapped human brains and bodies, diabolically experimented on almost every living thing, imported creatures from other galaxies as servants or slaves—'

'And do you have any proof of these wild accusations?' she asked.

'The proof lies all around you. The proof lies in the cursed and rotting deadness of our cities, the crushed abandonment of our suburbs, the detritus of rusting weaponry poisoning the shorelines, the acrid death of forests, ocean and air!'

I almost added, 'For fuck's sake', but desisted. It was an international broadcast, after all. Creatures would be forced to watch, from G6 to G30. As for my vow to maintain a Zen-like calm – you'll have noticed how long *that* lasted.

Ravene returned, in a weird sing-song voice, 'How strange you are! The land all around is nothing like your description of it!

The cities rise majestic over the horizons while the nourished countryside flourishes!'

And here the walls absolutely glowed with improbably sweeping cityscapes, rich with parkland, along with countryside views practically throbbing with long-extinct bees, sweetly playful lambkins and chirping birds.

How dim did the Xirfell think we were?

'These are dead pictures from a dead past,' I replied, with all the patience I could muster. 'You can scroll down as many historic pictures as you want, but it's not like that anymore, and everybody bloody well knows it isn't. You're inviting us to admire something as distant from today as ancient Egypt or pre-Christian Rome! You weren't around – you wouldn't know – but the Earth was once a beautiful place. There really were lambs like those, and valleys as green as that. There really were fish in the rivers – you could even *swim* in the rivers – and there were hawthorns in springtime – while floating through the sky in a zelopod was a glorious thing, the land undulating below, the stars just emerging from a cream-pink sunset—'

'And so it is now,' she said, a little unsteadily, with that nervy flutter of eyelid. There was also something weird about her voice. But I had no time to worry about Ravene. This was my chance – almost certainly, my only one.

'Listen, you have no idea what it was like! Before your father and his disgusting friends invaded, the air was clear enough to see the hills from the cities – at least, it was in Australasia. People used to enjoy swimming pools and tennis courts in places where these days nothing but kudzu, ivy, insects and monstrous predators can survive. Some of us lived in pods looking out over seas that were still mostly blue. There used to be stadiums, right out in the open air – stadiums filled with hundreds of thousands, watching great sportspeople from every continent—'

She suddenly stiffened, as if prompted by someone or

something. Could this be a clue to the opacity in her eyes? And was Daddy calling the shots – or somebody else?

I was playing chess with an invisible opponent.

Suddenly, she whipped, 'And I suppose there was no violence in those halcyon days, Mr Tenten?'

'No, there was plenty. There was the oligarchy, still in control, the rigged elections, massive social unrest, racism, poverty and inequality. The government before the invasion was fascist – no question – but it wasn't hell-bent on worldwide destruction. They stopped educating people who couldn't afford to pay but they failed to wipe out whole cities, hunt the underclass or experiment on living humans. Instead, they contented themselves with lowering taxes for the richest, disenfranchising the poorer classes, and perpetuating the occasional judicial murder.'

'How fascinating that you should mention murder!'

'Humans can be murderous,' I said impatiently, 'but with the Xirfell, murder is the default mode!'

'What fantasies you have! No wonder people say—'

'What do people say?' I asked dangerously.

'Well, to be quite honest, they say that you and your followers are no longer sane! You must know that the Earth was ruined in your last World War! You must know that the Xirfell found it so. There were no flowers, no green hills, no soft blue skies. We came, we found it ruined – and so... and so... we are rebuilding! All around the world, we are restoring nature and beauty! On the screens all around you can see—'

'You have rebuilt nothing!'

'Then you have failed to look! Obsessed by a single, poisoned, corner of Earth, you have failed to see all the improvements, the amazing changes, that the beneficent Xirfell have already accomplished! Throughout the world, we have planted trees. Throughout the world, we have restored damaged wildlife. Throughout the world – except in a few places, which have proven so stubbornly resistant – we have ruled all creatures with gentleness, consideration and respect!'

For a wild second it seemed to me – that lilting voice, that dreamy intonation, those ruddy lambkins – that she was right, and I really was crazy. After all, I hadn't travelled beyond G13 since I turned eighteen, when Duncan very decently shelled out for a Mediterranean island-hopping cruise with four of my better friends.

What if I *had* been brainwashed, and the rebellion blindsided by vitriol and hatred? What if Sebastian Nevsky had only been out for himself, if everything I'd ever fought for was wrong? What if G13 really was only the last holdout of creatures too reckless or stubborn to give the long-suffering Xirfell a fighting chance?

It must have been thanks to the remnants of the drug that I gave this even a moment's thought. As it was – thank you, 7784 – I fought back. Ravene had shaken me – or some devilry had shaken me – but my breath was back, my belief was back.

'Listen, I don't know what you're smoking, but I lived on Earth eighteen years before you were even conceived, and I know exactly what the Xirfell have done to it, thanks. The King may be expert at manipulation, but nobody on Earth believes him, since he's done nothing but lie in every speech, in every communication, in every broadcast. You want the truth? –The truth is that he's planted nothing, restored nothing, and cherished nothing. Instead he's used creatures – of all sorts – in ways too horrible to mention. He's destroyed almost every sector of the overland – *not* merely rebel strongholds – and it isn't only Earth that he's murdered but planet after planet, in galaxy after galaxy! The King won't stop – the Xirfell won't stop – until they've laid waste to the universe, and enslaved or corrupted every living thing! The truth is—'

The reason I paused had nothing to do with Ravene. The screens had morphed. Tiny alpine flowers, bathed in a nostalgic late-afternoon glow, had given way to – to me. Not gussied up, not neatly suited, not with my every scar expertly disguised, but in prison gear, frowning, and bending over – Ichthus.

A raw chill swept through my body.

It was the moment: the moment when I'd taken a deep breath, measured my exact distance from the King for the millionth time, and placed my fingers on Ichthus's scraggy neck. But as I watched myself – what a strange expression I had! – part-pity, part-raw determination – the recording didn't stop.

Instead, *I killed him.*

Yes, in every Earth sector still capable of receiving live broadcasts, I was shown, not nailing the King, but committing murder! – We even got the death-rattle, as Ichthus's last breath collapsed under 'my' fingers.

Fucking bastards! Someone must have strangled him and superimposed my template digitally. This wasn't Ichthus's real death – and yet it was. This, almost certainly, was how Ichthus had died.

I had heard about people 'seeing red', but I'd never done it before. Enraged, I tried to spring to my feet, forgetting the invisible bands, which jerked maliciously against me. Probably looked as if guilt was tying me in knots.

Ravene spoke again – if it *was* Ravene, because there was something weird about the voice. 'Can you deny the evidence of your eyes, Mr Tenten? For you are yourself a murderer – and in cold blood, too! You were filmed strangling Ichthus Dmitrios, a fellow member of your precious rebellion! What a chilling example of bitter jealousy and vitriolic hatred!'

'The Xirfell killed him. That recording has been doctored!'

'Easily said, Mr Tenten,' returned Ravene, with a taut little smile. 'But the evidence is before us. Can you deny it?'

I said, as steadily as I could manage, 'Yes, yes I can. Ichthus was brought to me, here in prison. He'd been tortured so badly that he begged me to kill him—'

Those bifurcated irises looked torched from within. 'Really, Mr Tenten, can you seriously expect us to believe that the poor fellow begged you to kill him? Have you any evidence for such a wild claim?'

'How could I? – I'm only a prisoner here! But—'

'A prisoner of your own imagination. You came of your own free will.'

'– but this deed I could not do. I tried – and failed.'

'You seem to have overcome your squeamishness quite remarkably, Mr Tenten, considering the result. And it's easy to say that he begged you to kill him – as well as convenient. Not the slightest evidence for it, of course.'

She was attempting to sound condescending, but her voice still held that tinselly note. I briefly wondered if she might be dead herself. I'd vaguely heard of body blending, body borrowing – but I'd never been interested enough to learn more. Could her stepbrother Uval have triumphed? Could this stunning part-alien be merely a robot, or a shell? But I hadn't got time to think about it; I still had work to do.

I said, as quietly as I could – for millions were watching and I'd probably been tried and convicted by most already – 'Tortured by the Xirfell to the point of longing for death, Ichthus begged me to kill him. I just couldn't do it.'

'An ingenious fantasy!'

'Listen, Ichthus was old. He was always pedantic – he could be pretty fucking annoying. But the Xirfell tore out his tongue, tortured him and finally strangled him, digitally imprinting me over whoever really finished him off… But you've made a massive mistake in releasing this faked recording. Everyone on Earth knows enough to guess what really happened – and, in G13, at least, we will rise, because we've had *enough* – of your lies, of your King, of all your kind! Sooner than you think, you'll find you've taken on the combined fury of creatures, not only here in Australasia, but in every corner of the planet!'

I wasn't surprised that, just as the old juices were beginning to flow, we were suddenly plunged into darkness. I heard the whirr of an approaching robotnik and steeled myself for the blow – which never came. Instead, pundlings started padding past on their dimpled feet, the lights slammed back on and suddenly there was a tester simultaneously releasing me and hauling me back to my chair, on purpose – or so it seemed – to viciously score both my wrists with his filthy fingers.

Great. Probably, I'd wind up infected.

Every second there was more activity – testers barking orders, robotniks dismantling the set, broadcasting operatives rushing about – while I fizzed with impatience – impatience to know, mostly. If only I'd guessed that they would ambush me with Ichthus! Had they cut the transmission before I'd justified myself? Had I persuaded anybody that I hadn't killed him? Yet if I'd been *too* persuasive – if I'd unnerved the King – this day would certainly be my last.

I also regretted my instinctive attempt to rise – was it obvious that I'd been restrained, or had I merely looked like a trapped fish? Was it possible that I'd inspired anybody, even lit a couple of little lights?

I also recalled pundling 7784, with a rush of guilt. He and his garnet-starred drink had saved my wits, but already his soft sweet innards might have been awarded to some reeking blurg, that luminous gaze doused forever. What *hadn't* he risked, for me? I felt so distressed – or perhaps 7784's liquid had been so warmly powerful – that I didn't recall for ages that I was hungry.

When the pundlings finally returned, it was back to the gruel, but I was too tired to worry and swallowed it, almost with

gratitude, for the combination of nerves and an empty stomach
had been horrible.

16

The next day opened on a dullish morning. A few listless drops of rain skimmed just past my feet.

The previous day had altered everything. Before it, I'd been an anonymous, imprisoned rebel operative. I awoke as the most famous face – possibly the most infamous face – of the rebellion, recognisable over most of planet Earth. There could be only one topic of conversation, from Death Valley in G22 to what used to be called Australasia, which was: 'What a pathetic wanker Aiden Tenten is! And what a chance the fellow had! After all the misery and humiliation the Xirfell have inflicted on us all, how could he have stumbled so feebly? And how pathetically he weaselled when confronted with his crime! Not to mention that fake grandiose bit at the end. What a prat!'

But I still retained a sliver of hope that other creatures might be generous enough to be thinking, 'What a spot that poor fucker was in! Probably framed for the murder and then shoved into prison – almost certainly zuged by this time. No, well, he didn't do fantastically, but who's to say that I'd have done any better, in front of the whole freaking world and with that rather gruesome beauty needling me?'

And then suddenly, MF was back, six testers with him. After I'd snarled a bit and he'd got connected, I sneered voicelessly,

–So where's the rest of the execution party? Caught in traffic?

–This almost happened. There was a crisis meeting, the Golden Circle, the whole bit.

–Including the mermaidy-one?

–You dwell too much on Leelack.

–So, did I do OK?

–Why else do you suppose the transmission was halted?

–Really?

My self-satisfaction must have been obvious because MF twinged me. After I'd abused him, he continued, a little grudgingly,

–You did very well. There have already been movements.

–What do you mean, movements?

–Uprisings – in the southeast and southwest quadrants, big ones. As far away as G7 and – especially – G9.

–Could it be serious? For the Xirfell, I mean? And are the uprisings coordinated by our own cells?

–These appear to be spontaneous, and altogether new. Though the Xirfell have already dispatched whole army divisions, testers, robotniks – it could all be snuffed out within a week. And there are also rumours of the King's sending you to the Creature, without a trial. Could you yell?

I duly yelled. Then,

–What creature do you mean?

–I forgot that you wouldn't have heard. A sea monster, basically, which has become, overnight, a media sensation. I don't know where the Xirfell found it, but several victims have been publicly sacrificed to it since your arrest. Until your interview yesterday, almost nothing made the news beyond the Creature.

I wasn't fussed. Maybe an alien whale, maybe a giant sea-snake plied with growth hormones – whatever. All I could think was that I'd finally done something useful with my life.

–So, no trial for me?

–Almost certainly not. Although the rescue idea is again being considered.

I'd almost forgotten about it. I said,

–What will I have to do?

–Whatever you're told to do at the time.

–Tell them not to send Petra.

–I have no say in the matter. It's up to McNamara and the council.

Then I remembered 7784.

–MF, was I drugged before the interview? I felt drugged, and 7784 –

–7784 discovered that you had indeed been drugged. What he brought you was a pundling home remedy, and entirely on his own initiative.

–Well, it fucking worked!

–He took a tremendous risk.

–But is he all right?

–I don't know – I haven't heard.

–Could you at least thank him for me?

–Not without arousing suspicion. He will, I am sure, guess your feelings.

–Cautious bastard, aren't you?

–Indeed. Could you protest again?

I could, but I was struggling to feel sore and angry and ill-used, just at that moment.

–Who really killed Ichthus, MF?

–A tester, at a guess.

–And he really is dead? It's not just another trick?

–I'm sorry to say that he is certainly dead.

As I'd suspected. Poor old Ichthus.

–So why were you ordered to come?

–For the Xirfell, to plant fears in your mind about the Creature, and to tell you that you had been entirely disbelieved. For Martin,

to alert you about the possible rescue. As far as the trial's
concerned, I'm sensing that you're a little disappointed, having
had such a confidence boost yesterday.

–So you think I'm just sitting here feeling smug, do you?

Without answering, he unbridged himself – I thought of it as a
bridge, somehow – and oiled away, the old toad, leaving me with
my thoughts.

Fact is, I've never considered myself a particularly confident
person.

An Academy professor once described me as 'arrogant without
foundation' but I often think that I've spent most of my life
covering up for the insecurity I'd been born with, the sense of
not being good enough that I've never quite lost. Never quite
clever enough. Never quite sporty enough. Never quite handsome
enough. A perpetual runner-up; never quite snaffling the prize,
whether the prize was being captain of rugby or winning the
most lusted-after female – except for Ravene, and Ravene hardly
counted, given that the downside involved lifelong infertility.

But maybe out of all this had come that determination Sebastian
had identified when he'd first taken a chance on me?

17

A few years after Sebastian recruited me, I was asked to assist in blowing up a high-security scientific installation – a mission that had already been in planning for several months. Then twenty-four, I'd been a replacement for a more seasoned team-member who had lost hope and plunged into the outback, never to be heard of again.

We met in an abandoned plant nursery with most of the roof missing, cleared of reptiles and poisonous spiders by one of the support groups.

Our team was led by Ichthus. He was already fussing with his old-fashioned notepad when I arrived. However, none of us so much as rolled an eye, for Ichthus possessed all the lustre of a founder member. There was a mystique about these: Priscilla, Ichthus, Malthus – Sebastian, especially.

The bomb had been made by 'Clement' Dane, whose real identity was known to a mere handful, not including me. Presumably, they had sourced some secret stockpile of fertilizer somewhere: gold dust.

Our mission was to bomb the factory, the only Earth-based manufacturing source for the signature component of the infamous robotniks. We had two 'sleepers' in the factory: Joan, a toughie in her forties, and her nephew Milo, a raw and rather excitable youth of nineteen, vouched for by his aunt.

Ichthus greeted me with sardonic eyebrow. 'A little late, are we not, Mr Tenten?'

Supercilious old mummy, I thought, disrespectfully. Joan and Milo were already seated. She would have passed anywhere for a typical harassed office worker – I secretly pencilled in young Milo as rather a squirt.

'Right, let's run through the plan again, now that Mr Tenten has deigned to join us. Joan has assembled the device created by, ah, Clement, which is currently at her home. There's a massive shipment due to leave the factory on October 20th, so we're hoping to mount the operation on October 19th. As the factory tests every consignment on the factory floor, Sebastian thinks that our best chance would be for Milo, who works in electricals, to transport, with the false box nestled in amongst all the others.'

'I could maybe carry it?' suggested Milo.

'No, I'll have already assembled it and hidden it inside the consignment,' Joan intervened. 'It's far too heavy for you to manage. Then, because we need something to distract security—'

I said, 'Wait, here's a wild and crazy thought. What about a fly-past from Theo's famous dinosaur-birds? What are they called again? – Piacentors.'

'Still untrained,' said Ichthus shortly.

It seemed to me that, if Theo hadn't blinking trained them by that point, they were never likely to be of any use – but I had my doubts about Theo. Great guy – heart of gold – but too dreamy by half.

I started considering another angle. 'But surely robotniks would normally transport the boxes?' (I secretly thought that Milo might as well hoist a large flag with, 'This is a bomb, assholes' on it, as stagger around doing a robot's job, solo.)

'Meaning?' inquired Ichthus.

'Meaning that it would look strange for Milo to do it, even if they'd know his face.'

'That's why you're here,' Joan told me. 'We need a diversion, so the guards don't get suspicious. I mean, the paperwork should be perfect – I doctored an invoice from a genuine consignment. But the ognyites might still be able to smell the fertiliser, and you're spot-on about consignments generally being transported by robotniks. So, it's your job to create a diversion.'

'But I don't even work there!'

Ichthus intervened. 'That's the point. You, Aiden, are playing a tramp. Joan's stumbled across you in the canteen, looking for food. She hauls you to security, just as Milo emerges with the consignment.'

'And my backstory? Was I dropped down the chimney by Santa Claus?'

'You're starving,' said Ichthus, sighing, probably at the depths of my stupidity.

Now this didn't strike me as unbelievable. I was between jobs at the time and often hungry – though I could imagine easier ways of getting food than breaking into the canteen of one of the Xirfell's highest-grade scientific establishments. I said grudgingly, 'OK, right, but it'll have to be perfectly timed. And what if their testers zuge me on the spot, just to be on the safe side?'

'They can't, not in public, anyway. Ever since, well, you know.'

We all probably thought, No, but they could still arrest me, shove me in some nearby room and zuge me there. But nobody was tactless enough to mention it.

Each one of us was taking a massive risk. The bomb could blow up, either in Joan's home or in Milo's face. The Xirfell's creatures might sniff out the incendiaries. The testers guarding the premises could – if their lunch had disagreed with them – take me away and execute me. The timings could go awry.

The odds were stacked against, no question, but I wasn't fussed.

I was very young – I was extremely angry at having been dismissed from the Academy without my degree – I was tired of drifting from job to job – and I hadn't had a mission in a while. (Probably, I'd also seen too many Telepod series glorifying the resistance during WWII.)

So I only asked, 'How do I get smuggled in?'

Joan replied, 'That's the best part – there's a tunnel! It was my finding the tunnel that gave Sebastian the idea for the operation. A couple of tramps dug one from outside the perimeter walls all the way to the canteen – and they've been using it ever since, though nobody knows but me. They never take much food – I even put a bit aside for them when I can, as one of them lost a leg during the war. The only downside is that this episode will end their scavenging! But, as far as the operation goes, you just sneak in through the tunnel and lie low in the canteen until I come in and pretend to discover you.'

'How wide's this tunnel?'

'Narrow, but then, so are you. If I can use it then you should have no trouble at all.'

'Any other questions?' snapped Ichthus.

'Is the food worth the swiping?' I joked, but Ichthus hated jokes.

'With regards to the actual retreat,' he told me stuffily, 'the tunnel will be the exit route for both Joan and Milo. You'll have been kicked out of the entrance by then. And you'll all have no more than twenty minutes before the entire premises will be blown sky-high, so I would strongly advise you not to dawdle.'

I secretly thought twenty minutes didn't leave a helluva lot of leeway, but I didn't want to raise more objections. I've noticed the same hesitancy with younger rebels, now I'm thirty. Some of them would – quite literally – rather die than look a fool.

All I asked was, 'Do I get to fight back while they're kicking me out?'

'If you don't value your life, yes,' was Joan's opinion. 'My advice – and remember, I see these testers every day – is to take whatever's meted out to you. Anyway, you're not supposed to be a fighter. You're a starving tramp!'

I secretly reflected that at least the starving part was true. I could count my ribs in those days.

There were a few dried biscuits on the table and Joan had brought some turnips – some people still planted vegetables, if they could avoid the surface contamination. There were still a couple of turnips left, and I was hoping to swipe one before Milo demolished them all. (As I recall, we divided the last one between us. He was probably starving too.)

On the day appointed, I showed up at Joan's, which turned out to be one of those shelters slung up right after WWIII, that had only become homes after most real homes were demolished. It was immaculate, if notably short of personal possessions.

Joan surveyed me with approval – I hadn't washed, my shoes were falling apart and there were a couple of holes I'd worked on in the elbows of my shirt and trouser knees.

Poster-boy for an Indigenous netty tramp.

'And you'll look even fouler once you've crawled through the tunnel,' she observed with pleasure. We took a circuitous route around the barbed-wire barrier, ending up in a thick copse, where Joan, after a bit of trial and error, eventually located the leaf-ridden hole we were after.

As tunnels go, I found it unappealing. A sensible person might have thought about all the poisonous nasties that could be lurking inside, but my only concern was that it didn't seem to allow for much air. I took a few deep breaths as Joan patted me maternally on the shoulder.

'See you inside,' she said and then, under her breath, 'Remember what we're doing this *for*.'

Personally, I was doing it in hopes of undying fame, but still, her words stirred me. Yes, what a chance – what a fantastic chance – to bite back at the regime that had taken our whole world away!

And so down I scrabbled, full of hope, full of vim. Luckily, there had been no recent rain and the tunnel, if not exactly roomy, was mostly dry. Also on the bright side, the earthy smell was not unpleasant and there was no immediate sign of snakes (the monstrous ones wouldn't have fitted, anyway). I did have one moment of breathlessness, before my torch picked out the metallic plate that was the finish line.

'A little push'll do it,' Joan had promised, and Joan had been right. The barrier gave way with a short grind of protest – my heart momentarily stopping in case it had been heard. However, the canteen was entirely empty, if ghostly in the half-light. I replaced the metallic cover carefully and, feeling extremely grubby but very cheerful, wandered around in search of food.

A bonus. Even a perk.

Each door looked identical, though I slammed one back sharpish that turned out to have live kopets behind it. Finally, I found some potted meat. It tasted great if a bit gritty, but my standards those days were pretty low. After stumbling on a few bits of rather curious-smelling cheese I curled up on the floor to sample them.

Meanwhile the bomb should have been smuggled in by Milo inside an otherwise harmless consignment. And at exactly 06:45 Joan was going to 'pop in for a cup of tea' – really, to discover me.

Food never tastes as good if your stomach is nervous, and mine heaved after the potted meat and cheese, so I shoved the remaining cheese deep in my pocket, just like a real tramp.

Method acting.

It seemed to take forever for 06:45 to arrive and I had several false alarms, including the kopets getting overexcited and bashing restlessly against their compartment. There was also a smallish tester – small for a tester, anyway – who swung past almost noiselessly while I was browsing the bakery, causing me to lose a couple of years of life and a stale croissant. By the time Joan hove into view I couldn't have been more pleased to see her had she been my birth mother personally.

'Well done,' she said under her breath, before snapping restraints on my wrist and starting to drag me down various mainly empty corridors to the entrance. I used the moany sounds I'd practised, though we met almost nobody: 'Miss, miss... I wasn't doing nothing... There wasn't no harm done, miss! Ouch, stop it! I'll come easy, miss!'

Joan moved fast. 'To the second,' old Ichthus had instructed us, about a quadrillion times. Although, in retrospect, I felt guilty for thinking him a boring old stick. He was probably sweating as much as we were – and with nothing to do, as well.

Around the final corner was the entrance, a meeting-point of about ten separate hallways, heavily guarded and heaving with robotniks, pundlings, humans and half-human workers. Out of the corner of my eye I glimpsed young Milo emerging from a different wing, grinning fatuously. I wanted to punch that smile off his face.

I also spotted my first ognyite – famed for their sense of smell – whom I ardently hoped had a lousy head-cold. Lumpy, lizard-like, greenish-grey, with a long snout and still longer tongue, even the testers gave it a wide berth. Their tempers were also legendary, as whose wouldn't be, having been swiped from one galaxy and imprisoned in another?

Would Tim's smell disguiser deceive the ognyite? – If not, I'd get to hear that famous ognyite shriek. Was it true that they distrusted Indigenous humans, or was it just an urban myth? – I didn't want to hang around long enough to find out.

Meanwhile Joan, pulling me, was panting as if I'd fought her, though I'd been hugely submissive, not wishing to give anyone an excuse to zuge me. She spat, 'Look, street trash! In the canteen!'

'Street trash? Probably a dig spy!' sneered a tester.

Oh fuck, fuck, fuck.

Milo was getting closer, still wearing that boy-scout-like expression of good cheer. I adjusted my own expression to cravenly apologetic and whined, 'I didn't do nothing! I were only hungry, mister!'

'Human filth!'... 'How could he have got in?'... 'Why don't we give him to the blurg?'... 'Nah, not even they'd eat such a piece of scum!'... 'What's the fucker stolen, then?'

'I didn't steal nothing! – Tell 'em, miss!'

One tester kicked me in the balls, laughing, while another spun me upside-down, using just one gigantic hand. The cheese fell out of my pocket. I scrabbled for it blindly, still reeling from the blow.

'Typical half-breed!'

'Thought you said you didn't steal anything, fucker!'

Out of the corner of my stinging eyes – though my whole body was singing with pain – I saw the ognyite slouch suspiciously forwards.

'Consignment,' I heard Milo say, briefly. Personally, I thought his nerves visible from an intermediate galaxy, but the testers were busy guffawing at my humiliation, so maybe our timing was perfect.

The ognyite retreated; the guard stamped Milo's papers and Milo was in – not to mention the bomb – the other testers ignoring him entirely in favour of glaring at me. One said to Joan, rather threateningly, 'How'd the worm get inside?'

'There's a tunnel!'

'From where?' he grated.

'How do I know? I only just found it! – and this creature. But could he have made it? – Impossible!' She looked disdainful. Meanwhile, I glimpsed Milo moving back the way we'd just come.

Then the ranking tester got busy. He started firing off orders: four testers were to inspect the security breach with Joan, fourteen others were to alert the external border guards, the tunnel was to be cemented up within the hour, an investigation was to be launched, and the 'snivelling little git' was to be taken into custody.

My heart stopped. Custody meant death in 17.45 minutes. My whining became virtuosic. 'Please, sir, I jus' found it, I dint mean to! Don't zooj me, sir! You don't want to zooj someone like me, what's never done nothing!'

His contempt increased. 'Oh, sod him. Fucker's not worth the trouble!'

I have never, before or since, been so delighted to be kicked about three metres in the air. I thought gleefully, You've cracked three ribs and saved my life. Piss off and die, asshole!

And then, despite the glittering pain down my side and a suspicion that one of my ribs might have punctured something vital, I pelted out of the compound, leaving them practically wheezing with laughter behind me.

I didn't stop running until every ounce of breath was spent. Then I leaned against the nearest wall, breaths cracking, hoping that Joan and Milo had got out in time. (Oddly enough I didn't mind Milo, at that moment. Had he shown up, I'd have greeted him like a brother.)

I minded him even less when I finally heard it – a great grinding noise, which shuddered the ground beneath the street.

Passers-by took it big. Pundlings squirrelled around making chuntering noises; and there was human and half-human terror, even hysteria – plus a few creatures quick enough to guess what was happening. ('The plant! Jesus!'... 'Aren't there killer chemicals in it?'... 'Don't stand around! *Move!*'... 'Get underground and downwind – fast as you can!')

Though a few people started smashing shop windows, hoping to get away with looting – and good luck to them. One of the robotniks I saw was actually flattened – lying on the ground, its 'feet' still stoically gliding against a mid-air backdrop of smoked sky and acidic dust.

Personally, I wanted to punch the air. It had been Clement and Joan's bomb, and Sebastian's scheme – led by Ichthus – but still, I'd done my bit. Every one of those testers must have been blown to pieces, but what pleased me most was that the inner voice that kept sniping, 'You're not good enough/brave enough/smart enough,' had been drowned out, as the tumult all around grew louder, wilder and more chaotic... And that wasn't all. People were smashing windows with loose pavement tiles, grabbing the latest gear from shop windows, even hurling themselves at the upended robotniks. For one glorious moment I thought, *The revolution – at last!*

And perhaps it might have been, had the Xirfell not had a back-up plan.

Because shortly after the great blast, the Xirfell unleashed one of those sedating dust clouds over the whole area. I later heard that some older people had died because somebody had shoved too much sedative in, but personally I just trotted back to the homeless centre and took a long shower. I then bound up my ribs with help from a fellow lodger, content that, had I really punctured a lung, I'd have been dead already.

Other guys in my wing were bragging.

'I heard it – I felt it... It was wild! You coulda heard it in sector frigging 26!'

'Old Lenny got lucky, broke into one of those places off Democracy Row.'

'Where were you, Aiden? You must've been close, to have been frigging wounded!'

'Not too far away,' I admitted.

The next day, I was devastated to learn that Joan hadn't made it. As Milo reported at the debriefing, 'She pushed me in the tunnel first. Then she got called back by one of the testers. The only way she could've made it was if she'd run inside the tunnel in front of the tester, and then they'd have shoved a grenade in after us, so she just stayed.'

The tears were spilling down his cheeks and I had to swallow hard to fight down my own, as he repeated, 'She just stayed. She just – stayed and stayed!'

I later heard that Milo wound up doing very well: a rising guy in the rebellion. But neither of us will ever forget his aunt Joan.

We had a two-minutes silence after Sebastian put our decorations on, and I bit my cheek so hard I could taste blood when he said, 'Also, in absentia, hero of the rebellion, first class, Joan Marie Artington.'

I hadn't even known her last name.

18

After MF's visit I felt increasingly desperate for news. Once I thought I spotted 'our' pundling 7784 – once, down the corridor, I even imagined hearing MF himself. But I was left to my own devices: either editing the memory sliver or else experiencing alternating episodes of boredom, anticipation or fear.

It seemed to me very bad news that the initial bustle – or had I imagined it? – had given way to such torpor, unless of course testers, army, the lot, had stormed off to stifle sudden rebel uprisings – which I found just too cool to believe.

Increasingly restless, I also longed to be out there – fomenting revolt, encouraging the troops, giving my opinion about operational objectives, even dying in combat. I wasted a lot of time imagining these kinds of scenarios. (Of course, I recognised that Joan's death had been every bit as inspiring; it just wasn't the kind of end I dreamed about.)

Several days passed. I'd gone through every play and book I could remember – I'd done memory exercises with every poem I'd ever been forced to learn at school – I'd played games with historical dates and re-enacted – in imagination – every conversation, every mission and every sexual act that I could manage to separate from all the others. I had also conjugated every verb and messed about with every character – whether personally encountered or else historical – I ever knew. By the time I was finished, Hitler had enjoyed a torrid affair with Goebbels, who was then murdered in a jealous frenzy by Eva Braun.

Yeah, you're right. I was pretty fucking bored.

At times the silence, the sheer emptiness, almost drove me mad. I desperately tried to engage the pundlings who padded into my room to shave or feed me, 'What's happening? Is there a war?' – but their gentle gaze told me nothing – not even lies, because I never knew a pundling to lie. Though even lies would have been better than solitary confinement.

I thought, 7784, where the hell are you?... MF, you bastard, you can twinge my spine as hard as you like, if you'll just come back!... Ravene, I'll give you the sex of our lives, if you'll just show up...

Sometimes my brain switched into fever-mode. Where was Petra now? Could the Xirfell have discovered MF's treachery? Had it really been Ravene in our bizarre interview? Who'd be picked to lead if Martin was captured?

Sometimes I felt stir-crazy with inactivity – sometimes I became almost torpid, as if my blood was slowing, like that of an animal entering hibernation. Then I felt fatalistic, almost calm. Perhaps nothing was happening. Or perhaps I was slowly going mad, staring up at that changeable but somehow changeless square of sky.

One night there was just a single star visible – the last star standing.

I briefly considered starving myself to death – that pallid gruel tasted thinner yet grainier by the day – but I was still sworn to the rebellion, and my trial might still happen. A week passed – I clocked every second of it – before MF returned. Petra herself could not have been more welcome. I could have embraced every centimetre of that revolting, bulbous, vein-filled mass; the effort it took to scowl at him ached my brow.

–Well?

–I tried to get here earlier, but all hell's broken loose, I'm afraid.

–I've been forgotten, anyway.

–Everyone's been forgotten, except for the rebels and the rebel cause.

–My lights?

–Are everywhere. Half the guard's been sent to put them out. Which is why your rescue bid is set for tomorrow night. Security is laxer than I can ever recall it being.

The rescue bid! Now I loathed this metallic chair and this metallic room with a monumental and metallic hatred. I absolutely yearned to stir my legs, to move, to run – yet to be cheated of my trial was still a disappointment. Yes, they'd kill me afterwards, no question. But death at a distance never seems very real, does it – whether you're facing a tester, a bomb or a zuge's string of gem-like eyes. I said gloomily,

–They don't think I'm up to it, Martin and the rest.

–It's simply that there will never be a better chance at a rescue. Nobody's here, I tell you. The King's gone to G9, and Ravene to G17. And what a blow for the regime, for you to escape just before your highly publicised trial!

–Highly publicised?

–It's been advertised everywhere.

–I thought it wasn't happening! After all, what's in it for them? I'm not the leader. Why give me such a platform?

–I entirely agree. You're both personable and articulate. If I were the King I'd drop the whole notion – in fact, if I were the King, I'd simply kill you.

In lieu of which he absently tweaked my back. I was almost too distracted to curse him in return. Because, the more I digested this news, the more cheated I felt. I was even obstinate enough to think that I might excel at my trial… After all, hadn't they pulled down the curtain on my broadcast because I was doing too well?

I said,

–Those uprisings –

–The sticks were dry as tinder, but you struck the flame.

–Then why shouldn't my trial kickstart a fucking conflagration? Is that such a crazy idea?

–Well, I expected you to think it. But still – Aiden, do you know the reason you've never been allowed a leadership position?

–No, I fucking don't.

–It was Malthus.

–Malthus! – You're joking.

–He believed you to have a certain psychological complex. I may add that I disagree with him – though, from my privileged position, I might know more than most. There's no question that you've done extraordinarily well, everyone says so –

–Everyone?

–I believe, everyone.

–Even though I'm supposed to have a complex. I don't suppose you could explain this so-called complex, in words of one syllable?

–It's called a Messiah complex. Basically, people who have it feel that it's up to them to save the world. Although psychologists quite often disagree about –

–But what if they really *can* do something to help the world? What if this might really be my 'time'?

–I suspect that most people would probably take that as confirmation of the diagnosis.

–So, I'm not allowed to help to save the world, because I have a fucking complex?

–I did say that I disagreed with Malthus' diagnosis, if you remember.

–You don't think I need rescuing?

–Well, only from yourself.

I considered this for a moment, then,

—But – when all the dust is cleared away – the facts are that tomorrow I'll be rescued. Or, if the rescue goes pear-shaped, killed in the attempt.

—Yes, I suppose that sums it up rather neatly.

—And, either way, no trial for me… So, what are my orders?

—To do what you're told, if your rescuers appear. If they don't make it through, then you have no orders. Now I must pretend to work you over.

—Must be great to have a job you love.

—Piss off, Aiden.

If only I could! – but once he'd gone, I found quite a lot to think about.

At first I felt pure resentment – resentment taken neat – against Malthus and anyone else who might vaguely concur with his opinion. Malthus had been a strong leader – in some ways even a great one – but how dared he claim to interpret anyone else's soul?

I also remembered his warning me off Petra, and couldn't help wondering if his diagnosis of this 'complex' had been the reason. I also remembered his rather reserved commendation at the ceremony when Milo and I had been decorated by Sebastian – and his preferring Martin to me, about a year before, for a minor mission in G6.

So much had suddenly been made clear! And yes, for a while I was almost unbearably angry. But gradually it all ebbed away.

Because – let's be logical, just to make a change – had I been Malthus, and Petra my niece, I might have felt exactly the same. A born netty, plucked from the street – never really belonged – never quite fulfilled his early promise – turfed out of the Academy without a degree – and probably only chosen by Sebastian in hopes of getting at Ravene. A guy too arrogant to take precautions about being outed as Ravene's lover – and too cocksure to go into hiding.

As for this complex – well, what if he'd been right? Didn't

I secretly think that I was meant to do something astonishing? Didn't I generally resent those in leadership above me? Didn't I imagine that I was supposed to save the world? No wonder Malthus had warned her about me. No wonder Martin imagined that I'd be safer – a loose cannon – gathered back to base!

Gloomily, I watched the light shift from dusty cream to washed-out navy, edging into night.

And remembered.

19

There was a new operation in the offing. At twenty-seven, I had rarely felt more positive, stronger, better equipped or readier. I was fit, powerful, enhanced. I strode through the wilderness practically hoping to meet some rabid creature and I found it increasingly difficult to fit in at my workplace, where I was – for a pittance – permitted to teach some hand-picked pundlings a hugely sanitised version of Earth history.

I'd begged Sebastian to choose me from the moment I'd heard about it – he had listened and smiled but promised nothing. I later learned that his wife, Priscilla, had resisted the idea of my teaming up with Petra on a mission. Luckily, Sebastian preferred at least one male to be included, even though most of the rebellion's greatest triumphs had been achieved by women. (The reason? The Xirfell were relentlessly, infamously sexist. They seemed to view human women as either sexual partners or domestic slaves, while – despite an equal distaste for human males – they treated us miles more seriously.)

The main reason I longed to be picked was because the goal of the mission was to assassinate the most repugnant member of the Golden Circle: the vicious blundicant who had christened himself The Enlightened One.

Others called him names rather less flattering. He possessed a sure political instinct and – despite being the fattest, ooziest, most repellent blundicant I'd ever seen – he boasted a following who idolised and even adored him.

The blundicants had been conquered by the Xirfell some centuries before they reached Earth. Androgynous, they're able to self-inseminate – if the notion takes their fancy, which can't happen very often, as I've never seen an infant blundicant.

I first encountered The Enlightened One – then known by his given name – at the Academy, where he scooped up most of the academic prizes. What impressed me most, though, was his deviousness.

I had been arguing with Ravene about the Roman Empire, about which she took far too rosy a view – but then, Ravene was always an impulsive historian, and famously prone to exaggeration. We were getting pretty heated by the time the blundicant joined us at the student bar. Now I happened to know that he shared my own opinion, so I welcomed him as an ally. Despite this, fixing his bulgy orbs impassively upon us, he proceeded to take precisely the opposite view, charming Ravene but thoroughly pissing me off.

The Roman Empire, which he had previously considered as containing within itself the corrupt seeds of irreversible destruction, he now reckoned an inspirational prototype for the glorious Xirfell, going so far as to praise other blinking empires in between, including Napoleon's and Putin's. As we were in public I chose to shut up, on this occasion. However, I took the first chance I got to tell him how appalled I'd been by his hypocrisy.

Now, blundicants can't really wink. Their eyes seem to operate very differently from ours, but, had he been able to wink, I suspected that this blundicant would have done so.

'You'll never get anywhere, Tenten,' he observed unctuously, 'without being able to simultaneously hold two opposing points of view.'

I had despised him from that moment, while considering his

political success a certainty. Though it took even him some years to worm his way into the Golden Circle.

Once elevated, though, The Enlightened One made an instant impact. Far from keeping a low profile, he was constantly in the news, a genial apologist for the regime, while remaining wildly popular among the people. He was the leader – at least he was according to your sturdy workingman – who 'tells it like it is,' 'doesn't kow-tow to nobody,' and 'sticks up for the likes of us.' And there was more. He combined this twinkly, blokeish air with a touchy-feely 'religion' imported from his home planet.

At some point between the Academy and the Golden Circle, he'd lost most of a limb, which he had turned to typical advantage by attaching a stamping brand to it. This stamp, he hinted, possessed strange powers. It all started without much fanfare, but – after two or three supposed miracles – The Enlightened One modestly admitted that his famous stamps were powerful, not only against illnesses, but even against ill-luck. Believers queued up to be stamped after his rallies, and fervently claimed to have been cured of everything from allergies to cancer. Soon the symbol on his stamp could be spotted everywhere, on doorways and shop-fronts, on T-shirts and bags.

Overnight, The Enlightened One turned into a cult. Books were sold, supposedly written by him, good-naturedly ridiculing such old-fashioned but still popular notions as tai chi, mindfulness and meditation, along with the more recent craze for free-dwelling. He gave wildly popular lectures, consorted with the Xirfell princes as equals, and was reputed to have become richer than all the rest of the Golden Circle members combined. Rumour had it that his dressing-room walls were encrusted with sapphires and gold.

His fame became sensational. There was something – in his voice, his persuasive powers, his flashes of humour, his aura – that appeared to give even the most downtrodden creatures hope.

And the King didn't seem to mind. In one broadcast, he even

referred to The Enlightened One as his 'most valued advisor' – a backhanded blow against several longer-serving members of the Golden Circle, one of whom was executed the following week. By this point, The Enlightened One was probably better-known than every royal, except for the King. One could buy Enlightened gems, Enlightened blessings, Enlightened every bloody thing.

And this cult-like status was rare, since the Xirfell never encouraged even members of the Golden Circle – some of whom elected to remain secret – to become public figures. Nor were the royals promoted in this way. They could easily have founded a cult of Ravenites, but they never did, for all her looks and style, petulance and panache.

But we in the rebellion had long thought very differently about The Enlightened One. His avuncular charm had never deceived us, nor his supposed cures. After all, it was he who had ordered the arrest and murder of Priscilla's parents; he who had overseen the genocide that polished off the G12 rebellion; and he who had recently started appropriating every set of identical new-born twins, in hopes of combining blundicant genes with human DNA.

This last was what caused the rebellion to target him for assassination in the first place; the plan springing into Sebastian's fertile brain when a rebel resembling his wife won three tickets to hear The Enlightened One speak.

'Simple plans are often the best,' Sebastian reminded us, in the musty cave where we often gathered. 'Priscilla, pretending to be Irene, is permitted two guests. I'm proposing that Aiden and Petra impersonate her daughter and son-in-law. We could utilise the templates for Troy and Elaine Smithson, as they've never been used.'

I slid my eyes around to Petra, who lifted her delicate chin and glanced elsewhere. Our relationship, often stormy, was in a rocky phase – the idea of pretending to be my wife did not impress her.

Sebastian continued. 'Hugh's got hold of a pretty exciting

poison, one that can be communicated on contact. Now, everyone knows about the Enlightened One's famous stamps. After every performance he normally agrees to stamp his imprint on a few dozen fans. You three should be at the front of the queue, holding out your pre-poisoned hands to be "blessed" – as the target dares to call it. The poison should be transferred instantly through the stamp although – and this is crucial – it will only gradually seep into his bloodstream.

'In other words, it should be impossible for his minders to discover exactly which groupie was the assassin – particularly since it will take time for the poison to affect such a massive specimen. We'll also need some respectful question to submit, at the entrance. Can anyone think of one suitably obsequious? Nothing sarky, Aiden, nothing clever – nothing that might get the invitation rescinded and such a chance wasted.'

'How about, "What have you got against infant twins?"'

Sebastian shot me a warning glance. 'The target considers himself a great spiritual leader. I was thinking something about his representing the revival of hope during the years of rebuilding?'

'Excellent!' was Priscilla's opinion.

'But there's *been* no fucking re-building, other than for the elite.'

'Spiritual rebuilding, Aiden.'

'Oh, I'm not objecting! – The great lump of gelatin'll love it.'

I said this in hopes of amusing Petra, because blundicants aren't really gelatinous. There are even people who consider them fascinating, especially those with constantly varying colours. I don't remember Petra smiling though. In fact, whenever I remember her, she's wearing that direct, serious gaze, above that almost too-pointed chin, with that straightness, like a silver birch… At the time, it was mostly a blind physical urge. I wanted her so badly. I always do when we're having a row. Basically, the worse the row, the more I want her.

Priscilla added, 'On the other hand, maybe Sebastian's question is just a touch too brilliant. We don't want our question selected. What we want is to blend in.'

'How do we get the poison on our hands?' asked Petra.

Sebastian said, 'I'm just getting to that. Only one of you need be the actual poison-carrier. My idea is that you all three leave the Centre early, after applauding wildly of course, or whatever you find that all the others do. But you don't immediately rush to the place where our hero deigns to stamp the faithful. Instead you grasp each other's hands and embrace, utterly overcome at the life-changing treat you've just enjoyed.'

'Who wrote this crap script?' I wanted to know.

'I did. Priscilla will have earlier doctored her hands with the poison. If you share enough of this between you, whichever one of you gets "stamped" will certainly kill him.'

I said, 'I'd like to volunteer to be the main poison-carrier – maybe even the only one, though Priscilla and Petra would be great for cover. First, because Indigenous people can be less susceptible to some poisons, and second, because Priscilla—'

'Sorry, Aiden, but the answer is no. The reason being that the blundicant *appears* to favour women and only selects about every third supplicant to stamp. A single volunteer doesn't give us strong enough odds... Incidentally, Hugh is also emphatic that, once one of you three is stamped, the other two must leave the queue. A double dose could kill him far too quickly, and then his bodyguards could start shooting everyone in sight. There are always hordes of fans, apparently. The place is regularly packed.'

'How does he do this stamp, anyway?' I asked.

'He presses the stamp at the end of his stump into the back of the hand. The brand rises, like the brand on an animal, and lasts about a week, during which time gullible people queue up to touch it, to benefit their boils, insomnia, indigestion, whatever.'

'But why should Priscilla have to endure the poison throughout the whole event?' Petra asked. 'Couldn't we just break a vial in the toilet or something?'

'A vial would never get through the security scanners,' said Priscilla, 'so our only chance must be for it to be on someone's skin already. And yes, it might be detected, though Hugh's pretty confident that it won't. But that's a chance I'll just have to take.'

Sebastian had been stroking his beard. 'Priscilla. I'm thinking that he won't give young Aiden here a second glance.'

'If Petra gets her hand poisoned, then I do too,' I said swiftly. 'But Priscilla's taking by far the greatest risk. The longer this stuff sits on the skin, the greater the risk that it might permeate. That's why I should be the carrier. I'm younger than Priscilla – and stronger than Petra, as well.'

I didn't like to remind them that I'd been enhanced, as it could freak people out. But, to my mind, it was no contest between a great but aging lady, a slender young woman like Petra, and me.

Priscilla gave me an oblique look, meaning, 'You're right, but I'm still not listening.' She said, 'Hugh says that Q578Z is far more toxic to oil-based aliens than to any Earth life-form. And I'm far less valuable to the cause than a fit young person like you.'

The argument didn't end there, but it might as well have done, because Sebastian, as I later learned, had already lost it.

The next week, Petra and I arrived, separately and disguised, at Hugh's.

I should just put in a word here about Hugh. Hugh was not quite a founder rebel member, but he was still mega-important, as he combined working on an elite team of Xirfell scientists with acting as an agent for the rebellion. In this instance, he not only accessed the poison but deployed the Xirfell's own techniques to transmute Petra and me into Elaine and Troy Smithson, a couple involved in a suicide-pact who had donated their bodies to the cause. The procedure involved an hour's operation and a couple of hours of moderate pain upon waking. Petra didn't complain, but I found

Troy's lungs stuffy and heavy, and his bulk annoying. Basically, I felt like a garden snail borrowing a too-hefty shell. Yet there was a palpable sense of excitement – noticeable even in the self-contained Hugh – that it was almost time, that the mission was almost upon us.

The next morning Priscilla joined us. Her disguise was quite successful: her own wrinkles had been cleverly exaggerated with some of the most up-to-date procedures (we had sleepers in several important factories). Her hair, an appalling colour on her, but one not uncommon in older people, was dyed a near-midnight black. Between her assumed limp, that awful hair and all those wrinkles, the quick, real Priscilla seemed completely lost.

I watched, almost jealously, as Hugh treated Priscilla's small hands instead of mine. It was leaden brown stuff with an astringent smell as he painted it, but both the colour and smell soon seemed to fade.

We set off for the Centre immediately afterwards.

The Centre itself might also be worth a mention. It's probably to this day Earth's largest unnatural structure, a mind-blowing combination of the Xirfell's engineering genius and their slaves' and robotniks' hard slog. It covers a ground area exceeding three thousand square metres although – through some trick of the brain – every seat gives the sensation of being in the very front row.

A little spooky, I've always found it.

Lining up for the security bubbles – which could supposedly detect point-zero-zero-five of a milligram of a banned substance – I found my pulse speeding. As agreed, Priscilla and Petra were keeping up most of the dialogue, discussing such inane topics as a row between 'Posy' and 'Jeff', some marvellous Xirfell initiative to build pods over the sea, and the problematic pregnancy of a fictional 'Elise'.

My own role was that of unenthusiastic attendant, though of course I had to remember to address Petra as 'Lucy' and Priscilla as 'Nana', and to display a rudimentary interest in their conversation. Every now and then, I thought I spotted a flash of Petra in Elaine Smithson's hazel eyes – otherwise, it was pure strangeness, pure unreality.

Our first setback came right at the beginning. Petra and I went through the bubbles seamlessly, but 'Nana' was recalled for a second inspection.

I felt boneless, and Petra/Lucy turned to me and whispered, 'Nana, fancy! Of all people!' with a quiver in her voice. I said, as comfortingly as I could, 'Her heart medication, I expect,' in a voice I bet neither of us recognised.

The actual wait – though it couldn't have been longer than seven minutes – seemed endless, as we wittered on about nothing, with me making bad jokes and Petra attempting to laugh at them. The moment Priscilla reappeared, serenely smiling, was ecstasy – she hadn't been arrested, the game was still on.

The surrounding hordes were certainly excited. In fact, so strong was the sense of expectation that my own secret anticipation seemed to slot right in. An almost crazy exuberance filled me. In my mind Sebastian was already decorating me. I was the envy of every younger rebel, tipped for the top, destined for great things ('Aiden? Oh, well, there's no stopping Aiden. Sebastian's blue-eyed boy, absolutely!'... 'Well, you must have heard about the assassination, didn't you?'... 'Old Aiden's got what it takes, no question. His nerve is second to none.')

This pleasing daydream was punctured by Petra's nudging me, and I hastened to add something to the inane conversation, saying, 'I've never even seen him before.'

'Ooh, we did, didn't we, Nan? Only from a distance, mind.'

It surprised me, Petra's uncanny ability to get in character. She had realised, as I think we all had, that the crowd was mostly what Sophia and Duncan would have termed 'lower middles' – the kind who had only left off voting for D. Justin Medlicott to fall for

The Enlightened One. Not highly educated. Not highly thoughtful. Basically, patsies for the regime. ('Ooh, Lizzie, Lizzie, have you thought of a question, love?'... 'If he just looks at me, I'm going to faint! How silly am I?'... 'They say he's beautiful and ugly at the same time.'... 'Whaddya call him? Your Honour, of course! They're all Your Honours, even the King. Just Your Honour, and you needn't bow, because he's as modest as modest.'... 'Does my hair look alright, Mikie? Does it *really?*')

Both Petra and Priscilla – herself probably the most highly educated person in the entire rebellion – were making a remarkably good fist of fitting in, a test I failed. But all the while we were creeping forwards, towards the preliminary 'show' – which was itself showy enough.

There were bugles and harps and alien instruments – some of these alive – in a strange mishmash of styles, but every one of them loud. There were humans and half-humans, one extremely famous, though he's become a non-person since: Lionel Messinge. His dancing was so good that even I forgot myself and shrieked along with the rest... There were visions of 'reality' too – 'real' people passing by in 2D, for example, and an alien who could make parts of his body appear, disappear, and appear again at will... Handy skill for an assassin, I couldn't help thinking. There was even supposed to be a gromeline – so rare as to be practically mythical – but I never saw it. Basically, all the fun of the fair.

Finally, they all buzzed off and then, in a blaze of iridescent light: The Enlightened One. I must admit that no representation I'd ever seen had really done him justice. Ugly, beautiful or simply unearthly, there was certainly something fascinating in the play of such vibrant colours. He was like a living work of art, with constantly shifting layers, from rainbow to sea-mist. It was hard to look away, and most people didn't, drinking in his aura as if hypnotised.

You'll want to know: what did he do? Did he perform? Did he teach? Did he preach?

Well, he did all these things – and none of them. In the strangest way, he simply *was*. It wasn't singing as the performers had sung, or teaching as most teachers teach, but – and this is the strangest part – everything he said seemed to make the most perfect sense while he was saying it. Immediately afterwards, while the next grovelling query was being floated, I recognised every word as the most utter tosh, but as the music emerged and the colours altered and the shapes took on timbres, I felt entirely convinced.

He would say – indeed, I believe he *did* say – that rebellious elements 'no longer existed', that all the universe had been 'united in the glory of the Xirfell's bloodless victory', and even that WWIII had 'never happened'. Instead – haha – it had been created by the Earth's vicious media, which had since been entirely discredited. And all the while some infinitely subtle technology created the illusion that he was addressing me alone, as if none of the others were even present – except as a spur to the emotion, an uptick in the pulse.

It felt odd to recall that we were only there in order to kill him.

Our question wasn't picked, so all the effort that had gone into it was wasted. Wasted too – much more worryingly – was Priscilla's face by the end of the first hour. The colour seemed to drain from brow to chin, leaving a greyish tinge behind it, and the skin under her eyes seemed to darken ominously. Petra alertly proposed taking her home.

'No, no, dear. How could we leave when he's so beautiful?'

'But you're chilled! Let me feel your hand,' said Petra, a serious meaning in those borrowed eyes. Her 'Nana' responded by shaking her head fiercely and burying her hands in her pockets, meaning, 'I'm the poison carrier. It was decided.'

'I don't feel chilled,' she added, while Petra's eyes met mine over her head and a guy behind us said simply, 'Who could leave, with *him* still here?'

This certainly summed up the feeling of the masses, and as the procession of fake questions and false answers continued, the crowd's fever, amounting to intoxication, only increased. It reminded me of those famous films of Hitler's rallies, as if the crowd had been brainwashed into ecstasy, practically drugged. Also, Petra and I both had elevated temperatures, due to our DNA having been overlaid with the Smithsons'. I felt weighed down, as from a major germ, or some serious blow.

Of course, the event didn't only consist of the Enlightened bastard. In between the questions there were fierily rhythmic songs glorifying the beneficent Xirfell, our loving King, the caring Golden Circle and the immortal Enlightened One, and such was the power of the singing, in that glowing space, that even I felt – for a fraction of a second – almost captured. I certainly felt no inclination to leave – other than my worries about Priscilla.

The trouble being, of course, that Priscilla outranked both Petra and me, and that all methods of inter-creature communication had been banned, post-invasion. I was desperate to know what Sebastian would have ordered us to do, without a chance of finding out. Had he been there, would he have forced her to go, or not? Where did our first responsibility lie?

'She's so stubborn!' I complained to Petra, who raised one eyebrow expressively.

Got it.

At that point our surroundings began to ocean into midnight blue and to pulsate with stars, not just those iced blue ones visible from Earth, but wildly kaleidoscopic efforts from the Xirfell's own galaxy, and I swear that half the crowd believed that The Enlightened One himself had conjured them into being. A couple of people even collapsed in some kind of religious fit and had to be helped to leave by pundlings.

About fifteen minutes later, Priscilla must have finally come to terms with her situation. Because, after raising her hands blissfully skywards, she turned, levelled her gaze to mine and said, 'My dear, I grow old. Perhaps I may never see such another day! Let me bless you!' and with this she grasped my hands – with surprising power – in her own.

I returned the energy of those chilled little fingers with everything I'd got. I was telling myself that I wished to spare Petra, but I longed to be the one who polished off the great bastard. I doubt that much poison was left for Petra, as she in turn rapturously clasped hands with Priscilla, promising her 'Nana' that she would, 'tell your grandchildren about this, some day!'

'How beautiful!' said a misty-eyed observer nearby.

I was obliged to stand there, beaming, while feeling increasingly impatient. We had to get Priscilla out!

'Nana is becoming almost faint with excitement,' Petra murmured. 'You should take her home, dear.'

'You could take her. I'll soon catch you up.'

Petra's glance was eloquent. She was trying to remind me of The Enlightened One's preference for young women, and that she had the best shot at being chosen. There was some sense in this, so I pressed Priscilla's hand again. 'Nana dear, we'll meet you outside in the fresh air. The – thrill – has been too much for you, I'm afraid.'

'You do look a little ropey, love,' another woman advised.

We finally prevailed: Priscilla was assisted outside by a couple of pundlings, where she was met by a junior member of the rebellion. The moment she was out of sight, I found that I could breathe again – the worry had been pulling us both down.

The finale of the 'show' was shorter. This was lucky, as I'd begun to be conscious of at least something of what Priscilla had endured: a dulling of the senses, a reluctance to move, a chill at my extremities and a throbbing in my temples.

As we rose for the standing ovation, I felt something nudge itself inside my palm – Petra's hand. She suddenly looked more like herself, and less like the dead Elaine. As she brushed against me I even felt the old uprush of desire, as if the poison had galvanised my every blood cell into a struggle against oblivion.

We were among the first to slip out – I noticed that I no longer had any sensation in my toes – and headed to where the stamping was supposed to take place. There, for reasons of cover, we attempted to make conversation with the fanatics – though no fanatics, I believe, can equal cult fanatics, in terms of annoyance value.

'Wasn't he marvellous!'

'He certainly was,' said Petra fervently.

'I hope all you young people realise how you was graced!'

'Will he come here, Terry? Will he really and truly come just here?'

'Dunno. Hope so. That's what they say he does, anyway.'

'I can't wait. When he comes I think I'll just faint away!'

'I can't wait to see him either,' I told the fan. 'I can't believe that some people can just wander on home.'

Though I could, not least because about nineteen creatures had been crushed to death at the previous week's stamping. Which helped us a good deal in terms of reaching pole position, as there were fewer groupies than usual.

'Och weel, it was a long show, though it seemed to last but a second. Hark! He must be coming!' This from a hearty fellow with a foghorn voice.

The procession was arriving. First pundlings with the waif-like, wolf-like edoys, then a series of uniformed humans, the usual ranks of scowling testers, and finally… our hero. Even grosser up close, yet still possessing some curious, deeply personal, power.

The woman we had just met was right at the front. Lips parted, she pressed eagerly forwards, waving her hand. He smiled at her but instead selected a pudgy, freckled lad of around six, whose mother squealed with orgiastic pride. He passed a family, then a skinny young fellow – who looked, the poor sap, practically broken-hearted. He was almost upon us.

My heart sped until it seemed ready to jerk straight out of my chest. Choose me. Choose me. CHOOSE ME. **CHOOSE ME.** The Enlightened One seemed – or was it only my imagination? – to be gazing directly at me.

Pushing swiftly past Petra I eagerly extended my hand. He turned, made a strange gesture, almost of benediction, then wired the back of my hand with that thick blackened stump.

An instant surge of heat pulsed up my arm and throughout my torso. Then a wild swirl of fuchsia-slashed-with-orange flashed beneath my eyelids, as if the stars we had recently seen, fiery and spotlit against the black, had been injected into my brain. My every corpuscle felt separately fired, an almost intoxicating sensation, especially after the chill of the poison. I half-stumbled backwards, almost squashing a smallish alien, and only saved myself from falling at the last second.

Meanwhile The Enlightened One continued his regal progress, advancing, selecting, stamping and blessing like some type of alien pope. Through a haze – my eyeballs felt as if they were swimming in flaming waterfalls – I saw Petra beckoning, and moved towards her.

Of course. She couldn't risk being stamped, in case the creature died too fast.

As we walked the ornate brand began to swell on my hand – a warming, tightening feeling. The sense of strangeness accelerated, though this might have been from my borrowed DNA, the chilled poison in my blood, or the fiery stamp. But nothing could dent my happiness, because – I'd done it. I'd assassinated The Enlightened One!

Though not even he knew it. Yet.

At the far door, I dared to glance back. My victim proceeded implacably forward, still smiling, still glorifying, still stamping. I thought, Oh God. Don't tell me it hasn't worked?

Meanwhile, the celebratory crowd was eddying in two directions: the tardy hopefuls still towards the stamping zone, the rest of us towards the exits. Petra and I manoeuvred, as swiftly as we could, to the main exit, for sooner or later – unless something had gone badly wrong – The Enlightened One must fall.

When every one of us would become a suspect. And I'd have been caught on every monitor, as well. I recalled Sebastian's warning: 'In a young blundicant, perhaps half an hour. In one so bloated and unfit – just get out as fast as you dare.' It was mega-slow going through the waves of other creatures, or maybe it only felt that way. My body felt at war, the poison chilling my feet meeting the waves of heat worming inward from the stamp.

We were still surrounded by the lunatic fringe. 'Malcolm, I just felt it right here. I'm *sure* he cured me, just with that stamp!'… 'What a load of creatures there still are, war or no war!'… 'Hush, Mum, and don't complain. You've just seen a frigging marvel, haven't you?'

Gradually, I began to feel dizzy. The stamp – or the remaining poison? – vibrating through my blood, I felt cut off from my limbs and pinched in the head, as if my brain was being slowly crushed. Even my memory sliver felt strangely tight – I normally forget about it. I worried too that the chill in my feet might reach my legs. Then another worry surfaced, which refused to go away.

Petra had to get that stuff off her palms.

'You should go to the loo,' I told Petra, adding rather more loudly. 'You know how you always need to before a journey, dearest.'

'We haven't got time,' said Petra, not even glancing at me. By then her 'Elaine' face had the same bony pallor as Priscilla's.

Despite this she seemed utterly determined – and maybe she was right, given that my legs might have packed up at any moment.

And still no panic from the 'stamping' zone – though I was alert for it, every second. Finally, finally, we made it, with the multitudes, to the exit. Outside the Centre, I spotted Iolanthe – one of the most beautiful sights I'd ever seen, though she'd always had a snub nose and, just then, also looked wild-eyed with terror.

Oh God, Priscilla must be dead!

Then suddenly, just behind us, a tidal wave of rising cries, screams – some creature absolutely screeching – overladen by bellowed orders from every side.

'Shut every entrance! Let no one leave!' one tester roared, just as we, along with a great flood of humanity and other creatures, careered through the exit.

It was surreal. Out in the street people were still blessing each other in an ecstasy of quasi-religious fervour while – only ten metres away – others were in hysterics: locked in, frenziedly weeping, clutching each other for support, and banging against the barriers. Some creatures, separated from members of their party, were pounding helplessly back from the open side; while various robotniks and testers shouted for, 'Quiet, in the name of the King!'

We didn't hang about. Instead we followed Iolanthe, who led us down several side alleys and into a quadropod. The driver instantly doused the lights and sent us jerkily upwards, while Hugh lost no time in injecting Petra with the poison antidote, causing her to jerk instantly into unconsciousness. I was just reaching for her hand – was she annoyed? – when he, without warning, injected me. The quadropod's roof flickered, fizzled, and disappeared.

When I came to, my legs felt normal, but the sensation of weirdness remained. The skin around the stamp had ballooned to bursting point: the glorious motif of The Enlightened One had risen in all its repellent splendour. Petra was sitting up and drinking some steaming liquid; she gave me a long, level look that I couldn't read. We were absolutely racing – I couldn't see who was driving, but it was skilful stuff.

Hugh took my pulse.

'Priscilla?' I asked.

Hugh indicated and I turned around. She was ice blue, hoarsely breathing. I hadn't even noticed her as we'd piled in. I raised an eyebrow at Hugh.

He only shrugged, but I'd known Hugh a long time and there was hope in his eyes. He said, 'Good thing you shoved her out – else she'd have stood no chance.'

'But will she make it?'

'I think so. Can't you just sit still, just for one frigging second, Aiden? You're making my job impossible!'

I duly stilled myself. As we blasted forwards into the darkness, Petra's chin remained in her hands, her face averted. Then came the signal from Sebastian: a long flare followed by three short flashes. It glowed from the wilderness coordinates just as we were beginning our descent. The Enlightened One was dead.

On board, there was more relief than celebration. I'd been obsessing in case the Xirfell had somehow saved him – perhaps the others had, too.

Priscilla regained consciousness shortly afterwards. Hugh was beside her in an instant. Eventually he returned and caved in beside me – he's shaped in a rather concave way anyway – as if de-boned with relief.

'She'll do,' he muttered. 'Thank God.'

20

I had assassinated The Enlightened Bastard, but I was still miserable, because Petra wouldn't forgive me.

It wasn't, as Priscilla whispered – it took her weeks to recover her voice – that I'd succeeded and she had failed. Instead it was my 'sexist, belittling' pushing past her in the stamping zone that had infuriated her. She had told Priscilla that I had 'read' The Enlightened One wrong, that he'd been heading towards her, that I had pushed her brutally out of the way, that I was arrogant and self-aggrandising, and that she would despise me forever.

Priscilla's response was typical. It didn't matter which of us had assassinated him; generations of unborn twins would live to bless us, and it had been a matter of complete chance who had been chosen... I told Priscilla that, had I not made my move, all our efforts (and her own desperate illness) would have been for nothing.

Although – strapped to this bloody chair, three years on – I found myself wondering if this had been strictly true. As well as I can recall, the situation could have been read either way – either of us could have been given the nod. But Petra might have had a legitimate grievance. She might even have been right.

Either way, for some time afterwards she wouldn't speak to me – though we rarely met. Sick as we both were – from the poison-carrying and the borrowed DNA – we still showed up at our usual jobs: me at my teaching, Petra at the shelter, helping those the Xirfell had no use for.

I didn't know how Petra coped, but nobody at the college appeared to notice my exhaustion in the least. Instead, the rest of the college staff had trouble restraining their excitement, because sympathy for the rebellion ran deep, though there were always a few objecting, 'What good does it do?' and, 'Utterly useless, of course... Those airhead rebels again!'

The week of mourning for The Enlightened One seemed endless. There were four services a day, with representatives of every sector obliged to attend. Marie, who represented the college, reported that it was deadly – but we'd all guessed that already, because everyone in G13 had to stop working for several hours on the final day. As I watched the burial, I felt very strange: partly proud and partly frustrated. I longed to step forth in a blaze of trumpets and admit that I had been the assassin – instead, I had to mutter what a pity it all was, with all the rest.

I doubt that more than two of them meant it.

Meanwhile, the King was still combing the country for the Smithsons, whose bodies had immediately been zapped in Hugh's garage. The regime excelled itself with wild threats and crazy rewards for information, as tended to happen when the King felt challenged. Though he might not have been quite as devastated as he pretended. There was even a rumour that he'd arranged to have The Enlightened One murdered. There is such a thing as outshining one's master.

In the end, the regime arrested any number of attendees and released them all. It was the Smithsons they wanted, but that trail lay cold as death. There was also a massive reward offered for information leading to Priscilla's arrest, but, as she'd already been in hiding for two years, it didn't impact on her much, though it took her weeks to recover.

Our mission also seeded loads of conspiracy theories. The Smithsons were from an alien force that would eventually recover the Earth... We three were ex-Enlightened loyalists, bent on revenge after his 'cure' had failed us... We were even angels brought down to punish The Enlightened One, for hubris. As with the assassinations of John F. Kennedy in 1963 or Wang Li in 2045, conspiracy theories continued to abound long after the body was buried.

I wasn't worried about being arrested – but I was miserable about Petra. It was Sebastian who finally lost patience and insisted that she snap out of it, which she did, icily, after a cell meeting. She later sent a formal note, suggesting that we meet accidentally, in an ancient tree-fort in a devastated mansion, miles from anywhere.

It was a hot and humid day, almost unbreathable. I had killed one of those rodent-like mtjiks on the way, so I lit a little fire and barbecued it – it was gristly, but I was hungry. As I knew Petra would disdain the slightest morsel, I seasoned it with a few herbs from my backpack and polished it off, trying to imagine it was one of Sophia's lamb cutlets. In those days I often hungered after those comfortingly old-fashioned things at which Sophia Tenten had used to excel – scalloped potatoes, cheesy leeks, rhubarb ice cream.

Petra stiffened the moment she spotted me. She wore an I've-been-told-to-make-it-up smile, and grimaced as she spotted the skeleton.

'I didn't save you any,' I told her.

She swung herself lightly up onto the platform, where there was just a breath of wind. We were both wearing our grubbiest clothes and carrying backpacks full of wood shavings. (Our cover story was firewood collection, since wandering in the wilderness for amusement had been disallowed by the regime.)

'You were ordered to show up,' I offered.

'You're a ruddy genius.'

'And you don't want to be here.'

'Right again.'

Her clothes clung to her body, lean and sinuous as ever. Sweat dripped from her hairline, which the humidity had electrified. I hungered for the taste of her sweat.

'I'm really sorry I shoved you out of the way,' I said.

The Enlightened Idiot's stamp, which had initially looked as if a worm had burrowed into my hand – it had almost *hummed* – was mostly faded, while the medal Sebastian had pinned – on all three of us – was something I still thought about. My star was rising: I was a coming man, listened to, noted, consulted, even petitioned for advice by the younger members. The new respect was palpable. Though not yet twenty-eight, I'd come through seven times for the rebellion.

Petra, though, was unimpressed.

'I don't think you're sorry,' she said. 'I think you bloody planned it.'

'I didn't! It just happened. I just felt that – contact.'

Petra looked at me, actually looked at me, for the first time. There was a little mole, always had been, of course, just beneath her neck. I longed to kiss it. I longed for the smell of her, for the feel of that slim back. But I kept my fists clenched behind me, thumbnails digging into my palms.

She plucked a segment of bark from the tree. 'But, Aiden, don't you see it's always like this? You always have to be the first, the leader, the centre of everything! You resent Martin, you resent me – I bet you even resent Sebastian! Some new recruit shows up, and you're instantly on guard, like a dog in a pack: is she ahead of me or behind me? Do I have to worry about him, or not?'

I was stunned – because it was true. I muttered, 'But not you!'

She leaned back against one of the trunks – it was one of those tree forts without proper sides. 'Listen, me especially. I'm

perceived as a threat to your precious pecking order, so I have
to get shoved out of the way. What happened at the Centre was
utterly illuminating – of your mind and your feelings. Not merely
about the way you feel about women, but about the way you feel
about *me*!'

'But I love you!'

'Maybe a little. Maybe in some ways. But not nearly as much as
you love your reputation. You know what I think? I think you're
dangerous. I think you'd do almost anything to be famous. I also
think you're psychopathically desperate for attention. Maybe it's
because you were adopted. But it might just be the way you
fucking *are*.'

Her voice was soft but whipped, each phrase a swipe. Every
muscle in her body was tight with fury, small fists jammed in her
front pockets as if she longed to pummel me with them.

'But it wasn't premeditated! It just – happened!' I objected
feebly.

'Maybe it did, maybe it didn't. Maybe you're just a complete
and utter jerk. Ever thought of that?'

It was then that she attacked – an utterly pathetic attack. She
was far too delicate to do me any harm and I was way more
concerned – as I held her off – that I might damage her wrists. I
also worried that she might overbalance and fall the four metres or
so to the ground.

Eventually she started to weep – a good sign – and then she
collapsed, sobbing convulsively, and gripping my torso for what
seemed like hours. Something melted then, some hard little
residue. Something inside me had shifted.

I held her away from me and met her eyes. Then I said, 'You're
absolutely right. I'm an arrogant asshole. I don't know how you
put up with me, I really don't.'

Then we were both crying, and I was kissing her salty lips and
clasping her sweaty body and running my fingers over her, from

her small toes to the topmost crown of her head. And as I kissed her I felt as if every wave of feeling I'd ever felt had been slung together, wave after wave, into something large enough to drown a medium-sized city.

She moaned as I pulled her to me; we were both – for a second – in danger of rolling off. Then I assisted her to the centre of the platform and let the puzzled birds make of the scene what they would, as she pulled me deeper and deeper, until the rich ache in the centre of me finally ebbed away.

21

Looking back on this in prison, I felt bad about this. I'd apologised – but so feebly! Instead I'd covered up my misery with physicality and bluster; I'd also used sex as a weapon (perhaps as a shield). That meeting had been my best chance to persuade Petra that everything she'd heard about me was wrong. Instead, she'd probably been left with a residue of doubt. Was I really remorseful, thoughtful, caring, the kind of guy someone would want to be with long-term? Or was I arrogant, sexist, only interested in my own ambitions – basically, a bad bet?

Sebastian had persuaded her to give me another chance, but I worried that I'd failed to convince, and this thought tormented me.

I was hoping for MF to show up when 7784 arrived with what those hilarious pundlings liked to call lunch. It was the first time he'd been sent since the interview, when he'd taken the brunt of a tester attack – and also got that rejuvenating, claret-coloured drug to me.

He was still free! I quenched my delight with a black scowl, saying, 'Can't you idiots make anything that doesn't taste like a dusty cricket pitch?' 7784 stirred the gruel, touched the dish and then turned to his colleague, pundling 4682. Probably a great guy once you got to know him.

'It is cold, 4682.'

4682 appeared to object, in their light and fluty tongue, but 7784 prevailed and dispatched him to heat it up. He then moved as if to follow but swiftly returned, and bent down, pretending to tighten my bonds.

'The rescue is tonight,' he said, so softly that, for a second, I thought I had imagined it.

'Not so hard!' I yelled, and under my breath, 'And the revolt?'

'Is ongoing. Which is why.' And, aloud, 'There. That is better, prisoner.'

I was unsure whether he meant my bonds or the gruel, which had resurfaced, as had 4682, not looking very gruntled. I downed as many of those grey clumps as I could bear.

'Thank you,' I said significantly, looking straight at 7784, and meaning: thanks for the lot – the information, the claret-coloured stuff, not to mention that hit you took for me. He half-twinkled back.

I thought, Not your average pundling, by a couple of parasongs. And then, Tonight, I might even be free!

But, decisions, decisions. Which suitcase should I choose, the shek-leather one with the gold handles or the buffalo in muted brown? How many golf clubs would I be permitted? And how could I bear to leave that teasing window to the outside, at that moment drizzling rain with the persistence of grief?

After this, I got serious and attempted to test my injured knee against my bonds – I could move maybe a couple of centimetres in both directions. Then another fear gripped me: what if I was too out of shape to run, after weeks in the chair? – It was possible. I'd only been tortured once, but the knee might not be sound. I wasn't sure it would ever be perfectly sound again.

But then I imagined the bliss of freedom: nothing fancy, just the ability to scratch an ankle or to choose an egg in the morning. After a while, I drowsed. Next thing I knew, Petra was shaking me.

I thought this was probably just another dream – only then did I remember the rescue. But hadn't 7784 said 'tonight'? It was mid-afternoon, maybe not even that.

Wearing a Xirfell army officer's uniform, Petra looked thinner than ever, cheekbones sharp enough to injure glass. 'Quick! Before anyone comes!' she whispered, fishing out a key that skidded my bonds back.

I leaped to my feet and almost tipped backwards – even standing briefly dizzied me. Pupils glittering, Petra pressed an F86 into my hands. I glanced towards the nearest monitoring device but she stopped me with a fingertip. 'I turned them off. Just move! Do you *want* to be caught?'

My legs felt as feeble as a new-born calf's. Maybe I'd lost muscle tone in the chair? Could there have been some weakening agent in the mush I'd been downing for weeks? But excitement still buoyed me, while the lustre of the weapon comforted my palm. In fact, I simply couldn't resist. First flicking down the silencer, I took aim at that horrible chair and pressed the trigger.

Nothing. Zilch. Zip.

Suddenly, suspicion flooded me. I grabbed Petra, wrestling her arm behind her back. She bit her lip but didn't cry out.

'Wait! What if this is a trap?'

'Are you mad? Do you want to die?' she hissed.

'But what about the trial?'

'The trial will never happen now! Have you heard *nothing*? There are uprisings everywhere!'

'And MF?'

'What's an MF? We have to move!'

I'd forgotten that it was my name for the blundicant, but I still suspected her. Petra, losing her cool mid-operation? Petra biting her lip hard enough to make it bleed? – I checked her backpack and discovered a second F86, which I shoved hard against her temple. She was sweating, so this one maybe worked.

'Proof!' I snarled into her ear.

'Proof of what?'

'That you're with us. Priscilla's blood name.'

'You're playing *games,* at a time like this?'

'Only one game, sunshine. Priscilla's secret name. You get five seconds. Five. Four. Three. Two.'

More red flags. She was sweating – and the sweat smelled wrong. The angle of her ear was wrong, too. There was no mole beneath her neck. She was a good copy but not a great one: they hadn't got the fucking DNA, had they?

My grip on the fake Petra tightened. 'Your own name, then. I'll make it easy for you.'

The creature stiffened. It was far stronger than Petra: a powerful, tensile resistance. I rasped, 'Three. Two. One. Last chance saloon.'

It spat in my face and – simultaneously – I fired. What happened next was wild.

For a start, I hadn't killed it. Instead I found myself holding a small, spiteful, khaki-coloured alien, prickly yet slimy, with brackish blood streaming from a wound in what might have been some kind of a limb. I examined it with fascination as it repeatedly tried to bite me – I'd read about these. Show it an image and it could replicate it almost perfectly. Enough for anyone – except a lover.

But duty called. I had already dropped it and sprinted to the door when it transformed itself again, this time into an altogether more formidable adversary.

Oh, fuck. I should have ground it into dust, shouldn't I?

I should. I was now faced with a giant blurg – terrifying, oily, man-eating – but still, in my opinion, a strategic error, as blurgs are pretty slow and I'm pretty fast, despite my knee... And in a second I was back in the corridor I must have been dragged through weeks before, only half-conscious. It seemed both smaller and dimmer than I'd remembered. Left fork? Or right?

I chose the left, F86 at the ready, and pelted down it.

After perhaps five minutes two thoughts struck me: how fucking out of condition I was and a possible reason for the relative dimness – the lights embedded in the walls were blinking a dullish amber. There seemed to be no overhead lighting at all.

Did they normally blink amber – or was that a warning?

Also, where the hell was everybody – the pundlings, the testers, the robotniks, the blinking Xirfell themselves? Had the insurrection already triumphed? Had everyone rushed off to take part in the final battle? And, if so, who the hell sent the fake Petra to me? Could 7784 himself have been turned? Had the entire rebellion been betrayed?

I was still running, the blurg presumably lumbering behind me. I vaguely recalled that shapeshifters couldn't switch shapes very often, and trusted that its system might still be reeling from 'being' Petra, to returning to itself, to impersonating a blurg. But where was its blinking back-up? Surely a few testers should have been bunkered down at the door?

Or maybe not. MF had mentioned that security was in disarray, hadn't he?

Suddenly there were several paths, all unmarked, forking in different directions, a strong light pulsing from each. Instinctively I chose the one opposite, hoping for a snappy rise towards the Earth's surface.

Instead, I was almost instantly met by a tidal wave of noise. A great stream of creatures pushed towards me: humans, pundlings, testers, aliens, half-humans, a few species unknown. Even to attempt to wriggle past that little lot would be to invite scrutiny. I took the path of least resistance – and was tided backwards, descending deeper and deeper into Xirfell territory.

The crowd appeared in resigned-enough mood, and I heard

one half-human describing some fantastical inner chamber, 'with jewels, real jewels stuck inside the walls!' At the crossroads the masses quietened as we moved past the blurg, who was scouring the tumult with bloodshot gaze.

I crouched beside a muscular tester, hoping it would miss me in the crush. Immediately afterwards I heard a woman complain, 'Just a bloody annoyance, as far as I'm concerned. Some of us have work to do. Why should we be hauled off just to witness yet another execution?'

'Are you sure it is an execution?' asked a young guy.

'When else are we rounded up like sheep?'

'Maybe to be killed?' suggested an older lady, rather tremulously. 'There was that time in G7 when the Xirfell decided there were too many old and useless—'

'Who's being effing executed, then?' I asked a morose-looking fellow casually. Thinking, Please God, not someone I knew – Priscilla, for instance.

'Who cares? They just want a crowd for the bleeding broadcast, don't they?'

'Nah, you're daft,' objected another. 'They want us to watch so we mindlessly do what we're told, is all.' There was a vague murmur of agreement, with someone muttering something about brainwashing. Then I heard a hiss – 'Spies about!' – and the murmuring dissipated.

Although it remained noisy – with the nervy chatter, the juddering boots, the distant bull-horns of the Xirfell ahead of us – and disorientating, what with varying types of creatures randomly illuminated by those pulsating amber lights. Every corridor looked identical, while the intermittent flashes made my temples ache. (Could amber be code for 'escaped prisoner'?) There was no sign of the shapeshifting blurg.

Could he have changed into an edoy by now? Or alerted a platoon of testers? Changing into a giant snake would have had everybody screaming… 'D'you know who's being executed?' I murmured to the guy beside me.

'Nah, but they're all fruitcakes, anyways.' He lowered his voice. 'What the fuck can humans do against dictators with killer testers and zuges and blurgs? Utter waste of bloody time, trying to fight *that!* They want their fucking heads examined!'

Not one of my little lights.

Suddenly I spied a tiny corridor, shooting off to the left. I had a moment of feverish doubt. Should I try to escape or should I – secretly armed as I was – stick with the throng and take out the highest-ranking personage present at the execution? Maybe even the King?

This thought tantalised me.

The little corridor no longer held any appeal. Instead, I tried to guess how long it might be before my escape was noticed. Had the fake Petra really taken out the devices in the cell? Wouldn't the shapeshifter report straight back to the regime? – though even most loyalists lack access to instant communication; you have to be mega-elite for that.

And all the while the corridor kept on widening and widening, and brightening and brightening until – before my light-starved eyes – there dazzled the underground equivalent of the Centre, a place I had heard about but never seen.

The Colosseum.

It was – in its own style – glorious.

Here, in the heart of the Xirfell's underground kingdom, great craggy walls had been dug out, creating an irregular, wild, unXirfell-like beauty, with crystals and glowing stalactites studded across the top, while the walls seemed encrusted with serrated crystal.

Below all this, where tens of thousands of us were filing in, it felt like being inside a tourmaline or an onyx – for a second, I recalled Duncan Tenten's onyx paperweight with a nostalgia bordering on depression. But where were the security barriers? Or had I bypassed security, being underground already?

I couldn't believe that anybody's luck could be quite that good. Then, glancing back into the corridor, I spotted the shimmery, scummy, shapeshifting blurg, maybe ten metres away. I pressed forward, saying, 'Well, well, an execution, eh? Great! I love 'em!'

That was when I noticed that security was spot-checking, the major scans presumably having happened in the overland. The blurg, looking both savage and mournful, surfaced just behind me, raking the crowd with his gaze.

My pulse rocketed. How many Indigenous guys were likely to be in the mix, anyway? What if I didn't get the chance to do anything, after all, but instead got pinned and swept back to my cell, or awarded to a real blurg as a between-meal snack?

There was an older guy with a friendly face next to me. I begged, 'Can I have your hoodie, mister?'

He gazed at me suspiciously. 'Whaddya want it for? It ain't worth nothing!'

'I'm cold. I had bronchitis last month,' I whined. 'In the army.'

His wife gave him a nudge. 'Just give it to him, Albert. He were probably press-ganged, same as our Herbie.'

'How much?' Albert asked, striking the business note.

'I ain't got any. I were – press-ganged – same as what she said,' I said sulkily.

'Go on, Albert. He's one of the starving poor!'

'So are we,' said Albert, for which I, for one, couldn't blame him. But he handed over the hoodie, which reeked of tobacco, though I still breathed a good deal easier with its hood around my face.

The neighbour on my other side then caused my blood pressure to skyrocket, as I'd forgotten my recent notoriety. 'You know, you remind me of somebody,' she said thoughtfully. 'I just can't quite place you.'

'I just look like a lot of people,' I said hastily, easing sideways, for it was impossible to advance... Strangely, her query served to ground me. I was no longer merely the pursued, the half-panicking. Suddenly I was no longer an escaped prisoner, surrounded by whip-wielding testers and seconds away from death-by-zuge – I was the rebel Aiden Tenten, with his game face on.

And yes, still up for saving the world, thanks for asking.

The Xirfell music – a relentless throbbing, shot through by brassy howls – provoked an unsettling wriggling in my veins, as if they'd been invaded by ants. We were pushed forward towards the rows of granite seats, with some spectators hauled over for security spot-checks by bulging-muscled testers.

I prepared to sell my hidden F86 dearly as I approached the barrier. Then a scrawny youth in front of me was chosen, and I took my seat with a heart swelling with gratitude, improbably – even bizarrely – fully armed. Cheated out of my trial – the tiny but potent F86 hammering against my heart like an extra ventricle – this could be my last best chance. Although the sheer enormity of the place almost shook my resolve.

How could I be certain of hitting the right creature at such a distance? – though the newest F86s programmed instantaneously, of course. I also worried that I was showing off – even going rogue – by not having fought my way through the crowd to the surface, though I hadn't been given a whole lot of choice...

'Where's the King?' demanded a half-human big enough to be a tester. 'Isn't the effing King coming?'

'Trouble up-country, fathead.'

'But he's at every execution, right?'

'Not these days. Probably the princess. One of the princesses, probably.'

'Ravene's fighting too. Don't you listen to the frigging news?'

Ravene was fighting? The thought disturbed me unreasonably. I couldn't even begin to imagine it – what would she be wearing, for a start? Not even Ravene could fight in silks, slivers of emeralds in her hair...

But when the show, the qintoric dancers, the glitz and special effects had all ebbed away, what was left behind the last metallic blasts from the musicians was a medium-sized hole, perhaps four metres square. And through the underground hole rose what appeared to be a fish tank, iridescent and sheeny, mint-green, iced blue.

And suddenly I recollected the rebel alien in the Golden Circle – and leaned so far forward that the creature ahead of me pushed me back with an oath. All around us creatures were murmuring about the 'ice mermaid'. When she stepped out of the tank, with a gush of sea water, I understood why.

Now I – privileged to have boasted as girlfriend one of the most stunning half-aliens known to exist – might be considered relatively hardened to female beauty. But Leelack, who was a shimmeringly soft amber, still took my breath away. Perhaps it was the liquidity of movement, the sweep of flaxen hair and gilded gown. Perhaps it was those endless eyes, hugely dark and powerfully deep, shot through with flashes of gold. Or perhaps it was her patina, her sheen almost – presumably part of whatever genus she belonged to. I burned at the thought that the Xirfell – coarse as they were – had dared to seize such a creature, only to imprison her in the heart of a ruined planet. A murmur rose from the audience. So graceful, so impossibly well-formed – surely she wasn't scheduled for execution?

Another flurry from the Xirfell drums and... MF appeared.

But not the MF I knew – ugly, plain, unfussy. To be fair, he was as ugly as ever, but was transported in an imposing carriage savagely encrusted with heavy jewels, representing a regime he certainly loathed as much as I did. He was also wearing a strange crimson-and-black ornament around what he probably fondly imagined was a neck – an ornament I'd never seen before. Its scintillation punished my eyes.

Had they ennobled him, then? Had he, himself, ascended to the Golden Circle? Was that why I hadn't seen him? In that moment I was so desperate to 'speak' to him that I wouldn't care how much he twanged my spine.

But what if he'd been turned, or had sold out to the regime? What if he'd known about the fake Petra – had even sent her? Despite my disquiet, I'd missed him so much that he seemed almost to sense it. Perhaps he even *smelled* it, for he reared up, those see-through organs restlessly colliding, almost sniffing in my direction.

Instinctively I pulled the hood about my face and shoved out my lower jaw, with luck entirely altering my aspect, because we'd been taught that nothing alters the lines of a face more. Meanwhile, MF turned to the senior tester and they conferred for quite a while. Part of his role as the King's advisor – or could he be ordering my arrest?

Meanwhile the masses were unsilent. 'Right ugly bastards, aren't they?'… 'It's Leelack, Leelack herself! I saw a photo'… 'Just like a mermaid!'… 'Is the King coming?'… 'They have to live in ice'… 'Ugliest damn alien I ever seen, don't care how blinking important it is.'… 'I think it's part of her dress'… 'They can't execute *that!*'… 'Shh, you'll be reported!'… 'Henry, you never know what they'll do.'

But who was to be executed? Surely not – *that*? While MF was still engaged with the tester, I began to fret.

The Xirfell had blown hot and cold on public executions, just as they had on trials: sometimes preferring private executions to wildly public ones, sometimes preferring to snuff out resistance with publicity blackouts – most recently, seeking to deter sympathisers by making rebel executions as prolonged, painful and well-publicised as possible.

I recalled some famous instances: the Russian rebels bound to trees amid starved tigers and sheks, that Brazilian tribe whose brains were famously operated on in prime time… And kept continually testing the heft of my own weapon, while sweat kept scudding down the small of my back.

Suddenly there was a great grinding noise, and another tank – of a completely different order of magnitude – rose slowly and majestically from the floor. Taking up maybe half the gigantic stadium, it was probably the size of a couple of rugby pitches. I nudged the guy on my right. 'What, do they execute by great white these days?'

He stared at me, almost amused. 'Who said nothing about sharks? Where've you been? Ain't you ever heard about the Creature?'

I recalled MF mentioning it. 'I been abroad – G5,' I said hastily. 'What kind of a creature do you mean?' Then there was an enormous gasp, shared by around a hundred thousand others. My neighbour, triumphant, said, 'See for yourself!'

And well, there it was. Of astonishing length, over twice that of the largest-ever blue whale, with that vicious snout, those slitted eyes and a sage-grey, eel-like shape. Though it wasn't actually smooth – instead, it was scaly, almost crocodilian. And its size!

'Found it on the bottom of the sea, didn't they?' my companion continued importantly. 'Wonder why the G-fivers ain't heard about it? Hey, Agnes, they ain't even heard about the Creature, up in G5!'

Another gasp as the creature skimmed from one end of the tank to the other, with a flash of that mind-blowing tail. It had all the sullen grandeur that Tyrannosaurus rexes must have had, with the additional terror of speed.

'Months and months they was trackin' it – and when they captured it, it was all over the news.'

'When?' I snapped. 'When did they capture it?'

'Maybe two, three weeks ago?'

I nodded – but, personally, I doubted it, and gave grudging credit to the King.

What better opiate for the people – what better talking-point – what better object to steer the masses' attention from small but fiery arrows of insurrection – than a sea-monster the size of a smallish island? What better distraction for the overworked, undernourished overlanders, themselves battling oppression, pollution, and gigantic snakes?

The regime had probably been keeping the Creature secret for just such a purpose, for surely not even the Xirfell's engineering genius could assemble a tank of such sensational size quite that fast. And suddenly I thought (maybe I just have this crazy suspicious mind), What if it had been kidnapped from the Xirfell's own galaxy?

It *might* still be from Earth, as humans had yet to explore the depths of its own oceans – now largely poisoned – so probably we never would. But what if, somewhere in the Xirfell's galaxy, a dinosaur-style era might be in full swing? It wouldn't have amazed me. For all we knew, the planet concerned was massive, and crammed with sea-monsters. Perhaps, in its own galaxy, the Creature was only a baby sea-monster...

MF stepped away from his tester colleague, who gave a signal. There seemed to be something happening on the wide platform at the top of the great tank. Another tester – looking surprisingly tiny – stood there, beside a supplementary tank, this one about the size of a good-sized house. A second later, in a gush of seawater, a giant octopus was released from the small tank into the main tank. There was a great spillage of limbs, as each of its arms was about four metres long, but it still looked – in comparison to the Creature – notably unimpressive. It floated to the bottom of the tank, where it began to wave its tentacles.

The Creature slowly turned its great head to watch, that massive maw slightly ajar, eyes gleaming, tail twitching – causing plumes of spray to crash up into the tank's gigantic roof – a slash of purple tongue visible between those monstrous teeth. Then the giant octopus began to uncoil, to inspect the stony bed of the tank, feeling about tentatively with its suction-cupped limbs.

A second or so later, all that remained was one tentacled arm, still vaguely moving, amid a wash of purplish-brackish blood.

The audience gasped, nudged each other, screamed or laughed nervously, while the tester at the top watched, one massive hand still resting on the lever that had sealed the octopus's fate. Was he due to release another one? Or something else?

The Creature seemed inspired to show off. Probably itching for the freedom of its true home – wrecked ocean bed, alien seascape? – it tore from one end of the tank to the other, to the delight of its audience. MF watched, impassive as ever; Leelack had disappeared into her own tiny tank. But surely there would still be an execution? I felt a spurt of unease as I glanced at the other tanks at the crest of the monstrous one. What – or who – might be inside them?

The crowd was still contentedly marvelling. As for who might be about to be executed, nobody seemed to either know or care. I thought of Priscilla with a sick sensation: could they have discovered the false wall at Tim's house? I thought of the ever-reliable Hugh, the less reliable but brilliant Laurentia, good-hearted Bully the fug... Less warmly I remembered Harrison, who had denounced me at the Academy, resulting in my scrabbling for bread in rubbish bins as well as ending all hopes of a degree. But nobody'd heard from Harrison in a helluva long time.

My jaw aching from being thrust forward under my donated hoodie, I watched MF confer again with several officials before turning to address us. I noticed that his amplified voice sounded unlike itself, but maybe that's the nature of amplified voices.

'Living forms of the new world order! Behold the Creature,

largest and most powerful life-form ever found in any galaxy! But today the Creature is an agent of justice!'

'But it won't even be hungry! Just ate a whole effing octopus, didn't it,' a woman objected, but her partner overruled. 'That's why. If it was hungry there wouldn't be any toying with the victim – they'd just be swallowed, same as the octopus. That's the point – to make them suffer! Fucking Xirfell!'

Someone else suggested rather sharply that she 'didn't care to see a human being torn apart by those teeth, thank you very much,' but another observed that Leelack 'wasn't properly human but was one of those weirdies instead' – and anyway, 'must've done something pretty bad, for definite.'

They thought it was Leelack. Could they be right?

Hoodie pinned to my throat, I was still trying to analyse MF's tone. Was it really MF, and these doubts nothing but my own inflamed imagination? After all, he'd never said much in our meetings. We had 'talked' almost entirely inside my spine.

Then MF proclaimed: 'Treason! Treason, my friends, fellow citizens, and fellow creatures! Treason: the scourge of the new world order! Treason: most vicious of hate-crimes! And here amongst us' – at this point he seemed to be looking straight at me, as I shoved out my jaw like a blinking Neanderthal – 'we have one of the most vicious traitors of all time – and also someone who can give the Creature some sport, as she is completely at home in water—'

Leelack. A moan of horrified pleasure from the audience. Meanwhile, seaweed-coloured cuffs were snapped on her wrists, which she permitted with a movement of such grace that it tore at my heart.

'But first, my friends, you shall have proof.'

And with this MF gave the nod to the tester at the top of the tank. He released the springing door to the second tank, and there stepped out, in a gush of seawater, a youth every bit as beautiful as Leelack, and obviously her kin, though perhaps tawnier, less golden, in colouring. At the sight, her proud posture almost crumpled. I was shocked by my sudden jealousy, which was crazy. Of course she loved him! – They were both more like breathing jewels than anything else.

'Who is this?' demanded MF, while the tester's fist clamped down on the young man's shoulder.

'My brother, Yoreen,' Leelack whispered.

'Louder, if you please.'

'Yoreen, my brother,' she answered. Her own voice was soft but deeper than I'd expected, almost like a cello.

'But don't spare me on that account,' the brother said, setting his jaw far more appealingly than I'd set mine. I couldn't release my thrust-out jaw, either, because blundicants boast laser-like vision and MF might wheel back in my direction.

MF repeated, 'Yoreen, your brother. And he will die today if you fail to admit the truth – in this hour, before the very people you have betrayed. Admit the truth, and you have a shadow of a chance of saving him – so, listen well! Here are your crimes. You have conspired with rebels to bring down the democratically elected Xirfell government. You have given false counsel to the King, with the intention to mislead. You have broken your vows of fealty, loyalty and honour to your fellow members of the Golden Circle – and you have deliberately and maliciously betrayed your adopted country. But there is still hope – for your brother, at least. Should you choose to repent – now, publicly – your brother will be saved, and you alone will perish. Should you *not* repent, he will be the first to be cast into the Creature's tank, and you will follow him.'

The Creature could never have heard but still – as if on cue – it suddenly scudded from one side of the tank to the other, thrashing that mountainous tail. It must have been just my overactive imagination, but it seemed to me as if the entire hall rocked with the movement. There was still one octopus arm trailing between those gigantic teeth, but it no longer quivered, and I felt vaguely irritated that it was still there at all.

The youth spoke strongly. 'Sister, do not weep on my account. I am proud to die in the cause of freedom!' And, to MF, very fiercely, 'I am ready!'

But MF hastily turned to Leelack. 'Will you allow him to sacrifice himself, lady? Two words from you might still save him! If you but say "I repent", then I guarantee that your brother will be spared your own fate.'

She was silent, motionless. Even the crowd was utterly still.

MF wheedled, 'Let it be still simpler. Simply nod, lady, if you choose to repent.'

Perhaps she was tempted – I couldn't tell. Though I longed for the youth to live, all the same.

'Do not repent!' Yoreen fired back, making my heart jump. He seemed to almost glitter against those dead-black stones.

'Brother,' she whispered.

Again he commanded, 'Do not repent!'

MF began to weave his web once more. 'You see, Leelack? Only you can save him! Do you throw him down? Because it is you who will have done it, and not the King.'

She drew herself up, took a deep breath – and said, very sorrowfully, 'I do not repent.'

MF turned his face upwards. Was it a grimace of sorrow, even agony? Who could read a face like his? 'Your last words,' he ordered roughly to the youth, and turned away, either because he was washing his hands of the entire business, or else – was it possible? – because he cared too much.

The youth balanced lightly on the edge of the great tank, as if he could skim right off into freedom, as if the jewelled crags hid some opening into the overland, and he had been gifted wings. He said, 'Do not mourn me, for I go to a far better place than this. Instead, remember that there is, inside each creature, a spark, an inner light, which is unquenchable, irresistible and immortal. Nourish your light for ever! Nourish your light and live! Live as if you might die tomorrow, fighting for truth and freedom for every creature – while nourishing the lights in the centre of your souls! Then you will illuminate even the darkest places. And now, my dear sister, farewell – I shall see you on the other side!'

And with this he dived inside the great tank, a sleek feathered curve. The Creature was skulking along the bottom, but I'd already learned what that exuberant lash of tail meant, and I kept my eyes on my boots, rather than witnessing the quenching of that glow. Thanks to this I only saw the great thwack of that mighty tail and the wild splurge of waves clawing at the lid after the final octopus tentacle and the gilded youth had disappeared from the face of Earth forever.

The mood of the crowd had sobered: there were no cheers or laughter such as had greeted the demise of the unlucky octopus. I even spotted several testers, across the canyon-like hall, plying their glazed whips in hopes of prolonging the applause. But I couldn't get distracted. I had to think.

Now, Leelack belonged to the rebellion – so it came as no surprise to hear her denounced as a traitor to the King, the regime and the Golden Circle. No, the part I couldn't stomach was MF's composedly presiding over her death, and the death of her brother. Panic was rising inside me, in time with the waves gushing against that giant tank. What if MF had deceived me? What if he had ascended to Leelack's vacant place in the Golden Circle? What if he'd been the one to denounce her? What could that chunky, dark red necklace signify, if not promotion? *What if – what if – what if?*

As my fingers automatically traced the soft, almost pulsating, metal of the F86, MF's strangely flat voice continued, 'Citizens of the democratic republic! It is my deeply unpleasant task to inform you that Leelack, a member of the Golden Circle itself, has been tried and convicted as a traitor. You have yourselves heard how stubborn she is in her misguidedness – stubborn enough to sacrifice her own brother! Let her wilfulness and obduracy serve as a warning! For the resistance – the so-called rebellion – possesses many seductive and persuasive liars, liars who secretly foment murder, violence, even anarchy!

'Don't listen to them! Instead, recall your civic duty and give their names to the authorities. Then, once the rebel concerned is captured, you will enjoy a well-earned reward of as much as five thousand kadrills, depending upon the rank of the traitor you denounce – not to mention the gratitude of your beneficent King!'

Crowds: such curious things! While the sensational youth had touched and possibly even roused them, now a feverish titillation was evident, as if the masses had become almost instantaneously hardened to death and violence. Was it merely the prospect of getting a bit of money, or had they turned against Leelack because she had sacrificed her brother?

Unwillingly, I supposed that the second option was possible.

Some seemed utterly indifferent to this limpid beauty being dismembered. One workman did murmur, 'She's so pretty!' but the woman on my left was busily assuring us that their blood, 'wasn't red but goldish-coloured – perhaps we'll get to see it, this time. Swallowed the fellow whole, didn't it?' While a third observed gloomily, 'You can't never trust foreigners!' and another gloated, 'Wonder how many kadrills the creature who denounced *her* got?'

Meanwhile, a document was brought to MF to sign, while doubts hammered away at me. Perhaps she *had* betrayed the rebellion, as well as the regime? How else could MF appear so calm – he'd seemed more concerned about her brother! Or could his own hand have been forced? The King was capable of that – of almost anything.

Then, suddenly, it hit me. What if it wasn't MF at all? Any more than the 'Petra' sent to my cell had really been Petra? – I steadied myself, trying to remember.

Harpalian, he had called me, at our very first encounter: my blood name. He'd known Priscilla's secret name, too. He had to be one of us! But what if he was no longer? His voice sounded different, though that ectoplasmic exterior looked just the same.

Think logically, Aiden. For once in your frigging life.

If Leelack was with us – and I had only MF's word for that, though the regime certainly seemed prepared to kill her – it was my job to prevent it, if possible. But how? I could certainly take out a few testers, if no one interfered. But after that I'd just be recaptured – or else shot – my only chance gone.

Also, the propaganda value wouldn't be fantastic. The regime might even hush it up and pretend that nothing had happened – they'd pulled that trick before. In propaganda terms I probably needed to shoot MF himself... or else think up something too spectacular to hide.

My actual orders were as follows: 'If operationally solo, attempt to take out the ranking members of the enemy.' That would mean Leelack and MF, in that order – but what if they were ours? And what price MF's lurid new jewel? A reward for turning Leelack in, or just some bauble? – though he'd never seemed the bauble type.

'What are they *doing,* anyway?'... 'Do you think she's guilty, Hubert?'... 'Are we on live broadcast, d'you think? Should we wave?'... 'They don't have human feelings, you know. They're like animals, really.'

If they'd only shut up, so I could think!

Then a hybrid gloated, 'Creature'll have some fun now!'

I thought, Why don't we start with you, sunshine? Let's shove you down the Creature's great maw, see how you like it!

Instead, the drivel continued. 'Last week they fixed one of those oxygen masks, so the fellow could breathe long enough to suffer. It was like the Creature was just *toying* with him'… 'Must be torture. Specially not knowing when it's going to slice right through your whole entire body'… 'I'd have a heart attack the second I was dropped in the tank. I'd just have a heart attack and die!'

Hang on – the tank. Could one of the newer F86s – just possibly – pierce the tank? The idea of the gigantic Creature slithering out atop the crowd was dizzyingly glorious. The propaganda value would be incalculable. (Sebastian: 'Almost anything attracting publicity is worth doing. Publicity gives oxygen to every cell on the planet.')

Meanwhile MF permitted Leelack her last words, spoken in that entrancingly lovely alto. The crowd even shushed itself to hear her.

'I am not guilty of treason – or of spying, either,' she said, all shimmering amber. 'I am guilty only of attempting to do what I could for each one of you, in the cause of freedom and justice. If you must judge me, judge me by my actions, and not by what might be said of me. For I wish every creature, on every planet, in every galaxy, nothing but peace.'

She's got to be one of us.

I should have been reassured; instead, I felt clammy and weak. What if it didn't work? What if it failed and I was wiped out, without taking a single tester with me? I tugged my gaze from Leelack to MF, his expression unreadable. But then, that's the nature of blundicants in general, and MF in particular.

Inside its great tank, the Creature skirted around restlessly, in constant movement, now in view on one side, next – presumably – in view on the other. Its eyes were a smoky, orangey-red, its tail ridged with spikes like tiny razors. Each tooth, even the smallest, was the size of a quadropod. But it wasn't only the fact that Leelack was about to follow the giant octopus and her glowing brother down that massive mouth that chilled me. MF had been

– along with 7784 – my only friend, in prison. Could I really kill him? – because I couldn't imagine how a creature of such mass could possibly swim.

And what about the bystanders? Most of them sounded like disaster zones but I hadn't interviewed them individually. I could become, in the space of the next few seconds, a mass murderer – a mass murderer who had sworn, a decade ago, to protect and defend my innocent fellow creatures, in the name of the rebellion. I passionately longed to give Leelack a chance but – wasn't impulsivity one of the things I was supposed to fight?

'Why do you keep *doing* that?' demanded the woman behind me, and I realised that I'd been stroking the hidden F86 obsessively. But who else – out of the hundred thousand present – had the chance to do any bloody thing?

God's idea of a joke, that it should be me.

Meanwhile they were moving Leelack to the top of the tank. There was an annoying, 'Ooh!' as the pulley wavered, weaving her before the glass, like a child's figurine, like a mermaid keyring… MF was talking to a tester, slightly adjusting that red-black ornament at his throat.

Had his voice really altered? – And wasn't it most likely that the F86 projectile would simply bounce off the structure? Suddenly I wished that someone – even Martin – was there, just to take the burden of decision-making off my shoulders.

Just hand me the gun and tell me where the fuck to aim it…

Meanwhile, the half-human on my left jogged my elbow, not wishing me to miss a second of the treat in store.

Leelack had dived into the tank, without fanfare. Presumably she could only breathe air for a brief period – and indeed seemed to gain luminosity on contact. I watched, in what were probably her last moments, her colouring altering with the light, her face the frailest gilt-pink, her hair a sunny ripple of gold. Each of these colours was gradually strengthening, as if the water was renewing her. And suddenly I realised that I'd made my decision – and watched MF for a sign.

I also spot-checked the Creature. Rapturously full, it appeared in sportive mood, showing no interest in the glowing little shape following the octopus's trajectory to the bottom of the tank. Instead it splashed and dashed, even snapping at the side of the tank, as if disconsolate at being stuck between glassed walls... I felt almost sorry for it. Had it asked to be made so huge, so spectacular, so ravenous? It was as imprisoned as all the rest of us!

Still. Those jaws. There was a collective intake of breath as the Creature swirled past Leelack, that lethally spiked tail close to her poised little face. She sat composedly on the bottom of the tank, by comparison the size of a doll though entirely returned to her element. (Was she really amber-coloured or was there a more gilded sheen?) The crowd was silenced, mesmerised, and every camera extended greedily towards the tank, waiting to gather her in.

It was time. I picked a place as close to the centre as possible; there could be a structural weakness there. If it gave her just half a chance... I took one last glance at MF – pressing something at the centre of his new bauble – and felt suddenly certain, with an uprush of gratitude, that he wasn't the MF I knew. He had either been turned – or else corrupted. The MF I was about to murder was no longer ours.

The Creature made two more swift passes, the second accidentally pushing Leelack into the crunched gravel, with one careering pull of that gigantic tail. It was only as she righted herself that it seemed to notice her, for the first time. It halted at the top of the tank, baring those pod-sized teeth. Did it simply fancy a chance to play? It was preparing to plunge downward, was all I knew.

I pulled the trigger.

I was disappointed in the first milli-second: it was so nearly soundless, but all the new ones are, and I hadn't had an upgrade for ages. Then the power of the recoil shoved my entire body backwards. Amid a deafening cacophony of screams and yells, I watched the gap in the tank yawn open – its sides unfolding like gigantic origami – while the gush, rush, slush of sea-water turned, within a couple of seconds, into a great roiling torrent, sweeping up the whole of the audience in one effortless surge.

Salt water.

I was struck, from the left by a head, from the right by a shoulder. So many creatures striking in a frenzy for the surface. Salt in my mouth, salt in my eyes. As I crested the waves I felt a panicked swell beneath me – the freed Creature.

Even if it chose me, I'd still have launched one last blow.

Screams and yells seemed to echo weirdly across the water, but I kept my head turned towards that section of the gigantic hall where the closest exit was. The top of the water looked peppered with heads, like bubbles left by a retreating ocean liner, or pebbles in a stream. I swam as hard as I could against what felt like a tide, took one last swollen breath and dived. Behind me, I felt the pull of the Creature's next joyous uprush through the waves.

The released water was bulging in several directions, including the entrance I'd used, and the gate through which Leelack and MF had arrived. I kicked hard towards the latter, though constantly struck on all sides by panicked fellow swimmers, and pushed from behind by the water, also intent on escape. There was a long moment of suspense, as my lungs punished me. Then several of us were spewed out in a single breath, like a shoal of fish, into a corridor with a steep upward incline. Dizzied from lack of oxygen, aliens, humans, hybrids and pundlings were all released in a single sodden, beached mass.

A tester stamped to his feet, startling both myself and a geeky student-type beside me. It occurred to me, as he glared, that I might still – just – be recognisable, from the international broadcast. Hurriedly securing the soaked hoodie, I forced myself to run, though my legs felt like cooked noodles.

That bloody chair.

'What happened to the frigging tank?' a brawny labourer wanted to know.

'Dunno,' I responded. The water was by then only swirling around our ankles, the incline tilting ever more sharply uphill. There seemed to be no security – presumably they'd all rushed into the arena. As we emerged into the murky, smoky city twilight, just another two in a long tail of drenched creatures, I became conscious of advancing sirens. Though exhausted, I forced myself to push on, accidentally tripping up an ancient aged around 120, who gave me a blistering glare, as if it was all my fault.

Well it was, of course.

My damaged knee gradually began to protest, and there was a sharper pain in my foot, as I emerged into a watery, post-apocalyptic, late afternoon. Normally, the city disheartened me, but after prison even the sickly haze of the capital looked pretty good, so good that I felt strangely like weeping. A human beside me, also dripping, smacked my wet shoulder saying, 'Hey, mate, we made it!' and embraced me.

Maybe nobody would ever know what I'd done? I wondered how much the cameras had picked up, trained as they must have been on Leelack and the Creature. Would the regime pretend that the tank had ruptured accidentally? Would anyone in the rebellion guess that I'd been there?

A nearby street creature was selling something resembling cheese scones, though with smoky, alien spices. Hungry as I was, though, I had no money. Meanwhile, creatures kept pausing to stare at us, at the stream of sodden survivors pitched up from underground.

Xirfell drones lurked overhead. I also held my breath as a pair of armed robotniks stormed past. But we were so many – dust-coloured, grey-slimed – and nothing to set me apart from all the others. I trudged on doggedly, cursing my aching knee. (What if I'd murdered thousands – Leelack included?)

Kicking aside debris from rain-swollen gutters, I paused to take in my grim surroundings, including a ragbag army of nettys. A slit-eyed giant rat, too arrogant to care about being seen, shot across what had once been an important thoroughfare, almost tripping up one of those attenuated aliens.

The rat darted down a side alley while I paused to massage my knee. A woman asked me, 'What on earth's going on? Is it the revolution at last? Or have those shits decided to drown us all?'

Another woman responded, with gleeful energy, 'What a scene! The Creature's great fangs passed right by me! Let me tell you...' As a thrilled crowd surrounded her, I limped on, hoodie clutched around my throat, aware that my left foot was bleeding steadily. But by then I wasn't too far away – and I'd always known where I was going.

Bullivant Bulianturian's peeling door still boasted one of the old-fashioned key locks. He was there the instant I rang, apprehension in his eyes, ancient AK103 at the ready. Recognising me, his eyes almost leaped from his head and I was enveloped in an exultant, fuggy embrace.

I said, with deep emotion, 'Bully, you bastard, get the fuck off of my foot!'

(Background: Bully, a middle-aged fug, had served heroically in the past but was by this point merely the organiser of a safe house.) He was also near tears. I found myself, stale with exhaustion and crusted with seawater, cast in the role of comforter.

After Bully had recovered from the thrill of my escape, I was half-dragged to his remaining comfy sofa – much tattered – where he staunched the wound on my foot and tutted over the fresh scars on my temple, eyebrow and knee. Now fugs, kidnapped by the Xirfell from E865, are tireless, honest and brave – famously, they never let go. They're not specially renowned for first aid, but it was such a pleasure to see a friend – squat, stocky and fuggy as he was – that I didn't care.

My first task after Bully patched me up was to make my report – which was never going to be as correct or as tidy as Martin would have preferred – but I threw something together, dictating into Bully's ancient computer. Bully meanwhile was tearing joyfully around his kitchen, fetching me cups of tasteless tea and the kinds of mealy biscuits I'd disliked even as a child.

The doorbell was blasting every second with rebel messages, via the underground network of children, beggars and disguised resistance members. ('Lucky bastard! Never thought we'd see your ugly face again!' and, 'Kudos, you fucking bugger!' were two of the politer ones.)

To me, Bully's house felt almost homelike – despite its distinctive, sour-sweet, reptilian odour (he befriends lizards, actually catches insects for them). Even his dusty tea had a comforting aroma. It was wonderful to stretch my legs to their fullest extent, and soon my injury stopped bleeding, while the sores on my arms, flared by the salt water, began to settle.

Luckily, there were no monitors at Bully's, which was how it got approved as a safe house in the first place. The Xirfell would probably get around to spying on every overlander eventually– unless they decided to exterminate us instead – but the last dwellings they'd mess with would probably be in this run-down, mostly demolished, sector of the ancient capital. I reckoned Bully's house might be safe for a couple of decades.

Then I received the same message from Martin and Petra. 'On my way!'

Meanwhile Bully was constantly urging me to eat, food nasty to the taste yet gloriously wholesome compared to those grey messes I'd grown accustomed to. I demolished ancient riced lemballs, complaining, 'Bully, these taste like roadkill.'

'I didn't know you were coming! Nobody told me!'

'Nobody knew, fathead. Have you heard what line the regime are taking on it?'

'No, but Martin'll soon be here – he'll know all about that.'

With unease, I recalled the swell of salty water crashing into the hall, the Creature's tidal exuberance beneath me. Was there even the slightest chance that Leelack had got away? And what if they'd mostly died? – The lemball, already chalky, suddenly felt inedible. I put it down.

'Here's the next lot of messages,' said Bully gleefully.

He was absolutely on fire: all Bully's Christmasses had come at once. I flicked through the latest batch of messages under Bully's yellowish, pre-war lights. ('You're a tough man to kill, sucker!' And, from Priscilla: 'Never heard such fantastic news in all my life! Can you really have escaped?')

I recalled that I was the first creature – human or alien – ever to have escaped the regime and tried to quench a growing exaltation, though my itch to know more still maddened me. Suddenly I wheeled towards Bully, who was busy spooning out great globules of precious izntmawl paste – a delicacy frankly wasted on any dish Bully was capable of making.

'Surely it was relayed live on teleview?'

'Yeah, but I never put my teleview *on*.'

'Bully, it's *mandatory* to have it on!'

But I'd guessed his answer already. It was mandatory to have electronic entry (so testers could blast in anywhere without warning) – mandatory to have monitors (in case of being denounced) – mandatory to have the teleview on. But nobody bothered monitoring the ghettos: Bully scored again.

The broadcast would certainly have been pulled the instant the great tank had buckled open. But still, Petra must at least have heard about it, the Petra who had just scribbled, 'On my way'? (And was that all she could say, after the chair, the torture, the interview, the escape and the frigging Creature? She must have known *something* of these, thanks to MF?)

It was Martin who showed up first, leaner than I had remembered, and for the purpose of disguise sporting a fake beard, which obscured his strong chin and accentuated his rather drooping eyes. He looked half-amused as he put his hands on my shoulders – he was slightly the taller – and pretended to shake me.

'Only you!' was all he said.

As for Bully, he didn't know whether to linger over the prodigal me or to caper around our exalted leader. Unsurprising, really. It had probably been a decade since Bully'd been asked to host anything more thrilling than an accountancy audit in a heavy dust storm.

'Tea? Rice lemballs? Or would you rather wait? I'm making something really nice,' he told Martin.

I corrected him. 'No, he isn't. Bully, you know it all tastes like glue.'

Martin grabbed one of my lemballs. 'So. You got used to some fab dainties in prison, did you? This is yum, Bully – really hits the spot.'

Bully practically kissed his feet. The true leader, I thought gloomily. 'Would you be kind enough,' I asked Martin, 'to tell me what the fuck actually happened?'

Martin was skimming a message. 'Hmm, that's rather a nuisance,' he said. 'Well, you were there, right?'

'Yes, but what happened to Leelack?'

'Recaptured.'

So, I'd failed. Martin glanced at me curiously. 'You've never actually met Leelack, have you?'

'No. And the Creature?'

'Last I heard, it had survived.'

'Really?'

'Yeah, I was surprised too. They closed off all the entrances, so I suppose there was just about enough water. He's a real propaganda coup, so they'd certainly make every effort to keep him alive.'

'And MF – the blundicant, I mean – did he make it?'

'He drowned. But, Aiden, just so you know—'

'I think I *do* know. He wasn't with us at the end.'

It was somehow very pleasing to startle Martin.

'Who the hell told *you?*'

'Nobody. It was just an instinct.'

'Well, well.'

Martin brooded a moment, then said, 'He wasn't actually turned. One of those brain-hijacking viruses, is what I was told – very unpleasant, the whole thing. The only good bit is that it wiped out his memory at the same time. Rather than just burying him, the Xirfell inserted an artificial brain and *promoted* him!'

'Do you mean that his actual memory was wiped? Did they never know that he was with us?'

'We think not.'

So, the real MF had died before the deluge. In that case, did it matter that I drowned his body? – I was guessing not. I said, 'How did you find out? About his virus, I mean.'

'Someone on the inside. Can't recall who, just off the top of my head.'

I thought this odd – Martin had been celebrated, as far back as school, for feats of memory. Probably I wasn't operationally cleared to know. Another thing was worrying me, though, almost too much to ask. 'And what about all the spectators?'

'Oh, lots died, no question, but it was about a hundred, not several thousand. The Creature didn't seem hungry. Instead it just thrashed around, crushing a few creatures accidentally. They pulled the broadcast almost the second the tank opened up, though there's still been no statement from the government. Frankly, it's not going to look great, however they choose to spin it.'

That exuberant swell beneath me. About a hundred – and I might as well have stabbed each one personally. I wondered if the couple who had donated my hoodie had made it.

'So, did I do OK?'

Martin shrugged, taking another sip of Bully's foul homemade tea. 'Well, you were bloody dramatic, which was what you wanted, right? It was exactly the kind of thing we've come to expect – you know, flashy. Maximum bang for the buck. Never knowingly under-theatrical.'

'So, what should I have done?'

'Well, you were the only command operative present, the only armed member of the resistance, so you had to act. And you did act, I'll give you that. Ideally, you'd have taken out the blundicant – for publicity purposes, of course – and as many testers as you could manage before being recaptured – but you weren't to know that Myiqwewelf was no longer with us, and we'd got no method of getting that information to you. On the other hand, the propaganda value – Leelack, the Creature – the propaganda'll be worth something, no question. Something substantial, is my guess.'

I couldn't process even half of this instantly, but there was something else I needed to know.

'Martin, who sent that fake Petra to me?'

'Not a clue – I assume someone in the regime. I aborted the escape mission as soon as I heard about Myiqwewelf's virus, of course. The regime might have discovered all about it.'

'But it wasn't in the Xirfell's *interest* to give me a chance to escape – they'd just perfectly framed me for murder! Why should they risk freeing me – even momentarily? Also, they had no security back-up for the shapeshifter. I mean nothing, zero.'

Martin gave me a long, level look. 'What about Ravene?'

MF must have told him. I felt myself flushing, even as I

protested. 'Ravene took a massive risk warning me about my trial. She'd never have sent a shapeshifter to kill me!'

'I don't mean Ravene personally. I mean that, had the Xirfell somehow learned about your – encounter – with Ravene, they might very well have decided to dispatch you. The King could even have feared that she might be turned. You and Ravene have a past, as everybody knows.'

Could the King have sent the shapeshifter? – It wasn't completely impossible. As much as he cared about any creature, he seemed to care about Ravene.

I said, 'What about Leelack? What'll happen to her now?'

Martin hesitated. 'Well, you gave her a chance, but she's pretty conspicuous. She was always going to be recaptured. It's only in films that the gorgeous heroine swans out of the villain's lair without a bruise.'

'Will they just set up another execution, then?'

His look was sardonic, but not unkind. 'Well, what do you think?'

A wave of utter depression swept over me. Martin, though, was still pursuing his own line of thought. 'Why you weren't spotted by the security I'll never understand. I mean – nothing personal – but you don't look like everybody, and never did. It was a batshit crazy risk to take, going armed into an execution.'

Secretly, I admitted that 'batshit crazy' was not entirely undeserved. I said, 'It wasn't pre-planned. I was trying to find a route to the surface when I ran into this massive crowd. Believe me, I'd have been a lot more conspicuous trying to go the opposite way... Though I got some lucky breaks, no question. I didn't get spot-checked, and then this guy just straight-up gave me his hoodie, out of sheer good-nature, because I asked him for it. Also, half of the security detail had been sent out to quell the insurrections. And I'm a pretty strong swimmer. I was into the overland before they had a chance to miss me.'

Martin shook his head. 'Well, they're almost certainly going to announce your death, as your existence is such an effing embarrassment. Mind you, could still be handy for us, because – once you're dead – you can do whatever you like. Hang on, just let me check out this message.'

Bully, always hopeful, 'Aiden, I just found some pickled sausages.'

I pretended to fancy them, since he'd recalled – rather touchingly – the street food I'd loved in my Academy days and my tastes had evolved since. Still, they were nothing like as bad as the lemballs. But where was Petra?

Martin closed down his connection. 'Bully,' he said, 'could you possibly make yourself scarce for a second?'

Was I in trouble? – though Martin's expression was more embarrassed than angry. He'd changed, I thought gloomily, maybe grown into the job. There was a new authority even in the way he tilted his chair. The instant Bully closed the door, he said, 'Look, Aiden, there's something rather personal I have to tell you.'

'Petra.'

'Well, yes – it is about Petra. I'm sorry to say that, while you were in prison—'

I'd guessed right, then. I passed a hand over my eyes and leaned against the table.

'I think – I think I knew.'

Martin was extending his hand, presumably in manly sympathy. The Alpha male; the whitefella, the preferred. My fucking boss. I kept my hands buried in my pockets as he continued uncomfortably, 'It was just one of those things. A mission, not too risky but still—'

'It's OK,' I said. 'I understand.'

Really, I understood all too well. There's something so charged, in shared danger. I got up and moved restlessly around the room.

'I don't want to talk about it,' I said. 'What I want is something to fucking *do*. The chair was pretty awful but being stuck here isn't much better. You're the leader. If you're really sorry about what happened, you can do something. There must be *some* mission I could take on, some assignment – a long way away, with any luck. If I'm caught again, it's game over. If I'm not – who knows what I might do?'

I couldn't read his expression. Was he pitying me, admiring me, weighing me up operationally – or was his mind elsewhere?

Finally, he said, 'I'll give it some thought.'

'You do that. Meanwhile, I think I'll just go have a wander.'

'Not outside!' he reminded me sharply.

There'd be photos of me in every newsfeed, along with some level of reward – unless the King decided to pretend that I was dead. So, I turned into the adjoining room, where I paced for ages – ancient floorboards, threadbare carpet, powerful smell of live lizards – and tried to cool down.

Any relief I might have felt at having escaped official rebuke was torpedoed by Petra's rejection. I tried to be fair, to recall the dizzying aftermath of a mission – that rush of adrenalin – but I was trammelled by my sheer dislike for the guy. He was so patronising, so rigid, so humourless!

So they'd done some puny mission together – nothing noteworthy, nothing thrilling – and Martin had seized his chance. And meanwhile – as this sordid little drama had unfolded – I'd been tortured, half-starved, drugged and bound to that revolting chair. Also, with a little help from 7784, I'd nailed an international interview and managed to escape, gifting the rebellion with arguably the biggest publicity coup in its effing history.

She'd still dumped me.

Had it been because of Ravene? But what could I have done about Ravene? Ravene had initiated the whole business. Not to mention that, had I rejected her, she might have zuged me on the spot – she was so volatile, so impulsive! The very floorboards seemed to shriek in protest as I paced up and down, my clothes encrusted with sea salt and sweat. Really, I needed a shower, but I was too wound up to think about it.

The electronic doorbell – surprisingly, for such an ancient dump – sounded in every room, so I had plenty of warning when Petra arrived. I had no desire to share our reunion with Martin, so I waited for her. After what seemed an age there was a short knock and then… How lovely she looked! All the lovelier for sporting old-fashioned decorator overalls and sneakers, a dusty cap smothering her light-brown hair. She hugged me powerfully and, with a pang, I was reminded of the way her ears nestled into her neck.

I pulled away, saying rather bitterly, 'Kind of you to bother.'

She was about to hug me again, so I laced my gaze with an edge. She read this instantly and instead seated herself cross-legged on the floor. She was smiling up at me so vividly that I marvelled that I could have ever mistaken any imposter for her. Too brightly, she said, 'You did it!'

'Well, I took my chance. Not too well, I'm afraid.'

'You did wonderfully!'

'Press reviews were mixed. All those punters dead… I think I should've blasted a couple of testers and called it a day.'

'They'd only have caught you again.'

This was true – but it didn't seem such an evil, just at that moment. The trial – what a chance! I glanced down at Petra, at that challenging gaze, that pixie-like chin. What must I look like, exhausted and bandaged, salty and scarred?

I asked, 'Would you have cared if they'd recaptured me?'

She would have risen, but my gaze pinned her to the floorboards. She said, 'Oh, Aiden, if you only knew how I felt when you were arrested!'

'Tough day at the office, was it? Well, you seem to have got over it pretty sharpish.'

To her credit, she flinched. 'It wasn't what you think.'

'Oh Christ, spare me the details.'

Because part of me was remembering her, 'You don't always ... choose.' But she *had* chosen, hadn't she? – She'd chosen Martin. The injustice hit me again, but harder. Petra lowered her gaze, recognising me – correctly – as an incendiary device.

'Aiden, listen, you know that you and I had – issues.'

'Are you hinting that you'd have dumped me anyway?'

'I don't know! – I'm just saying that everything wasn't perfect, where you and I were concerned. Basically, only the sex was perfect.'

The minx. Could she have said anything more disarming?

'So I was just too frigging boring out of bed, was that it?' I said dangerously.

'God, no! I just felt, what with everything being so desperate, that I needed someone more... stable. More predictable.' This answer was also insanely, obscenely brilliant. I found myself revising my self-worth, always a sore point, all the way from screwed-up-risktaker-who-couldn't-even-get-himself-killed-properly to a-guy-so-effing-thrilling-that-the-poor-girl-couldn't-cope.

She continued, 'And how was I to know that you'd get out? No one's ever escaped the Xirfell before – only you! And then, you were so amazing in the interview.'

I'd been amazing. So, nobody was dissing me. And stuff happens. As I knew perfectly well. And – sometimes guys simply have to put our hands up and *admit* this – sometimes women have instincts that we lack. Perhaps Petra might be more of a Priscilla than would be right for me – someone requiring more stability than action, someone more likely to pull me back than to urge me forward. Perhaps Petra had always been fated to be the rebellion's First Lady – heir to Priscilla herself. Leaving operatives like me – admittedly always pushing the boundaries but frankly rather more interesting – to find other fish to fry. I'm not saying that the image of Leelack surfaced at this point, but what did surface was some kind of acceptance.

Also, I was just so frigging tired.

The day that had started with grey mess spooned to me by a pundling ended with a triumphant Bully uncovering a plate with a real, honest-to-God, historic, rogan josh on it. A rogan josh made with ingredients no longer legally available, courtesy of the son of a friend of a neighbour. (Basically, don't ask.)

It was all I could do not to hug the fat little swine.

22

It was the beginning of a week of readjustment, a week of being mollycoddled, petted, feted and generally appreciated. Martin and Petra excepted, most of the rest of the ranking rebels managed to beat their way to Bully's door, generally long past curfew, bearing gifts not only edible but emotionally consoling. In short, I was overwhelmed by the kindness of friends.

I ate mightily – maybe too mightily – and in idle moments I attempted to work out, in hopes of building up strength for missions to come. And if, in the middle of the night, lying on Bully's only comfy sofa, I cursed the King, D. Justin Medlicott and Martin McNamara more or less equally, there was still a growing sense, deep inside, that I hadn't been permitted to survive for nothing.

I was also showered with congratulations for having created a drama that not even the Xirfell could hide, and also for murdering MF's body, his mind having been invaded by one of those pus-like, mind-stealing worms that even the Xirfell fear.

Sometimes, when I woke in the middle of the night and watched the clouds rearranging themselves through the window, I found myself mourning MF – sardonic, annoying, real. Without him, would I have kept my sanity underground?

After a week, I was summoned to a council meeting. Though

dreading being in the same place as Petra and Martin together, I knew it had to happen at some point, and longed to get it over with.

We arrived separately and in various disguises. (Bully had procured me a zuge-keeper's suit, meaning that every creature in the world gave me a mega-wide berth.) In the roofless sports centre, we gathered around the remains of a fire. Petra looked flushed, dishevelled and more beautiful than ever. I had to force myself to look away.

Rebel meetings were generally informal. Laurentia chatted with Petra, Tim had a private word with Martin, Priscilla counselled me. But once Martin rapped on the table everyone instantly fell silent. Then he suddenly swivelled towards me. 'Are you better, Aiden?'

A mission, had to be. 'Yes, perfectly.'

'Up for a challenge?'

'You've got something?'

'Something for you to consider, at least.'

Martin was famously, even repellently, cautious. But what a strange expression in his eyes! Curiosity, doubt, guilt?

I said, 'Just tell me where to go, and how I can get there.'

'G9.'

The circle was silenced. Priscilla recovered first. 'G9!' she murmured. 'The King!'

'Exactly.'

'But how on earth—?' demanded Laurentia, just as Martin said, 'Ho Chi. He's hijacked a blinguard.'

And how the hell had he managed that? I thought, amazed. Ho Chi ran a rather modest cell up in G6. Younger than Martin and me: scrawny, geeky, clever.

As for blinguards, they were reserved for the Xirfell or their most exalted aliens. The largest ones could circumnavigate the

Earth in around ten hours. I'd used to daydream that I was flying one. Imagine the freedom, the power!

Petra objected, 'But can Ho Chi actually operate it?'

'He's done so already, and he's volunteered to take Aiden to G9. And back, of course.'

I wouldn't be coming back, I thought. I said, 'You're talking assassination.'

'It's an unmissable chance. We'll never have better intelligence – or a better person to take it on, of course.'

There was a drumming of knuckles around the table – that was for me – but I was thinking hard. Now, I entertained zero fondness for the King. I still regretted not breaking his neck when he'd ordered me to murder Ichthus, and – had he been presiding over Yoreen's execution-by-Creature – I'd have been in absolutely no doubt what to do. However...

I said, 'The blinguard bit is sensational – great work, Ho Chi! But how the hell can I infiltrate the Xirfell army, with my mug advertised on every continent?'

'As a tester. We've had a body.'

Of course, I'd borrowed a different body before, when Priscilla, Petra and I had dispatched The Enlightened One. Recollections flooded back – Priscilla's drawn face, the hefty sweat of Troy Smithson's donated body, that stamp tightening across my hand... But Smithson had at least been human. The idea of 'becoming' a tester – those enormous shoulders, those slitted eyes, those revolting spurs of hair between the fingers! Some of them had horns, even.

The idea made my skin crawl – a great sweeping shudder that I hoped nobody noticed. I had also heard – or read – that you can't always be restored after borrowing the body of a different species... On a lighter note, some of them had two pricks. Which sounded pretty cool.

Anyway, I'd have to be an idiot to turn it down. I was being offered everything I'd asked for – adventure, distraction, a critical mission, perhaps *the* critical mission – a chance to burnish my personal fame. Assassinating The Enlightened One could be regarded as a stroll in the park compared to infiltrating the Xirfell army and taking out the King.

I started to thank him, but Martin interrupted, 'You'll probably be killed, so no thanks necessary.' Then he added, 'You'll have all the support you want, and any personnel you wish to take with you – as long as they're willing; we're a rebellion, not an army. You're also under absolutely no obligation to take it on. But since you've shown a pretty uncanny knack for surviving impossible situations, you get first refusal.'

I suddenly recognised why all this was happening in public – in front of Petra, especially. No recriminations, should it all end in tears. ('Well hell, old Aiden asked for it, didn't he? It was effing *minuted*.')

Priscilla spoke up, 'I have a few concerns. First: we don't know that Ho Chi can really manage the blinguard. He says he can, but he hasn't proven it, that I've heard of. Secondly, we don't know that the existing fuel cells will last long enough to reach G9, not to mention giving Aiden, Ho Chi and whoever else is involved the remotest chance of getting back. And third – and most seriously – Aiden might suffer a reaction to the tester body, which could incapacitate or even kill him. Borrowing a body from a different species is still a relatively young science. Aiden, I think you're jumping into this with both eyes closed.'

Because Petra's dumped you, she did not say.

Petra said nothing but her eyes were also speaking. Don't sacrifice yourself on my account. Don't make me feel guilty for the rest of my life.

(You really *can* know people too well.)

Might they both be right? – I didn't think so. I had faith in the rebel surgeons, and I'd chanced my life with them before.

I could easily imagine spending the rest of my life regretting such a chance – and what operative wouldn't yearn for a bit of action, after weeks bound to that sterile chair? What better mission could I possibly be offered? And finally, after he'd had me tortured, messed up my knee, framed me for Ichthus's murder and – probably – sent that blinking shapeshifter to finish me off – I positively yearned to take out the King.

I said, 'Sounds ideal.'

More drumming of knuckles. Martin looked approving, others frankly envious, although there was something in Priscilla's expression that startled me. She was a famously intuitive woman. Was she 'seeing' my death, with that inward eye? – But then, everybody's dying – some slower, some faster. I couldn't imagine any of us younger rebels reaching a respectable age.

Then Tim was called on, in order to dispose of two of Priscilla's objections: the fuel cells were full, and apparently Ho Chi had once worked as a blinguard engineer. Tim also filled us in on how the actual theft had happened: the aliens ordered to guard it had been targeted by some passing rebels, just on the off-chance. But what almost unbelievable luck, not only to have a medium-sized blinguard fall into rebel hands, but into the hands of probably the only rebel who understood how blinguards worked!

As we discussed logistics I did wonder if Martin might not be taking the first possible chance to get rid of me. But *someone* would have had to take it on. It was obvious that Ulvers and Nathan were jealous, Laurentia too. Probably almost everyone was, to some degree – though extremely complimentary, possibly in hopes of being invited along.

At the end of the meeting I was invited – very unusually – to stand beside Martin, while the others filed past to shake my hand – in Priscilla's case, to warmly embrace me. Petra would have hugged me too, but I stepped back, and she whitened and half-bowed instead, shoulders downcast.

Afterwards, Bully and I were silent as we passed through reclaimed wasteland and the straggled wrecks of ancient pods, except when he careered off after one of those rat-like mtjiks, which escaped down a hole.

'Good eating, those,' he mourned, 'specially with a little sage,' but I only grunted, as I find them greasy, whatever herb they're cooked with. I was still agitated, thinking that I had rejected Petra's friendly gesture out of petty-mindedness. Not that it mattered, as – the mission approved – we'd probably never meet again.

I didn't notice Bully's gloom until he unlocked the door and I spotted tears blotching those fat fuggy cheeks.

'Hey, Bully. What's up?'

He stumped into the room, kicking his holey carpet out of the way. I couldn't figure out, from the shape of his shoulders, whether he was angry or distressed. With Petra on my mind, I suspected that loyalty towards her might be upsetting him – for Bully loved us all, which was both touching and irritating. Probably he'd found my rejecting her upsetting. (Hell, *I* found it upsetting.)

I followed him, humiliated, into his front room, with those pathetic, pre-WWIII lights and that crumbling sofa. I was perfectly willing to apologise but he wouldn't let me. Instead he hit me quite hard and burst into tears. Arm still aching – he still packed quite a punch – I abandoned the Petra theory and sat down, troubled.

'You're pissed-off that I'm going, aren't you? You think they're trying to get rid of me, right?'

But Bully sniffed and shook his great head.

'No? Then you're pissed-off I accepted the job?'

'No! You did right there.'

'Well, you shouldn't be, because – between us – I asked for it:

I asked Martin to send me away. I gotta keep moving, Bully-boy. Now especially.'

He scowled. 'You got no chance. The other testers'll smell you out and toss you to their blurgs for dinner. Might as well slit your wrists now, make a good clean job of it.' He was absolutely fuming, his cheeks a mottled, reddish colour. I don't think I'd ever seen an angrier fug.

'Look, Bully, I didn't ask for this mission specifically —'

'No, but you asked to be famoose, didn't you? Famoose! What fucking good does it do to be famoose when you're exploded by a zuge or roasted by a blurg?'

It was a weird way to pronounce 'famous' – but the boy might have had a point.

'What's the good of it?' he half-yelled.

I stalked around the room, managing to alarm one of the rampant spiders, the fluorescent ones, into legging it across the floor. Bully – he'll eat any bloody thing – scooped it up and chomped it, glaring at me all the while.

'I don't know why, Bully. It's how I was made! My mum—'

'That's the real reason? Just because your fucking mum fucking gave you fucking up and—'

'Fuck you, Bully. Fuck you!'

'—and so now you're doing this to spite poor Petra! You're throwing yourself away so she'll feel sorry! Just so, once you've burst through your own skin from a zuge you'll be able to tell yourself—'

'I'm not doing any fucking thing to spite any fucking person!' I yelled, careless of the fact that Bully had neighbours, both sides, and that we were supposed to shut the hell up.

'You are! You are! You are!'

Well, was I? – I forced myself to stop and think. Was I seriously taking on a critical mission in suicidal spirit, because I liked the idea of Petra's feeling sad if I died – and she *would* be sad, I knew – and even in hopes that she might make Martin suffer?

I looked down at Bully's lumpy face and knew the answer. Because I had already imagined it. I'd imagined Petra, ashen and sharply boned as she had looked earlier, her face marbled with grief. I had imagined Martin attempting to placate her resentment – attempting in vain. I'd even imagined her rejecting the rebellion, returning to the wealthy and privileged family who considered their beloved Petra irrecoverable. Because of me.

Bully was right, but it still wasn't the whole story. If I looked hard enough, I knew it wasn't. There was D. Justin Medlicott, for a start: the guilt that I carried, the compensation that I owed Australasia. There was Sebastian – what didn't I owe to Sebastian? And, deeper still, could there be a cause more worth dying for? Could there be any planet – wrecked as it was – more dear? The day I'd taken my oath to the rebellion – there had been maybe ten of us, Martin and Sefu among them – Sebastian had quoted Gandhi: 'Be the change that you wish to see in the world.'

I wanted to be the change, too.

What other cause could possibly equal this one – at least for my own generation – the generation who had survived WWIII only to face the Xirfell's iron rule and the end of all things? Without the rebellion there'd be nothing worth fighting for! And this was our moment, this was our time – the Earth so tinderbox dry with resentment that the King himself had been summoned to put out the biggest conflagration... If I could only take out the King, who knew what might happen?

'And now you're effing dead,' said Bully flatly.

He was calm again – how fucking mercurial he was – and checking the latest bulletins.

Not a flattering photo. I looked forty – glowering, furious, uncontrollable. A mass murderer on a bad hair day.

REBEL AIDEN TENTEN EXECUTED

The rebel traitor, Aiden Tenten, has been zuged, palace sources confirmed. Tenten's crimes include hundreds of murders, including the treacherous and cold-blooded strangling of two of his own colleagues, Malthus Montgomery and Ichthus Dmitrios. His other crimes included attempted assassination, collusion in riot, incitement to revolt, corruption of innocent pundlings and hate-speech.

'So, I'm dead,' I remarked – pretty calmly, for a dead person. 'But won't people want to know why my execution wasn't broadcast?'

'It probably was. You probably missed it, haha.'

I sat down beside him. He seemed calmer. Perhaps we could talk sensibly.

'Listen, you imagine that I've taken on this mission out of spite – but I haven't. Just *listen* to that rubbish on the teleview – and some creatures will believe it too, because they're brainwashed, because they're scared, because they're just so frigging tired. But it can't be long before there's nothing left worth saving. I personally suspect that the only reason the Xirfell are still kicking around the place – why the King and the rest haven't just moved on – is because there's no more liveable planet for blood-based beings *anywhere*! We probably have only a couple of years to get rid of them before it's all over – for the planet, as well as us. But should the King fall—'

I stopped, not because I'd finished, but because poor Bully was weeping. I patted his fuggy shoulder and tried to make out what he was saying, which was utterly incoherent. Then, with sinking heart, I realised what he really wanted. He wanted to come with me.

For a crap leader, I seemed to inspire a surprising amount of belief.

I stroked my chin, divided between pity, affection and gut-rock common sense.

Bully's powerful but stocky and slow, like all fugs – which are anyway one of those species that the Xirfell tend to disdain. He was never a very decent shot. Plus, as a fug, he'd be conspicuous – though, at the same time, he might be dismissed in a way that I – once locked into 'my' tester skin – would never be. But how the hell would it look for a tester to have a sidekick, let alone a squat little fart like Bully? Testers don't do sidekicks. I might as well shoot off to the army camp wearing a placard saying, 'With the resistance! Zuge me now!'

So, I decided that I had to be firm. I'd tell him this: 'Bully, you'll always be one of my favourite creatures. But this is probably the toughest mission of my life and I'm going to do it all on my own.'

Did I do this? I did not.

Instead I said: 'Of course you can come.' And he leaped up, all thrilled, and it was already too late to take it back, but I couldn't help suspecting that I had just made yet another massive mistake. Though Martin had said, at the meeting, 'as long as the creature was willing'. Well, Bully was willing, no question.

Next, we had to figure out what to do by way of a fug disguise. Doreen was the rebellion's go-to person – Doreen would think of something. But the same day we'd made the appointment to visit her underground warehouse, I got all kinds of crap delivered from Martin.

'Lay off the jokes. This is a serious business. M.'

'Aiden, get your fucking head together. Bully is not an option. Did you tell him what was really involved? M.'

'OK, OK, I accept that he's cool with it. But he's effing fifty, probably more. I'm not sending you both out there to croak. M.'

'Bully may very well be keen. But, Aiden, is this intelligent? Is this sensible? Is it even fair? Do you want to put him in harm's way, when he deserves a peaceful retirement? Fugs don't generally live as long as humans. Think about it. M.'

And finally, very testily indeed: 'Right. I wash my hands of the whole affair. You do exactly what you want to. You always do, regardless. Leading you is a mug's game and I'm through with it.'

I thought, Thanks, mate.

Up to this point I'd mostly allowed a dignified silence to speak for me, but his last faintly alarmed me, with its hint of my being reprimanded for insubordination. Though nothing was likely to come of that, mostly because I probably would never make it back. Though it'd be rather Martinesque to pass a motion of censure once I was out of sight – he could be a little underhanded. I also recalled his evasiveness during our last meeting, when he'd pretty much flat-out refused to tell me how he had learned about MF's virus. But then, he could well have intelligence sources he didn't want to share. After all, he must've got the King's coordinates from somewhere.

For the record, there were no messages from Petra.

Now Doreen, who was probably of Fijian ancestry, was aged maybe ninety, maybe a hundred, and a frigging genius. We ascended to her ghetto attic, where she measured Bully, jabbering all the while under her breath: '152.4... 152.4... I wonder whether I might not try... Can't quite put my finger on it, but don't you worry, it'll be here somewhere... There's this twitile outfit that might do you, Bully, but your arms might be uncomfortable. And then, there's the heat.'

'I can bear anything,' said Bully mulishly, 'as long as I can go.'

Doreen told Bully that he was 'a caution. But it's got to fit, otherwise you'll be cursing old Doreen, wherever you're off to!' Where we were off to, of course, was G9, but not by so much as a blink did Bully give this away.

He was utterly delighted when Doreen eventually emerged with a corriskidder husk. Now these rare fugs possess a spongy, bouncy outer crust, and slicked feet. Bully's enjoyment in that attic was a picture. He skated across the room, at first tentatively but with evident relish, at one point almost crashing into Doreen.

On the way home, he seemed to have taken on a new lease of life. His step was springier, he looked younger and he couldn't stop beaming – though I still fretted, in the middle of the night, that, in picking Bully, I'd screwed up, out of gratitude at having been understood at last.

For reassurance, I'd asked Priscilla if she would pop round after curfew. When she did, I got rid of Bully by requesting a roodoo cutlet. The second he'd gone, she said, 'Aiden, I hope you won't take this amiss, but I can't help thinking—'

'I know, and you're probably right. But I can't go back on it now. You wouldn't believe how thrilled he is.'

'I don't mean Bully. I think that part's fine – Bully's so solid, so reliable! No, it's the DNA part that worries me. It might not take. Or it might take too well – you might be part-tester for the rest of your life!' Then, catching sight of my set expression she burst out, 'If only Sebastian…'

We fell into each other's arms, as I remembered how he'd popped along – had it been a vision? – while I'd been stuck in the chair. Though I didn't know how to begin to explain it, even to Priscilla. I was also a little shocked how bony and fragile she felt. I held her carefully, as if she was breakable, and said, 'But really, I just wanted you to reassure me about Bully.'

'Martin thinks the result might be compromised. But Bully will be just fine.'

'So, I'm not guilty?'

'I suspect Bully's the guilty one, if there's any guilt involved at all.'

A great peace flooded through me. She wasn't holding me then, but I *felt* held. I said, 'I still feel I need your blessing, somehow, like you're the first woman pope.'

She laughed. 'I'm not your pope, or anybody's! But you are, perhaps, rather like the son I'd have liked to have had – honest, quick-feeling, flawed, but always true. And so, I do bless you – for whatever that's worth – and hope and pray for your safe return.'

We were interrupted by Bully, bearing a stinking roodoo and that beaming grin. The DNA top-up he'd been given in preparation for the corriskidder disguise had made him look both shorter and stumpier, but also tauter and more muscular. And was he happy!

I did a good thing after all, I thought, as we sat around, eating roodoo and talking over old times. For a fleeting moment, I even felt fine – until I remembered that I had only one more day of being fully human.

Here's hoping this works.

The next morning, I went alone to the coordinates I'd been given, in order to switch bodies with the dead tester. I'd already taken a pill that turned my skin a far richer shade. Combined with my zuge breeder's outfit, I was so brilliantly disguised that my contact failed to recognise me, and I had to prompt him.

'Atlantis?'

'Harpalian?' He relaxed. 'Chilly, isn't it?'

It wasn't, but I agreed, because this guy was just about to mess with my personal consciousness.

'This way, please. Just follow me.'

I watched the swirl of his old-fashioned raincoat as he led me through windings of side alleys that only the giant rats and mutant lizards know. (I only just missed nailing one mauve-olive tail.) The last door, which had an ancient, gated look, led directly into a staircase featuring the musty scent of rodents. As I followed him downstairs the air gradually improved. We wound up in a tiny space, all chilled stone, perhaps no more than a cell, perhaps religious or historic. There he fastened the door securely behind us.

I assumed that this was where I got turned into a tester – but it wasn't. Instead, a pundling appeared, bowed low, and ushered us towards a corner of the cell, where a still steeper, still narrower spiral staircase descended, seemingly endlessly.

Eventually I found myself in a room perhaps three metres by four, and bitterly cold. I instantly spotted a great lump, under a sheet which glowed like a pearled glacier. I pulled back the covering – and replaced it just as hastily.

A powerful shoulder, just the edge of a hairy tester limb. The pundling hastened to reassure me, saying in their curly tongue, 'He is dead, soldier.'

I couldn't answer. I suddenly longed for Bully's stolid and fuggish support, because – for me – becoming a tester felt far nervier than any mission. I experienced a surge of attachment to my scarred and flawed but tried-and-tested thirty-year-old body. It wasn't perfect, but it was mine. How could I entirely trust anyone else's? Though I *had*, when assassinating The Enlightened One – I kept reminding myself of this.

As if reading my mind, the fellow assured me, 'You'll be stronger – even stronger than in your prime. Effortlessly strong, and effortlessly fast. You'll feel as if you've been enhanced.' I didn't mention that I already had been, thanks to the Xirfell's early enthusiasm for human experimentation, but I secretly wondered if my original enhancements might affect my new, tester self.

I could be the most powerful tester who ever lived. Super-tester! Until, of course, they killed me, in which case I'd certainly be the strongest damn corpse in the graveyard.

I might also have two pricks, but was too embarrassed to ask.

Atlantis then left to change into his surgeon gear, while I was moved into a room with metallic walls, which reminded me of my prison. Staring up at the ceiling, breathing in the chilled, drugged air, I gradually began to feel increasingly disconnected. A curious lightness unspun my brain and I received a vision.

It wasn't a normal dream but maybe that's how it goes with drug-induced slumber. While my transformation was taking place, colours swirled: lurid fuschias and bloodied crimsons, salty oranges and oceanic purples. I seemed to be floating on some gilt-foamed sea, being gently rocked rather than swimming, the air spacious, as if the very ceiling of the sky had been lifted… I was conscious of a deep resistance to coming back, to being pulled from this place. Had I ever felt so peaceful before?

When I came to, I seemed to be breathing, bizarrely, from the bottom of my stomach. My nose itched, but when I moved to scratch it, this gigantic hairy digit reared up towards me. Then I remembered.

'Are you back?' asked Atlantis.

'Yeah. But I feel – strange.' Though I felt much more than strange, as if a part of me had died, and my inner panic was indescribable.

He said calmly, 'Well, obviously, it worked – well done! Now, first, you'll notice that your lungs are lower, your stomach is roughly where your kidneys used to be, and your heartrate is far more powerful, also much slower. Also, your two hearts aren't always quite in sync, which is normal.'

'The deeper lungs I definitely notice.'

'Stamina will probably be the greatest improvement, but you won't notice that yet, of course.'

'Look, while I was under—'

'Yes?'

'I had this dream.'

'Sexual in nature?'

'Not at all.'

'Fascinating! I'll just make a note, if you permit. Of course, it's a very rare operation – it's only been done three times before, I believe – and the second time it didn't take. Could you take me through it? Would you mind?'

I did, and he recorded it on one of those thumb-sized devices. Afterwards he asked, rather hesitantly, 'Would you say that you're normally subject to visions?'

I remembered Sebastian and the ruined tennis court. 'Maybe.'

'How would you describe yourself spiritually?'

'Confused.'

He almost asked me something else but decided against it.

He wasn't on the operational list so I said nothing about the mission, but he must have guessed that it was serious because he grabbed my hirsute hand at the bottom of the staircase and muttered, 'Good luck, friend!'

As I ascended the circular stairs and emerged into the city, I tried to analyse all the differences beneath my tester lieutenant-grade uniform. My vision was certainly brighter, my hearing superb. But it felt weird to walk so heavily, burdening the ground, not to mention scattering the citizenry in my path. I got dirty looks as well as fearful ones – and I wondered if the tester whose body I had swiped would have noticed the resentment, the wariness, along with the respect. It occurred to me that one way of identifying possible rebel sympathisers might be to simply wander across the capital, in tester-mode. I could almost *smell* which creatures longed to murder me, which ones only hoped to get away without being challenged, and which weren't fussed either way (mostly depressed). The sense of power was thrilling: my prime had returned – that effortless flexibility of eighteen.

The oddest part was simply breathing. Not that it was difficult – I think I'd have found it tough to get out of breath, however long I ran – but simply from the strangeness of having my lungs in a different position. My voice also startled me. I dodged a small netty in my path and from my cavernous depths came a hilariously gravelly, 'Sorry!'

The lad peeled off in terror, but I reminded myself that a true tester would have sworn instead. Then a rather vicious-looking fug came up to me, tugged his forelock and requested orders.

'Get lost, toad. I'm busy,' I glowered.

Would this keep happening? I wondered. And wouldn't it seem suspicious if I never had orders to give? What if I had to order some creature to be punished, or even arrested? I tried to forget about this as I muscled my way through the city, shoulders thrusting as if through water, towards the byway leading to Tim's own safe house, part of a ruined church. Bully was already on the watch, and I was whisked inside.

He had prepared two dinners – and the oddest part was that the Indian curry held no appeal for me at all. Instead, my tastebuds zeroed in on a sinewy pulp resembling congealed fish food.

Bully eyed me sympathetically. 'It's what Tim said you'd want. Any good?'

'I find myself strangely drawn to it, even though you cooked it. But what's in it?'

'Do you really want to know?'

'Was it ever human?'

'Good God, no!'

'Then I don't want to know. Um, who else is expected?'

'Just Tim. Not Petra.'

Sometimes I thought Bully a shade *too* acute.

Later, with Tim, I brought up matters arising. 'Why am I constantly being asked for orders by random creatures?'

'Well, testers rank third in the hierarchy, after the royals and the Golden Circle. It would certainly be unusual for a minion *not* to ask what you wanted, by which I mean a pundling or a fug. Saves time, energy and getting kicked a couple of metres in the wrong direction.'

I recalled being kicked – though in the right direction – outside Joan's factory, my wildly mingled pain and relief.

'OK, so what do I tell them to do?'

'Well, you could pretend to be obsessed with nocxmow gambling, loads of testers are, but normally their fellow testers invite them to play. You could also develop a reputation for greed. Ask the pundling – or whoever – to procure various dainties, or what passes for dainties with testers. I sent you the list, didn't I?'

'Mtjik bladders?'

'Those are pretty fatty. Why don't you pretend to a ravenous passion for globster bites?'

'Insects fried in blood? Think I'd prefer the bladders.'

'Be careful. Tester fat transitions almost instantly into muscle – but you might find that it transitions right back into fat once you're human again.'

Bully teased, 'All his women'll run a mile!'

I ignored this. 'Also, how do I figure out whom to kow-tow to?'

'Ear-pins and epaulets. The list should be in your file. It's really straightforward – except for blurgs. There, you'll simply have to memorise their colourings – there's no other way. The King's royal blurg is easy, with that bizarre neckpiece that only the elite are granted, but the rest can be complicated. Have you tested any of your new capabilities yet? Running, jumping, reaction times?'

'Not really, but I feel springy somehow, and constantly hungry, and, well – very much like a teen.'

'Testers are extremely highly-sexed,' Tim observed. 'The trouble being that almost all the female testers were left on their parent planet. Meetings between male and female testers are rare but mostly spontaneous and immediate – practically a chemical reaction.'

'Tricky for the males dragged down to Earth, then.'

'Indeed,' said Tim, rather drily. 'But there's nothing stopping male testers from swiping human women, as they do. You might also become aware of tester summonses. That faint buzzing at the top of the spine.'

'Not yet I haven't.'

'Well, even though you're a lieutenant, you probably will. Any tester who outranks you can summon you, within a radius of about a hundred metres, just as you can summon any tester whom you outrank. If they do summon you, you have three choices: to accept the task, to reject it – in which case you need a pretty persuasive reason – or to stall for time.'

'What would happen if I rejected it?'

Tim fiddled with his papers. 'I would strongly recommend you alternate between acceptance and stalling. Though, should you stall too often, you'll be assigned a fledgling tester to shadow you. In which case your card will be marked. Just showing up on the Xirfell radar equates to awaiting the denunciation to come.'

'Which would mean curtains.'

'It would mean either death or deportation – the deportation being to some planet where life expectancy would be measured in weeks, at the outside. The King tends to be extraordinarily vicious towards testers and to have what amounts to a soft spot for humans. His first wife was human, of course.'

The night before Bully and I departed, we were flooded with messages, and received a visit from Martin. When I regretted the cancellation of my trial, he was dismissive.

'That would never have happened,' he said, attempting to swallow a little of Bully's own homemade brew. 'At the time you had already wounded the King, defeated Ravene during an international broadcast, and helped to reignite resistance in the provinces. Since when you've murdered a King's counsellor – along with about a hundred bystanders, up-ended a state execution and become the first person ever to escape the regime.

'Don't kid yourself, Aiden. If you were ever arrested again, you'd be zuged within the hour. In chess terms, we're in the endgame now. And so, listen up. You've got to keep your concentration on this mission. No going off-piste, no screwing the princess, no messing about. As for Bully—'

And here Bully sat up very straight and stuck his chin out pugnaciously.

'Well, he's not the companion I'd have picked, but he's not such a bad choice for all that. So, if you and Tim could just buzz off a second, I'd just like to have a word with Bully on his own.'

I lumbered off, breathing deeply from my stomach, apelike arms dangling from my heavy shoulders. (Only one prick, though. Bummer.)

I found Tim in the kitchen. He asked, 'Can you still hold a pen, Aiden?' And when I agreed that I could, though I would find it far simpler to crumple iron, he asked if I could autograph an engraved card for him.

I didn't know he fucking cared and said so. He responded, 'It's not for me. It's for my daughter. Dina. Please write "For Dina" on it.'

Turned out she'd loved my interview with Ravene. He showed me a photo: red-gold hair, maybe eighteen or nineteen, delicate, pretty. I thought, Wait for me, kid, in case I make it back alive. Although the notion that Petra hadn't been willing to wait still needled me, all the same.

The next night Bully and I made our separate ways from his house to the bleak wasteland by the former cricket pitch. Together with Martin and Priscilla we watched Ho Chi neatly land the blinguard. As Martin shook my hand, he said, significantly, 'Remember.'

Priscilla hugged me as Martin watched, rather a strange look on his face. Ho Chi stepped out to have a quick word with him, while Bully-as-corriskidder-fug jumped in, practically bouncing in his seat. I secretly felt a bit like doing the same, though I had noticed – which I liked – that my tester self mostly appeared to be frowning, even if chuffed to bits.

Something to do with the eyebrows – eyebrows express such a lot.

Ho Chi returned, saying solicitously, 'Can I get you anything?' and I growled in the negative, simply for the thrill of staying in character.

Tim's crash course in being a tester had left me both sickened and conscious of a sneaking respect, because testers are hard – bottle-chompingly, zuge-bendingly hard. They outrank every other known humanoid in terms of strength, even though their diet consists mostly of invertebrates. They combine raw and steely power with roughly enough brains to fill a medium-sized coffee mug, making them hugely useful to the Xirfell, particularly since they're also loyal to a fault.

The ideal servants – dim but loyal, thick but strong.

What else had I learned? Their hierarchy is both simplistic and irrevocable. They are literally born into their ranks, which never alter – the ancient Indian caste system has got nothing on the testers'. They're exploited, being forced to slog for the Xirfell without the smallest say in their personal fates, but they never seemed to resent it, and even appeared to possess a vague but potent sense of mission.

Thanks to the consciousness transfer, their language came readily to me. It was in manner where I messed up, forgetting to roll my shoulders like a gorilla, forgetting to glower, forgetting to muscle through the world without apology. All this zipped through my head as the blinguard lifted straight into the air, tilted, hovered for a second and then lurched dizzily forward.

'How come they don't just shoot us down?' Bully asked. 'Don't they *know* we stole the blinguard?'

Ho Chi chuckled. 'Not yet. We hacked the log and recorded it as in need of a battery upgrade in G13. Once we get back to inner space – and assuming they inquire – I'm going to submit that's it's OK, except that the visuals aren't working. After that, well, we'll just have to see how soon they realise that their crew is captured, their blinguard's AWOL and we're not following orders!'

Our route at first lay over the familiar ruined suburbs, and the
sun had set gloomily over the mostly deserted hinterlands before
we broke through the fog blanket. But then, stars! – Not just the
odd singleton through clouded dust: the real deal.

How I'd missed stars!

'Jesus,' Bully whispered. 'Never thought I'd see the Southern
Cross again!'

It was shocking, somehow, that there were so many, that they
were all still there. Also, the contrast between their charged
brightness and the thick surface of Australasia – the dead soil,
the enveloping, choking, oxygen-starved air. And, as we climbed
higher, I was struck by the contrast between that navy skyline and
those pure, knifing stars. The glory of it. The sheer, ridiculous,
expensive glory of it.

We climbed and climbed. Bully clocked the horizon with
kindling eyes and I recalled those evenings after school when
Duncan Tenten used to take me out in one of his zelopods, to see
Acrux, Centaurus, Carina… I released my safety harness in order
to see the stars behind us. Suddenly the blinguard dipped. Ho Chi
carolled, 'Nothing to worry about, but I'd better just zip you in for
safety, OK?'

Now call me neurotic but, ever since that blinking chair, I'd felt
allergic to restraints of any type, but I submitted. Once it was clear
again, I asked, 'Could we lose the belts?'

'Better not,' counselled the co-pilot, Darius, a fellow
Indigenous guy.

Eventually I dozed off. Bully woke me, some hours later,
saying, 'We're going to have to stop, just briefly, at their home
base.'

'Why? Is something wrong?'

'Nothing to worry about!' Ho Chi answered, with a laugh. 'Fuel
cell's dipped a little lower than it should have. It won't take ten

minutes to check whether we need to boost it. We'll have it sorted before you know it.'

I'd thought the fuel cell was supposed to be full, but I had to assume they knew what they were talking about... Soon it was a cheery, 'Almost there, guys!' from Ho Chi, but I'd already sensed the descent. Gradually, the faintest misty-moisty, yellow-green sunrise broke, displaying fields below. There's generally a hiatus when a blinguard cuts out on landing, but Ho Chi's landing was pure silk. It was only after we were cradled to a stop that things started to happen.

Before the engine hissed to a halt, I impatiently pressed my release valve – which didn't respond. Then a flare of light slammed into my face: Darius. But what the fuck was he holding? And why was he wearing that half-exhilarated, half-nervy expression?

Dizzied by a scintillation of light, I lost him – and indeed everything – except for a sharp serrated pain, as if part of the Southern Cross had swung down and crashed into planet me. I just managed to yell, 'Bully! Watch out!'

Then every star turned black.

23

I was registering a metal-on-metal sound, and a strange smell. I opened my eyes to Bully, who was stirring something in a small pan, something that made my stomach heave.

'What on earth—'

'We were set up,' said Bully matter-of-factly, still stirring. As I seemed to be lying on solid ground, he must have hoicked me out of the blinguard. Was that why I was aching all over?

Drowsily I took in the scene, which was – frankly – glorious. A long river, framed by grasses damp with either rain or dew, stretched into the distance under a fresh, peach-apricot sun. Nearby were copses of kale-green trees; in the distance, steeper hills were thumbed by early morning shadows.

On the downside, Bully's food smelled foul. Trust Bully to locate some local creepy-crawlies… Suddenly I whirled towards him, remembering. 'I was attacked! Ho Chi—'

'Ho Chi didn't attack you. That would have been Darius. Ho Chi attacked me. You want, by the way, to look out for snakes – little ones, but I'm guessing poisonous. I spotted two already.'

'Ho Chi?' I repeated stupidly.

'And Darius. They overrode our safety release mechanism and blinded you. Darius stabbed you, while Ho Chi had a go at me. Hey, look, I was there.'

'Then why aren't you dead?'

'It's tough making a fug black out. We got fat necks.'

'I was stabbed?' I tried to sit up, suddenly conscious of the bandage around my chest, but everything swirled sickly around me, so I lay down again.

What could have made Ho Chi attack us? And how on earth could Bully have defeated Ho Chi and Darius all on his own? I remembered Ho Chi's notable cheeriness – could he have been brainwashed, maybe? Meanwhile, Bully, chewing thoughtfully on some herb, scattered a few more on whatever he was cooking.

'A set-up,' he repeated. 'I'm guessing Ho Chi was turned.'

Was it possible? – It was always, of course, possible… but I couldn't get my head around it.

I said, 'What's that godawful smell?'

'I caught a few things. Nothing that looked poisonous.'

'Bully, you have to be the world's crappiest cook. But I think you just saved my life.'

'Well, my belt wasn't tight and Ho Chi didn't know that corriskidders can skate on their feet. I tripped him up – he went down beautiful, cracked his head on the wall. Then I had to fight Darius. What do you mean, the world's crappiest cook?'

I attempted to rise again before falling back, clubbed by a soaring pain.

'So, my little fugglet, you upended Ho Chi and defeated Darius! Not just a pretty face, are you? But where's the welcoming committee? Where are the local troops? Isn't this supposed to be Ho Chi's home turf? In short, why do I wake to find you cooking something unmentionable – hope it isn't Ho Chi, by the way – over a slowish fire?'

He gave me a long, steady, pitying gaze. The pain as I finally hauled myself upright speared my entire torso.

'No *way* could we have been betrayed by everybody!'

Please God, not Petra.

'Dunno. But I only just managed to stop your bleeding, so you'd better lie the fuck back down.'

Bully doesn't normally swear. Curious, I checked under my bandage. The actual wound startled me – the knife had gone straight into my massive muscles, inches deep, almost exactly where my human heart would have been. My tester body had sensationally withstood the test, and the bleeding – what brackish blood testers had – was mostly over.

'You're lucky you weren't still human, Aiden. Else you'd be dead,' said Bully, unnecessarily.

'Yeah, but I still don't get it. If Ho Chi's cell is infiltrated, they could have waited until we'd landed to overpower us – we wouldn't have stood a chance! And if it *isn't*, then where is everybody?'

'I'm guessing we're not quite where we're meant to be. No sign of anybody.'

I said, without enthusiasm, 'I suppose I'll have to try to raise Martin from the blinguard.'

'Are you sure?' asked Bully sharply.

Good point. There was at least a chance that we'd been stitched up, both ends. Stitched up to be quietly dispatched – by Martin, in league with Ho Chi. Although the elaborateness of the scheme still seemed crazy. Why bother to deploy the precious stolen blinguard, just to kill Bully and me on another continent?

I recalled Martin's strange expression as we'd boarded the blinguard, something I'd vaguely connected with Petra. But Priscilla had been beside him, and there was no way that the Xirfell could have infiltrated our top leadership, as long as Priscilla was a part of it. And was Martin – annoying as he was – really capable of murdering fellow rebels in cold blood?

Automatically, I felt for my weapon. Then I said, 'Shame you didn't spare at least one of them. We could've stuck lighted matches between their toes and found out what's going on.'

'Funny, I just didn't think about that, at the time.'

'And what about the blinguard? Was it damaged at all? Not that we know how to operate it, of course.'

'It looked OK to me, but I haven't really examined it.'

'Well then, I'm going to.' Despite Bully's frown, I heaved myself over, and mounted the steps to take a look. Bully had bagged both the bodies but blood, mess and breakages were everywhere, though the controls themselves looked to be intact. Bully, who had followed me inside, silently towed out one body bag. I moved towards the other.

'Whoa, lemme do that,' said Bully, alarmed. Brushing me aside, he retrieved his second victim personally. He returned to check my wound, but it was still hardly bleeding.

I said, 'Why didn't they just frigging shoot us? Were they worried about making holes in the blinguard?'

'Dunno,' said Bully and returned to his fire. Frowning, I decided to search every compartment, for something – orders, drugs, weapons – for a clue, just a single frigging clue.

Nothing. Clean as a whistle. Until my massive hand grasped hold of something, something which must have blended into its background so perfectly that I hadn't even spotted it. Something alive, nestling under the co-pilot's seat.

I couldn't believe it. A live gromeline. Trembling, possibly with fury, and trying in vain to squeeze back. Grabbing my trophy – I could feel its hot little heart throbbing like an injury against my palm – I hopped out of the plane so fast that my wound protested.

'Bully!'

Bully raised one eyebrow. Two would have been overkill.

'Bully, you are not going to believe this. I found a gromeline!'

The gromeline – only about fifteen centimetres – bit my finger, hard, even though I could have easily crushed its entire body with my fist – and probably would have, were I a real tester.

Feisty little gromeline. I flicked it lightly with my sausage-sized finger. When it protested, I growled, 'Cheese it, munchkin,' though I could feel it struggling obstreperously against my palm. Bully was intrigued.

'Is it genuine?'

'Of course it's genuine. It just fucking bit me.'

Bully probably considered this no proof. But they're rarer than clean air these days and his fascination was obvious. (In case you – accessor of my memory sliver – are unaware, gromelines come from the farthest galaxy so far discovered, can speak any tongue and own enviable mental powers. They are also brave to the point of stupidity and ludicrously small. This one was mouse-coloured – they can be spectacular – with tiny red eyes. Few humans have ever seen one.)

'What on Earth was Ho Chi doing with a gromeline?'

It was a reasonable question. A mission was no place for such a valuable alien. Could have been bounced to pieces, even during that feather-silk landing. I leaned down. 'Did you stowaway on Ho Chi's blinguard?' I asked, but it just slit its eyes, pursed its lips and glared at me.

Bully trotted to his backpack and removed a small bag.

'Shove it in here. Not even a gromeline could tunnel out of that. Once we've had something to eat, we can find out what it knows.'

With some difficulty we succeeded in loosing the little creature inside, where it immediately started gnawing on a corner.

'You sure it can't just chew itself out?' I asked.

'Not unless it's got a small but serviceable nuclear device. The bag's made of one of those new materials, can't remember what it's called.'

The animals, herbs and stuff Bully found tasted OK, in the end. It's tough for any creature, stranded in some foreign country and catering for two different species, to get the cuisine spot-on. I found it too tender and tasteless; he too chewy and fiery, at least judging from all the water he kept gulping.

We didn't chat much. There was no way, in that lush river valley, that a giant snake could sneak up on us, but there were strange little rustlings that could well have been the tiny adders Bully had already spotted, and also unnerving howls, maybe from timber wolves. I watched the gromeline inside its sack. It had been busy with its sharp little molars, but to no effect.

'What'll we do about little Harvey here?' I asked.

'Better find out its real name before you alienate it completely. They're fluent in about a quadrillion tongues, you know.'

'Let's find out.' I spoke into the bag. 'Sir, what is your name?' It ignored me completely. It might even have stuck out a minute tongue in my direction. Hard to tell when their bits are so little.

'I tried being polite. It still treats me like rubbish.'

'Well, not even a tester's mother loves a tester, which is why they get taken away before their mothers can eat 'em,' said Bully reasonably. 'Lemme have a go.' He shoved his friendly fuggy face towards the hole in the bag and said, 'I realise that you probably don't care for testers – or for fugs, come to that – ouch!'

The thing had impaled his nose with a needle-like nail. The gromeline crossed its insect-thin arms, practically swaggering inside the bag.

'Cute – but annoying,' was Bully's verdict.

'Bully, have you considered that there might be some crucial info in this bird-sized frame? It could've been there for the landing. It could've seen the attack, maybe overheard Ho Chi talking to Darius, even!'

'Yeah, but how can we make it cooperate?'

'For a start,' the creature piped, 'you could take me out of this bag, which is stifling. You could also stop calling me "Harvey".'

'Whoa,' said Bully, astonished. 'A female gromeline! They're super rare!'

I inspected it as well as I could: fuzzy fur, twitchy nose, hot-bright eyes, padded feet, tiny rounded ears. Each of its four kidneys must have been the size of a dust mite. My very first gromeline.

'Forgive our stupidity, lady,' I said, as suave as dammit, 'but if you would be willing to tell us your name, we would be delighted to use it.'

That tiny foot tapped dangerously against the bag. Then, 'I give nothing to testers, or to any member of your corrupt, fraudulent and nefarious regime!'

'That's cool,' I soothed her. 'Know, O small, pugnacious and fabulously rare creature, that I am no ordinary tester – and nor is my colleague here your average fug. We're both prominent members of the rebellion. I'm actually human, and Bully—'

'But she must *know* all that,' Bully objected. 'She was on the ruddy blinguard!'

'Indeed, you are mistaken,' returned the gromeline frostily. 'I entered the empty blinguard on a reconnaissance mission, after it landed. You stand on my personal territory!'

In which case, it probably didn't look too good. Inside the blinguard she'd have spotted a couple of bagged corpses – after which she'd been kidnapped by a great hairy tester and a great lumpy fug. Fugs could be independent, but testers, by definition, were servants of the regime.

'So, you sneaked onto the blinguard after we landed?' Bully asked – but suddenly that tiny mouth clamped back shut and the tiny eyes smouldered, as if the bat-like creature was cursing herself for having told us anything. 'Probably, she slipped into the blinguard while I was cooking. What a perfect spy she'd be! Tiny, clever, smaller than a starling. And those claws, like mother-of-pearl... I never saw anything so neatly made!'

The creature, unappeased, slashed at him, fruitlessly, with those mother-of-pearl claws. 'I am no spy!'

'I really don't think she is,' I said.

'Yeah, but what proof can we give her that we're not with the regime? We show up in a blinguard – and whoever heard of a *rebel* blinguard? – Plus, our uniforms, our looks, even your voice is against us! You sound like a bag of rusty nails.'

Which was too true for argument. Softening my vocal cords, I turned back to the gromeline. 'What can I do to convince you that we aren't what we seem? We'd have to be pretty ruddy crazy to carry around written assurances from Sebastian himself!'

'Sebastian?' she whispered.

'Sebastian Nevsky, lost leader of the rebellion, based in G13. Ever heard of the professor? Or Malthus, maybe?'

I thought those ruby eyes just flickered, but perhaps I was imagining it. The different rebel cells had been constructed almost entirely independently. Probably only Sebastian or Malthus could have assisted us – and both were dead.

As if reminded of this, Bully said, 'Well, I'm off to dig a shallow grave.' I offered to help, but he gestured gloomily at my bandage and buzzed off.

I considered. It had seemed to me that there might have been another little spark when Ho Chi was mentioned, which gave me an idea.

'Wait!' I yelled, and Bully turned back. I leaned down to the gromeline and grated, as winningly as I could, 'Ho Chi. Do you *know* Ho Chi?'

A bright red glare. The little lady loathed Ho Chi, was my guess. On impulse, I grabbed the bag we'd put her in, and headed towards the corpses. Pulling back Ho Chi's canvas, I said, 'Look! We did that, in self-defence. Now can you trust us?'

There was an attentive little nod. I carried her back towards the fire and lowered the bag onto a tuft of grass. The gromeline was squeaking; I had to bend down to hear.

'Return me to my previous position immediately!' she commanded. 'Carry me back!'

'Where to? To Old Virginny?'

'To the corpse of Ho Chi! I wish to dance on the grave of the fraudulent venal spawn of a tree frog!'

Well, after that, of course, everything was cool. We reminded her that Bully had first to finish the grave before any creature, however delicately built, could hope to dance on it. And she unbent to the extent of introducing herself.

'I am Pavlina Dafina Evangelija of Macedonia.'

'Macedonia!' cried Bully. 'The ancient name for G6! Are we in Macedonia?'

'It is the correct name,' retorted Pavlina. 'G6 is a revolting Xirfell construct.'

I bowed, which reminded me of my wound faster than Bully. 'Lady, forgive us our rough treatment. We believed that you might have been Ho Chi's companion and witnessed his attempt to murder us.'

I didn't want to remind her that she'd kept trying to bite us.

Her posture eased a little. 'It is understandable. I have indeed travelled in Ho Chi's blinguard. But I am delighted that he is dead. It was he who handed over our previous leader to the Xirfell – Lord Rafael, of whom you must have heard.'

'Handed him over?' asked Bully.

'Betrayed?' I suggested, and she assumed again that I had heard of this Lord Rafael. So I pretended I had, as she was so fussed, and then asked, 'How long has it been since Ho Chi was turned?'

'We have known for eight weeks and two days,' she said sadly. 'But I accept that this is not a precise answer to your question. He might have been false for longer.'

And so might Martin, I thought grimly – but kept this to myself.

'Are there many in your group?' Bully wanted to know.

'Rebel humans, half-humans or gromelines?'

'Gromelines.'

'Perhaps only two hundred now,' she admitted, 'but the group itself flourishes. Over the past month we've recruited new members almost daily. What happened to Lord Rafael roused many – and then, just the following week, there was that wonderful interview with the G13 rebel, Aiden Tenten. Waverers re-joined, newcomers surfaced, there was suddenly a new energy, new drive. An interview with the ranking princess, I assume you saw it?'

'Um, yeah,' muttered Bully.

'Did you never meet this person?'

'I met him once,' I said hastily. While Bully – bless – stood by, not giving away the truth by so much as a flicker of a fuglike ear. Then I said, 'Forgive me, Pavlina, but we're very short of time and we need to decide what to do. Are you the leader of your local cell?'

'Cell?' she repeated, bewildered.

Yet again I was reminded, not just of time zipping past, but of the difficulties of communication. Though, to be fair, how could anyone have foretold that we'd end up in lesser blinking Macedonia?

'Who is the leader of your group?' Bully translated.

She frowned. 'Lord Rafael was betrayed by the corpse, Ho Chi. On whose grave I propose to dance.'

'But who ordered you to inspect the blinguard?'

She bridled. 'No one! I saw a Xirfell blinguard on our territory, and came to inspect it, on my personal initiative. Since I was captured, I have not yet reported it. But now I know that you have disposed of that spawn of a tree frog—'

I intervened, 'Lady, allow me a moment with my colleague here... Bully, what the hell do we do?'

'We take her with us,' said Bully, clearly starstruck. 'If she'd come. I mean, what *can't* she do? She can fly – she can fit into a pocket – she can talk a blue streak—'

And, weirdly enough, I agreed. It might have been dead against protocol, but what could be handier, on an assassination mission, than a pint-sized creature of exceptional feistiness and vocabulary? My main concerns were that she might get mistaken for a bat or mouse or accidentally crushed. And then, there was her natural haughtiness. Bully – or so I imagined – would obey me, most of the time. I felt less than confident about the Macedonian munchkin.

'But she does her own thing.'

'She might refuse,' said Bully, missing my point. 'But I think she'd be up for it. Specially if I tell her that you're her hero Tenten, haha.'

One of my little lights. A very little light. I felt another surge of pride, along with a twinge of nerves. How could I measure up – in person – to the me she admired, the public guy?

I couldn't, was the answer. That interview had been a one-off. The occasion had inspired me; 7784's garnet-coloured drink had inspired me. I said, 'Listen, Bully, don't tell her who I am. Just call me "boss" or something. Keep it simple. We're after the King – we don't know where the hell we are – and is she game to come along? My guess is she's game for anything. My finger's still hurting where she bit it.'

'My nose too. That nail rasps like a wasp.'

And so, our little symposium concluded, we returned to the gromeline, who was tapping those minute feet dangerously.

'Lady, we have decided to share our purpose with you, in hopes that you can help. I am a disguised human, known as "boss", and this is Bully, short for Bullivant. We're on a mission to take out the Xirfell King.'

'To take out?'

'To eliminate. To assassinate.'

She said, 'In that case, may I assist?'

'We were hoping you might.'

'I'm sorry that I bit you,' she said meditatively. 'It is extremely thoughtful of you not to hold it against me.'

After we competed to reassure her on this point, I said, 'Lady, once we get power back on the blinguard, we'll need to know how far we are from the King's coordinates. We also need to find out if we can somehow work the blinguard.'

Her tiny nostrils flared. 'If you know the King's position, then all is well. For' – a toss of that tiny head – 'I can fly a blinguard.'

Well, she couldn't, of course, unless somebody created a special, munchkin-sized one, in which case I would have frankly backed her. But – and this really was a slice of luck – she did know *how* to fly a blinguard. She knew, at least, how a blinguard worked.

She was mega-bright – one of the smartest creatures I'd ever met – but, in addition, blinguards weren't as complicated as I'd imagined, being scintillatingly well-designed. We could probably have figured it out with no assistance at all – though with the joint risks of either messing up the engines or stranding ourselves in Macedonia.

More crucially, we were running out of hours. We needed to be at the coordinates Martin gave us before 16.30 local time; and, after Pavlina had finished instructing us, by about half-one we were good to go.

Given the time constraints, Bully simply shoved some leaves and detritus over the corpses, while I attempted to find some strapping for Pavlina. In the end, the gromeline herself improvised, chewing and tying fragments of thread together.

The day was beginning to heat up as we settled into position onboard, Bully's human-sized chair well forward, mine pushed back as far as possible. Pavlina was wedged in a corner, wearing that disdainful expression I was already beginning to recognise. There was a brief spasm from the engine as I pressed the final start button, but then – with the usual lurch – we were airborne, gazing down at the river valley, itself fired from end-to-end by sunlight like a gigantic golden snake. It seemed to me, at last glance, that some wolf-type creature was already pawing at the bodies, but I had no time for more than a shiver of repugnance before it was miles behind us.

Bully had locked in the coordinates, and, aside from monitoring the controls, there was soon disconcertingly little to do. Suddenly he said sharply, 'Um, boss! The communication link is connecting!'

'Where to, the White House?'

'To any bloody place, look! Well, shall I feed in Martin's address? The others'll be wild to know what's happened.' And, as I hesitated, a clear little voice wished to be told who these others were and why, precisely, we should inform them of anything.

I liked the way she was thinking. I didn't want Martin raining on my parade – I didn't want Martin, end of story – while the idea of Petra's being worried held rather a fascination for me. I said, 'Martin saw us off, remember? He must have known we were about to be murdered!'

'I know but—'

'But what?'

'Well, I've been thinking and I just can't believe it of Martin, is all.'

'Is this Martin your lord?' Pavlina wished to know.

'You could say that, but it's not a term we use in G13.'

Bully said chattily, 'We normally just say "leader" though up north they're called "captains" and in G20—'

'Lords can be turned. I strongly recommend that you do *not* share our plans with this creature.'

'Well,' Bully admitted, 'we don't have to. After all, we're just getting on with the mission – we're just doing what he ordered us to do. But now that this link has started functioning, what's to stop him from calling us?'

'Not a damn thing – but we don't have to answer. Pretend there's too much interference to get the signal.'

This was not, by the way, quite as stupid as it sounded. When I was a teen, there was no interference to speak of, even in outer space. By the 2070s, even in inner space, it was a different story: dust clouds, radioactive matter, detritus from some long-spent weapon or ancient satellite, any bloody thing.

I rather enjoyed the idea that Martin couldn't reach me; I also enjoyed the idea of being in complete command. But, not having slept more than an hour the night before the mission, there was one idea I liked even more.

'Bully, I don't know if it's because my stomach's in the wrong place or because the wound's still bleeding, but would it be OK if I slept a bit?'

'I will take your place,' said Pavlina.

'How'd you learn so much about blinguards, anyhow?' Bully inquired respectfully, and I fell asleep to those Thumbelina-like tones: 'Lord Rafael... Xirfell... small enough to be smuggled under... various situations of a serious nature...'

And so the gromeline took my place, twig-like arms folded, staring critically at the computer before her, while I bunkered down on the floor, shoved some rough canvas over my tester head and slept.

24

When I woke up, a creamy sunrise swelled iridescent over the whole sky – not just a square of it. I'd forgotten how lovely the Earth was, when not obscured by acidic dust and a patina of cloudy film.

Then Bully spoke. 'Um, boss? We're maybe twenty minutes away.'

I was on my feet in an instant. Martin's intelligence was that the King was due back late afternoon, local time. But it would have been madness to fly straight in. Instead, the plan was to land in a nearby clearing and to make our way on foot to the encampment, hoping that the blinguard would still be there if we ever got back.

'I'll just get my jacket,' I said.

Bully was still wearing his, though it was a little too small, and his ample belly forced the mid-section open. Basically, he looked like a street fug with a craving for sweets. Buttoning up my own, I grunted, 'And Pavlina? In your backpack?'

'We voted you shove her in your pocket.'

I was about to object when I caught sight of those ruby eyes. 'Assuming the lady is willing,' I said, while secretly thinking that her best chance, if captured, would be to play dead, close her eyes and look as much like a local bat as possible.

Landing was bound to be the trickiest bit, as none of us –

not even the gromeline – had ever landed a blinguard before. She showed me the grey switch that 'shadowed' the blinguard, cloaking its contours and muting its engines so that we would be less noticeable during the preparation stage. The instant I pressed it the windows darkened as if a silver-grey film had been dropped over us, and I worried that the engines had cut out entirely.

As we pushed lower over the area, I spotted the royal blinguard. Several floors high, stupendously gilded and lavishly ornamented, it reminded me of the jewel-encrusted equipage that had carried MF to his death in the Colosseum.

Good taste was never a Xirfell thing.

The field we'd targeted was only about fifty metres square, and almost denuded of grass but it turned out there was a thorny bush in the middle that hadn't appeared on the satellite. Either way, it was too late to abort, so I gritted my teeth and pressed on.

'First the left bar, all the way down,' ordered Pavlina. 'Now, very slowly, the right one forward, but not too far.'

There was a nervy moment when the engine really did cut out, and the blinguard made a rather sickening swoop as we scooped down to Earth. Mindful of the bush, I decided to ease to the left at the last second, but still we grazed it, ending up at a slightly weird angle. A second later I heard a soft, 'I feel slightly unwell, Bullivant.'

Bully rushed to release the gromeline while I stilled my dancing heart. *We did it! We landed a frigging blinguard in the heart of enemy territory!*

This was before nerves kicked in. Then: *we've landed a frigging blinguard, etc., and are about to be surrounded and foully murdered.*

Weapon in hand, I pressed the door release and, well, it felt just like home – though after the green, sweet light of Macedonia, the air hit my nostrils sourly. We were probably about as far from G13 as we could be, but the atmosphere had the same swampy humidity and heavy radioactive content as the giant-snake-ridden G13. But there was no time to drink in its delights, because the sooner we got away from the stolen blinguard the better. I wheeled round. 'Everybody OK? Then I'll swipe Pavlina and we're off. Bully, remember, two steps behind me. Not an equal. Oh, hang on – weapons check.'

Silently we both checked and double-checked. Then, just as I turned, Bully asked, 'Could we…'

'Could we what?'

'Could we maybe shake hands, or something? I mean, just in case—'

My 'Yeah, right' – because I was itching to get on – dead-heated with the lady's rather stiff 'Naturally!' but Bully and I were both as delicate as porcelain when brushing that tiny paw, for fear of breaking miniature bones. Then I placed her in my coat pocket and strode off, with Bully trudging a couple of steps behind.

I was actually far less confident than I probably appeared. While secretly wondering whether we shouldn't have camouflaged the blinguard – just in case we got lucky, needed to swipe a snappy getaway and discovered it missing-in-action – I was busy processing Tim's advice: 'Power walk, power feel, power drive forward. Basically, stride like a bear.'

Of course, if Martin had really been turned, there remained the possibility that he had tipped off the local testers to zuge us on sight. Despite this, I'd rarely felt more alive than when striding through the waste ground towards the edge of the army encampment. Until I was challenged, anyway.

'Password?'

For one black second it was gone. Then, I told them, 'FJN354.'

A grunt, then, 'What the fuck's with the fug?'

'My father's fug,' I glowered. 'I swore never to desert him, the odorous louse. When does the King leave?'

'Not till the princess arrives.'

'Which princess d'you mean?'

'Ravene, of course. Wounded at the front. Don't you listen to the fucking bulletins?'

I was secretly shocked but stayed expressionless. Perhaps Bully didn't, because my brother tester instantly hit him. 'As for you, keep your ugly eyes straight ahead, jackass!'

'Hands off my father's fug! Was the princess badly injured?'

'I don't know. *Yeruwoq!*'

'*Yeruwoq!*' I responded. (Meaning: 'May right prevail!') As we moved on, I muttered, 'You OK, Bully?'

'No worries.'

'Pavlina?'

'I am prepared.'

I was challenged at several other checkpoints but they hadn't altered the passwords. Each time this happened I felt a trickle of relief, and even an uptick of faith in Martin... Most of the testers we met were my inferiors, but, eventually, we encountered a tester colonel. 'Are we so desperate for workers we have to put up with fugs?' he joked, to sycophantic laughter from his mates. 'Have you come from the front, brother?'

I growled, 'No, brother. It goes well?'

He cursed, then, 'They're like grass in June. We cut them down and new ones spring up!'

My heart constricting, I couldn't help marvelling at the stamina and determination of these gutsy locals, when we in G13 remained so feeble and so few...

Bully's appearance seemed to arouse a grudging respect. One tentacled alien even cursed him, adding, 'Blasted fugs! Best fighters those fucking rebels have. But I'd keep yours out of sight, if I were you. The King's blurg likes 'em, barbecued.'

'Nobody barbecues my father's slave,' I rasped. 'Any grub?'

'Not until the King's ass is out of sight. You might get a snack in the far tent.'

As I turned to stalk off, hoarse laughter erupted behind me. ('Jackass! Imagine believing that we'd be fed at this hour! What a *tortif!*') Furious with myself I walked even harder, until the gromeline raised a point of order. 'Is it completely necessary to jam your hand in your pocket quite so hard?'

'So sorry. I forgot.' Then I turned and pretended to upbraid my 'slave'. 'Fucking *tortif!* Can't you keep up? I *thren* my father for my promise to protect you!'

Hoarse laughter and tester applause were my reward – I felt accepted again. But I had no time to relish the appreciation of my fellow assholes, because there was suddenly a stentorian blast, as if ten or twelve discordant morumbas were being sounded simultaneously. I sank to one knee with all the rest, my hearts hammering hard enough to deafen the hidden gromeline.

The King! – and, almost certainly, my death.

But it wasn't the King, after all. Instead a canopied carrier appeared, and on it a patient, waxen though still stunning, her irises precisely bisected, her brilliantly-lit hair haloing her pillow.

And here, unknown accessor of my memory-sliver, I must ask you to recall your own first love, in order to understand my confusion. Because my own first love was before me – impulsive, impetuous, imperious – though always faithful 'in her fashion'. There she was – to make it worse, wounded – the half-human I'd always cared about more than I'd admitted. For all these reasons, as I knelt, there could be no more messed-up tester than me.

Languidly gazing at us, she suddenly said, 'Wait! And which are you?'

Publicity I could live without.

And I, half-glancing round, half-rising, could only query, 'Lady?'

Because there was nothing to distinguish me from all the others, other than the hidden gromeline. OK, one tester might have a rather higher hairline, another slightly burlier shoulders, but –

believe me – we were all testers. Visually speaking, an acquired taste. Though I couldn't help wondering, might Ravene have acquired it?

'Attend me,' she murmured.

The suspicion of my fellow testers was brutal. I was bumpily escorted by about six of my fellows, along with Bully, who was escorted more viciously still. (I had no idea that fugs were so despised – I should never have brought him!) Inside the chamber – a hastily slung-up tent – the princess's litter was lowered, while pundlings rushed to provide her with delicacies, including tangerines, avocados, roasted artichokes and several imports from some other planet which I couldn't put a name to.

Close to, she looked pale, those bisected irises flooded with colour, which I seemed to remember was a symptom of rebirth. A pundling offered her some drink which appeared partly alive – I had to force my eyes away, as its movement dizzied me. Then she fixed untranslatable eyes on my face.

'Strangely,' she said, 'I feel that I know you, *horvel*.'

She was calling me 'underling'.

'Lady?'

The looks of black hatred from some of the other testers were so threatening that Ravene ordered them to depart, while I hastily told Bully, '*Tortif*, remain.'

'I wish to see this tester alone,' she said curtly.

I tossed my coat, the gromeline still inside its pocket, to Bully, who caught it just before he was bumped away. Then I said, 'Lady, I am true to your *ywitr* father, may he live forever.'

The lie, of course, did not concern me. What did was a sudden, passionate feeling rising irrepressibly inside. (Tim: 'A tester is pretty much up for doing it anywhere, anytime and with a paper napkin. Annoying in some ways, if rather convenient in others.') I attempted to keep my gaze from straying to those spectacular legs. Where was her blinking wound, anyway? She looked still more appealing with this fragile pallor – perhaps more like the late queen?

Ravene shifted into a sitting position and flinched. She spoke almost to herself, as if I was too stupid to understand. 'You're ugly, of course, but then, you're all ugly. But there's something different about you. You remind me of someone I first knew years ago.'

Might not have been me, of course. Always sought-after, Ravene. The legs, mostly. She turned her head, reminding me that her profile was tops, as well. My erection was, I hoped, disguised by my uniform.

She continued, 'He was human. Good-looking – not stunningly good-looking, but still handsome – well-built, clever, amusing. Tenten was his name, you might have heard of him? He was only recently executed.'

So the King had lied even to Ravene, his favourite child and acknowledged heir.

As some answer seemed expected, I rasped, 'A known rebel. A known traitor, lady.'

'A traitor to us, perhaps, but utterly true to his own people. You must realise, *hircht*, that I am part-human? My siblings constantly remind creatures of this, in hopes that I might be discounted in the succession.'

I knew all this, of course. Whether most testers would have, I hadn't a clue. I stood in the approved tester pose: staunch, wooden, dull.

Ugly too, I bet.

'Perhaps that's why I remember him so warmly. Of course, he was impulsive, stubborn, in some ways difficult, but his humanness somehow spoke to me. I've never since—' She lapsed back into thoughtfulness, while I kept wondering why the hell she was telling me this.

'He had such feeling! Everything with Aiden was always so

wonderfully in the moment! There was a time, I remember, we were on a balcony—'

Oh God, I remembered that too. Almost fell off the bloody thing.

I shifted uneasily as she said, almost dreamily, 'And then, and then, another time – we were on a picnic with other students. It was autumn in the overland and somehow one could still sense it, even deep below – perhaps some movement in the air, some atmosphere, some sense of leaves being trodden, decaying, into the dark earth... The picnic was in one of those *kycnm* fields with false-rainbowed skies and grass that never smells right. Aiden and I drifted away from the others. We had been dancing – did I mention the music? – but why on earth am I telling you this?'

Search me.

But beneath both my hammering hearts I was still bewitched. That rainbow-textured sky, that music, that day... Sternly, I attempted to think of Bully, of Pavlina, of any bloody thing, just to break the spell.

This didn't work. Instead, I was also caught up in remembering. Ravene, casting her gaze backwards in the Academy corridor. Ravene waiting in the disabled loo, hair already rapturously dishevelled. Ravene winning the badminton tournament, with that perfected eye. Ravene sliding her palm into my pocket in the refectory... I tried to remember Petra, but she lacked vitality, in comparison. It was as if Ravene had tossed diaphanous silks over everything that wasn't ourselves – young and handsome, young and full of hope, young and full of glory, the way the young are.

She sighed, stirred, and continued. 'We left the others, just the two of us. We – oh, I don't suppose you understand for one single second what I'm talking about! – but luckily, you're far too stupid to understand. At any rate, we left the others under that great canopy of false sky. And above it there was a crack, and through it

– like a gift – a slice of real sky. And he took me, just there, under that—'

She had been gazing into the distance. She glanced over at me and wriggled discontentedly. 'What an apish expression you all have!'

As for me, I was still trying to look like the dimmest tester going. As much as I was feeling glad about anything, I was glad that I had shoved Bully out with the gromeline. My erection was – and here I must apologise for being graphic – completely overpowering.

(Sometimes I wish I'd been born female, though I bet I'd have been rubbish at it.)

'Lady, just tell me what to do,' I growled, as politely as I was able. 'Command me. A drink, a pundling, an attendant—'

She half-rose on her elbow, staring at me. Both of my hearts stopped.

'Say that again!'

I glowered – with any luck apishly. 'A drink, a pundling? You may command—'

'Aiden! It *is* you!'

I retreated, my hearts leaping like a pair of racing trout. 'Lady—'

'Come here,' she ordered, as every atom in my body tugged me towards her. 'Closer!'

I obeyed. She smelled like the sea. My soul – my shining youthful soul – glowed in those bisected eyes. She said suddenly, 'It is you, it is!'

I recalled Bully, Pavlina, the vow I had made to Sebastian. I also remembered Martin's orders ('No going off-piste, no fucking the princess…') I said, desperately, 'Lady, I am Technior, satellite 532, lieutenant of Amber 421.' And then, as loud as my ratcheted tones would carry, 'The princess is faint, and mistakes me for human scum! Assistance! Assistance!'

Why nobody heard – why nobody came – I'll never know.

'Shut up and do it,' she hissed. And how could I refuse? I was already all sensation: her feverish urgency overwhelming any objections – which were anyway notably unimpressive. About the next bit I don't remember much: a swirl of tumultuous sensation, an attempt not to press against her bandage, a sensation of overpowering sweetness. I also remember imprisoning those endless legs, and a struggle to control, even to throttle back on, the kind of urgency which I'd never before imagined possible. Holding back – holding back – poised on the edge of torrential glory – eventually overruled with internal white-water rapids, an electric fury fired within the blood.

Lucky bastards, these testers!

Afterwards, I was again embroiled in internal combat, not with my tester drive but with my human soul. More conflicted than I'd ever felt in all my life, it was as if MF – and not only MF, but the entire rebellion – was striving against me.

–An ideal chance to kill her. That perfect throat is at your mercy. She throbs with pleasure, back arched, body glowing – you couldn't have posed her any better!

–No way. I was sent to kill her father, after all.

–No rebel in the history of the world will ever have a better chance! And she's weakened, too – probably reincarnating, partly in love…

–I can't kill any creature in cold blood.

–You mean, you still care about the witch.

–You sound like MF!

–I am MF. I am Sebastian, and Priscilla. I am the voice of the rebellion that owns you, body, mind, soul… Your duty is to kill her, for the good of every creature on Earth, for the planet's own last chance!

A great wave of sorrow ached my throat. Ravene stirred. 'What's wrong, Aiden?'

'Nothing to do with you,' I said roughly, because, as for pretending that I wasn't me, that would have been as impossible as killing her.

I'm not saying that I was in love with Ravene – I'd have had to be insane, as she was so changeable, so tempestuous, so blinking superficial – but I'd been in love with her once, and I couldn't forget it. Plus, there's this massive difference between 'being in love with' and 'loving'. Ravene and I had been in love once, and I'd unwittingly been tipped into loving her since. Which was probably why it had shaken me to learn that she'd been fighting. But what should I do?

'Take me again,' she whispered, her soft breath tickling my ear. But I couldn't. Not even a tester could, once feeling takes over. Instead, I sat up, sharpish.

'I still can't believe you effing spotted me!'

'People have – atmospheres, Aiden. Auras.'

'They also have purposes. At least, some people do.'

'Have you come for my father?' she whispered. A tendril of glowing hair tickled my cheek; my tester prick disturbed me once again.

'I have,' I admitted, more harshly than I had intended, recalling my rash leap from beside Ichthus's litter. Then I remembered something else.

'Ravene, was it really you, in that interview? You sounded so strange!'

'No,' she said, reaching over for one of the artichoke slices. 'It was *not* me. My father thought, since we had been lovers, that he should use my double instead. She could be trusted to say exactly what he ordered, was the reason. Do you want a slice?'

'No, thanks. And afterwards he sent that shapeshifter to kill me, right?'

'No, my father wished you to stand trial for those murders. He blamed Uval for the shapeshifter. They shouted and shouted about it until I got tired and went away… But how did you escape?'

'I shot the Creature's tank,' I said shortly.

'I *thought* it was you!'

'To be honest, Ravene, it wasn't such a hot idea. Lots of people died – and Leelack was recaptured. You probably weren't told all that.'

'No, we were told,' she said, with that casualness I recalled so well, 'but – I knew it was you!'

'But your father still told you that I was dead. Doesn't that bother you at all?'

'He lied to us, but I can understand it. You were too dangerous, after the interview, after the escape. Your name had to die; your *power* had to die. You had got up to number three.'

'Number three what?'

'Number three of wanted creatures. Your price in kadrills was something fantastic!' Then she added mischievously, 'Now that you're alive again I should denounce you – but I don't need any money, do I? So instead you must tell me about your other women, and how they're not as good as me.'

'Ravene—'

'Oh, never mind! Then, just do it again. Just in case.'

She meant, in case it was the last, the very last, and her warm, warm hand moved down between my massive legs. But I didn't think that the shot was on the board.

Although – oddly enough – turned out that it was. The tester me could probably do it all year long. While the real me kept thinking, with that constriction in my throat, *the last*. Within the hour, I would either be dead or else estranged from Ravene – this time, forever.

But, before you write me off as the feeblest – if possibly the sexiest – operative in rebel history, I was also hatching a back-up plan, and, even as she was aching with pleasure so deeply as to be immobilised, I was trapping that turquoise hair inside one hammer-like hand and swiping that silk belt around her mouth with the other.

Ravene struggled furiously but stood no chance. Her belt also provided an admirable gag, the only risk being that she might still be able to moan – but then her bodyguards hadn't exactly distinguished themselves when I'd yelled for assistance, had they? I had her trussed and bound to the bed in no time, secretly hoping that the King's guards would prove as pathetic as the princess's… Finally, just to be sure, I tore an extra bit of cloth from her skirt and knotted the belt tightly around it.

'Sorry,' I told her, 'but you know the alternative.' Her shapely bum twitched furiously – but by then I was already listening at the door.

Cracking it open, I spotted maybe twenty testers at the far end of the tent, but they all seemed noisily intent on their gambling. As I entered, the tester sergeant swivelled round, registered my ID on his device, and urged, 'No, no, you fool! Seven! Go for *seven*!'

I slipped out of the outer door, swinging my shoulders in the approved fashion. This exit was also guarded, but only by a junior tester. I shoved him powerfully against the tent. 'You! Where's my father's fucking fug?'

'Unharmed! They took him to the pits.'

'Where the fuck are the pits?'

He stared, surprised. 'Level sub-eight, of course!'

I didn't dare ask where level sub-eight might be. 'And the King, may he live forever?'

'Delayed.'

'Until?'

'No one knows.'

I stalked off, as apishly as I could manage. The next junior tester I spotted I clouted on the jaw. 'Where the fuck's sub-eight?' I grunted.

'Side escalator fifteen, sir!'

'Then go there instantly and fetch me the fug, Bullivant. Now – or your eyeballs to the blurg!'

'Yes, sir! At once, sir!'

Frowning blackly, I strode towards the centre of the camp, where Ravene had appeared. We seemed to have been gifted a little extra time. But what if Ravene was – even at that moment – in the process of being freed? What if somebody had spotted the gromeline? What if Bully and Pavlina had been separated, even imprisoned? What if the junior tester couldn't retrieve them in time? And – if I nailed the King and was immediately cut to pieces – how would the others manage to escape? Bully should still be armed, but everything else would be against them.

There seemed to be a new sense of urgency and purpose in the centre of camp, and nobody was messing about playing nocxmow anymore. Instead, it was: 'Get out of my way, *tortif!*'... 'Where the fuck's the music sergeant got to?'... 'Only a few minutes to go!'

Heart pounding, I thought that it could only be a matter of seconds before Ravene was discovered, the alarm raised, and every lieutenant of my order either shot or arrested.

Suddenly those discordant instruments could be heard, closer than before, and everyone again paused in order to go down on one knee – or the alien equivalent. I lowered myself with the rest, my hand just above my weapon, just as a bizarrely extrovert royal litter rolled into view. And, in that moment, my every worry quietly vanished. I'd been transformed: from a nervy operative to an agent of rebel vengeance.

I couldn't help recalling the chilled millimetres I'd been calculating the last time I saw the King. Then I'd been guarded, unarmed and gifted with nothing beyond enhanced calves and personal fury – now, I was unguarded, disguised, fully armed and braced at point-blank range. Barring some last-second intervention, this had to be the last moment of the King's life.

The royal litter edged closer, closer. But just as I silently removed the electronic catch on the gun, I felt a little tug on my boot. Glancing down, I spotted the gromeline, neatly inserting herself between sock and ankle.

Little fathead. I longed to pick her up and kick her like a minute rugby ball. I hissed, 'Get away from me! Do you want to fucking die? In about two seconds, I'll be cut to pieces!' But she'd burrowed herself securely, and – suddenly – there were no seconds left.

The King's wide-set eyes and robust build were just as I remembered, and so was that self-satisfied leer. He waved a dismissive hand in acknowledgement of our tributes and said something – a flash of teeth – to the tester walking beside him.

Time was telescoping. ('Brace the left thumb, allow for recoil.')

Closer, closer. ('Hold fire till the last possible second.')

Now.

I whipped out the F86 and fired, perfectly, into the exact centre of his chest. The King seemed to fold in on himself, almost in slow-motion, just as something heavy landed on my back.

What the fuck was Bully doing on top of me?

Then about a million things started happening at once. The testers were all shouting and yelling, all pretence at discipline lost. Caring little pundlings were rushing towards the King. The ranking tester was raking the area with shots. That strange spider-creature swivelled its every eye in my direction.

Suddenly *everything misted over*. Had I been shot? Was this what death felt like?

It was as if a gossamer sheath had been inserted between the world and me. Even the sounds, even the shots the other testers were blasting, some at short range, seemed eerily muffled. While humans, Xirfell, testers, robotniks and aliens were randomly shooting, yelling or firing off warnings – 'What happened? Who shot him? Where's the fucker gone?' – I had to strain to hear anything above the anarchy of my twin hearts.

This moment seemed to last for several weeks but was probably only a fraction of a second. Then, with Bully bouncing on my back and Pavlina's claws spiking my ankle, I was sprinting out of that smoke-blasted madhouse and into the humidity outside, passing bellowing testers and panicked pundlings. My boots gradually clogging up with mud, I was running – running faster than I'd run in the entire course of my life – away from the encampment, across a couple of fields and towards our abandoned blinguard.

And, in a shorter time than seemed possible – I could probably have run for decades, even with Bully on my back – I'd burst through the hedge and there it was – an exquisite sight – our dusty, dented blinguard, still angled jazzily atop that bush. We tumbled inside – the gromeline somersaulting, Bully ungracefully, me in a single bound – already reaching for the lever. For a second I thought, *What the fuck do I pull?* – Then, blessedly, remembered.

And it was bloody lucky I'd been nippy, because just then Bully yelled, 'They're after us!' just as two of my fellow testers loped into the field and started firing. One shot jarred the blinguard but failed to alter our trajectory as we zigzagged upwards – *not* a great take-off – but within seconds we were out of range of any hand-held device. Though, if they had raised the alarm fast enough, we could still get nailed by a missile.

Bully, as if reading my mind, started weaving. I heard a little moan and warned, 'Careful! Pavlina's bouncing around back there!'

'Sorry,' breathed Bully, and I managed to push Pavlina back into her space and wedge her in. As so often, she was slightly frowning. She was also injured, a trickle of spangled liquid slipping down her ear.

'Should I be doing something about that?'

'Just get back to the controls!' she snapped, and I obeyed, adding, 'Thanks for saving our bacon. I didn't know you could do – whatever it was you did.'

'Humans are extremely ignorant of what gromelines can do.'

'So are fugs,' said Bully fervently.

After another ten minutes I declared us out of range of any ruddy thing and leaned forward to catch my breath against the controls. The sense of relief was, briefly, overwhelming. I was intensely curious about Pavlina's 'trick' but first I had to know, 'I did kill him, didn't I?'

'No question,' Bully told me. 'Sebastian is avenged!'

Sebastian. Malthus. Ichthus. Priscilla's parents. My own adoptive parents. The whole of broken Earth. And by then, perhaps, Petra might even have heard what we'd done. My adrenalin levels, which had dipped, skied again. I asked, 'So what happened underground?'

'Well, I've been to better parties. We got dragged below by a couple of testers, me clutching your coat with Pavlina in it, the testers all pushing and shoving. One of them had my ear – still feels as if he fucking tore half of it off. Anyway, down below was this ancient, abandoned coal mine, full of cells, mostly with prisoners in them, all damp, dark and horrible.

'We just got dumped in a room, not a cell. Then a tester tried to grab the coat with Pavlina inside, so I howled as how my tester would kill us both if I lost it, and he saw sense. It was freezing, but way better than being locked up in one of those rancid cells. And after a bit this young tester rushed in yelling, "The fug, where's the fucking fug?" and someone told him, and he dragged me out. Once he got us upstairs he got a bit panicky trying to find you, and almost every tester who saw me kicked me. One even yelled, "It's a fug spy!" but I just sat there looking dim until he decided I was too thick to be any effing thing.

'Then I spotted you, and that was when Pavlina took over.

She ordered me to wait until you appeared to vanish and then to jump onto your back and hang on. She was amazing, so calm and assured! She never hesitated. Instead, she—'

'Might I inquire which of you is in command of the blinguard?' a rather disapproving little voice interrupted. Bully switched to the controls as I leaned down and solemnly shook that tiny paw, and I thanked her. Then, while Bully was piloting, I started searching for a newsflash, a bulletin – for any confirmation that the King was dead.

But there was nothing. Perhaps Ravene was too busy taking over – unless something serious had happened since. After all, several of her half-siblings – Uval particularly – were capable of mounting a palace coup.

Unless the King wasn't dead after all?

'What coordinates, ah, boss?'

'East.'

'But where east?'

'Macedonia, of course. After that, we'll go home.'

'Home?' Bully echoed, and suddenly any remaining elation seeped out of me. Because, until we learned whether Martin really *had* set us up, did we even have a home? – And exactly at that moment, Martin surfaced on the screen, leaning forward as if intent upon invading our physical space.

'Ho Chi? Darius? Aiden? Is anybody *there*?'

I mimed slitting my throat with my hand and Bully instantly cut the connection.

'Aiden?' demanded the gromeline sharply. 'Aiden *Tenten*?'

It seemed churlish to deny it, to this self-contained little creature who had just saved my life. I said, 'Um, yeah, that's me. I told you I was just borrowing this body.'

'I see.'

I couldn't tell if she was disappointed or if she had already suspected that her hero might really be the swearing, nervy, real-life tester-me. Or maybe she was just annoyed I hadn't trusted her in the first place? – People can be odd that way. Barring the faint wheeze from the tester's bullet-hole, it suddenly felt pretty quiet in the blinguard.

'Well?' asked Bully. 'Do we contact Martin – or not? You're in charge.'

That almost primeval pang that I wasn't. That Martin was. I said, 'Just give me half a sec.'

'If I might venture a suggestion, *Aiden*,' piped up a voice from behind, with rather an emphasis on my name. 'I would like to propose that you lay a trap for this Martin person.'

'What kind of a trap?'

'I suggest that Bullivant pretends that you were actually killed in the Xirfell encampment. You might, conceivably, be able to tell, from his reaction—'

'Brilliant! Aiden, you should be dead!'

'And that could easily be arranged,' added Pavlina, 'should you not take evasive action. Look at the screen.'

'Another blinguard!' yelled Bully.

I was on it in a millisecond. In the history of the universe, no tester has ever moved faster than me.

'What, Bully, only one?'

'Yeah, yeah, there! There it is, on the right! "Blinguard, registration unknown."'

'So why are we still heading right? Push left!'

'It won't *go* farther left!'

'There must be a force field. See if there's a lock – quick!'

I struggled, battling an increasing sense of hopelessness. The unknown blinguard edged closer and closer. Were we already within missile range? Would this be the moment I went down with my ship?

Down, I thought. I said, 'Bully. Couldn't we head downwards and swerve just at the end, simply to elude the force field?'

The idea seemed to be a good one – until the ground reared up towards us, mountainous, volcanically bleak. I yanked the handle up just in time, breathing fast. What if we were surrounded by force fields? Who knows what fields the blinking Xirfell might have thrown up? But there had to be a way. We couldn't have come this far for nothing!

'It's closing on us,' said Bully tonelessly. 'It's probably bigger than we are. Way bigger, maybe.'

Was Ravene inside, watching her captain leaning on the controls? Somehow, I couldn't imagine it. But every blinguard on Earth belonged to the Xirfell – except this one. In short, there was zero possibility of there being, in inner or outer space, a neutral blinguard.

Pavlina said, 'There's something else, just on the edge of the screen. What is it?'

'Dunno,' said Bully. 'Seems to be shadowing the other blinguard. Maybe a back-up?'

I wheeled around. 'Could *we* do that, Pavlina? Shadow ourselves, I mean, the way we did when we landed past the encampment?'

She frowned. 'Perhaps. Try pressing the little button underneath the silver arrow, the one resembling an eye.'

'Whoa, stop!' yelled Bully as we soared vertically upwards.

He actually staggered while seated – never seen anyone do that before – and I thought I heard a little *pffft* noise, like air leaving a balloon, from the gromeline. But Bully was still searching. Suddenly he said, 'No, that can't be right. I bet it's this one.'

I had very little hope by then, but the renewed roar from the engine – and what I spotted on the screen – made both my hearts leap. 'No, no, it's good! It's all good! That button's turbo-charged us! We're as fast as they are now! Hard left, Bully, hard as you can!'

This time, it worked. Bumpily, roughly, we made it through the force field.

'Amazing! It must have overridden some safety mechanism!'

Bully clearly wanted to stop everything and take the blinguard apart, but engineering has never fascinated me. We all watched until it was clear that the chasing blinguards had ceased to gain on us – though they weren't exactly falling behind, either.

Then Martin re-surfaced on-screen and Bully, with an oath, blocked him again. I noticed that Martin looked rather drawn. Despite Bully's snappy shut-down, I also had a weird feeling that he was still watching me.

'Martin can track us, right?' I asked, uneasily.

'Of course,' said Bully. 'Anyone can track us, as long as they've got a working reyto – and even some kids have those. But we'll just be registered as another Xirfell blinguard, so it's no big deal. I'm thinking this car chase could go on and on. What do our fuel cells look like?'

Pavlina said, 'The larger gauge on the lower left. It looks fine, at the moment.'

'But the chase might *not* go on and on,' I objected, 'because we've only got one blinguard. The Xirfell must have thousands. So why haven't they scrambled any others to intercept? Three or four from triangulated coordinates and we've had it. Unless it's Martin chasing us, and not the Xirfell at all?'

'That's daft,' said Bully, dry-lipped. 'Where would Martin get more blinguards from?'

'Might I suggest that you weave about and attempt to lose the others, rather than wasting time in idle speculation? Assuming Bullivant is correct, we might possess the smaller and more nimble blinguard.'

I gave Bully the nod. Then I started to think.

It couldn't be Martin. But the Xirfell still had blinguards on every base. I simply couldn't fathom why they weren't cornering us. Was the regime in such turmoil that they couldn't scramble a few blinguards? They still had the frigging Golden Circle. They still had my old playmate, Ravene. Or could they be – at this very moment – organising a reception party for us in G13 instead?

I had strangely mixed feelings about G13. G13 was my home. It had been my home when I'd lived for rugby, when I'd lived for girls, when I'd lived to be famous. I could still remember it between WWIII and the invasion, when the seas were swimmable, when an evening in the city was a thrill. I even had a little nostalgia for the post-invasion Academy. (I know, I know, one of the lucky few.)

Of course, G13 had never been beautiful the way Switzerland – G4 – was beautiful; I'd always longed to do some mountain climbing in Switzerland. And I also recalled Macedonia – the green copses, the sloping hills, that curling river – with envy. But G13 had a spare, rocky, astringent beauty all its own. A red dirt beauty, a bare bones beauty, an Australian beauty. Never to see G13 again, to be permanently on the run…

I suddenly had to swipe a handrail, as Bully was taking his orders seriously. The next ten minutes were wildly confused. Down… up… left and down… right and up… powerfully straight up – then, a terrifying near-miss with a fragment of some long-abandoned satellite.

And repeat, barring the fragment.

Then a breathtakingly hard right. A nippy backward left.

And just as I was thinking that we were running a serious risk of stalling, Bully whooped, 'We lost 'em! We – no, wait, hang on. They've turned around. They've both turned around! They're heading back the other way!'

I whirled. 'But why? Why on earth would they suddenly quit chasing us? They can't *both* have a technical malfunction!'

'They've slowed right down now, look! They're just – dawdling in inner space. Doesn't look like they're very keen to rush back home, does it?'

Bully sounded gleeful; I wished I was.

'New orders?' hazarded the gromeline.

'That's where I'm going with this. Ravene, assuming she's in charge, would have tracked me to the end of the solar system. I tied her up, is why.'

'How?' Bully wanted to know.

'Never mind how! But take it from me, she was pretty pissed-off.'

'But if the King—'

'The King's *got* to be dead. Right, Bully? You saw it all.'

'He may have died' – that cool little voice – 'but the Xirfell can achieve rebirth.'

I recalled Ravene's words: 'He is anyway dying.'

I said, 'They can, of course, but the King's had his chips. This was his last go – which was why we were sent to assassinate him in the first place. Unless he had some special protective device, maybe?'

It wasn't the first time I'd fretted about this. Until the pursuing blinguards had shown up, it had been right up there with, 'What if the Xirfell have some new procedure that could have saved him?' and, 'What if he'd been wearing some kind of special barrier underneath?'

Pavlina said, 'I consider that extraordinarily unlikely. Instead, I suspect that the captains of the pursuing blinguards have just been informed that the King is dead – or that a coup has occurred. It must have been something crucial for them to abandon the chase with such suddenness. They're probably moving slowly to give themselves time to consider their political position. To back the princess or the ranking prince, perhaps?'

Bully agreed, 'Yeah, the succession is not a given. Ravene has always had enemies.'

'Ho Chi? Darius? Are you there or not?' Martin zipped back into view, pushing his thick hair off his brow, eyes bloodshot. 'Ho Chi, what the hell's going on? Aiden, answer me at once!'

Bully blocked him, while I briefly remembered those wolfish creatures I'd seen pawing at Ho Chi's corpse. Then I called the meeting to order.

'We don't know why the Xirfell blinguards were recalled, and why no other blinguards have intercepted us still strikes me as strange. But, since Martin clearly knows where we are, we need to decide whether we still trust him. This seems to me to be the crucial issue. If we trust Martin, we need new orders. If we don't... Listen, Bully, could you lie? I kind of like Pavlina's idea of your telling him that I was murdered after shooting the King.'

'Of course he can lie. Lying is an elementary accomplishment.'

Bully looked dubious. 'Couldn't I just be pissed-off?'

'Sure you could. In fact, you could be effing furious – that Martin allowed us to leave the base at the mercy of a couple of his hired assassins, and that your best mate – that would be me – was murdered in the Xirfell encampment, not four hours ago. But remember, Martin might not know that *we* know that Ho Chi and Darius were turned... He might not even know *himself* that they were turned! It's not likely, but it's still possible.'

Pavlina said thoughtfully, 'I suspect that there was some signal that this Martin expected to receive from Ho Chi – some signal that Ho Chi never lived to send. If so – *because* he never received it – he might have guessed that Ho Chi is dead, however much he might still pretend to wish to reach him.'

Bully was gazing at Pavlina with something like hero-worship. He said, 'Yeah, no wonder Martin's frantic! He's guessing that his precious plot failed, and that we continued on without Ho Chi! Maybe the whole mission was never meant to happen at all!'

Pavlina said coolly, 'Anything is possible, but perhaps the truth

– one way or the other – might soon become obvious. Perhaps you could rehearse?'

I agreed to 'be' Martin, while Pavlina took over the controls. Then I said, 'Martin here. Is that you, Bully?'

'Martin normally says—'

'Concentrate! Martin here. Is that you, Bully?'

'Martin is extremely sensitive towards the issues surrounding fugs' identity as—'

'Bully! It's fucking Martin here! Are you fucking there or not?'

'Um, hi Martin.'

'Go on.' (Pavlina, from the bleachers.)

'Hi, Martin. Yeah, I'm here all right. And am I ever fed-up!'

'What's happened?'

'What's happened is – well, you know! You set us up!'

'What on earth do you mean?'

'Martin would never—'

'Bully, you are trying my fucking patience!'

'Are you being Martin – or you?'

And so sad was his expression that I lied. 'Martin, of course!'

'OK… Right, well, you set us up! You sent us off with Ho Chi and Darius, and they tried to murder us!' And, in quite a different tone, 'You know, I still find it pretty hard to believe.'

'What do you find hard to believe?' This from the gromeline.

'Well, you don't know Martin, of course, and he's not a very warm person – but still, he follows every rule, he ticks every box, he gets everything right. He's just not imaginative enough to betray anybody! It's just not the kind of thing he would *do*!'

Me, sharpish: 'Bully, you never know what people will do until they frigging do it. Look at Ho Chi and Darius – and what happened to Pavlina's friend Rafael! You need to treat Martin as if you were surveying unknown territory. Is it safe? Is it ours? Can we go there?'

'OK, thanks. I'll try. Where was I?'

We persisted a little longer, but Bully's first attempt had probably been his best, so Pavlina and I decided that he was to stick to stolid fuglike fury and not to get frigging distracted. Then we retreated well out of sight, while he moved to the pilot's seat, opened the communication, keyed in the connection and cleared his throat like a blinking yengij singer.

There was no immediate response. Instead, it was the usual, unfocussed, chaotic, rebel turmoil from the other end. ('He *has* to be dead'... 'I don't believe it'... 'But if you're right, who the fuck swiped our intercept?')

Bully had to yell to be noticed. 'Hello? Hello? Anybody there?'

Then it was all, 'Get Martin!'... 'Where's he gone, for chrissakes?'... 'Well hey, at least Bully's still alive!'

Sometimes the rebellion seemed such a pathetic, two-bit operation.

Eventually Priscilla was shoved on as Martin's back-up. She looked exhausted, with the same pinched expression as when she'd been carrying The Enlightened One's poison. 'Bully? Bully, it's me, Priscilla! Can you see me? You look blurry.'

'I can see you, Priscilla. It's just the usual interference.'

'So, you're back on the blinguard? But what about Aiden? Surely they didn't capture him again! And what about the King?'

'He killed the King. But then—'

'He did? Oh Bully, you've all done wonderfully! But was he recaptured?'

We'd all done wonderfully. I let that sink in. I forced myself to remain perfectly still, a great lump of muscled tester covered by canvas – the gromeline, like a soft-furred little bat, beside me.

'No,' said Bully and then huskily added, 'No, they didn't capture him, exactly.'

Give that boy an Oscar. Priscilla seemed to almost crumple.

'Get Martin,' she whispered. And, almost a shriek, 'Get Martin!'

Meanwhile I huddled, cheek pressed to that chilled, shuddery floor, feeling absurdly like Tom Sawyer overhearing his own funeral. Eventually, Martin arrived. He was frowning, and behind him were a whole slew of creatures, most of whom I recognised.

'Shoot, Bully,' said Martin heavily. 'We can guess what you have to say.'

'Can you? Can you?' Bully was working himself up nicely. He suddenly seemed to be a bigger, bolder street-fug.

'In that something's happened to Aiden, yes, we do guess.'

'We lost him!' said Bully with subdued ferocity.

'You mean that they captured him – or that they killed him?'

'He was jumped by five or six testers and *murdered*. I saw it! I was there! But that isn't even the worst!' His voice rose, in honest, fuglike fury. 'Just listen, listen up, everybody! Aiden was murdered, but he knew that might happen. What we *didn't* know was that Martin himself had already set us up to be murdered – before we even reached the King's encampment! Ho Chi was turned – and Darius too – and Martin knew all about it! Because—'

'Enough!' snarled Martin. 'Cut the connection! Cut the connection! CUT IT, I tell you!'

If I hadn't already been on the floor I'd probably have jumped as high as poor Bully. I'd never heard Martin's voice whip like that, and I'd known him since our schooldays. His face looked almost contorted, as he screamed about the connection.

For whatever reason – other than the trademark rebel confusion – this didn't immediately happen. Instead there were all kinds of noises off.

'*What* did he say Martin did?'

'Ho Chi would never—'

'Cut the connection! Cut the effing *connection!*'

Over it all Bully stoically continued: 'You ordered Ho Chi and Darius to kill us! You set us up! You set us up! You set us up!'

Then, suddenly, everyone disappeared with a shallow hiss, leaving nothing behind but the hum and buzz of our engines through inner space. I rose and gripped Bully's shoulder, maybe harder than I'd intended. I said, 'Well, I don't know what you think, buddy, but it seemed to me that Martin's heart remains unbroken.'

'I rattled him, didn't I?' said Bully, looking up with hope.

'He seemed pretty fucking rattled, to me. What do you think, Pavlina?'

'I do not know this lord. But he appeared both guilty and angry, to me.'

'Angry at being found out, you think?'

'Exactly. You did very well, Bullivant.'

I agreed. 'Absolutely! Not even Martin could shut you up!'

Bully, embarrassed, shoved the Xirfell teleview back on. Then he suddenly cried out. Because – yes! There I was, at last! Though not even my closest friends would have recognised me. (What a plug-ugly tester I was!)

The announcer declaimed: 'The King has today survived an attempted assassination by a turncoat tester. The rebel, whose identity has yet to be released, can be observed here daring to attack His serene and beneficent Majesty, before being overcome by the King's own valiant forces.'

I was among about thirty other testers and perhaps a hundred other creatures I'd mostly failed to notice at the time. (What *was* the spidery one, anyhow? The latest Xirfell weapon?)

As the King appeared, there was the usual mass obeisance, fanning out from that glittering litter. One tester accidentally backed into a pundling carrying a diamond-covered goblet, and there was a brief comic turn as both pundling and goblet were upended.

When I fired, the King folded in on himself, precisely as I remembered. But then reality bowed out, because an enormous tester thudded onto my back – where Bully had really been clinging – after which about twelve other gigantic testers – sparing no effort – leaped right on top of him. Basically, think an old-fashioned rugby scrum with self cast as ball – the kind of test not even a tester could have survived.

Even though this was utter fabrication – as much a lie as Ichthus's death rattle beneath my fingers – the very idea of being smothered still stopped my breath. Then, 'The fucking cheats! There's no *way* he could have survived!'

'They've made what I told Martin *true!*' Bully gasped.

'I can well believe it,' said Pavlina.

We watched and listened all over again.

As for a turncoat tester, the idea was absurd – testers couldn't be turned. You'd have more luck trying to 'turn' a table! But maybe the average creature might not know that? The average worker, the citizen in the street – what did they really know about testers?

'Wait, look!' marvelled Bully. 'How weird is that? We're not even in camera-shot, Pavlina and me! I should have been *there* – just behind that robotnik – but I'm not!'

Our silence sobered him instantly; his fuggy face fell. 'You mean, we got spotted, and excised from the record books?'

'Well, *you* got spotted and excised. There's still a chance that the gromeline wasn't.'

'You mean, before she turned invisible.'

Here Pavlina tried, for about the fiftieth time, to explain that the gromeline's talent was not actual invisibility, but something to do with fooling molecules into exactly matching the colouration adjacent to them, and sharable only with creatures in direct contact.

Whatever.

I suspected that the Xirfell hadn't a clue about the gromeline's party trick, mostly because they weren't interested in delicate, subtle little aliens like gromelines. The creatures that fire the

Xirfell's blood are mostly insanely powerful, mega-bloodthirsty or super-showy. Basically, the Creature is a Xirfell thing – gromelines, not so much. There was something almost comforting in this – something feeding my hope that someday we should be able to overthrow the regime, deploying subtlety instead of power.

Although the result – the real result, not the doctored result being broadcast – must surely have screamed 'gromeline' to at least a handful in the regime, at least. No other creature I'd ever seen or heard of could have enabled us to escape unmolested – as even the Xirfell were bound to discover at some point.

We checked the clip twice more, in search of clues. The King's body was certainly hustled off. (The old bastard, dead by my hand. Though there's always something horrible about *any* creature doubled up, head drooping like a ragdoll's, eyes curtaining.)

I pressed the off switch. 'So. They know about you, Bully – and they'll soon guess about Pavlina. You'll probably both make the regime's "most wanted" list, now I'm dead.'

I repeated what Ravene had told me while we shoved down some food. But I still felt vaguely uneasy, so I switched the teleview back on. And there he was – the King! – speaking straight to camera.

'Today an attempt was made upon my life, which I was extraordinarily fortunate to survive. Every creature throughout the galaxy will rejoice to learn that I continue to rule as head of the beneficent Xirfell, supported by my devoted princesses and princes, alongside the deeply loyal members of the Golden Circle.'

He intoned this maddeningly, over and over, especially as his voice rose irritatingly on 'throughout the galaxy' and he was backed by faux-heroic music. For a second he seemed to shimmy before me, as if fury had shaken my vision.

Could I have failed, at such close range? – Impossible!

Admittedly, I'd been on an adrenalin high. I'd also been

distracted by the advent of an unexpected gromeline inside my sock. But I happen to be a crack shot and I'd drilled his heart at a distance of four or five metres. No creature could have survived it!… But then I was assailed by returning doubts. What if I hadn't shot the King, but some body double, instead? What if instead I'd only killed a robot – a double, like the fake Ravene in our interview?

Frustration boiling over, I punched the wall. Hurt like hell – but recalled me to my senses.

Bully, very quietly, 'We didn't see him die, Aiden.'

'I couldn't have missed him! Sophia Tenten couldn't have missed him, and she couldn't shoot a balloon in a bin! My roommate at the Academy, who—'

'He looked younger,' mused Pavlina.

'Younger than what? Springtime?'

'Younger than he looked four hours ago.'

I stopped and had another look. My memory of the King while I was in prison was unclear – I'd been utterly absorbed, I'd been calculating millimetres – but I recalled that smug smirk in the encampment perfectly. Did his jaw here seem less jowly, his eyes less heavy-lidded?

'And isn't it at least possible' – this again from Pavlina – 'that they're simply *pretending* he's still alive until they get the succession sorted?'

'They could have faked the whole thing,' agreed Bully, brightening. 'It'd be pretty simple, given a strong template – which they're bound to have of the King.'

'But they can't prop him up and stuff him and expect him to lead in a war zone!'

'Of course not, but it could still buy them time – and prevent the rebellion from getting the wind in our sails.'

'Shove it on one more time,' I ordered. I watched it idly, cudgelling my brain. Trouble was, whenever I had seen the King, it had been through an adrenalin haze: to kill him or not? To kill Ichthus or not? To stay alive – or not?

And even through a haze of the more vital Ravene. Whenever I tried to conjure up her father, I could summon up nothing more than a fit-looking guy of a certain age, those bisected eyes perhaps just a fraction *too* wide apart. What had she said? 'You were far too dangerous to be allowed to live. Even though you had escaped, your name had to die...'

Could that be what was happening, but in reverse? I was alive but had been forced by the Xirfell to 'die' – was the King, now dead, being forced to 'live'? After all, it had been decades since people had been able to mess about with the templates of iconic actors. Personal versions of the classics – with anyone you wanted in the title role, including yourself – had been around since forever. Since my interview, the template to mess about with my own face and voice must also exist – but, luckily, I was dead.

It felt weirdly freeing, being dead.

We argued the toss a bit longer but then we three decided that the King must still be dead, haha.

Yes! We bust open some of Ho Chi's beer – even the gromeline had a little – and made toasts to my death, and to the King's, and to the triumph of our mission. The beer had probably been in the blinguard since the Final War and tasted diabolical, but we didn't care.

My biggest issue was that I was stuck being a tester until I could get hold of Tim, Hugh or Atlantis without the risk of Martin's finding out. But this was a minor inconvenience, compared to the thrill of being dead. No responsibilities. No orders. A whole new astonishing life.

I did an imitation of Bully's acting. Then Bully did an imitation of me, walking. This was extremely funny. Testers' walks really are extremely funny. It's as if they all have two pricks and they're terrified that the left one might bash into the right one. Even the gromeline giggled, after her third thimbleful.

About an hour later Bully asked, 'So, where are we heading, then?' and Pavlina dictated her home coordinates. That was when I registered, for the first time, that our home wasn't the same as Pavlina's – that it wasn't even on the same continent. I tried to hide my disappointment while watching the dead King assure his rejoicing people of his continued existence, for about the trillionth time.

Of course she was going. She'd only signed up for this mission, which – though its upshot remained a little murky – was clearly over. Still, I think I'd stupidly supposed that we three would hang together, using the blinguard for other missions, perhaps. Bully was politely asking Pavlina what her plans were.

'That depends on the situation once I return,' she said crisply. 'Previously, we were ordered to assist with intelligence regarding the insurrection at the border. My group will be missing me.'

'Are you its leader, then?' asked Bully respectfully.

'Of course.'

'So we deprived your cell of its *leader*?'

'This was my choice,' she said, adding sadly, 'I had only recently been elected. Lord Rafael was our leader before.' I remembered asking her the same question in Macedonia and getting some oblique response. But – to be fair – I hadn't confessed to being Aiden Tenten, either.

As for corresponding or anything like it – well, pre-invasion, we could have kept in touch, but the interpersonal communication network had been the first thing the Xirfell had destroyed. Unless we could hang on to the blinguard, or access some similar piece of Xirfell kit, we'd never see or hear from Pavlina again… Meanwhile, Bully was eyeing her with awe, probably thinking, 'Wow, not even Aiden's a cell leader.'

This did not make me feel good.

I took over the controls while the others slept. As the blinguard surged through the darkness, it felt as if I was navigating through perpetual mist, from iron-grey to almost pearlescent, from towering thunderclouds to a few stray wisps encircling the moon. Hours passed, during which I stayed glued to my post. Strange, disconnected thoughts flickered through my mind – though the monitor insisted I was good to fly, so it couldn't have been the beer, could it?

I found myself remembering a day at school, when I'd been maybe six, maybe seven, and the last one standing when the captains were choosing soccer teams. I'd been the last, the very last, even after Toby Summers, who shied away from the ball as if it was alive and could somehow kick him back.

All I could think was, if ever there had been a calculated insult, this was it. So I shinnied up a tree, high, very high, far higher than any teacher could hope to climb after me. I watched the soccer game from the top of the tree, wondering if anyone would miss me if I jumped down and died – until I gloomily recalled that this might sink my hopes of being captain of rugby forever.

Because I never saw myself as a bit player. No, I had delusions of grandeur even at seven, with scabby knees and a ferocious frown. And when the bewildered Sophia zelopoded in and demanded an explanation, I just sat there, silent, mutinous and desperately afraid that – if I told anybody anything – I'd commit the worst possible sin for my age and sex, and cry.

That was the first time I made my vow: Someday, everyone would know my name.

So maybe it wasn't so strange that I'd 'got up to number three' – assuming that Ravene had got that right – because it takes a pretty single-minded obstinacy to become famous. And yet the people I most admired – Sebastian, Priscilla, Malthus, Joan – never seemed to care, either way.

And yes – since you asked – my birth father *had* fought off half the cabinet in order to become prime minister – but surely there comes a point when you can't blame your genes for every bloody thing?

Suddenly, the whole blinguard jolted sideways. Mugs, plates, paraphernalia were all jerked to the floor – one railing even crashing into the far wall. Bully was spilled from his seat, dead heating with my oath. Then the door blasted open and we were boarded, along with a laced whip of iced air.

Boarded, without a single warning? How was that even possible? Didn't the monitors work on this fucking machine?

Then – oh shit, a blurg! A howl from Bully – the gromeline had already disappeared.

Good call, Pavlina.

Suddenly everything went swimmy – a shock of blood in the back of my mouth. The cabin seemed crowded with creatures: testers, that blurg – and the weird spiderish alien that I'd first noticed in the Xirfell encampment.

Poor Bully had been flattened by a tester. Meanwhile, the giant spider-thing swam, first in, then out of focus. I hadn't even figured who or what had hit me before something shovelled in my massive brow.

Bye, world. The strangest sensation of release.

Along with a sense of stepping off the highest branch at last.

25

I was bound on the floor, a metallic taste in my mouth, staring up at the blinguard's silvery ceiling. Caked blood drying on my temple, my brow was still on fire, and – still worse – that fire was burrowing into me, like one of those worms from Lakdusia.

I smelled rain so I guessed we were on the ground – an oily rain, the way rain had smelled for most of my life. Still, it was a contact with the Earth and I breathed it in with a hope which was itself a joke, because what else could have happened, except that I'd been recaptured and poor Bully likewise?

I lifted my head – hurt like hell – and glanced around. I was being watched by the spidery creature: purplish-black, body about a metre square, ten or twelve legs, bulbous eyes.

Was it this that had crumpled me without actual contact? Or had that dream – so common among rebels – finally happened? Could we have been boarded by aliens capable of deceiving the Xirfell's highest level of security, who would themselves overcome our Xirfell conquerors?

No, seemed to be the answer: because I was flanked by two Xirfell testers, because this was never more than wishful thinking, and because I'd eyeballed the spidery alien – or one of its body doubles – back in the encampment. A couple of metres away was a snuffling Bully, unbound but guarded, a Tester beside him. I felt a rush of fury – what had they done to him? And what about Pavlina? Could Pavlina have escaped?

Stupid with pain, I pretended to be still stupider. I closed my eyes, opened them, closed them again, and groaned. The light did seem pretty vicious. But so would any light, considering what my brow had just been put through. There was a harsh glimmer in those multiple eyes as the giant spider thing hissed, 'Are you the traitor Tenten?'

There didn't seem much point in denying it.

'And your co-conspirator?'

I forced myself to sneer. 'You mean my slave? His hand was forced!'

'His *name*?'

'That's for him to say.'

A sheet of pain crisped through my head. The spider creature seemed able to inflict torture with a mere thought. The flame torched my tongue, even my vocal cords. For a moment my mouth wouldn't even work properly: 'I b-b-blackmailed the fug into c-coming with me. He's n-not to blame!'

Again, my whole weapons-grade tester-body shuddered. My yell emerged in instalments, in time with my two hearts, which spiked on colliding schedules, as if racing each other. Every nerve in my body felt separately blasted. Had I a suicide pill – yet another rebel fantasy – it'd have been down me so fast that the spider thing – what oiled and glistening legs it had – wouldn't have had time to blink.

We're in the endgame now.

'Where's the gromeline?' hissed the thing.

'Where's the *what*?'

This time the pain was only down half of me – but one more shot like that and half my face would be paralysed. A stroppy teacher had once advised me to remove my rebellious expression before it 'got stuck' that way. Maybe this was finally happening.

'It was seen,' the thing glared. 'It was *monitored.* Where's it gone?'

My brain raced. Could they have opened the door since the landing? Pavlina was squirrel-fast. She could be so far away that they'd have to dragnet half a continent. But what if she was simply watching from the roof of the blinguard or was quietly blended into that canvas in the corner? Even more worryingly, what if she had exhausted her invisibility or blending capability and was trappable, as she'd been when I first grabbed her?

The creature's eyes were also purplish, with a touch of glowing scarlet, just rimmed with sable. In its own way, I suppose it might even have been beautiful... My fried nerve-ends having gifted me with an idea, I mumbled something about not being able to breathe.

The thing rasped impatiently, 'Open the door, one of you!'

'No! The gromeline!' snorted the blurg. The reward for my inspiration was another stunner, this time on the reverse side. My every nerve was singing, the wound on my brow operatically.

Fuck, fuck, fuck.

The blurg said, 'What about the fug?'

'Too stupid to know anything,' was the spider thing's opinion. 'Just a slave.'

'No, no. I mean, we could torture the fug. Then Tenten might—'

'Oh, do as you please!'

The blurg's eyes gleamed with an almost lascivious light. 'I'll chew off a couple of toes. The toes are often particularly toothsome. And the testicles.'

As the blurg oiled towards Bully, I yelled, 'All right, all right, we let her out!'

The spider creature was onto this, instantly. 'What? The gromeline? It's *female?* And you released her? Where?'

'Just – just over the last border. I think.'

'Which border?'

'I – I can't remember.'

It was giving me the creeps, spindling around on those delicate legs, as if probing the blinguard's walls for secret passageways. (Where *was* Pavlina, anyway?)

'Which border?' breathed the blurg, rancid breath in my face.

'G14 – and – G7,' I gasped, as if it had been corked out of me.

This lie might buy me five minutes to think of something better. One of the testers was ordered to check out the computer log – but at some point he was bound to notice that we hadn't stopped at any effing place. Suddenly it occurred to me that the coordinates Bully had last entered – for Pavlina's home cell – would still be registered. We'd unwittingly put her entire cell in jeopardy! What had happened to the frigging alarm system, anyway? Could the blinguard's security have been hacked?

To my overheated brain, the next few minutes seemed to last forever. Then, the tester spat, 'They stopped nowhere!'

Oh, fuck, that was fast. The blurg splurged towards the controls, releasing stinkloads of bile, seized the log and then shouted, 'Search every centimetre! The gromeline must be inside!'

Now I've never been one of those humans who avidly collects random information about aliens. But I still found myself ransacking my memory for anything about gromelines that I could remember. (Almost wiped out on home planet… Wide variety in terms of colouration… Reproduce like seahorses, the father does the tending… Far greater likelihood of infant mortality in females.)

Those females would be rarer still any second now.

Meanwhile every centimetre of the blinguard was being searched. Was Pavlina invisibly thumbing her nose at their clumsy efforts? Could she possibly have slipped through some gap in the frame, and already be miles away?

The blurg was losing patience. It grunted, 'We could shut the door on the traitors and gas them. That would dispose of the gromeline immediately: their lungs are tiny.'

'We were ordered to capture the gromeline,' the spider-thing objected, still groping. 'Tenten also.'

Who did the ordering? I wondered. Could it have been Ravene?

'And the fug?' the blurg proposed. You could practically hear him salivating.

'Oh, do what you like,' returned the spidery thing impatiently, still probing, probing, with those glossy legs, into every cranny.

Was I about to see poor Bully lose a toe – or worse? The blurg advanced, dripping lumps of stinking ooze behind him, while I kicked myself for having let him come.

'Leave my slave alone!' I yelled.

And, in that second, with the wildest swoosh, we were suddenly thousands of metres in the air, and – just as when the turbo-drive first kicked in – I was seeing spangles, despite being bound to the floor.

We lurched to a halt even more sharply, and almost certainly on purpose, as most of the Xirfell testers smashed their heads so hard on the ceiling that they weren't going to bother anybody for a while – maybe ever. One of them appeared to be having some kind of a seizure. I had him shoved up against the wall the second Bully razored my cords. The spider creature was crumpled in a leggy heap.

Pavlina, of course. Who else could have started up the engine unnoticed? Though how she'd got it to kick-start in turbo I hadn't a clue.

Which just left the blurg. I spotted it out of the corner of my eye making a grab for Bully and kicked its great oily gizzard with my boot, while grabbing the nearest tester's whip. The whip – sickeningly – went straight through the blurg, which collapsed in a slew of oily rings and putrid flesh.

Bully shuddered, and then said, 'We better swipe the weapons off the testers, just in case they come round.'

'I'll bind 'em,' I said, and had just started on the first when Bully – skidding on his borrowed feet from the second tester to the third – suddenly yelled. 'Aiden!'

The spider creature was no longer stunned. It was too fast for me, and too fast for Bully. It pulverised me with a single thought – both sides, no prisoners – but just as it advanced for the killer thrust Bully blasted its head open with the second tester's gun.

Its blood was navy with pustule-like globs and carried a stench like a week-old corpse. Bully and I both vomited, and Pavlina, suddenly visible at the controls, humanely damped down the engine thrust. We all just breathed, for a second, then I turned to Pavlina.

'Taking as read all that crap about how good it is to see you – first, can you tell me how we got boarded without warning, and, second, could it happen again?'

She frowned. 'We omitted no available safeguard, and the security checks were all in order. The gauge with the orange circle in the middle – see? – is still showing green. Can you think of anything that might explain it, Bullivant?'

'Hey, don't mind me. I'm still counting my toes over here.'

'But what that means is—'

'Precisely,' said Pavlina. 'They might board us again, once the regime learns that their first attempt failed. They could be massing back-up boarding parties at this moment.'

'What about that blinguard-shadowing thing you pulled at the encampment?'

'That's only available when coming into land. This particular blinguard has no capacity to shadow while in flight. Whether others might be able to – I couldn't say.'

'Meaning that it could just be one long fun afternoon of fighting off blurgs and spider aliens, while having testers club our existing wounds?'

'It's possible.'

'But how'd they get access? And wouldn't another vehicle have to lock onto our docking system, in order to board?'

Bully offered, 'A disposable launchpad, maybe? I'll check.'

Bully's hunch was right – he dismantled the connection and gloomily dispatched the disposable launchpad into inner space. After that, he checked our injuries. Pavlina was untouched and Bully merely battered, but the wound in my brow would have killed anybody human and Bully fretted that my earlier scars, neurologically lashed as they had been, might worsen.

My own concern was the stench, so we decided to head straight down again to terra firma, where we could shadow the blinguard long enough to unload the bodies. Turned out the nearest bit of land was an island entirely gutted during WWIII.

It was a place of chill deadness – deserted, black-ashed, crumbling. We landed after dark, which didn't help, nor did the grit beneath our feet, which was very rough. Pavlina refused to even get out. I said, 'I vote we just shove them all out and let the bodies rot.'

'We don't want the captured testers, either,' observed Pavlina.

They both looked to me for a decision, which I liked. 'Then they can buzz off here as well.'

Nobody disagreed. Bully and I, with some difficulty, unloaded the dead, along with the surviving testers that we had strapped to the floor. Bully – usually the least vindictive of creatures – kicked the blurg's body in parting. His boot entered one of those disintegrating oily rings, and it took ages for him to scrape off the residue. The instant we were back inside he was checking the screens, as if still blaming himself.

'Give it a rest, Bully,' I advised. 'We're shadowed while we're down here – and I really think nothing could have prevented it.'

On the teleview, the King was still rejoicing the hearts of his delighted subjects. There couldn't be a single creature on Earth not wanting to heave a brick at him.

Bully then forced us to eat – lumpy tester muck for me, and Ho Chi's remaining supplies for himself and for the gromeline, who hardly ate anything. Even then, I couldn't prise him from the computer, sandwich clenched in his left hand, right fingers punching away. He was absolutely convinced that there must have been – somewhere – some security check that he'd omitted.

I felt a little guilty as we took off, leaving live testers in that dead-ash place, but Bully had already bleached the floor and it felt cleansing to get going. Soon though, I felt restless again. 'Bully, isn't there any real news? Maybe about the uprisings?'

'There's no other news, end of story. Oh look, only a few hours to go before we get back to yours, Pavlina.'

She had gone very quiet, maybe drowsing. Bully turned the lights down, possibly as the next-best thing to some quiet beach, waves rolling in, an orange-pink sun suffused over the horizon. I was piloting, with Bully by the door, F86 cradled in those stocky arms, just in case. Creatures don't take advantage of Bully twice – especially the ones with a taste for fug toes.

'When we arrive, I hope that you will consent to leave the blinguard and meet my people.'

So, she wasn't asleep.

'We'd be honoured, Pavlina. But are you sure you want us to? What if the regime's still tracking us, and attacks your own cell?'

'If they do, then they'll discover that we're stronger than they think!' was her light response. Then she seemed to curl into an easy sleep. While Bully stayed by the door, I remained at the controls. I'd volunteered for this task because I couldn't relax. I didn't even feel tired. Instead, an obscure sorrow gripped me.

For some reason I found myself remembering Sophia Tenten and her lumpy piano playing.

I suddenly saw my birth mother's wild dancing for what it was – for hubris, read desperation. I also recalled climbing that tree to get away from – what? And recognised – for the first time in my life – that it had been to get away from me.

Nobody else. Just me.

And I didn't want to be that angry little kid anymore. I didn't want to care if I got picked or not, or seen or not – or famous, or not. I wanted to be like Sebastian – someone giving themselves for the cause without being fussed whether anyone noticed. Like Priscilla – insisting on taking the poison on her palms – or like Joan Artington, waiting collectedly for the bomb that she knew would kill her.

I almost died today, I thought. The testers' wild shots in the encampment... the scramble to the blinguard... that crushing blow to my forehead... the fried nerve-ends from the spidery alien – that day, I had frankly seen the lot. And yet – *had* I died – what would people have said about me? ('Poor fellow, it was a risk too far'... 'Well, shit, at least he *tried!*'... 'You gotta hand it to Aiden for nerve! Say what you will, he always had nerve.')

But nobody would have said, 'Aiden had a great soul'... 'Aiden always cared about others,' or 'What an inspiration Aiden was – talk about dedication to the cause!'

How I longed for Sebastian, in that moment!

And bizarrely enough, as if he'd heard me, I was transported back to that snake-ridden, cicada-infested ruined tennis court, where Sebastian-as-gale-force-wind had first felled me. And what he seemed to be telling me was this: You can release all the worries, the regrets, the anger. But you have to choose to do it. First of all, you have to choose.

I'll give it a go, I promised, and then – with everything I had, with every breath I could summon up – I visualised *release*.

The strangest part of all was that – as I 'returned' from wherever I'd gone – I felt warmed from head to foot, almost lifted. And I thought, deep into the night, about many things, while skirting space detritus beneath the stars.

As we closed in on the coordinates, I said to Bully, 'We're almost back. Shouldn't we get Pavlina to warn her troops not to shoot us down?'

'Yeah – good thinking.'

When I did this, though, Pavlina only smiled. 'We're not that kind of a people,' she said, as Bully and I – we were getting far sharper at this – lined up the coordinates, keeping a wary eye out for bushes. As we rocked to a halt, Pavlina advanced to the door. I'd have preferred to have checked first how the land lay but – as it turned out – any such concern was wasted.

The moment our battered door shuddered open, there was this enormous cheer. The welcome party consisted of gromelines of every possible hue – and not only gromelines. As we descended I noticed a couple of hundred humans and a few aliens, one hurting my hand with the strength of his own. It was as if they'd all worried they'd never set eyes on Pavlina again.

There was a vehicle there, of delicately worked iron. Bully, Pavlina and I were ushered into it, and escorted down a deep tunnel, into what appeared to be an underground garden.

Turned out it really *was* a garden – not a joke – though how it worked, sun-free, I hadn't a clue. Here were feathery grasses, tremulous wildflowers, tender mosses – and gromelines, gently pulling us towards some feast. I caught Bully's eye and he was mouthing, 'Are we even awake?'

I wasn't sure. Even the air smelled different down there.

There was also a luminous light and an underground stream, studded with the tiniest alpinesque flowers and bordered by wild grasses of every shade. We gathered around crystalline tables burdened with glassed fragments of crisped grapes, silvery slivers of delicate fish and iced curling shapes I couldn't identify, that shivered like sea foam on the tongue.

Just under the surface, so unobtrusive that at first I hardly noticed it, there was music. It seemed to seep from the earth-walls, mingling with the trickling of tiny waterfalls and the almost inaudible hum – a power source, maybe – from the walkways.

Then the gromelines danced. How to describe the gromelines' dancing? It was nothing like any dance that I'd ever seen – nor was it like the natural dance of sea creatures, though perhaps it most resembled these. Instead it was simply the glad expression of physical joyfulness, an outward depiction of a powerful, inner spirit. The child gromelines – some very bright-hued indeed – danced first, and then the adults, until the music went lower and lower and deeper and deeper and Pavlina stepped onto the stage.

She was of course still mouse-coloured, and not in the least showy compared to others of her people, but she seemed to glitter with an obstinate inner light and the crowd fell absolutely silent as she started to dance… Her partner joined her. There was nothing staged about it: they danced just as their underground flowers grew, with some inner light. And then we were all dancing on the surface of the music – with Bully in a puddle of joyful tears. He had gone somewhere I couldn't follow, but I felt a powerful tide of affection, for his loyalty and his honesty and his sheer fugginess.

And for the whole of however long it lasted, I forgot to worry about the rebellion or Petra or Martin or whether I could ever go home again. The music was luring us into releasing everything into the moment – this moment – which would never occur again. At one point I found myself beside Pavlina and she asked, 'Are you happy, Aiden?' and I said, 'Yes' – and meant it.

Perhaps for the first time in my life. Not striving, not rushing, not wondering whether anybody might be catching me up or not acknowledging me. Not worrying about the last impetuous deed that I'd committed. Not fretting about how the hell we were going to get out alive. Just *being*, inside the moment. The 'here, now, always' from Duncan Tenten's favourite poem:

Not known, because not looked for
But heard, half-heard, in the stillness
Between two waves of the sea.

Duncan had mentioned that T.S. Eliot had always 'spoken' to him, but he'd never spoken to me before – or if he did, I'd managed to push it away.

And later, much later, Pavlina asked, 'What do you *want*, Aiden?' And I thought about saving the world and going down in legend and song, but for some reason I answered her, as honestly as I've ever answered anyone in my life: 'To be the person I was meant to be.'

She said quietly, 'But you already are. You've been that, all along.'

Which I doubted. But I refused to contest the issue. And, soon afterwards, tiredness took over, and everything began to whirl in a vague haze of fountains, colours, music and gold-orange light and I fell onto a velvet that surely couldn't be made of the stone that it seemed to be, and I slept and slept as if I'd been drinking the dew and the music and had fallen asleep, mid-dance.

26

When I woke the music was gone, and I was enclosed somewhere small, but so warm and light that not even I felt claustrophobic.

I tested my wounds – starting with the shovelled-in forehead. To my amazement, it was almost scarred-over. I could still feel some strangeness, a curious imbalance – or more imbalance than usual – between my human self and my tester body, but the forehead seemed practically restored.

I glanced around. Earth in every direction, spider-silken sheets over the sponge-like bed, which smelled of spring and herbs. I felt the most tremendous longing to curl back into sleep again, but my eye caught a movement in the corner, where some creature slumbered.

'Bully?'

'Yes?' – very sleepily.

'Just checking.'

'Thought I'd stick around, as you're wounded.'

'Well, thanks. But I'm not sure that I am.'

A dishevelled fug was beside me in an instant. 'What do you mean?'

'I think it's the place. It's got healing in every inch of it.'

'Aiden – your forehead! It's almost closed up!'

'Thought so, though it still itches. I want to get at it with nails.'

261

'Itchy is healing, Aiden. Maybe we should stay here forever,' said Bully, with the same longing in his tone that he'd evidenced during the dance.

'That would be extremely cool,' I replied, swinging my legs out of all the warm herbiness, 'but it wouldn't advance the cause, would it? D'you think we should check that the blinguard's still there – or did you sabotage it in the night, so we'd have to stay?'

'I'll check, Aiden. You stay here and rest.'

Part of me was hugely in favour of this plan, but it seemed pathetic to let Bully take the strain, so we both got dressed and sneaked up the stairway, past bud-like cubicles on every side, pearled-pink from that inner light.

The view on the surface was far prettier and less scarred than poor old G13, but there was still a sharpish wind blowing from the river. The blinguard, wet with dew and grimy from all its travels, remained where we'd left it – unsurprisingly, as several guards were there, presumably having been ordered to haunt the place.

'Quiet night,' one of them told us, her F86 still off its catch.

Swiftly, we ran some checks. 'Fuel cell's good to go,' Bully told me. 'Around three-quarters.' Which was impressive, considering all our efforts to outsprint the opposition.

The computer also passed every check. Still, the question lay before us: where were we travelling to? (Come to think of it, isn't that always the question?)

Bully was extremely quiet, maybe sad. We sat down and watched the great curve of river, a wavering sun trying to percolate through the clouds. I plucked a daisy and, bit by bit, pulled its petals to pieces.

'So, we're going back?'

'It's not about staying, Bully. Staying isn't going to happen. Either we go home and face the music, or else we think up something pretty radically off-piste we could accomplish with a stolen blinguard. Preferably something I can manage while being dead.'

Bully considered this while my stomach rumbled – I think that testers could eat nine meals a day, and still be scrabbling around for scraps at the end of it. Then he said, 'Why don't we check the news?'

Back inside the blinguard, which still reeked of Bully's chemical warfare against the spider alien, I shoved it on. 'Probably the usual,' I said gloomily, 'and if that smug git shows up, I warn you—'

But there *was* something new. Amidst all the propaganda – according to which the beneficent regime was adored and exalted throughout every bleeding sector from G1 to G53 – an announcer informed us, 'The King has decreed that the traitor Leelack is to be executed. Once a privileged private member of the Golden Circle itself, Leelack has recently been tried and convicted for crimes against the state. Her execution is to take place in the Centre, in G13, at thirteen hundred hours, tomorrow. Queues are already forming.

'Leelack, of the genus peitrel, which is unique to planet E356, must float within special chemicals at least once an hour while on Earth. One of only seven beings from E356 to survive their initial transport, she was the only peitrel elevated to serve in the Golden Circle, by order of the King. Tragically, Leelack eventually fell prey to the malicious fantasists of the so-called "resistance", sometimes termed "the rebellion"…'

I recalled the Creature's great tail lashing her to the gravel, those navy-black eyes – and the ache in my jaw as I pushed it forward, with MF practically sniffing out my presence. But this was followed by a surge of revulsion.

No! – They'd murdered Sebastian and Malthus and Ichthus and her brother Yoreen. They weren't getting Leelack too!

I leaped up from the pilot's seat but, recalling the last time I

punished the blinguard, I smashed my fist into my meaty palm
instead. Then I noticed the sombre look on Bully's face.

'What's the matter with you? They said *tomorrow*!'

'Aiden, listen.'

'Tomorrow! We've got to move!'

'But what if it's a trap?'

'What trap are you talking about? They've already got her!
She—'

'A trap for you! You tried to rescue her before, remember? You
have *form* where Leelack is concerned! You even released the
Creature, just to give her a chance! And now they're thinking,
how do we get hold of that bastard Tenten – the guy who just
assassinated their effing King – and, really, what better way could
there be? But listen!'

'Go on,' I said dangerously. 'But faster.'

'So now they're thinking, *this* is how we get our blinguard back
and Tenten zuged and the entire rebellion decapitated! Because
Aiden Tenten's the last guy to sit on his bum and let them execute
Leelack – who's probably been dead for a frigging week already!'

I paced a bit, forcing myself to think. Could Bully be right?
– I had risked a lot to try to rescue Leelack from the Creature,
and my instinct was to try to rescue her now. My instinct was to
take this blinguard – and remember, the Xirfell probably knew
exactly where it was, just as they knew that we'd disposed of their
famous boarding party – and to ride to the rescue like Superman
and James Bond and Zulfiqar and every other frigging superhero
all put together.

Aiden Tenten: always up to save the world.

There might also be something almost too clever about using
Leelack as bait, as if someone in the regime could guess my
innermost feelings. How moved I'd been by her brother!
('Nourish your light for ever!' And finally, to her alone, 'I shall
see you on the other side!')

Certainly, if it was a trap, it was a trap perfectly calibrated to catch at my feelings. But why should the regime bother to trap me if I *hadn't* assassinated the King – if I'd just nailed some stand-in instead? I wavered, sometimes thinking that I must have succeeded – sometimes imagining the execution's timing mere coincidence.

I also recalled Martin's dry response when I had wondered aloud what would happen to Leelack. ('Well, what do you think?') But I still refused to accept that she was already dead. For a start, no regime would privately zuge someone whose public execution would send so charged a message. Leelack was, almost certainly, curled in some small, icy tank, waiting to die.

Bully was waiting too, not without hope. 'Are you still mad at me?'

'Well, you're not just a pretty face,' I told him peaceably.

He beamed. 'No, I never was pretty.'

'I just bet you weren't. On the other hand, I think it's possible that you might be – at least partly – right. But we can't let it happen, all the same. You – you didn't see her brother die, Bully.'

'No. I—'

'And you didn't hear what Leelack said, either.'

'I know. But—'

'Breakfast.' It was Pavlina, standing in the entryway to the gromeline's underground domain. I whirled round.

'We don't have time.'

Bully began to explain but Pavlina interrupted, 'We'll discuss it over breakfast.'

It seemed to me almost criminally negligent, to have dawdled as we had already. I said, 'Thanks, but couldn't you just ask a couple of your friends to swipe a few supplies for us and wave us off?'

'Wave who off?'

'Us.'

'You mean *us*,' said the gromeline, very quietly, and Bully's eyes had never shone more radiantly. He practically *was* pretty, in his fuggy way.

'Do you mean—'

'I mean that I'm coming. I don't believe,' and here she looked almost amused, 'that you're quite safe without me.'

'Pavlina!'

'So glad you're pleased, Bully.'

'Lady, I thank you,' I said, with a little bow that tugged at my scar. I felt as if a weight had been lifted, as we followed her through the entrance, and into that glowing place.

27

The first thing we agreed was that it was pointless even to attempt to sail into G13 in the blinguard. Ours was a marked vessel. It might as well have REBEL BLINGUARD – AIM HERE scribbled over it in the common language of every galaxy – though, ever since the King's first decree on the subject, most other languages were dead or dying anyway.

Instead, we needed to trash it, and to secure other transport to G13, to have a tiny chance of succeeding.

We also needed a plan.

It was curious, though, that Leelack had yet to be interviewed on air, as inevitably happened with disgraced members of the Golden Circle. Instead the regime was just serving up the usual relentless propaganda – though perhaps with a touch more spin on the ball. ('No one except the beloved King can be trusted, for he loves the world like an uncle, like a father, like a tender lover'... 'World peace can only be secured through recognising the innate wisdom of the all-divining Xirfell'... 'Earth's salvation lies in obedience to the King's unique and beneficent vision.')

Oh, pass the sick bag. But it was still the King this, the King that, which bugged the hell out of me. Between that and the mental image I had of Leelack, curled quietly up on the ice, it was tough for me to drag my mind back to the practicalities of the meeting.

267

Where Pavlina was saying, 'Even assuming all the transport worked, I can't see how either of you could get through security. Every fug will be inspected from now on – though they'll be looking hardest at the corriskidder ones, of course – and Aiden's tester uniform and number are certain to have been circulated – though presumably only as some renegade tester, as they claim to have executed him.'

'So, I lose the frigging uniform. I hit some other tester from behind and swipe his. Haven't you ever seen any action films?'

Bully objected, 'Yeah, but even if that worked, what about those tester passwords? Do you really suppose that the Xirfell will decide never to change them again?'

We're stuffed. Testers did need passwords. Still, there had to be some way… My brain wriggled like a mtjik in a cage.

Bully continued, 'If you could get to Tim, you might get switched back to being human. But Tim might just pass you straight over to Martin, and the look on his face when he screamed about the connection…'

'But would Tim really turn me in? Last I heard, his daughter wanted my blinking autograph. And as for Martin, he might not be in a great position himself, at the moment. How do we know that Bully wasn't believed? That was a pretty comprehensive denunciation on the blinguard.'

Pavlina was considering – how well I'd come to know that little frown! 'We're running out of time, if we are to do anything. You'll probably have to let Bully and me go – with a couple of stronger creatures, of course. You might not be destined for this particular mission, Aiden.'

Now I absolutely hated this idea. I was trying to think of a polite way of objecting when Bully said, in alarm, 'I'm only good for back-up – and not even for that, half the time. You wouldn't believe how my knees were knocking in the encampment. And as for that awful blurg—'

Pavlina said warmly, 'I disagree. Who saved Aiden from Ho Chi and Darius? Who shot the spider alien after we were boarded? Who figured out how to make the blinguard go into turbo-drive? You did, Bully.'

'Pavlina's right, but there's still got to be some way I could come. There *has* to be!'

She fixed me with those piercing red eyes. 'There is one method. Which is that we medicate you ourselves, using a drug that will entirely alter your appearance.'

'Into a young Denzel Washington?' I quipped, but not without a dawning of hope.

'I'm perfectly serious. We can restore you to being human. However, in order to overwhelm your tester body we'll have to flood your system with the cells of seven or eight dead humans. This is the real problem. The consciousness can be transferred comparatively easily, as you know.'

'*What* problem? What are we waiting for?'

'It's only experimental,' she warned. 'It's not an operation. Instead, it's a drug. Much easier – but also even less safe. You wouldn't be exchanging one body for another. Instead, you'd be drowning your tester body with your own still-remaining cellular structure combined with those of seven or eight other humans.'

'So what you mean is, I might wind up being half-me and half-tester at the end of it? Because Hugh and Tim couldn't guarantee that all of me would make it back, either. I mean, I get that.'

'But it's entirely experimental. It hasn't even been *trialled*, Aiden.'

Bully said fervently, 'Is there nothing you people can't do?'

'There are plenty of things we can't do, mostly due to being inconveniently small. Which is one of the reasons why we need other creatures – and why this procedure was invented in the first place. So. Are you really willing for us to experiment on you, Aiden? Because that's what it amounts to. And I am *not* recommending it.'

I said slowly, 'So, what you're really saying is, I might wind up fifty percent Denzel Washington but one hundred percent dead.'

'Exactly. Precisely.'

I'm not saying that both my hearts weren't springing about a bit. I'm just saying that there was nothing by way of serious soul-searching going on. If the choice was between being side-lined as tester Technior, satellite 532, lieutenant of Amber 421, or running a mission to save Leelack, there was absolutely no contest. It would have to be impossibly bad luck for me to die.

'I'd like to go for it.'

'Wait! On the clearest understanding that you might wind up only partly human, only partly yourself or even only partly sane – in which case we'd have to imprison you here in perpetuity?'

Bully: 'No way! Aiden, they haven't even *tried* it before!'

I said, very formally, 'Lady, I do.'

Pavlina gave me a very odd look, almost said something – and stopped herself. Then she turned – we were still at the breakfast table, various strange and fiery fruits before us – and mentioned something to a passing gromeline, who blanched, and even dared to lodge a minor protest.

Pavlina dismissed him, taking another bite of a ribbon-like fruit. 'Is it because Leelack is one of the peitrel?'

I wanted to ask about the peitrels but then I realised that she was doubting my motives.

'Listen, I've never even met Leelack! The only time I've ever seen her she was being thrown to the Creature. All I knew was that she was with us.'

Pavlina leaned towards Bully. 'It may be pure infatuation,' she said, just under her breath, but – that tester hearing – I caught every syllable. 'I think you might be better off staying behind, Aiden.'

'And I disagree.'

'I think that your – feelings – for the prisoner might put the entire mission in jeopardy.'

'And I think I know exactly what I'm doing.'

She was silent for a moment, then: 'In my galaxy, the peitrel have a name, one untranslatable in your tongue, though perhaps the closest might be "the desired ones". But there's far more than desire. There's untouchability, unreality – sometimes torment.'

'I can well imagine. But whatever planet Leelack's from, and whatever she happens to look like, she's still a member of the frigging rebellion. A member who sacrificed her liberty, her peace of mind – even her own brother – to help the cause! For all these reasons, it's my job – not just because I'm pissed-off with Martin or to pass the time of day on a dullish Sunday – to save her, if we can.'

'Very well.'

'What do you mean?'

'Very well. As you will.'

And with that she just – absented herself. Instead of arguing, she just – submitted. It felt as if, in the middle of a fight, my fist had slid through my assailant into empty space. Though there was something else too, that unspoken issue – one extraordinarily typical of the rebellion – of who outranked whom. Technically the gromeline, as leader of her own cell, outranked me. In practice, we were equal.

'So,' Bully said, with a hopefulness that rekindled my own complicated longing, 'we're going home?'

Those bombed hills, that demolished coastline, that radiation-cracked sunlight, those wrecked swimming pools, those giant snakes… I was getting all choked up.

'Yeah, but not with all guns blazing. Here's where I am with it. First, we crash-land the blinguard into a fiery wreck. It's almost certain to be tracked, so maybe the sooner we do this, the better.

But, in real life, we don't get burned to a crisp. Instead, we abandon ship just before the fireball, in a zelopod – I assume Pavlina can access a zelopod—'

'And get shot down! Bravo!'

I glowered at the gromeline, her arms crossed, the size of a fruit bat.

'You have a better idea?'

'Two zelopods – zelopods are not a problem – and two gromelines. A far better chance of not being shot down, especially if both are clouded.'

'You mean invisible!' said Bully, thrilled.

Pavlina attempted, yet again, to explain to Bully that it wasn't true invisibility, but Bully wasn't listening and I knew it already.

'So. You choose another gromeline—' I said.

'The gromeline chooses herself: Gulzar, my partner. She was extremely impressed when you killed the King.'

'OK, great. So, we exit the blinguard in two zelopods, leaving a bomb in the blinguard. We buzz off, the bomb does for the blinguard and the watching Xirfell assume we've all been blown up with our ship. We then meet on the ground and make our way to the city – we need to think long and hard about how and where that might work. And we'll need some passable disguises.'

'Perfect!' said Bully.

'Don't get too excited. The drug might fail.'

'Yes,' said the gromeline serenely. 'But if it does, then you must be replaced.'

She was right, of course, but I didn't want to think about it. Instead I said, 'I also think we could do with a diversion. Something to take the Xirfells' minds in some completely different direction. If only we could still trust the local cell! If only we could press the communication button on the blinguard, summon Martin, and say, 'We need a little help. One of your younger guys, one of your glory-boys—'

'Or girls,' Pavlina interrupted, rather coldly.

'Or girls – no question! Is there any chance you could fire them off on some minor mission, for distraction purposes?'

'Theophilus,' said Bully suddenly. 'Theo would do it.'

I banged him so hard on the back that he gasped. (It'd be very cool to stop being a tester before I accidentally killed somebody.)

'Theo! Just the man!'

'Who is this Theo?'

'Theo is with us but not one of us. Lives in the wild, all on his tod, trains hawks and zillions of other birds, including ancient alien ones. Does crazy things to help animals but refuses to eat them. Forgets to eat at all, half the time. Meditates, sometimes for decades. Soulful type, not your man of action.'

'And what can he do?' Dead sceptical.

'Theo doesn't "do" anything. But he sends his birds out in a good cause, on occasion. Some of them are sensational, like dinosaurs – enough to distract any bloody thing. Theo loathes the Xirfell, because of the way they treat animals – and the way they treat the planet, of course. He thinks that the Earth is a living thing.'

'The Earth *is* a living thing,' Pavlina returned crisply. 'But surely the Xirfell will simply shoot down any flying creature – or even give it to their blurgs?'

Secretly, I was betting that Bully was wriggling those fat little toes of his in his boots.

'I think you'll find that Theo's birds are… different. Their technical name is piacentors. And I'm not even sure you *could* shoot them down.'

The crimson gromeline – Gulzar? – appeared, with a huge pill on an engraved plate. I rose, adding, 'The only downside of Theo is getting word to him. Probably, you'll need a zene – illegal, but possible. Bully, I'm going to have to leave that up to you. And now, if you'll excuse me, I'd better get this pill down.'

'Are you absolutely sure about this, Aiden?'

I bowed.

'Then – if you're absolutely sure – at least sit down. Please.'

And suddenly everyone was watching, not just Bully and the two gromelines but humans, pundlings, aliens – everyone, all around the hall. As if they all somehow sensed that something serious was happening.

Now normally the more attention I get, the more alive I feel – but my stomach for some strange reason was reminding me of a medicine Sophia Tenten used to make me swallow, which I once vomited all over her perfect hair. ('Oh dear!' she'd wailed, having never grasped the value of a really good swearword.)

Bottoms up.

First the right-hand side of my head swelled up, crashed into my skull and numbed it. Then my left-hand side crashed likewise. Suddenly a sliver of ice crystals started to descend, irresistibly, from the top of my crown through the whole of my spine, while my mitt-like hands and muscular calves started quivering, as if freezing ants had invaded my veins.

'To the cells,' ordered Pavlina. I seemed to have a very strange view of her, as if X-rayed, all cleverly interlocking bones. Then my vision was skidding and sliding... I was officially losing my brain.

Bugger.

Suddenly I was back in that metal chair, where Ravene was caressing me inside, rhythmically, gloriously, tumultuously. Bully's mouth was moving but I could hear nothing for the strange crashings of air. Was I falling or did it just feel that way? And why was Bully there, while I was pleasuring Ravene?

Still falling. Still falling.

28

Creaming through heavy, wild-tossed seas, I was pushed back, carried along, pushed back, and carried along again. I could see, but only sporadically, lightning flashing over oceanic darkness.

Ravene was leaning over me, her hair a darker turquoise than usual, streaming into the waves, deep claws of frothy purple crashing into that wild hair. I rose and she rose with me, that turquoise curtain lashing my face. My eyelids fluttered open and I discovered that those great eyes belonged to—

Bully.

Ravene, the lightning over the sea – nothing but imagination. Though I was still alive, which seemed good enough for the moment.

'Whatthehell?'

'You made it!'

'Whaddyamean?' My lips seemed to have been numbed by that ice-spewed spray.

'We thought we'd lost you!'

I'd thought that Ravene had found me.

First thing I really noticed was that poor Bully was a wreck – his clothes were in shreds and his brownish-grey hair dishevelled. Bedclothes, bloodied bandages, tester clothes and bonds were everywhere.

I wasn't in great shape either, but at least my stomach had returned to where, in my humble opinion, stomachs were supposed to be – and only one heart was churning away, where two had sometimes felt as if warring with each other.

My meaty shoulders had slimmed down, while my calves no longer represented a marvel of muscular strength and power. Only my hands still looked a little heavy, as if they had intended to switch back but voted at the last second to stay tester-sized, though thankfully not tester-hirsute.

Still, I felt like me. I thumbed my face, my slightly more aquiline nose, my former chin – and a wild gratitude seized me for being – mostly – me. I pushed myself upright, noting my lighter weight. It had grated on me, leaning quite so heavily into the Earth.

'Bully-boy, I'm back!'

'Wait, wait! Your bandage!'

I flinched as he adjusted the bandage across my brow.

He worried, 'You wouldn't lie still. I'd put it on, you'd swipe it off; I'd put it on, you'd swipe it off. And your forehead's worse again. It had almost healed before.'

'Testers are super-tough,' I reminded him. 'Even their skin is tough! But I still get to come, right?'

'They've gone to get a second opinion. But the first medic was OK with it.'

We're in the endgame now. My jubilation tempered, the adrenalin – familiar as my single heartbeat – flooded back. 'Is that my blood all over you?'

'You thought you were drowning. You kept saying you were drowning, anyway.'

'Poor Bully. What I put you through!'

'Yeah, well, *that* should stay on.'

'The zelopods?'

'They're fine.'

'Weapons?'

'Ready. For definite.'

'Do gromelines even have weapons?' I realised that, possibly due to their size, I'd been imagining the gromelines as anti-weapon – without a shred of evidence. For all I knew, they were armed to the teeth and the peril of greater Macedonia.

'Dunno. Their back-up troops certainly have plenty.'

'Has anybody figured out exactly how we trash the blinguard?'

'The gromeline engineer – Gulzar – she's onto it. She was installing something, last I heard.'

'The drag's the problem.'

'Yeah. We'll have to stall the engine in order to leave, and then we might get pulled into its death spiral.'

'Well, aren't you the frigging genius?'

'You really are back!' he said, thrilled by my rudeness.

'Bet I don't need to ask about disguises.'

'No, you don't.' Bully started tidying. 'Though I'll still feel sad leaving my corriskidder husk behind.'

'When can we go?'

'Soon as the doctor passes you as fit, I think.'

I lay back, suddenly. I felt like a small boy. ('Behave, young man, or no pudding'… 'No backchat – or no rugby!')

'Has anyone contacted Theo?'

'We sent zenes, but you know what Theo's like.'

Knowing Theo, he wouldn't even check where the zenes pitched up. Instead he'd be out wandering the bush, helping giant snakes out of thickets and getting chunks bitten out of him for his pains.

I started considering alternatives. Creatures I could trust not to report straight back to Martin. Creatures I could trust not to go straight to the regime. This did not leave a whole lot of creatures.

Then I heard a heavy tread coming up the stairs, pausing at the door. The doctor was tall, Black and wonderfully well-built. He had a scar down his jaw and a frown like a gromeline's.

'Tenten?'

'That's me.'

'Turn on your left side, please.'

'His wound's still bleeding slightly –' Bully began, but the doctor cut him off.

'Thank you, but I'll take over here, Mr—?'

'Um, Bully.'

'Mr Bully, thank you. Please wait outside.'

Bully, dissatisfied, ankled off. The doctor checked all my injuries, at one point flicking my knee almost callously, probably on purpose. Then he said, 'You've done remarkably, on the whole. Crazy idea, to run an experiment on an injured patient – and not what one would expect of Pavlina. Also, the hands are clearly wrong—'

'I noticed. There could be a reason. I was experimented on, years ago. One of the Xirfell's bright ideas. They decided to enhance—'

'That's interesting. So was I.'

I believed him. He could have been half-tester, with those remarkable abs, those enviable thighs. I shut my eyelids against the harsh light. There was something about this guy… Then it hit me.

'Sefu!'

'Hold quite still, please.'

'Sefu fucking Zwane!'

'This particular wound has barely closed over.' But then he smiled.

'I was wondering how long it might take.'

'I can't believe it! What the hell are you doing in lower, or possibly upper, Macedonia?'

'I got married.'

'Well, well.'

'She died and I stayed on. The gromeline are a remarkable people.'

Could he have married a gromeline – or one of their human supporters, maybe? People can be funny about their private lives, so I didn't ask. Anyway, I was too busy remembering.

Sefu ruddy Zwane. We'd both been adopted, thanks to the widespread infertility following WWIII. But while mine had been merely a local arrangement, Sefu had been brought in from G2, then still called South Africa. We'd attended the same school – really the only school, for the over-privileged – and later the Academy. There, on one never-to-be-forgotten day – on impulse – he'd wandered down for the rugby trials and bloody well been given the nod, right over the heads of all the rest of us wannabes. And gone down in legend and song.

Otherwise, I hadn't seen much of him at the Academy – but their medical department was famously tough. Once reckoned one of the rebellion's rising stars – I knew Sebastian had cherished great hopes – Sefu might have slipped off of the radar for a few years, but he'd returned fitter, stronger, better qualified and better-looking than ever.

I said, 'Hey, do you remember that day at school when we bunked off into town and ran straight into the deputy head?'

Sefu's smile told me that he remembered – but there was a new severity, too. The dead wife – or just the Xirfell? At any rate, it was probably this – along with the scar, and the voice, perhaps – that had prevented me from identifying him instantly.

He said, 'This is not the time for nostalgia, my friend. But – if you insist – I will allow you to go on the mission, upon two conditions.'

'No action-man rubbish, right? I mean, I'm not a tester anymore.'

'That's the first. And the second is that you take me with you.'

Suddenly, all the remoteness was gone. Those huge eyes – what lashes he'd got! – entreated me.

He was almost begging, old Sefu. He was a doctor, too – and he looked very fit. He still had that little indentation in his chin, he still had that sideways smile. How could I not have recognised blinking Sefu? – I looked at him and loved him. I gripped his hand hard, practically tester-hard. He gripped it right back. Then, in that startling baritone, he said, 'You won't regret it. To death or glory!'

To death or glory. I liked the sound of that.

29

Bully was unhappy at first. I had to talk to him like a brother.

'Listen, Bully, it's your basic suicide mission. Even more than the last one, because they'll probably be waiting for us. They can broadcast whatever they like, but they know that I'm not really dead.'

'I know, I know, I get all that.'

'Which is why we need all the power we can get. Ideally, a division of testers, a handful of nuclear warheads, couple of giant snakes, just to make up the numbers. As it is—'

'As it is, we get Pavlina's mate Gulzar and this doctor guy, who's great. It's just that it started out with just the two of us, then it became the three of us – and we three have been through a lot together – and—'

'And we'll still go through a lot together. Only with five, instead of three.'

'That isn't what you mean, Aiden. What you really mean is that I'm just weak and feeble, compared to this doctor guy.'

'Well, so am I,' I reminded him.

(Wrong thing to say. Did I lose half my brain with those astonishing tester balls?) I tried harder. 'No, listen! Sefu's great but you're the one I picked, remember? And Martin disagreed. But I told him, "Bully's the one I want."'

'You told Martin that?' His face had gone all glowy.

'Of course I did! And I had to take a lot of abuse too, because he didn't want to hear it. He gave me all kinds of grief. Probably he hoped I'd choose blinking Ho Chi, so he could get me killed quicker, haha.'

'I didn't know Martin didn't want me to come,' said Bully suddenly. 'Though he did say I wouldn't have been his first choice, or something like that. It was just before he asked you and Tim to buzz off, so he could have a private word with me.'

'When was this, again?'

'The night before we flew off with Ho Chi.'

Buoyed by the imminent mission – or still sore about Petra's desertion – I'd entirely forgotten this. But I asked, with a quickening of interest, 'So what did he say to you, then?'

'Well,' said Bully, not quite meeting my eyes. 'He said – he said that he believed that you had a condition, some kind of a mental issue.'

'He did, did he?' I said sharply.

'And that I was to watch you carefully and make sure you didn't decide that you're the only person who could fix the world.'

'You know, don't you, that this condition – it's called the Messiah Complex, by the way – is widely regarded by people in the know as a load of complete bollocks?'

'He didn't tell me that.'

'I bet he didn't.'

'He just advised me to bear it in mind.'

'And have you?' I asked, genuinely curious.

Bully said, 'No. I thought it was a load of bollocks too.'

(And that, friends, in a nutshell, is why I was so lucky that Bully really picked himself.)

I said, 'Bully, once all this is over – once the regime is overthrown and we're running the show – this is all assuming we both come out alive, which might be an even longer shot –

we're going to hire a blinguard, just the two of us, and wander around the parts of the world that are still worth seeing. I'm thinking Siberia and the Antarctic and the outer Hebrides and Bali – and call in on Pavlina in whatever-the-hell section of blinking Macedonia we're currently standing in and—'

'Really, Aiden?' asked Bully wistfully. 'Are you just joking, or do you mean it?'

'It's a promise.'

I empathised with Bully's inferiority complex where Sefu was concerned, having struggled with jealousy when we were younger. Still, to be honest, the more people I have under my command, the better I feel. Not that Pavlina was really 'under' anybody, and Gulzar appeared to possess the same cool independence. But Sefu's calmness, bulk and power was very reassuring, especially when I considered that we might get boarded again.

The second we took to inner space, this could happen. Or instead they could choose to simply blast us to pieces with some missile, leaving our shredded DNA over whatever godforsaken chunk of the planet they decided to pick. Arrogant as I was, I still found it hard to believe that Ravene would order my death – but it might not be Ravene's decision. She might be forced to agree, just to keep various warring factions onside.

On the other hand, the Xirfell now had issues with Pavlina and Bully, as well as with me, which argued against their blasting us to fragments in inner space. They almost certainly wanted us lingeringly tortured and eventually executed – though in my case privately, having already told the world that I was dead.

For all these reasons, the plan was that somebody would be permanently posted just inside the entrance. Where we'd got caught out the first time was in being gathered, like prats, around the controls, and I still couldn't quite believe that we'd got away with it.

We'd decided to detonate the bomb as soon as we were over the ocean. With any luck the Xirfell would imagine us buried under the waves, while we were really in Pavlina's zelopods, bouncing towards G13... Unless, of course, it all went pear-shaped. Those turquoise storms in that vision – was that where this day would end? Was I fated, metaphorically at least, to drown in Ravene's hair?

About an hour before take-off, I was snacking with Sefu in the gromelines' underground refectory and trying to keep as calm as possible. I was – I must admit – a little curious about his 'missing' years, but he had something very different on his mind.

'Aiden, look, this business about McNamara being turned.'

'What about it?'

They had been pretty friendly as kids – I seemed to remember that young Martin had invited young Sefu home for the holidays – but schoolboy friendships so often dwindle into nothing, or worse. I think I was expecting Sefu to say that he just couldn't get his head around it.

Instead he said, very quietly, 'Haven't you ever wondered if Martin might have wanted you dead for other reasons? You must know he always hated you.'

This almost made me laugh. I said, 'You're crazy. He doesn't hate anybody – Martin doesn't mess about with serious emotion. He's *ambitious*, no question, but passion just isn't his style.'

Sefu only shook his head. 'It's odd, you're normally so sensitive – it's as if you both have blind spots, just for each other! Aiden, do you happen to remember that day when we were picking teams for soccer and you never got picked – the day when you got into all kinds of trouble for climbing up that swamp gumtree?'

'Strangely enough, I do. I was remembering it only recently. But you're never telling me I didn't get picked on *purpose?*'

'Aiden, Martin *organised* it! He convinced everybody that you needed taking down a few pegs – and he bullied anyone with any doubts into going along with it. *That* was when I first realised...'

I thought, He'd organised it? He'd frigging *organised* it?

Sefu continued, 'But a school like that one is such a warped, intense, unnatural setting... Kids take against each other – stuff happens. I'd forgotten all about the episode, until the day when we were all at the Academy and McNamara stopped me in the quad. There he told me that you were having an affair with the ranking princess – and that something had got to be done to stop it.'

I stood up – I sat down again. I stood up again, took a couple of deep breaths and thought about release. (Release?! Who the fuck was I trying to kid?) Then I said, through gritted teeth, 'Sorry, but just let me get this straight. Are you trying to fucking tell me, Sefu, that it was *Martin fucking McNamara* who denounced me, at the Academy, for being with Ravene?'

'And that he told me he was going to, before he did it. I'm just so sorry I couldn't get word to you in time!'

I forced myself to sit down again, half-blinded with fury. I recalled my lost degree, my years struggling with joblessness. I remembered the week I was turned out of my lodgings – the week I'd had to bunker down to sleep in a shop doorway, because I'd been too proud to let anyone in the rebellion know. I even remembered, during that tunnel mission, swiping a few mouldy chunks of cheese from the factory kitchen – probably all I'd got to eat that day. And yet I'd never – not even for one second – imagined that it was Martin who'd done this to me.

Ravene had certainly led me to blame Harrison, but Ravene had always been utterly useless at names. 'Boring' had been specified – but Ravene thought almost every human boring, and when she'd mentioned that we'd been betrayed by a history student with dark brown hair – also, I'd *always* suspected Harrison. It had never occurred to me to recall that Martin's hair was almost exactly the same dark shade.

Suddenly it seemed to me that Martin had always been there – at school, at the Academy, in the rebellion – setting me up to suffer, eloquently pretending to sympathise, secretly relishing my pain.

Sefu continued, 'To be honest, I hadn't even *heard* about you and Ravene. I never went to parties – I didn't hang out with the other medics – really, it was my final year, and I was working my arse off. But when McNamara said that something had to be done to stop it, I said it must be operational, maybe even Sebastian's own idea.

'But he swore up and down that you were volatile, unreliable and a risk to Sebastian personally – and that you had to be denounced before you brought the entire rebellion down. In the end, I pretended he'd convinced me. Then – because I had an exam, unfortunately – I sent my roommate with an urgent note, to warn you.'

'You sent a note? I never got it.'

'Well, I still sent it – though I suppose someone might have intercepted it. But you do know, don't you, that you were bloody lucky to get out of the Academy alive? The King wanted you executed, but Ravene wheedled him out of it.'

I'd always wondered how I'd escaped – now I knew.

But I'd also heard – more than once – that McNamara had only a single blot on his record as far as the rebel leadership was concerned, and my personal bet was that this was it. After all, Sebastian hadn't minded my being with Ravene – he'd almost encouraged it. I'd even wondered if it was the affair with Ravene that had made him recruit me...

It took a massive effort to thank Sefu, and to get a grip on my feelings. In the end I went outside to the blinguard, to re-run the same checks that Bully and the others had already done perfectly – for no reason other than because I had to keep moving – to keep distracted.

I just had to try to keep my mind from rehearsing – over and over – what Sefu had told me.

The launch went perfectly, with Bully and Pavlina at the controls, Gulzar and me buckled in, and Sefu by the door. Once airborne, Bully instantly shoved on the teleview. The broadcaster seemed intent on rubbing it in: not only was the beloved father of his people speedily recovering, but the King was even expected at the execution of the traitor Leelack, who was shortly to be interviewed at last.

'Thanks, Bully,' said Pavlina evenly. 'Now turn it off.'

I overruled, maybe to see if I still could. 'No, I want to see it.'

I suspected that Bully and Pavlina were exchanging glances, but I figured we might get an insight into Leelack's state of mind.

Leelack was seated beside a tiny tank containing only a cocoon-like structure, which could have been woven from seaweed. She looked thinner than she had in the Creature's tank, those luminous navy-black eyes more soulful than ever. The guy lobbing the questions was a half-human in a Xirfell army uniform. He got right down to business.

'Welcome to all our viewers, on Earth and beyond. You have joined us for the final interview with the traitor Leelack, previously of the Golden Circle, who is to be hanged today. Lady, the King has, with extraordinary kindness, awarded you this opportunity for the purposes of a public confession. Are you prepared to confess?'

'To what am I to confess?'

Her voice was soft and rich, like flakes of gold, like the ones covering G18's Shwedagon Pagoda, the one burned down in the 2043 riots. I found it perilously hard to look away.

'You are to confess to treason, lady. For betraying the King, and the King's noble purpose.'

'And if the King's purpose was itself treason?'

'Lady, the King's purpose can never be treason! You have been brainwashed by the leaders of a cult, a false rebellion—'

'I have been brainwashed by no one. And there *is* a rebellion, a true rebellion. Which is why the King is dead, though this is being covered up by the regime.'

'You are, I'm afraid, entirely deluded. The King is not dead. He was admittedly shot, by a renegade tester—'

'He was shot and killed' – how my heart leaped – 'by the rebel leader, Aiden Tenten.'

Pavlina glanced at me, which was annoying, as I was probably flushing from my half-new face to my brand-new feet.

The interviewer remained unfazed. 'Forgive me, but this is pure delusion. Thankfully, the King still lives. May he live forever!'

Leelack shrugged. 'You are, of course, entitled to believe whatever you choose.'

'You will see the King yourself at your execution.'

'The regime may rig up something plausible – I'm sure they will try. But the King is certainly dead.'

That subversive curl of lip was irresistible. She was taunting him, on the very day of her execution. Was her composure related to her dead brother? She seemed to fear her own hanging no more than she had feared the Creature, eyeing her from the other end of his tank, swishing that pod-sized tail.

'Lady, you have been misled by malcontents, those witless few who only exist to spread lies, to foment discontent, to disempower aliens and to stealthily reassert the dead hand of human rule over the planet. They hunger to return to those days when a handful of obscenely rich humans despoiled the Earth, demolishing hope and fostering despair.'

His tones were almost hypnotic. Recalling 'Ravene' in my own interview, I found myself wondering if the latest Xirfell gambit might not be mass hypnotism. Of course, they'd always blasted the airwaves with propaganda, which was one reason – the others being utter exhaustion and pure raw fear – why it was so tough to inflame the masses to revolt. Or maybe the Xirfell were simply betting on the truth that, should people hear something often enough, they tend to believe it?

Leelack's huge eyes glowed. 'I think just the opposite! The rebellion wants to preserve the Earth; the Xirfell only wish to exploit it. You must have seen what they've done to the seas, to the atmosphere, to the Earth, and to other planets – including my own!'

'Lady—'

'But the Xirfell power is waning – and that of the Earth is rising. The rebels grow daily stronger. Leaders are emerging, leaders with the determination to shake continents. The moment is coming for Earth to rise, and for the Xirfell's kingdoms of misery to fall forever!'

'Lady, I fear that—'

'Finally, finally, this is starting to happen! Only a few creatures are even aware of this, but on planet E856, once called Galippo, the resistance has already triumphed. The universe was not created for those who seek to destroy, exploit and choke life from other living things – to choke the very air from the skies! Instead, the universe was made for—'

'The usual rebel propaganda!' the interviewer almost spat, but instantly collected himself and smiled very thinly, instead. 'Some creatures are entirely unable to accept defeat! They prefer fairy tales of the sort that have always existed, though believed only by the deranged, the feeble and the poorly educated. The Earth before the Xirfell—'

She said sadly, 'I was not here. Before our capture we had never even heard of Earth.'

'Which explains everything! You could have no knowledge of the dark times before the Xirfell came, with no elections, no democracy—'

'But there's no democracy now!'

He smiled again, this time pityingly. 'Dear lady, there are

elections in every sector – except for the wastelands, of course –
and compulsory voting. What more could any government do?'

'When most votes are altered, miscounted or ignored? When
the pundlings and the poor are denied the vote altogether?'

'Yet again, you've been seduced by propaganda – by those who
would use your beauty for their own purposes! Why, I personally
witnessed the voting machines being tested before the last
glorious Xirfell victory!'

Now brainwashing humans was never very hard, especially
humans half-starved of food or sleep, as most humans were. But
not *every* human – or every creature, either. There was a serene
steel inside of Leelack. She was lighting little torches all over the
Earth, even as we watched.

The interviewer continued, 'Of course, you were not here, but
before the Xirfell there were no great underground cities,
magnificent urban centres, superb structures for artistic events—'

'But there were methods of communication, a permitted
opposition – stars that creatures could see, air that creatures could
breathe!'

He frowned. 'Lady, I must remind you that you have been
permitted this interview purely for the sake of confession. Your
cultish drivel is of no interest to those who understand the Xirfell's
unique achievements, their beneficent salvation of the planet, the
grand sweep of history!'

Then his tone suddenly softened, becoming almost caressing.
'But it's not your fault that you've been deceived and
manipulated. You were a mere child when first invited to this
planet. Our ever-generous King could still show you mercy.'

There was a flash of steel in those dark eyes. 'I do not expect
mercy. I know better, having been the regime's prisoner for so
many years. Instead, as you propose, I will confess.'

'You will?' he repeated, taken aback.

'Indeed. I confess that I am a true member of the intergalactic rebellion, loyal until death to Professor Sebastian Yaromir Nevsky, our founder, leader and inspiration – whom the King ordered to be zuged. I also confess that I have secretly fought the regime from the moment it captured E356, where I was born.'

'E356 was your home planet?'

'E356 is my home planet: I am not yet murdered. It was Sebastian Nevsky who first convinced me that the rebellion represented—'

At this point, the connection died. Bully tried several times to get it back, but no luck. Of course, we were in turbo and there was no shortage of interference. It was even possible that the Xirfell hadn't pulled the plug – though it was much more likely that someone had realised that Leelack was responding a bit too well.

It had happened before. I happened to know.

Gulzar recovered first. 'A great lady, a very great lady. We must do our best for her legacy, if not fated to save her.'

We have to save her.

After a moment, Bully asked, almost in wonderment, 'Are we really part of an intergalactic rebellion, Aiden?'

'That's why we're resisting – that's what Sebastian taught us to do! Assassinating the King, saving Leelack – these are just the beginning. Once word gets out – once most creatures understand – there'll be insurrections that not even the Xirfell can cover up. Instead, there'll be uprisings, of humanity and part-humanity, of aliens and hybrids – of every single creature who's been oppressed for long enough!

'There'll be a new world order, a world released to freedom – for the first time since the rise of fascism. There will be rallies and celebrations; the Earth itself will be dancing! And there'll be a statue of you, Bully – the fat little fug who helped to save the world – and one to the glorious gromelines, to the stalwart Sefu, and maybe even me – because we didn't just sit back and say how sad it all was, but we fucking *did* something!'

And while Bully laughed aloud at the absurdity of his ever being 'famoose', Pavlina said quietly, 'Well put!'

It was my turn to be co-pilot, where I forced myself to check and recheck our plans. We'd be split into three zelopods: Bully with Pavlina, the burly Sefu on his own, myself with Gulzar. Sefu alone was left without gromeline protection, so he was getting the cloud-coloured zelopod.

The hovering, polluted fog should be in our favour. We were also using a clever device to escape the drag from the failing blinguard. Gulzar's own invention, it fired the light little zelopods wildly sideways, as if from a slingshot, about nine hundred metres into the ether... As the moment neared, though, I secretly thought that fifteen hundred might have been safer. The butterflies in my stomach were back – my old, adrenalin-fuelled friends.

What if the regime's forces just picked us off, one by one, mid-air? What if the powerful Sefu was too heavy for Gulzar's device? What if – the moment we landed – we were captured by some Xirfell loyalist or brainwashed creatures? What kind of nutcase could have dreamed up such a mission? – But the others were sane, right?

I'd yet to meet a creature saner than a gromeline.

About an hour later we were buckling ourselves into the zelopods. Gulzar was calm but I found myself wishing that I knew her better. Pavlina could be bossy but at least I *knew* Pavlina – Gulzar was still a bit of a mystery to me.

Bully and Pavlina were fired first into the mist. Sefu went next, with a steady look I found reassuring. (Surely Sefu wouldn't have come if this was just one of my 'batshit crazy' ideas?)

Finally, it was our turn. I cast one last glance around – at the seat where I'd been strapped when Ho Chi and Darius had attacked us, at the corner where we three had giddily toasted our success, at the spot where the spider creature had finally disintegrated, at the chilly section of floor where I'd hidden while Bully lied...

It all felt as if it had happened to someone else, a long time ago.

As Gulzar and I emerged onto the blinguard's launchpad and climbed into the zelopad, we were greeted by a frigid blast from inner space. Stalled, the blinguard was already starting to drift, even to sink. I checked the timer on the explosive one last time, activated it, and instantly released the catch on Gulzar's device. Our zelopod was fired sideways, slickly fast, through the white, oiled atmosphere... It felt fantastic, like a ziptilter ride. But then we jerked to a halt, and endured a nervy moment before the battery kicked in.

It's always cramped in a zelopod – they're jet-propelled toilet seats, basically – and chilly too. The moment the battery fired, Gulzar caused that silvery mist to descend.

I asked, 'Can you spot Sefu?' but she couldn't.

Basically, just making conversation, bracing ourselves for the blast.

When it happened, it shivered our little zelopod – maybe even our whole section of inner space. A moment later a great fireball sizzled upwards, shuddering us backward. Colours – cobalt, lemon, mandarin orange, brackish crimson, inky blue – spewed feverishly in every direction. Then there was a glowering sizzle as the blinguard's fuel cells ignited, spiking a whipped flame skywards, a pulsating fist of fire.

The final stage was disintegration. Small chips of blinguard were whizzing off in every direction, though – eventually – each was pulled, irresistibly, back down towards Earth.

Thank you and goodnight.

They're jerky little buggers, zelopods. Ours stuttered a bit, thanks to blinguard debris, before it stabilised. Then we sailed on uneventfully, though I felt a rush of sentiment as I glanced down at ugly old G13, having wondered if I would ever see it again.

Gulzar was too polite to say anything, though she was probably thinking, 'What the fuck? Where are the rivers, the sweet grasses running all the way down to water's edge, the undulating hills?' Though, looking on the bright side, there were also no fiery blasts from Xirfell ground bases – and no pursuing blinguards, either.

Were the Xirfell really going to swallow the theory that we had suffered some fatal malfunction or rogue space encounter? Or were random messages already being blasted all over the sector: 'What happened? Was it shot down? Who shot it down?'... 'Where are the remains?'... 'Could they possibly have escaped?'

Perhaps searchlights were already combing the thick clouds above us – perhaps Xirfell robotniks were already submarining through black-blue ocean, in quest of gromeline bones.

For obvious reasons, we couldn't choose any of the usual rebel haunts as rendezvous point, but Bully had recommended a promising spot from his first days on Earth. As Gulzar and I closed in on the coordinates, it soon became clear that things must have changed for the worse since Bully's day. The circle of deserted high-rise pods had rusted to fragments, and the whole area was choked over with the kind of plants that not even the Final War could demolish. The ancient hubs – erected for earthbound vehicles – had been ivied over too, but at least there was no evidence of wildlife (I was thinking of giant snakes).

The moment we landed, I jumped out and almost fell, as if my legs had been filleted by the death throes from the blinguard.

'Stay here, Gulzar. I'm going to do a recce.'

The whole area – where the first fugs had been transported, direct from their own planet – looked as if it had been deserted for far longer than a decade. The dwellings were pitilessly identical, resembling mid-twentieth-century tower blocks, all evidence of individuality ground down at source. They had never been allowed actual gardens but – poking around – I found evidence of wistful little vegetable plots sandwiched between the gaol-block housing.

By the time I returned, the others had arrived. Sefu had endured a roughish landing – there was a long crack down the side of his zelopod – but Bully had managed brilliantly: not a hair on Pavlina's head was out of place. (Not that it ever was, what with her being such a neat freak.)

'Looks OK,' I reported. 'No sign of snakes.'

'It's too horrible even for snakes,' said Bully bitterly. As I'd suspected, he was taking it hard. He kept clocking one of the concrete ruins too, as if it might once have been home. Sefu said, 'Never mind, the blinguard crashed in great style. And it certainly seems pretty quiet here.'

'Dead, you mean,' said Bully, with a ferocity that I completely understood.

Now the Xirfell had never cared for dated things – dated technology especially. The appeal of Bully's earliest haunts lay in its underground railway connection. It hadn't worked for years, but we hoped to be able to track it almost to the Centre itself. It had been Bully who'd remembered the disused underground. And it was Bully who led us to the entrance, calling back over his shoulder, 'Aiden, look! It's perfect!'

Perfect was not the first word that I'd have picked. The tunnel was dusty, filthy, flaking and partly subsided, its once state-of-the-art movement-activated paint crackling and crumbling. Still, it had gone half-two, local time, so we had to get weaving. I strapped Gulzar to my belt and Sefu did the same with Pavlina. Then the two of us jogged inside the tunnel, as fast as we dared, with Bully sturdily bringing up the rear.

For about an hour it was all OK, except for my stumbling once on a chunk of fallen roof. But then, suddenly, just as I reached a forked bend, I was conscious of a heavy instinct of unease and halted so sharply that Sefu almost crashed into me. I grabbed my F86 just as Sefu yelled, 'Duck!'

I ducked, and the snake's massive grey head, about a metre wide, just missed me.

Then came the explosion – the second of the day. But this time it was the snake's huge head that was exploding. Sefu had shot it – at excruciatingly close range – and the gore went everywhere. It was dusky-brown gore, with a glutinous yellow sheen, but the snake was still writhing powerfully, and we all had to dodge those massive coils – coils heavy enough to strangle a human – as it thrashed itself to death.

Once it was finally dead, I had to help Bully up and over. Even Sefu and I found getting past the corpse tough, mostly due to the slippery blood. All in all, we probably lost a good fifteen minutes. I did feel a little pang as the rest congratulated Sefu but told him, 'Great work, Sefu! Sure you don't want the head for your mantelpiece?'

'I think I'll pass.'

'This is excellent,' Pavlina observed, as we set off again.

I said sardonically, 'Just remind me what's so great about it?'

'A snake that size must have commanded the tunnel. It could scarcely support more than one of that size.'

'Well, hey, it's a point of view, but I'm not going to start tap-dancing quite yet,' I said, before remembering to hearten my troops. 'Still, it's not as bad underfoot as I thought it might be. Let's keep moving!'

We made such good time from there that, apart from Bully tangling with a giant mtjik – Bully's fault entirely – we reached the finishing line earlier than I had expected. Close to the end of the tunnel, I gathered everyone together and said, 'Maybe we all look a little the worse for wear. My suggestion—'

The word 'worse' had hardly left me before Gulzar handed me a flat pellet a couple of centimetres square. As I touched it, it melted into a large, warm, thyme-infused cleanser. There was more than enough to clean everybody, even Sefu and me, who had taken the brunt of the snake.

Bully was desperate to find out how this worked, but I cut him off, with one eye on the clock. 'Great! Thanks, Gulzar. Weapons check.'

Only three of us were armed: the gromelines, as I'd guessed, didn't do weapons.

Certainly nobody in the rebellion was likely to recognise us. Sefu and I were outfitted as Xirfell miners and Bully as a plumber, while the vivid Gulzar had dusted herself to a faded pink, markedly increasing her resemblance to a baby gopher.

And then, at the last moment, there was a hitch. Just as we'd feared, the final section of tunnel was in ruins. Whether through structural weakness, human neglect, or the fallout from some WWIII fire-bomb, not even a gromeline could have wriggled through that rubble to the surface.

I swiftly removed an incendiary from Sefu's backpack while Gulzar took readings and judged distances. Not the kind of thing that could be rushed, of course. But I kept thinking of Leelack's interview, of the way her eyes had fired, of that flowing material – was it really material? – of dark sea-gold. We had so little time!

Finally Gulzar made up her mind, and two separate incendiaries were measured, laid and primed. We all shuffled back, past the last few sharp bends in the tunnel.

The detonation sounded apocalyptic underground. Rocks and debris powered towards us, covering us all with a thin layer of ashed dust. For a moment I waited for the whole road to cave in. Only when it didn't – only when we found ourselves surrounded by the scudding, scuttling settling of debris – did I remember to breathe.

Sefu and I clambered over the rubble and gave the ceiling a few experimental prods, revealing a small but perfectly serviceable hole. Then Bully said, 'Gulzar, you don't happen to have another of those thyme thingies on you?'

Bully's such a tidy creature.

In the end, most of us chose to leave a little dust, as camouflage.

We were just about to split up when he added, 'Can't we say goodbye? Just in case?'

Superstitious creatures, fugs! I lifted Gulzar and Sefu assisted Pavlina. Gulzar appeared entirely impassive, but there was a serious expression in Pavlina's eyes as she said something to Gulzar in their own tongue. Into the rather nervy silence that followed, I felt moved to cry, 'For the rebellion!' which everybody echoed.

We emerged from the tunnel at intervals, with Gulzar and me leading. The level of street noise shocked me, as we'd moved from the steady tramping of our own boots and the tunnel's fetid heaviness to the tumult of voices, metallic skidding of robotniks, hoarse cries of street vendors and rasp of vehicles along the overland's decaying roads.

There were three entrances to the Centre, and the plan was that Bully would head to the east entrance, Sefu and Pavlina to the north, and Gulzar and me to the south. As I followed the signs, I found myself scouring the mud-coloured sky for piacentors. If only we could count on Theo! But who could count on impractical old Theo? The only method we had to get a message to him was through the notoriously unreliable zenes – though they had the advantage of destroying themselves instantly if intercepted.

Suddenly – last thing I wanted – I was accosted. 'Aiden! Is it really you?'

Milo, of all people: Joan's nephew. Last encountered around seven years previously, during the bomb mission at the factory. At the time I'd found him faintly annoying, but – to be fair – he'd probably been all of nineteen. Since which time he'd been seconded to an important cell in G6, and done rather well for himself.

My first impulse was to try to lose him in the crowd – it was thickening by the second – but nothing would have been likelier to engage the attention of monitoring devices, drones – perhaps even passing testers. Instead I slowed my pace to a crawl and said – with all the conviction I could muster – 'Milo! Fantastic! Really great to see you, but I'm a bit behind schedule at the mo. I'm borrowing a bed in Green 389 if you might want to catch up later?'

To be frank, I wasn't even convincing myself, let alone Milo. He hooked my elbow into his and said, presumably for benefit of any drones, 'Sounds great! Let's just get away from all this fucking commotion for a second!' And under his breath, 'You're not going anywhere near Green 389 – you're on your way to the execution – but I really need a private word. A serious word. Not a joke.'

There was absolutely no shaking him. So I towed him into a dead-end alley, did a snappy check for devices, and said, 'Listen, absolutely nothing personal, but some other time, OK?'

The noise from the road suddenly soared – a Xirfell ambulance was weaving through human traffic, its wails spiking my adrenalin. Milo waited until it had passed, then he said, 'Aiden, it's about Martin – Martin McNamara. You *have* to know.'

I paused and said grimly, 'Go on.'

For a second he resembled the old Milo, a little lost, a little boyish. Then he collected himself.

'Aiden, I've – I've stumbled on something absolutely awful. I've got irrefutable *proof* – not on me, of course – at home, but proof positive. Martin McNamara has been turned!'

Me, roughly: 'But when? When was he turned?'

'You *knew*? I thought nobody – OK, sorry. Well, I'd been given the mission to rescue you in prison – but you'll probably know all about that. At any rate, Martin called it off the day before – he thought there'd been a leak, for some reason. But through a series of pretty strange coincidences I learned that he'd been lying. The whole rescue mission had never been intended to happen – it was all just a blind. Instead, without telling a soul, he'd accessed a shapeshifter – a real one! – and ordered—'

I'd heard enough – and cut him off.

Not Uval. Not the King. Martin.

'Milo. Have you told anybody else about this – anyone at all?'

'How could I? I didn't know who I could trust to tell!'

I had so many questions! But I also had a discreet nudge from beneath my third button, from Gulzar – and Gulzar was right. So, I grasped Milo's hand and then – probably to his astonishment – embraced him.

'I have to go. But listen, Milo – thanks!' Then I moved swiftly back to the main road, already thick with creatures.

Now, ever since Ravene's airy comment in the army encampment, I'd shoved the shapeshifter onto her stepbrother Uval's charge-sheet. But if Martin was capable of sending a shapeshifter to kill me, why would he have thought twice about handing over Bully and me to be dispatched by Ho Chi? (Though perhaps *Bully* had caused Martin some regret? – Could that have been why he'd so strongly resisted Bully's coming in the first place?)

As we approached the entrance, we were increasingly slowed by the crowd: humans, robotniks, aliens, the occasional scowling tester. The execution had attracted the usual clueless enthusiasts as well as long-suffering workers whipped in to make up the numbers – but then, governments long before the Xirfell's had done their best to turn humans into machines.

'Keithie! Keithie, as I live and breathe! Haven't seen you since – was it the last execution?'… 'Effing foreigners deserve all they get'… 'Oh, yes, very. Very good-looking indeed, but odd too, the way they are'… 'I saw her brother's execution and I don't believe for one second that the Creature's tank was faulty'… 'Dunno why they picked her in the first place, it's not as if there weren't humans they could have picked! D'you know how those creatures in the Golden Circle *live*?'

Really, just the usual. But, having been insulated among the gromelines, it jarred, it really did. The queueing process seemed endless, though surely nothing could happen until the audience was all assembled; my impatience tided and ebbed. We were passed overhead by observation drones, casting a very literal shadow on proceedings – though not much of one, due to the pollution. Meanwhile, the drivel continued: 'He was fired, don't care what they call it. Testers just took against him, didn't they?'… 'She just don't fancy someone like that. S'all there is to it.'

I was alert for anything political, but most creatures are wary in crowds.

By degrees, we were approaching the security barrier. At this point I was meant to prepare Gulzar to slip us into shadow mode with a subtle tweak, after which I was to pretend to have dropped something, and to stoop down, for the purpose.

The reason why I pinched her so frigging hard was because – while memorising the positioning of the testers' edoys – I'd spotted Petra, maybe seven metres away.

Because it was Petra? Or because she was so lovely, hampered as her boyish beauty was by her work uniform, the hair scalped back, those cheekbones sharpened? I was reminded of the moment when I first noticed her, when she spoke so boldly at that meeting. Now our eyes clicked together exactly as they had then, despite the crush of creatures in-between. And I sensed that she had seen right through the disguise, pill and all. ('People have – atmospheres, Aiden. Auras,' Ravene had said, but I hadn't really believed her.)

Almost instantly, I was back in that glittery fringe again, that half-world, as if a textured veil had descended. Somebody shouted – probably some creature chancing to spot me blending into the ether – but I was already skimming beneath a robotnik's probing limb and weaving between those waif-like edoys – though I was still pretty sure they smelled me. Two swivelled their bleak, hyena-like heads in my direction, and one made that disgusting grating half-howl, before its tester smacked it and I breathed again.

Was Petra still where she had been? Was she alone? And why was she even there? – Surely Martin couldn't be mounting his own attempt at rescue?

Most creatures were absorbed by the pre-execution entertainment, though several started or even turned to object as I skidded past – only to find no one there to protest to. I slipped like a breath of wind between testers and pundlings, humans and aliens, with just one thought in my head – to get as far away from Petra as I could.

(Strange thought. Wasn't I in love with her?)

Glancing behind, I couldn't immediately spot her. Once safely inside a pocket of tall robotniks I stooped down and gently squeezed the gromeline's foot. The swimmy feeling disappeared, reality solidified...

'So sorry, I didn't see you,' a stout lady apologised.

That would not have been possible.

'Too many fucking aliens. Not enough space for normal people,' grumbled her companion, who seemed to be pretty anti-diversity, reading between the lines. But I was busy scouring the sky for a sign from Theo, or, failing that, from Sefu and Bully. (Bully alone would have endured security, having briefly handed his own weapon to Sefu for the purpose.)

I spotted them at last; and something about the set of Sefu's shoulders cheered me.

Keep Pavlina safe, buddy.

Before us reared that enormous stage. The enhanced ligers had just finished their stratospheric leaps and we were currently being favoured by one of those yengij singers that can whine across the entire vocal range – something that never fails to make the back of my neck crawl. There was no sign of any tank, whether for

Leelack or for the Creature, who was still imprisoned in part of the ocean, last I'd heard. (No sign of a scaffold either. Her interviewer had said she'd be hanged, hadn't he?)

That lovely neck.

'You are supposed to be dead.'

How on earth had she tracked me down so fast?

'Sorry to disappoint. And the boyfriend, of course.'

'You're mad,' Petra murmured, though I felt sure she was lying. 'Listen, we knew *nothing* about Ho Chi!'

'We've been through this, Petra. Don't know where you were. *We* were on the frigging blinguard.'

'Where Bully lied to the entire leadership!'

'Yeah, well. You've heard that crack about love and war.'

She bit her lower lip. I tasted a surge of desire – as if I was a blinking tester still. I could have taken her there, in that gap between the rows. There was a vibration between us, though, not all of which was sex.

I said rudely, 'Now piss off. Some of us have work to do.'

'You're never attempting a rescue?'

'I gave you your orders, Petra. They started with piss off.'

Petra, just under her breath: 'Don't you dare to give me orders! Don't you know that Leelack *wants* to die?'

Suddenly I recognised this as my secret worry, all along. What if Leelack refused to be rescued? What if she'd simply had enough, after years of homesickness and sacrifice, not to mention her lost brother? – I recalled that self-contained little figure curled at the foot of that tank – the Creature's great shadow above – and said, 'If you aren't attempting a rescue, then why the hell are you here?'

'To honour her, of course. You wouldn't know – I didn't know until recently – everything that she's endured for us. Her isolation, her desperation, what the King forced her to – oh, it was disgusting, horrible!'

I didn't know, of course, though I could imagine, but before I could answer Petra flashed, 'So, listen, whatever mad plan you've got in mind, just call it off! You're not even a member of the rebellion anymore, let alone an officer! You were expelled even *before* you made Bully lie to everyone. You're not even one of us anymore!'

For a moment the unfairness of this literally deprived me of breath. This blow went deep, desperately deep, representing (as it did) the loss of the only place I'd ever really belonged, and the only family that had ever entirely accepted me.

The last few weeks rushed past my brain – my torture, my being drugged pre-interview, my nervy operation to 'become' a tester, Darius's knife thrust where my heart was meant to be, the neurological weaponry of that spider alien and – perhaps especially – that second when I'd steadied my aim against the King, knowing that, if the next moment proved to be my last, then the rebellion, at least, could be trusted to honour me.

For a second I wondered if this was what a heart attack felt like: mine was certainly attacking me.

Petra went on, furiously, 'You even stole the blinguard!'

The man behind complained, 'Just shut up, people. Something's happening!'

Leelack's ice-tank had emerged, along with the same tastelessly gem-studded carriage that had transported MF. But I was so stirred that I hardly even registered it.

If Petra's word could be relied upon – and she'd always proved reliable in the past – I'd lost my family, my identity, my reputation – everything I'd ever had that really mattered to me. The entire frigging rebellion had betrayed me! And, to be honest, I really couldn't answer for how I'd have reacted, before everything that had happened in the past few weeks. As it was, I somewhere found the resolve to steel myself to a – comparative – calm.

I said, very steadily, 'Petra, you're making the most appalling mistake. I don't know what Martin's told you, but he really *did* know all about Ho Chi.'

And when she protested, I added, 'Also, I've since learned that it was Martin who denounced me at the Academy, ending my academic career and almost getting me executed. And even that isn't all – Martin sent a shapeshifter – a fake you – into prison to murder me. There's independent evidence for this, by the way – from a rebel you happen to *know*. So it's got nothing to do with my obsessive jealousy or any kind of psychological complex – in fact, it's got nothing to do with *me*, at all. This goes *way* beyond me! The fact is, Martin is a traitor. You have to believe me, Petra. This is the truth.'

For a second she stared – in disbelief – possibly even in despair. Then we were scuffling and tussling, her slim fingers grasping the middle button on my jacket and furiously twisting it, in hopes of reaching my gun. That was when I noticed the silvery syringe in her other hand.

She was fucking *armed!* Who knew what might be inside the syringe? One of those incapacitating drugs – or worse? How the hell had she wangled that through security? She couldn't have, was the answer. There *had* to have been collusion with the regime. In other words, Petra must also be guilty...

We were still fighting, still struggling together, but I was handicapped – not just because I hated the idea of hurting a woman, but because I hated the idea of being *said* to have hurt a woman. But I was also driven by fear – that Petra might just succeed in inserting that tiny needle and – end of story, and goodnight.

Suddenly that familiar mist descended: an alarmed Gulzar – unable to see, perhaps even to hear – had tossed her tiny gromeline hat into the ring. My disappearance disconcerted Petra just long enough. The syringe slipped from her fingers to the ground just as the crowd erupted all around us.

Several of our neighbours, probably relishing the drama of our 'tiff', gasped as I skidded, still shaded, between them, but every other eye was on Leelack, who had emerged, quiet, composed, a tawnier shade than I'd remembered.

By then I was rows away from my previous position and the entire Centre in uproar. I couldn't spot where Petra was – probably she'd guessed the wrong direction, like a tennis player stranded mid-court. Maybe fifty metres from where we'd struggled, I risked a glance towards the stage. Out of the royal carriage stepped two figures. The first was Ravene, in a scarlet sari-like dress. But the other, the second?

The King. Himself, not a picture.

How many times did I have to fucking kill the bastard?

There was not a shadow of doubt in my mind that – God and the Xirfell medics alone knew how – the King had survived a blast in the chest from point-blank range. He had survived the encounter with the Chieftain in 2085; he had survived that anonymous attempt on E649 several years later – and he'd survived a shot, in a G9 army encampment, that had buckled him in two, courtesy of Aiden Tenten, tester.

I was still unsure about the 'King' in the broadcast – probably, the real King had still been recovering – but *this* King was real, that smirk unmistakeable. Yes, he looked a little drawn, and he appeared to be leaning on a cane covered with living gems but still – he was alive. The wrecker of planets. The breaker of living Earth.

Was the bastard immortal, after all?

I had been wrong. We'd all been wrong – even Leelack had been wrong – and her patronising interviewer had been right, at least about the King. Though Leelack herself appeared as tranquil as ever, those soft waves of gilded hair shielding that heart-shaped face. She looked like a guest attending a palace garden party, not someone preparing to be hanged.

Gulzar asked, bewildered, 'What was *that* all about?'

'Um, nothing, just an old flame. Thanks for going incognito. Would be cool to stay under cover a bit longer if you could manage it.'

'I could manage for rather longer if I had more air.'

'Of course, sorry.' I opened a few buttons.

Meanwhile Leelack was moving, in that lightly swaying way of hers. (Did she look suicidal? What does 'suicidal' look like, anyway?)

And as I watched I realised that she simply *was* – perhaps the clue to her allure. She wasn't attempting to be anything in particular, or troubled about what anyone else might be thinking. She was entirely self-contained and self-sufficient – which was vaguely passion-dashing, though I recognised this as my own issue, rather than hers.

If only Theo would come! Had the zenes even reached him, in his wilderness? Although – even so – there might still be enough time, because the King always gave his victims a chance to speak, having read it in a book somewhere. A bit like his frigging elections. Waste of time, waste of money, but still they had to happen, because of a book someone had once told him about, written centuries ago.

I spotted Petra, perhaps fifty metres away, just pushing that soft-lit fringe from her eyes. And, weirdly enough, I suddenly missed her. (How crazy was this? She had betrayed me, in every possible sense, and, had Gulzar not acted, she might've killed me, not ten minutes before.)

Finally the music started to fade, the crowd to quieten. The great stage slouched, like a large animal, back into its pit and in its place rose a scaffold big enough to hang a tester, though equipped with only a child-sized rope.

A Leelack-sized rope. My mouth dried in an instant.

The zelcams feeding the great screens zeroed in on her as she stood, utterly collected, waiting to be told when she might speak. Then they switched to the King.

I had to admit, he didn't look terrific. He moved gingerly, while his craggy, handsome face appeared rather craggier and not quite so handsome. But how was he even fucking *alive*?

He began, 'My beloved people! As you know, I have practically been raised from the dead.'

Many cheered – those seated nearest the testers with the wildest enthusiasm. But, 'Bless!' sounded from one pudgy fellow nearby: I felt Gulzar stir, in disbelief.

'I was recently shot, at point-blank range, by a traitor, a terrorist, who had already murdered two leaders of his own. The rebel Tenten is now executed' – wild applause, for which much thanks – 'but many, many more traitors still live. We urge you therefore to be watchful and ready, for who can be sure where the next terrorist might be? He might be working beside you today; she may be sharing your lodging-place tonight! Therefore, be vigilant and watchful – that we, your beneficent and caring rulers, may continue our ardent ministrations to this suffering planet, warped as it has been by your futile and self-destructive wars.

'Meanwhile we continue to work tirelessly, to rebuild and renew, to clear the seas of detritus and the air of decay. Another decade – just a single decade, dear friends – and you will not be able to recognise the Earth you see about you!'

Here he paused for the applause to die down, or – was it possible? – to summon up strength, before continuing. 'Today, therefore, is a day for sadness, rather than for revenge. It gives me no pleasure to execute anybody. I – along with my beloved children and the entire Golden Circle– only long for everyone to live peaceably under our loving and democratic guidance. For who could wish to harm someone like Leelack here? Only an ogre!'

Thunderous approval, while my neighbour marvelled, 'He understands everything!'

You might have noticed that the party line had subtly altered: during my interview, it was that everything was coming up roses – except for a few wilfully stubborn sectors of the planet, notably G13. At this point, by contrast, there was still a helluva long way to go, but the Xirfell were tirelessly bustling about rescuing the Earth, with a heart for any fate. Presumably the King had been persuaded that this switch-up would go unobserved, and his advisors were probably right.

Gulzar indicated that she was tiring so I bent down and flickered back into view. She whispered disconsolately, 'I don't know why it's so hard.'

My own guess was that, used to green swathes of lesser Macedonia, she was probably missing the air.

Several creatures near us were bobbing their heads in vigorous sympathy. 'Gotta do it, hasn't he?'... 'She didn't ought to have done what she did, and her in the Golden Circle too! So disloyal!' Some creatures were even stamping their approval, though most of this felt faked. I was suddenly certain that some of them were pretending. They were stamping their approval, black hatred in their eyes.

The King attempted a noble expression. 'So, who would wish to harm Leelack? Certainly no one in the Golden Circle! But when a creature nefariously conspires against us, when one of our own leaders is proven to have been corrupted, we can have no other choice. For there are threats, including threats to the Earth, that we can no longer ignore. We must pull together, for we are surrounded by perils, including perils not yet detected, in galaxies yet to be discovered.'

I guessed that this was a clever-enough pitch, to the stolid fellow in his plumber's outfit, to the young matron fearing for her child, to those creatures aged 130 or so, worn into resignation, and to the poor, hope already doused in their eyes. As one fellow muttered, more to himself than to the rest of us, 'They're no worse than the last lot, really. Just keep your head down and survive!'

And then we were all applauding – because we had to, because we must – and this seemed to trigger something in the King that had been missing before – because even bastards yearn to be loved, even if the love consists mostly of fear.

'And so, my beloved creatures, I can trust you to hear the last words of the traitor with generosity, recognising her delusion and pitying her for it. And recognising that our vigilance for your security is as constant as is our royal love!'

At this Leelack stepped forward and addressed us, in those soft, deep tones. 'Friends, my story is simply told. Eight years ago I was kidnapped from my own planet, and brought to Earth, by the King. Here I was forced to join the Golden Circle and made to endure things I found desperately hard to bear. I have never been happy – I have always been deeply unhappy – ever since being robbed of my planet and my home. But I did what I could – I fought where I could – I put my love to such uses as I could find. But the regime was too strong for me, the death-in-life was too strong for me.'

The masses seemed entirely bemused, but there was an undercurrent of gathering bewilderment, even unease. ('Is she a religious, then?'... 'Her fight? She couldn't fight a cold!'... 'I don't think they ought to hang her. I feel sorry for her.')

'And so now I must leave you. I beg you, therefore, to resist. Resist those who would distort your truth or crush your spirit. Resist hatred, resist separation, resist oppression. Resist loudly or quietly, depending on your nature, but never resist your inner truth, for *that* is the only death that can endure.

'I leave you with these words: Resist now. Resist always. Resist forever!'

I had to swallow hard – and even the toughie who had

complained before coughed and suggested that the lady was, 'probably just a little misguided'.

She turned to her guard, asking for the bonds on her hands to be released – then, it happened. A hoarse tester cry – a slim flash of silver – and Leelack lay in a gilded heap at the foot of the stage, already limp mid-fall.

Automatically, I moved towards the barrier, then halted. The crowd was in turmoil. ('A needle! She'd got a needle!'... 'She's gone and injected herself!'... 'No, the fucking tester – they effing poisoned her!'... 'Dead by her own...')

A needle! Provided by Petra, maybe? – Or even slipped to her by 7784 in her cell?

The King snarled something to his confederates: Ravene swayed and had to be steadied by her bodyguard. Immediately, Leelack's colour started to soften – she was losing that gilded edge, it slipped from her in waves, like water. And I experienced, along with regret, a kind of glory because she'd cheated them – a transcendence, because she had escaped. Resist now. Resist always!

Between two waves of the sea.

Then, without a piacentor on the skyline, it was time – it was probably more than time – for the last blow I could make for the cause that had expelled me. Making eye contact with Sefu – who nodded grimly – I whipped out my F86, anchored it straight onto that powerful neck and fired. And the ruler of every known galaxy fell, whipped backwards, and hurled by sheer force of impact to the ground.

At last.

Gulzar was trying; she could not have tried harder. But even before she confessed, I knew that I was going to have to fight our way out.

But just as I was preparing myself for retaliation from a tester or worse, I heard the sound I had been waiting to hear for over a decade: the swelling roar of a great mass of creatures – human, hybrid, alien – pressed beyond endurance. From behind, from in front, from every corner of the hall, came the sound of the masses rising, the sound of a million creatures who had been beaten down long enough.

I had never heard it before, but I recognised it instantly. It was the sound of riot.

There was a great tidal swell towards the stage – despite testers furiously plying their weapons in all directions. The security forces also rallied – edoys, ognyites, blurgs, robotniks – but the crowd was roused, implacable, and bent upon destruction.

Ravene was plucked up by a tester who was himself blasted – by Sefu, for sure, for who else could have been armed in that direction? But the tester contrived to bound up the tunnel with Ravene, slashing viciously at everything and everyone in his path.

Then there was a great animalistic roar as a whole slew of creatures started tearing at the King's corpse, using hands, claws, even teeth. Another group surrounded Leelack and lifted her, because she had touched them, before choosing her own, intensely personal, abdication. Surrounding her there was a/circle of calm, but everywhere else was in absolute turmoil – with creatures screaming, screeching, fighting, bleeding – as the royal blurg was pulled to pieces, as creatures wrenched the living gems from the royal carriage, and slashed the rims from its golden wheels. There was a constant sizzle of bullets – some from testers, others – I guessed – from Sefu and Bully. I blasted two testers personally and maybe a third just as the blurg's last rubbery coils were torn apart. Then Bully rushed up and embraced me, the gun in his fat palm banging my shoulder.

My brother.

But then his eyes, looking past me, widened in dismay, and I whirled round. A tester, spotting his gun, was aiming straight at Bully.

I clouted Bully out of the way, only just in time. The bullet, which penetrated the front of my thigh, I hardly even registered – (where'd Gulzar got to?) – because someone or something had shoved me to the ground from behind. I turned in disbelief.

Martin fucking McNamara? Was the whole effing cell here?

But there was – believe me – nobody on the planet I was keener to see. We closed instantly, wrestling, scrabbling, twisting, with first one getting the upper hand, then the other. Locked together, I managed to twist my boot around his ankle. Locked together, we crashed – locked together, we fell.

At ground level it was wild: all boots, blood and claws, accompanied by the screeches, shouts and roars of the rioting masses. Someone accidentally landed a blow on the back of my head, but I still had an intuition that I was winning. For the first time in our lives, I was winning. My half-tester hands coiled around his neck as I hissed, 'Admit it!'

'Admit – what?' he gasped.

'You set us up with Ho Chi! Admit it!'

I shoved his head back: his throat was working like a trapped fish's. I hardened my heart as I heard – from a distance – another animalistic howl from the crowd.

'What'd they offer you for Bully and me, then? Or was the thrill of losing me just too tempting to resist?'

His only answer was to knee me in the balls. Then we were again twisting and flailing all over the floor. The pain in my thigh was nothing; the blood down my thigh was nothing. I felt fit and powerful and astonishingly strong. There was *nothing* stronger than what was fuelling me.

'Let – me go! You can't – kill me!' he panted.

'Why the fuck not? You betrayed me at the Academy. You sent that fucking shapeshifter to my prison—'

'I did – nothing of the—'

'You saw Bully and me off to die!'

'You're mad!'

'You *expelled* me!'

I trapped his legs – though my own were slippery with blood – and grabbed his neck again. It felt nothing like Ichthus's – it felt young, robust and probably not unlike my own. But my hands were human-sized no longer. There was a touch of tester left in me.

'You m-m-misunderstand!' he coughed. 'Let me – go!'

We swirled dustily together again, like lovers, like brothers – creatures seemed to be giving us room – but I'd got my thumbs on his artery and I was going nowhere fast.

'You're a fucking *traitor!*'

'I – never – meant—'

'Admit it! The truth!'

'I – I – I never—'

'The fucking *truth!*'

Suddenly he went all floppy and slack beneath my fingers, just as something blackly booted my temple. *But I didn't do it!* I thought, pulling myself upright – dizzy, bleeding, confused.

And locked eyes with Petra, amidst the riot and the madness, the syringe in her hand – empty.

Just then, above the tumult, rose another sound I had never heard before and will probably never hear again, the untamed screech of a creature from ancient days.

Theo's piacentors had arrived: fastest creatures in the galaxy, dinosaurs of the air.

Theo's piacentors had come – too late. At last.

30

It hadn't been Theo's fault. Plan A had been for his piacentor to swipe Pavlina from Sefu and then – thanks to the gromeline's party trick – to pluck up Leelack and sweep her to safety. But by the time Theo had picked up the only zene to make it through, it was just too late.

Plan B was due to be activated if no rescue had arrived and Leelack was about to be hanged. In this case Sefu and I were to assassinate the ranking members of the regime – as it turned out, the King and Ravene – though Ravene escaped. The riot, nobody had planned.

Our getting shot, as Sefu had been in the torso and I'd been in the thigh, had always been a possibility – but we'd still been incredibly lucky. Pavlina would have been killed outright had the tester's bullet hit Sefu only two centimetres lower, though Hugh assured me that Sefu was also going to pull through. My own wound, having missed the main artery, was nowhere near as serious.

You might be bewildered at my even mentioning Hugh and the rest – having been reliably informed that I'd been expelled from the cell and even the entire rebellion.

But – I'm back!

It was partly Martin's death at Petra's hands and partly thanks to Priscilla – who had always fought my expulsion. It was also Milo's denunciation of Martin McNamara having been researched, acknowledged and accepted. I also owe a lot to Pavlina and Bully, who apparently made the strongest possible representations, though I know that 7784, Gulzar, Sefu, Tim, Hugh, Doreen and Atlantis also spoke up for me.

It might also have had something to do with that moment over Martin's body, when Petra's eyes met mine.

The truth is, I don't know the full story – either of my expulsion or my rehabilitation – and it might be better if I never do. What matters is that things are moving, all over G16, G8, G9 – even G13. The regime in meltdown, this is our moment: this is our time. As Sefu had said, in Macedonia, his great eyes shining, 'Death or glory!'

And it really is *our* time. Because, if I've learned anything, it's that I can't do anything all on my own.

'Aiden Tenten,' says Priscilla. 'Do you swear to uphold the rebellion to the end of your life, to lead with no thought of self, to protect – to the best of your ability – those given to you to protect, to follow in Sebastian's footsteps, and in the footsteps of those who have died for the cause before you? Do you swear all this?'

And it feels as if I'm back on that tennis court again, and Sebastian's tweed-jacketed arm heavy on my shoulders, and I remember that the only person who can save me is me, along with that kernel deep inside, that immortal core.

Pavlina had found it, and Sebastian had found it, and Bully had always possessed it, but some people never find it – the recognition of that truth, that humility, where we can merge, from all our separate selves, into the person we are meant to be.

And suddenly I understand at last.

The rebellion had been blindsided; only Martin had truly rejected me.

My birth father's crimes were his and his alone – and nothing I have to atone for.

My birth mother had never wanted to give me up; I had been collateral damage.

I've spent my life rebelling: against my abandonment, my race, my status, my nature. And they're all still me – at least, they're still a part of me – but I find that, at last, I can embrace them all.

I'll probably always struggle a bit, but something has shifted, I can feel it – had shifted even before I took that hit for Bully, even before that wave surged through me, releasing the part that always had to come first.

'I promise,' I tell Priscilla – just as, ironically enough, she makes me the leader, the first.

The applause ricochets around the cave.

It's a heavy night, with no visible stars, but I sense that somewhere all our lights are shining, the lights that Leelack planted, that Sebastian planted, that we all plant.

And now – if you'll excuse me – I'm just off to save the world.

THE BEGINNING

ACKNOWLEDGEMENTS

First, I have to thank my very dear father, John M. Taylor ('Doodie') to whom I dedicated this book, for continually urging me to write a pacey, thriller-ish book with an identifiable plot. (This one's for you!)

Second, I have to thank my wonderful husband Simon for all his encouragement, belief and endless editorial assistance – and our amazing daughter Rachel, for beta-reading while locked down with us during her final term at Oxford.

Third, I am also eternally grateful to Sam Boyce, for her inspired developmental editing. Sam is a brutally witty, inventive and intuitive editor, especially with regard to genre, pacing and character development. She understood me from first page to last.

Fourth, I'm very grateful to everyone at Unbound, particularly Anna Simpson and Julia Koppitz, for their assistance, understanding and support, and also for providing the patient and thorough Melissa Hyder as copy-editor and Sophie Scott as proofreader.

Finally, I'm grateful to all my friends – especially to those who pre-ordered this book and funded it, and to those who encouraged me to return to writing fiction.

Guess this one's for you, too…

Unbound is the world's first crowdfunding publisher, established in 2011.

We believe that wonderful things can happen when you clear a path for people who share a passion. That's why we've built a platform that brings together readers and authors to crowdfund books they believe in – and give fresh ideas that don't fit the traditional mould the chance they deserve.

This book is in your hands because readers made it possible. Everyone who pledged their support is listed at the front of the book and below. Join them by visiting unbound.com and supporting a book today.

Annie Ashton
Linda Blain
Jane Broadbent
Alison Brown
Judy Brown
Elizabeth Byrd
Ann Callison
Elizabeth Catchpole
Melissa Charleton
Angela Chillingworth
Sue Clark
Winifred Collarbone
Katherine & Alan Copley
David Coronel
Antoinette Davies
Hazel Davis
Helen Drayton

Rachel Dubourg
Diane Ellis
Jean Eubanks
Wendy Everett
Rebecca Fage
Ian Fosten
Bill Gaskarth
Clare Glenister
Anne Greenidge
Clive Griffin
Jehoash Hirshberg
Johari Ismail
Dan Kieran
Jayne Ryan Kuroiwa
Rob Lake
Phil McKerracher
Michael and Karen

320

Nicholas Miller
Simon Miller
Rachel Millington
John Mitchinson
Allison Morey
Anna Morris
Carlo Navato
Laura Nielsen
Nicky Pattrick
Janine Peake
Justin Pollard
Sarah Pope
Joan Pulliam
Dame Janet Ritterman

Julian Robinson
David Rodker
Kathy Shaibani
Doris Shank
Mark Sheridan
Margaret Slaton
Nadene Snyman
James Taylor
Chris Terepin
Vanessa Townsend
Anita Tucker
VM
Alison Westmacott